WAR OVER DISEASED BLOOD

Blue Lysis carved into their ranks with *Ferrus Eviscamir*, its blade slicing only their bones, invisible to metal and flesh and incapable of being parried or blocked. He tilled them as he had tilled the Land!

Dozens of bodies writhed.

Yet more Augurs advanced.

They pressed Lysis back by virtue of their sheer numbers!

Performing the theurgic rites of the elders, he danced with his blade and spoke aloud in arcane, insectan languages.

And the minions of Haemarr responded. Burrowing into the fallen Augurs, they animated the dead.

Thus Lysis commanded over thirty crippled corpses. As Haemarr's magic animated the dead, his avatar fully grasped the power of possession and reanimation. His victims rose. Empty eyed. Arms contorted. Spines twisted, bones piercing their husks. And Lysis set them upon their friends.

"Feed!" he demanded.

Terror rendered the remaining ranks of the Carver Guild useless. Many ran hysterical off the battlefield. Others fainted. The dead fed upon themselves, some dumbly eating truncated limbs, others gnawing into the warm flesh of the living...

LORDS OF DYSCRASIA

LORDS OF DYSCRASIA
GRAPHIC SWORD & SORCERY
S. E. LINDBERG

Lords of Dyscrasia
Copyright © 2011 by S. E. Lindberg
ISBN # 978-0-615-39286-8

Dyscrasia Fiction™ is a trademark of IGNIS Publishing LLC
Cover Art by S.E. Lindberg

IGNIS Publishing LLC
P.O. Box 1841, West Chester, OH 45071

The MORPHEUS FONT is used with permission from Kiwi Media.

Photoshop brushes from Obsidian Dawn were used to enhance some images (www.obsidiandawn.com).

SELINDERG.COM

Pleased visit the companion website _www.selindberg.com_ that features interactive maps, additional illustrations, video book tailers, and more!

The LAND and SKY

Avian Aerie

Abandoned Land

Clan Lysis

Gravenstyne Fortress

Insectan Five

CLAN TONN

CLAN QUAL

CROMLECHON

NORTH

ONE DAY'S
WALK

The UNDERWORLD

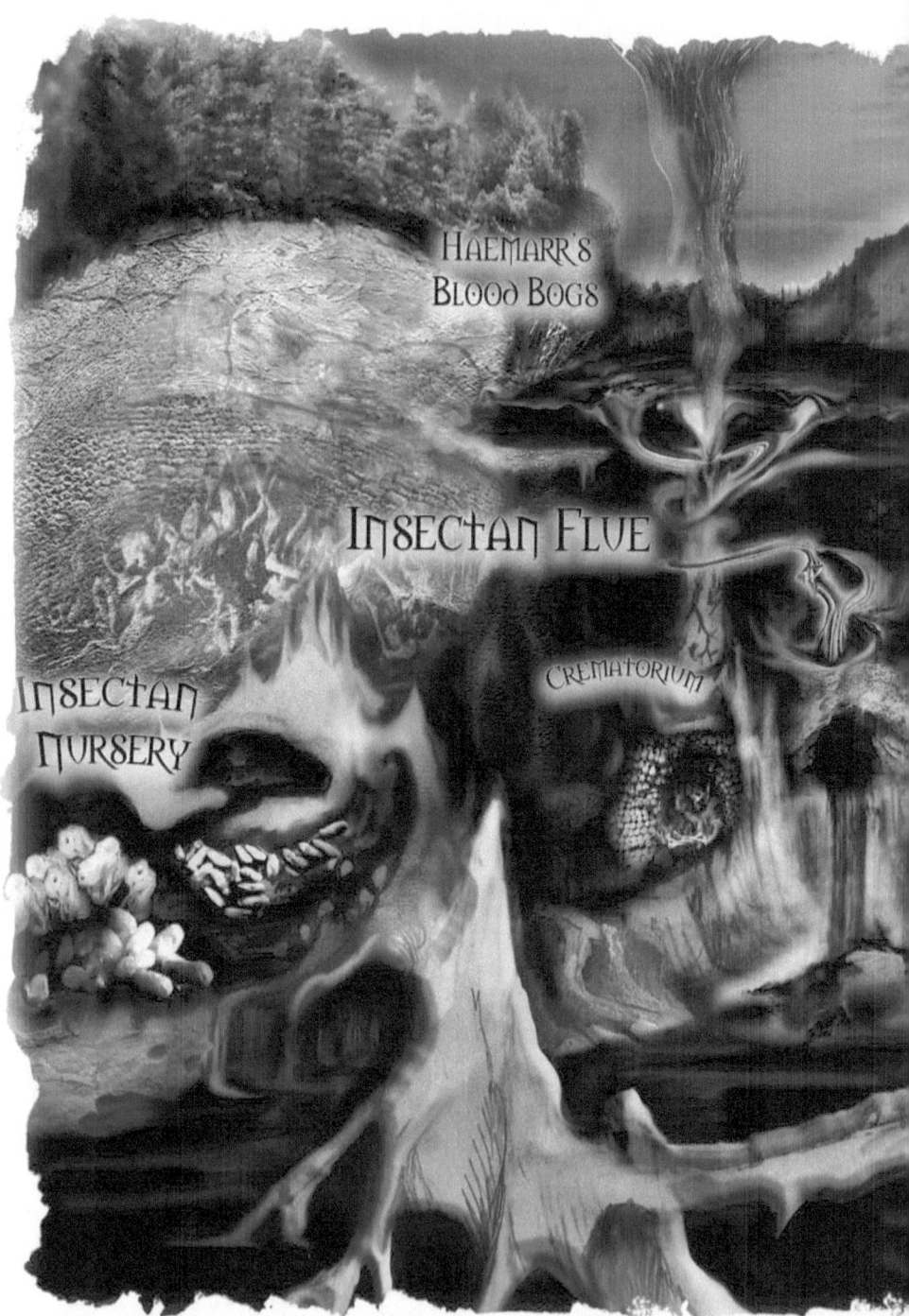

HAEMARR'S
BLOOD BOGS

INSECTAN FLUE

CREMATORIUM

INSECTAN
NURSERY

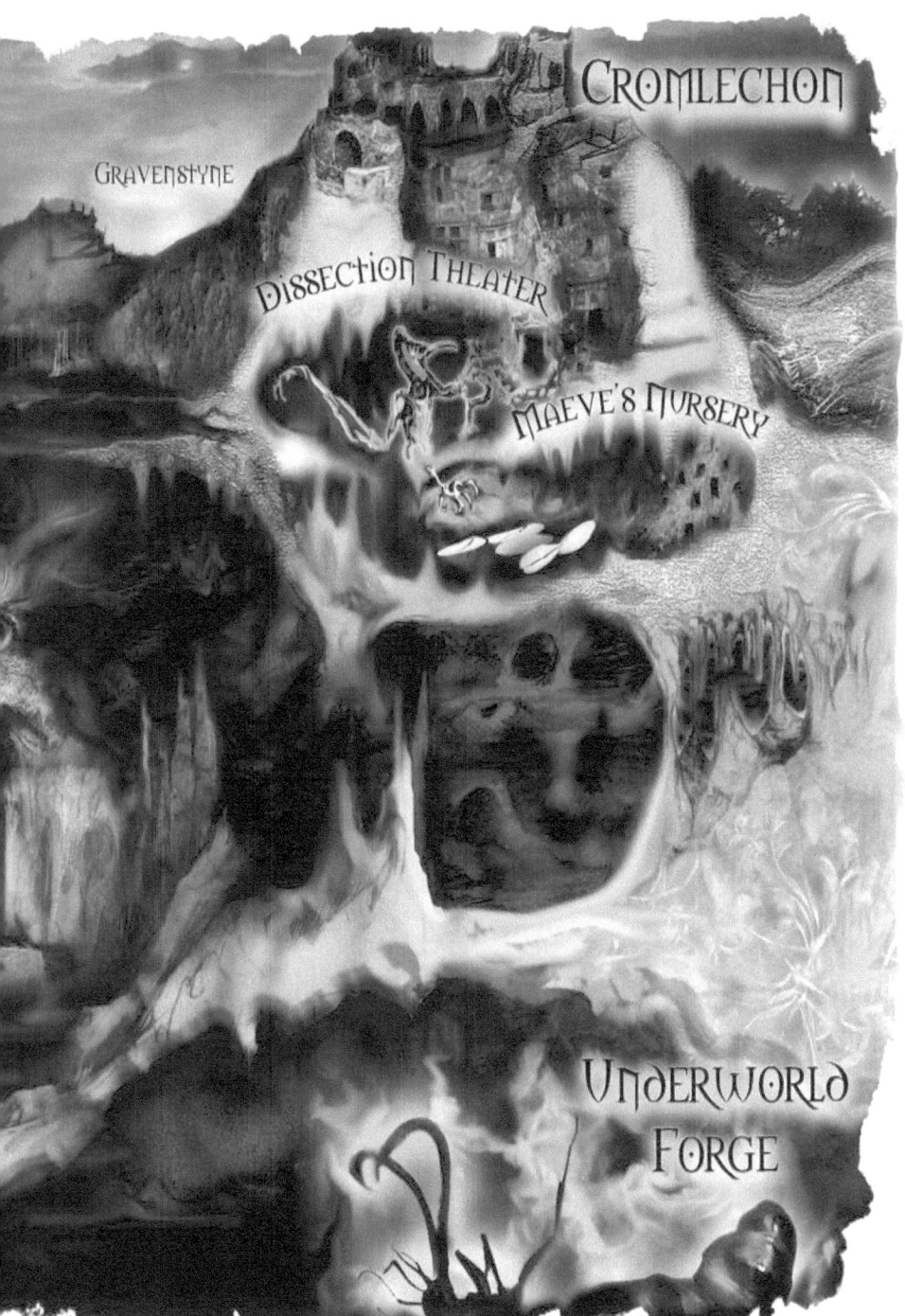

CROMLECHON

GRAVENSTYNE

DISSECTION THEATER

MAEVE'S NURSERY

UNDERWORLD
FORGE

Contents

PROLOGUE: DEY'S DIARY

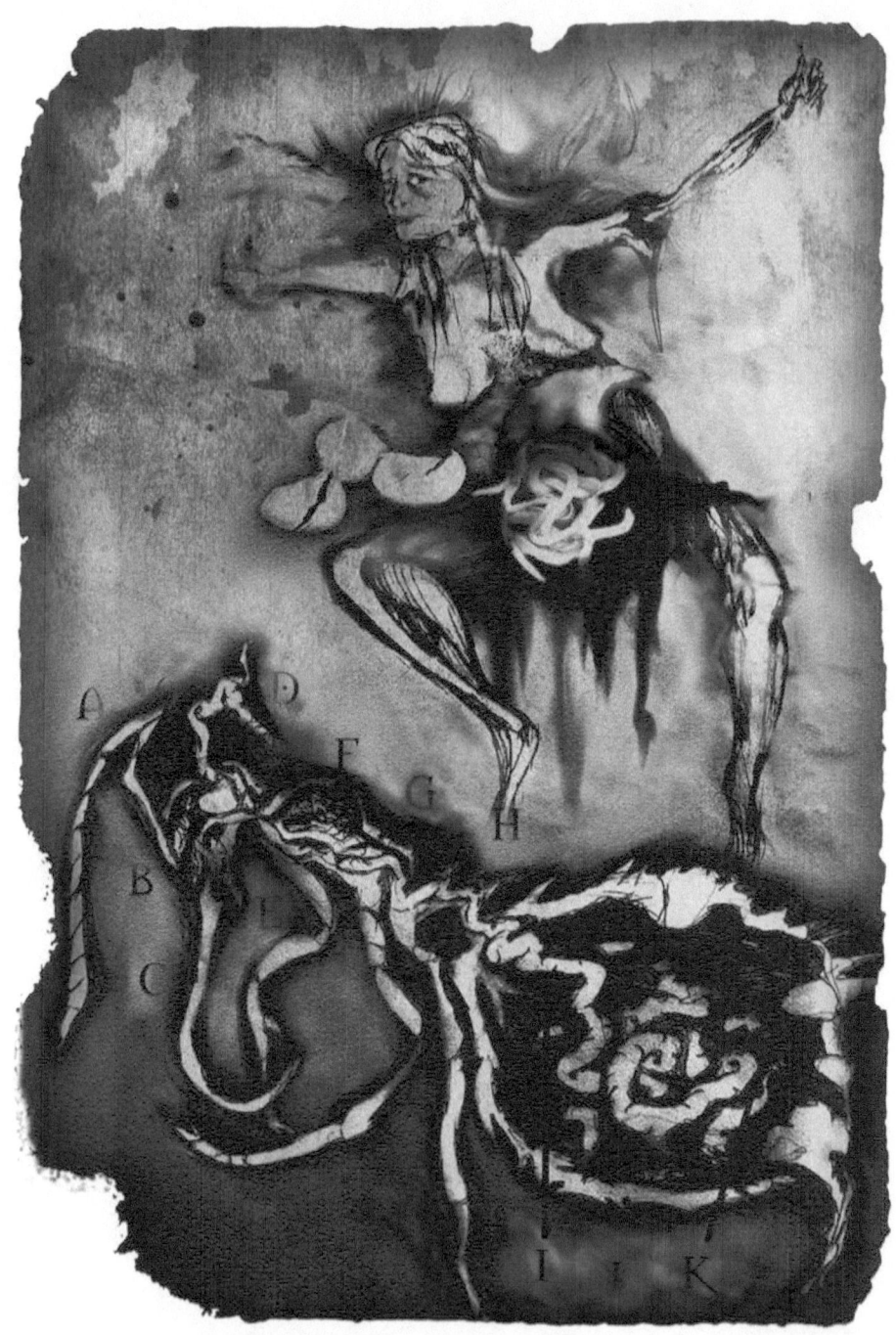

Dey's sketch of a dyscrasia victim

Prologue: Dey's Diary

Diary, I tallied the Dissection Theater's subjects again. Three and ninety female corpses. One and eighty pregnant. Forty embryos not quite human— plagued with dyscrasia. Doctor Grave has brought the fresh batch, magically collecting the victims from afar, and now his minion barbers labor to render the flesh, blood, and bone.

Dyscrasia has affected the Land for decades. All clans contribute victims: Clan Qual, the tailors and dyers of the central gorge; Clan Tonn, the metal workers, jewelers, and stone cutters of the northeastern ridge; and Clan Lysis, the painters and craftsmen of the western highlands. Even the godless folk of the Cromlechon cave colony, under which this Theater rests, donate lives. The scene before me represents the Land's dire health. Dead mothers piled in heaps. Their orphaned, lost children seeking refuge here. Victims of dyscrasia: a disease of blood and spirit.

The lifeless embryos exhibit the disease explicitly. The stillborn mutants present eldritch traits, all unique and terrible. Beaks and downy feathers adorn the avian ones. Translucent, soft-shell exoskeletons wrap the invertebrate insectan type, which are always infected with worms. They are actually larvae, as Doctor Grave often corrects me. Larvalwyrmen, he calls them. They get much larger as they age, as testified by a mummified example suspended in the Theater by five iron rods—it is nigh a fathom long. When he sees these embryonic larvae Grave becomes emotional, stroking their skins as if to comfort them. He would nurse them to maturity if he could. I know not the extent of his necromantic powers, but it is clear he is motivated by some fascination for the insects.

Doctor Grave is an ageless figure who reeks of smoke and is armored with distressed leather made of human flesh. I have never seen his face owing to the fact it is forever concealed behind his hood of oiled skin. The cloaked barbers of his guild dissect and prepare the bodies. It has never been clear where the bodies are eventually buried. Before they leave the Theater, I sketch as many as I can. For example, consider the sketch of the woman before me now. Inside this dead mother's womb, I discovered three eggs. Two of them were cracked, filled with misshapen embryos. These specimens had transmuted to stone, petrified into fossils. One intact egg, more fragile and not yet calcified, concealed a developed, tusked nymph, itself infected with larvalwyrmen.

I see my mother's reflection in this lady. Perhaps I will see her again, brought here to the Theater as one dead. That possibility terrifies me. It would be fitting, however, for her to find me here to judge me for leaving her to battle my drunken father alone. I ran away from him, not her. She probably has been searching for me for years. But I cannot go back. My fear of him is more than my love for her. This dissection theater within the Cromlechon colony is my home now. Doctor Grave had welcomed me here years ago, and there seems no better place for me in this desolate Land. I am safe here. I seem to be immune for I have often contacted contagious fluids without consequence. Grave says there must be something in my blood that protects me. For some reason, he laughs when he says that.

Doctor Grave says the tribal Picti are responsible for the disease. He promises to take me to one of their mysterious rites soon. I can hardly wait to see a ritual. A ritual promised to demonstrate the intangible link between the humans and elders, and perhaps reveal mysteries like how their worshipping propagated the disease. Now the avian and insectan elders are nearly extinct. Those living are mutated. And their symbiotic Picti die with them. These humans persist only in pockets, primarily within the Lysis clan.

Grave says that the insectan elders were once large enough that people could ride them like horses. Now only the miniature variety survives, and these appear as common insects. Grave pats me on the back, laughs, and says, "Be wary of the ones that glow in the night. The fireflies. The lightning bugs. They bite!" I never understood if he was warning me or ridiculing me.

The avian type is all but extinct. There is at least one survivor, a female harpy who haunts the Land preying solely on men. Sometimes Grave gathers the few victims she leaves to decompose in nature. Their injuries suggest having fallen in a battle before being raped and eaten. She is a vampire, a succubus, and a predator. Grave has been tracking her for a long time, but she evades him. He is not skilled enough as a hunter. I hesitate to predict the outcome of their confrontation if ever he caught her.

The emotional force of a hundred corpses suffocates me now. My only home—my very life as an artist of anatomy—cannot be sustained. It is all I have, but it is rotten. In order to have some protection from the elements, the orphaned children don themselves in the bloody aprons of the barbers. Whereas once I was saddened by such desperate measures, now I find them strangely familiar.

I am not the only one in need of salvation. The entire Land needs a healer. I am no healer. Nor does Doctor Grave seem to be a candidate. He claims to want to cure the disease, but seems more concerned about resurrecting dead insects than saving humans. Grave seems to welcome the loss of life, as if he needs to harvest blood for his own mysterious rite. He is a bit like the raven that feeds on carrion, tending to death but not preventing it.

One day I will leave the Theater. I will look for a savior that will resurrect the vitality of the Land.

Anyone who could conquer this disease, which is rooted in the fabric of the Land, must be likewise terrible. Perhaps there will be a hero, a warrior who will vanquish dyscrasia, only to usher unforeseen horrors into this world—horrors that will make us all suffer so much we will wish dyscrasia to return…

I: Endenken Unchained

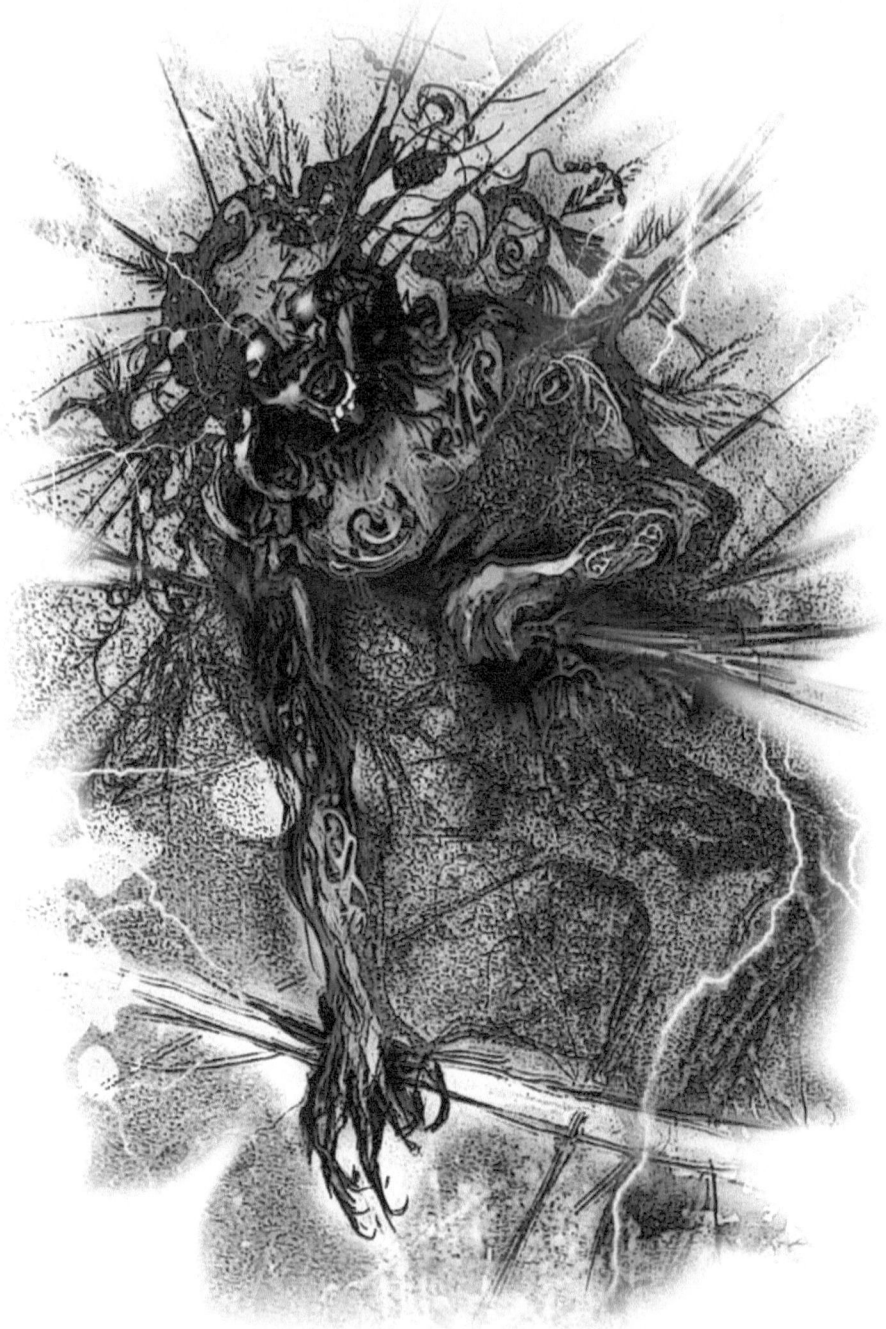

Endenken Lysis chained

I: Endenken Unchained

ENDENKEN LYSIS PUSHED his mother away.

"Enough about Lyhhana!" the stooping Endenken snapped. "You distract me from preparing father's body."

Lady Iriana retreated half a step. Her hair was a voluminous bouquet of thick strands resembling extruded wire. So streaked it was with silver and black, many retainers of Gravenstyne Fortress whispered that the mass was a wig of wrought iron and served as a nest for vultures. She approached her son again and adjusted his hair, exposing her milk-white arm. A train of arabesque tattoos of cinnabar and crimson ink blended with the bundle of veins wrapped beneath her pallid flesh.

"You must accept her along with your future, Endenken," she whispered, braiding the loose locks of his mane. His hair, though finer than hers, was no more beauteous. His hairline was receding, and the grotesque, lustrous curls that poured from over his ears were waxed and braided so as to appear a mane of flaccid, knotted worms. His skin had less color than his mother's.

"Enough!" He slapped her hand away. "I am overwhelmed about performing the Rite and leading the Picts. I'll not listen about Lyhhana again. Tonight we will begin the Inheritance Rite, but I do not feel like the leader you expect me to be. I am a hunter and protector, Mother. Not an artist like you others."

Endenken's quill dripped black ink onto the stone bed as would a scalpel blood. Lord Issynmerz stared blankly from the altar at his wife and son. Issynmerz's body was a still, dead audience. His soul had something to say, but could not be seen or heard by the living.

"You decorate his skin well enough, so you are an artist despite your determination to be different. Strangely, this legacy weighs heavy on your heart.

Perhaps your grief for your father's death confuses you, but you will realize your duties soon. You will carry on our bloodline. You have no choice. You are the only successor."

She moved to clasp his forearm to comfort him, but Endenken stepped away. "My heart simply is not dedicated to the Picti..."

"Nonsense. Although you do not specialize, you are an artisan at heart. You are as fine a Pict as your father was. And after the Rite, you are arranged to marry your cousin, Lyhhana—"

"I would sooner marry one of the servants of the Fortress who do not worship." Endenken held his quill before him like a dagger, the tip shedding dark, indigo drops.

"Endenken, you have always known that loving others would trigger disease. We are blessed to carry the Muse of our ancestors, as only we Lysis can. You must eventually have a child."

"She is barren! We all know that."

"Doctor Grave claims there are ways. There may be eldritch spells that can restore her womb."

Endenken was silent. His head swelled with fever and desperation. Defeated, he asked, "Is there not some counselor who can guide me?"

Lady Iriana shook her head. "You are the one to guide others now. Endenken, accept your role. You are leader of the Picti, and your cult is gathering now above ground. Shortly they will come for you."

Endenken's head swam. *Leader of a dying culture I care not to progress. Let the Picti faith die with Issynmerz. Let him be the last to carry the burden.* He wrestled with the notion of denying the Muse the others worshipped. He had always known this day would come, but he never prepared for it. Now the time of the Inheritance Rite was upon him, and he felt desperately cornered. It was his turn to carry the Muse, the god of the Picti.

"You don't seem to be listening to your heart," Lady Iriana said, "since it pumps the blood that houses our god. Obey it. And take heed, your choices as leader will affect your and Lyhhana's children, as mine and Issynmerz's have affected yours."

Lyhhana's children? Revolted, Endenken regained his senses. "I'll finish preparing Lord Issynmerz's body, but only if you leave me alone. Grant me some space."

So beneath the stone fortress, deep within the catacombs under the conical hill of Gravenstyne, Lady Iriana crawled away like a spider, leaving her son alone so he could finish tattooing her dead husband, former Lord over the Picti,

Issynmerz Lysis.

Endenken could turn his mother away, but he could not turn away the four dozen Picti congregating in the Gravenstyne courtyard. They amassed to escort him to a sacred ceremonial site. The momentum of tradition, and the lack of alternatives, pushed him toward a future he did not want. He would have desperately looked to his courters for help had they been available, but they hid away from the mysterious, masked entourage infiltrating the Fortress. They knew their place, and they were not part of the mystery cult. Endenken may not have felt part of the Picti either, but he was embedded amongst them.

An hour passed and then the funeral masquerade began. Iriana and Lyhhana led the Picts through the subterranean tunnels of Gravenstyne. The women wore colossal skulls of the ancient, avian elders as masks, their feathered headdresses adorned with pheasant quill plumes. The male Picti donned the hollow heads of extinct, eldritch insects. Many of these Picti came from beyond the Clanhold's reach. They were shaman and alchemists from adjacent tribes and recluse clans.

The elder birds and insects had once coexisted with the Picti tribes who worshipped them. Originally the insectan elders were purely mammoth ants, but as they grew diseased they took on avian and human aspects, such as wings and fingered appendages. The ancient Picti had sacrificed hundreds of people to their living gods and were rewarded with enhanced creativity. The more the Picti humans worshipped and crafted art, the more the elders got sick, took human form, and died. The human sacrifices became insufficient to sustain them. In fact, human contact and offerings seemed to poison them; the sharing of blood between man and eldritch god spawned the dyscrasia. The more diseased man and elder became, the more they birthed hybrid creatures—humans gave birth to babies with six limbs and fragile wings; the elder ants hatched from their eggs with human torsos and feathered wings; the elder birds hatched from their eggs with human legs. These diseased young had high mortality rates. Those few that survived were infertile or could not survive the act of mating, which was complicated by the disease. Genuine elder creatures had not been seen in decades because of dyscrasia. Over time, all the colonies and nests fell to ruin.

So now you dress yourselves up in the bones of the dead. You do not honor the elders! Instead, you parody those stricken with dyscrasia! Endenken declared to himself, struggling to contain his anger.

Dyscrasia was transmitted by blood, intercourse, or consumption. Doctor Grave and his Guild of Barbers at the Cromlechon determined that the Lysis clan carried a strain of the disease but were not contagious unless they mated outside the family. The fact the Lysis family could bear living children with the disease was a testament to their sacred lineage. They were specially designed, it seemed, to carry the eldritch powers. If Endenken started a family with one of the non-Picti, as he wished, his offspring would undoubtedly exhibit the disease. Be misshapen. Have crustaceous skin like a roach. Die. His ancestors had tested this time and again, giving birth to mutant humans that resembled insectan larvae. It was why Issynmerz mated with his sister Iriana. It was why Iriana knew Endenken had to mate with his cousin Lyhhana, last female of the Clan aside from herself. The Picti had isolated dyscrasia, their faith, in the Lysis clan. Their blood was sacred. They had few left to carry it. And it was Endenken's turn to inherit the burden.

So why must I accept it? I do not want this! I care not for my cousin. I do not want to carry on Issynmerz's duties, to be burdened with yesterday's promises and beliefs.

But Endenken had nowhere else to go.

And the masked grotesqueries swarmed him now, their human frames transfigured by ornate markings and hollow eldritch skeletons.

He could hardly deny the press of his masked visitors. All greeted him in silence, one by one, and bound themselves to him with hooked lines of fine wire and silk cords. It took several hours to tether each member to Endenken to make tangible the ethereal connections among the cult members. Flocks of birds and colonies of ants seemed to share single spirits, and so did the Picti, who honored the avian and insectan elders. Endenken had thought bitterly, and with apathy, as needles were sown through his skin for hours on end: *You pretend to be social insects married to some grand monarch via spiritual bonds. I am not your monarch for if I was, and you could read my thoughts, you would know I would abandon you. I just need to know where to go. I need a cause.*

Light-headed from dozens of bleeding wounds, Endenken was pulled along like a chained prisoner by the masked parade through the catacombs following the borne corpse of his father. Like ants in procession they scampered through the subterranean tunnels, Lady Iriana leading the way.

E NDENKEN CRIED.

    On the stone slab before him lay Issynmerz's flesh and bone, now reduced to liquids, wax, fine powders, and scrolls of rendered skin. Notably absent from these offerings was Issynmerz's skull, which had been removed earlier along with his heart and blood for special preparation.

Endenken and the sundered remains of Issynmerz were now exposed atop an earth mound north of the Lysis clanhold. The red glow of an autumn moon illuminated them before an audience of nearly fifty Picts. Endenken could not have felt more confined. For three days, he and the Picti cult occupied this sacred dolmen, performing the Inheritance Rite. The heir of leadership was chained to the altar with braided wire, consuming only fortified cider to sustain himself as the body of his father, Issynmerz Lysis, was meticulously dissected into its elements so that Endenken could work them into a portrait of the new leader: himself. The time to complete the portrait was nearly at hand.

Hooks tugged at the scabs in his nipples, brow, and hamstrings. He was ensnared by the network of silk cords and fine iron wire connecting him to the scores of Picti members. Many of them were similarly immobilized, chained to one another and to the megalithic stones, some held aloft by iron links dangling from on high, mimicking flight. The shoulders of the females were winged with shawls wove of eagle and crow feathers. Several death-masked ladies were free from the tethers and tended the braziers filled with smoldering white sage leaves; they also mended wire and hooks when flesh yielded to tension. Endenken could not identify all of them, especially since some of the members came from outside the Lysis territory from the northwest regions of the Land where the Picti roamed as nomads.

All but Endenken Lysis wore a mask. Endenken thought to himself: *You honor the elders. But they are extinct. Your gods are dead. Their time is done. We are done.* Then he stopped thinking, his eyes shut, stinging from smoke.

Lady Iriana was easily detected being that she helped orchestrate the ceremony and her wiry hair escaped the confines of her bird skull helmet. She approached from beside a cauldron that had been used to boil the fat from Issynmerz's bones. The bones and fat had already been collected. The fat had been skimmed from the surface of the boiling water and rendered so that it could be used as an oil binder for paint; afterward, the bone, having been cleansed of sinew, was collected from the sediment, sintered, and crushed to produce a brilliant white pigment. Iriana began opening the urns on the altar before Endenken. Wisps of fine powder took flight from earthenware vials.

Endenken coughed, and cried out in pain again. He had broken the rhythm of the swaying men, and suffered. As one swayed, they all swayed. The hooks tugged on those who failed to synchronize. It took all his will to maintain breathing. He became nauseous and focused on the physical pain to keep him alert.

The swaying Picti men chanted as they rocked in their net of wire and inhaled the smoke of incense. Those men on the ground began to bellow and strike empty kettles with iron ladles. They drummed a hypnotic beat, each note allowed to fade before another tremor was issued.

The vibrating hum resonated in the wires harmoniously with the chanting. The booming choir sedated Endenken. Humming. Drumming. Foreboding.

The ancient Rite was a testament of eldritch powers for it instantly summoned swarms of flies, wasps, and carrion birds from the neighboring wetlands. The buzzing matched the frequency of the resonating drums. Pounding. Repeating. Throbbing. Endenken absorbed the sonic pulses from the vibrating chain and through his ears.

All became dark as the storm of insects suffocated the moon. Only the kindling fires from the braziers provided any light... until Endenken discovered the glowing wasps.

Wasps with fiery blue eyes crawled on his forearms and nibbled at his wounds. Some tried to burrow under his flesh where the hooks opened up holes. Endenken looked close and could hardly believe his eyes. The wasps had miniature hands capping their appendages! And the rear legs had five talons each! *Are these the elders? Have our gods evolved into miniature gargoyles? What manner of sorcery is this?*

And there came more glowing man-wasps. They were drawn to the bleeding wounds on his legs, torso, and neck. And they were also drawn to the urns containing the corporeal elements of Issynmerz.

The hooks and wire prohibited him from crushing them.

Before Endenken could examine the insects further, Lady Iriana approached carrying Issynmerz's rendered skull. Her hands were gloved with mammoth pincers, the hollow, fossilized hands of an elder ant. These chitin gauntlets protected her hands from the human-like wasps, which grew excited at this procession and flew at Iriana. But rather than attempting to bite her, they escorted her to the altar.

Kerning. Pounding. Compounding.

Endenken wanted to warn her that something was not right with these wasps. But she seemed unalarmed with their presence. Yes, she was familiar with them. *They recognize the power in the skull. And they recognize her. She expects them to be here.*

He wanted to call for help. But he had no one to call to.

Iriana deposited the skull containing Issynmerz's blood beside the containers housing the purified pigments.

Endenken wheezed.

He tried to focus on the offering before him but could not, for he swayed in accordance with the vibrating tethers, and the smoke stung his eyes and blurred his vision…

"Time to begin your portrait," she commanded.   She leaned back Issynmerz's head to expose the heart cradled in its mouth.

Then it was as if the sun had abruptly risen!

Red, boiling blood!

So brilliant was Issynmerz's bloody heart, it made Endenken squint. The radiance pulsed as if it were still alive.

Winged insects rushed forth to drink Issynmerz's blood. But as the aura of blood contacted the wasps, they dropped like rocks and shattered on the stone. Puffs of powder were all that remained. Endenken did not have time to clarify all these observations. He knew only that he did not feel a part of this ritual. He did not want to lead others in this dyscrasia-riddled faith. He wanted out. He did not want the poison that was in Issynmerz's skull.

Iriana flapped behind him and with her insectan pincers cut the dozen cords restraining Endenken's hands and arms. This signaled an end to the swaying, though the chanting continued and the smoke remained thick.

"Now, accept your lineage. Sculpt an image of yourself from your father's remains! Drink his blood!"

I did not ask for this burden. I seek my own path.

Endenken clutched his hands to regain feeling. Then he stared directly at the infernal Muse. He could not deny that the Picti's faith had substance. The mutated, eldritch wasps had been called to it. He could feel its presence, for it gave off an eerie heat as if it really were on fire. Their Muse was real. It was terrifying.

Invisible tongues of flame lashed from the mouth and licked Endenken. It was hungry. The heart wanted him.

In desperation Endenken redirected his gaze beyond the confines of the ceremonial earth mound.

Cannot move. Breathe. They are not honoring me. They are sacrificing me. They are going to kill me! But I cannot move. Trapped.

Confused by the weight of expectation and the intoxicating smoke, he could not break free on his own accord.

If only this moment would pass. I could awake tomorrow elsewhere. Safe. Away. Not bound. Not dead. I need more time. Or, I need time to pass. Let the night pass and bring day…bring me the sun…Let the day come…

Then the cries of a woman pierced his thoughts.

Oh, let day come…

He heard the despairing voice scream, "Day!"

The mysterious maiden called out as she stumbled. It was as if she were reading his mind. Was she real? A hallucination?

"Day! Day?" she begged the Picti on the dolmen, but they simply ignored her incoherent plea. Their god was exposed and ready to embody a new custodian, and she dared to interrupt the climax of their Inheritance Rite with her plaint. She demanded attention. It did not occur to Endenken that she had not strayed here by chance, that she may have been called here like the insects were drawn to the scent of Issynmerz's blood. Nor did it occur to him that the path of her journey might have been orchestrated by evil beings that hunted her and steered her here.

The maiden pressed forward insisting on a response. Delirious and weak, she fell to her knees and crawled, reaching into the air as if to grab a hand. No hand was offered, so she collapsed.

"I need to save her!" Endenken cried out. *I need to save me!*

"I reject Lyhhana. I reject Issynmerz's blood!" Endenken flexed his grip on the wire tethers and started pulling, loosing flesh from his own body and that of the Picti anchoring the opposite ends.

Chaos erupted.

Lady Iriana approached, but Endenken twisted the beak of her death mask and then pulled it downward to send her rolling aside.

Chanting turned to wailing as hooked chains were torn out of those who sang. Picti dangled haphazardly, swaying like ensnared animals with wrists, necks, and ankles caught in nets. In an instant, a score of men hung from the stone scaffolds.

Endenken went berserk.

"Never!" he cried as he chewed through osier strands. He was deliberate with his rage, injuring only those who restrained him.

The skin of his chest was torn free, from the nipples outward. Endenken took no heed of this.

Wires he could not snap he tugged at fiercely to injure those attached. This broke many Picti bones and hailed a storm of blood from countless wounds.

Several feathered females tried to restrain him. One he swiftly kicked into a cauldron. Another went down as he manipulated a chain rope to twirl around her neck, coiling it like a whip to snap her skull mask and split it asunder. In a span of seconds Endenken disabled four more.

Then the vibrations ceased. The air grew suddenly still. He was completely disconnected. He was free. Liberated. Focused. Unstoppable.

Endenken departed in a flash to rescue the unknown maiden. Physical wounds could not deter him. In moments he would lift her off her feet and bear her to the protection of Gravenstyne Fortress. He would leave his vulnerable cult behind to recover without his guidance.

Lady Iriana arose wounded and contemplated protecting Issynmerz's blood versus running after Endenken. The Rite was left incomplete. Both her husband and the cult's Muse had been forsaken.

Cousin Lyhhana crawled out from the cauldron, her ceremonial costume ruined, looking for support from the Lady.

Iriana silently closed Issynmerz's mouth and looked up to witness the arrival of an immediate threat. Two shadowy figures stalked toward them. One prepared a bow with an arrow. The other hefted an ax.

The mysterious maiden had been chased here by these malicious beings that now breached the perimeter of the sacred mound. They had come to prey on her but found better game.

"You trespass," shouted a Picti male. But he said no more as one of the trespassers clove the man's insectan mask in two.

The bewildered and injured Picti were simply not prepared to defend themselves. Doom was certain.

Iriana caught a glimpse of the ax wielder's face and her heart sank. She recognized the outcast. These visitors had not come here by chance. She did not recognize the maiden, but understood the supernatural attraction of those with special blood toward the ceremony.

"Husband, our outcasts have come to claim an inheritance they do not deserve. Surely they come for you, as your Muse speaks to them. They follow invisible tethers to your power, but they shall not have it. They are not the proper heirs—"

In an instant, she ran away with Issynmerz's skull. She would protect the Muse at all costs, and for now that meant hiding it. Her only hope was to reach the Picti underground tunnels that connected to Gravenstyne's catacombs. As she retreated, her ears absorbed the horrible sounds of slaughter.

DAYS LATER, PALE as a corpse, Endenken departed the courtyard and descended into the porous core of the stony Gravenstyne. The arcades that welcomed him were at once primeval and ornate, with sculpted pillars intermingled with raw stone. Half-artificial. Half-natural. The architecture permitted streams of sunlight to pierce sections of the corridor and illuminate dust clouds otherwise left unseen. Servants muddled to and fro, buzzing like disturbed bees conjuring the storms of dirt. Endenken snaked his way through the honeycombed foundation. He had a mission. The servants of the estate kept an appropriate distance, too afraid to approach the Lord but too obedient not to attend him. Most were brooding over what would become of the Fortress, in fact the Clanhold, without a proper ruler. Lord Issynmerz had passed away just days ago. Iriana, Lyhhana, and Endenken were to return after the funeral rite. But only Endenken came back, injured, carrying a mysterious maiden in his arms. Whatever had transpired, it was tragic.

"Sexton Julian Kar?"

"Yes, Lord." The servant approached, holding a pick in one hand and a torch in the other. Grime coated him as though he had been exhumed from his own grave.

"Share your light and come with me to the bath chambers." And so the pair went. "Are all the remains taken care of?"

"Yes. Lyhhana's remains lie in her designated niche. The bodies of the Picts from outside your Clanhold have been collected and placed in the catacombs alongside her. Do you expect someone may claim them?"

"No. The Picts are a dead cult. Their souls shall rest peacefully once I catch their murderers. So you confirm that Lady Iriana and Lord Issynmerz's niches remain empty?"

The sexton Julian Kar nodded. "They were simply not present at the dolmen when I arrived."

"Iriana must have run away with Lord Issynmerz's elements. No matter. The Picts are finished. We are starting anew. We have been sent an angel to lead us forward."

"The woman?"

"Yes." Endenken clasped his servant's shoulder. "You are tired. I should not have postponed your rest. Go now. We have arrived at the bathhouse..."

"Shall I stoke the furnace? Boil the bathwater?"

"I am not here to bathe. Only to check on the woman and Doctor Grave, who tends to her."

Endenken marched around the bend and into the echoing chamber, the flickering light of beeswax candles illuminating the chamber from a chandelier. She lay in a bed beside the pool, which reflected the fiery lights from its mirrored surface. The Doctor demanded this arrangement in case she grew feverish and required immediate immersion into cold water.

Endenken stared at the maiden's dark veins bulging through her skin between her bandages. His own body had been wrapped like a mummy to contain the letting of blood from all his wounds. She looked no better.

"Does she have dyscrasia? She looks frail."

"Her blood is dark. She is merely melancholic, but generally healthy," Grave answered. The Guildlord barber kneeled to inspect the woman. His leathery hood cloaked his entire head, as if it were an executioner's mask. It matched the texture of his hide apron: quilted flesh, tanned and waxed to repel contagious fluids. A mysterious, icy fog accompanied him everywhere. "What you really want to know is if you can be with her without getting ill. Without giving birth to ill things. Your boyish attraction seems ill placed given the slaughter at the dolmen."

Endenken replied, "Surely I am spellbound since I am drawn to her more so than I was the Muse. Sorcery or impulsive love blinds me, so I must know if we are compatible."

"We must perform a test. I will need a sample of your blood to mix with hers. If it reacts, then it means you two are carriers. Then you shall be without hope. However, if the blood blends peacefully, then it means the strain of dyscrasia you carry is not activated by her blood. You shall then have hope of starting a family, assuming she awakens and you win her heart. As of yet, you do not even know her name."

So the Doctor unwrapped a dressing from Endenken's shoulder, ruining the burgeoning scabs. He collected an aliquot of blood into a miniature vial, and then retrieved an equal amount from the unconscious maiden. He shook the vial vigorously.

The two liquids mixed homogeneously without effort or effect.

"You shall be hopeful. And you should be gracious. Many Lysis have wanted a family but could not. You, at least, have a chance with her."

Endenken paced.

"What is the problem? You are not excited by this news? Your blood is miscible."

"Lady Iriana claimed I could not mate outside our family, and the maiden is not of the Lysis clan. Can we trust this test?"

"The test is certain, though history supports your mother's claim. Dyscrasia has turned many of your ancestors into mutants. So you are right to fear it. We who study the body do not understand everything about the disease."

"I would feel better if you confirmed the test. Can you show me what happens in the alternate case?"

Doctor Grave rummaged through a pile of bloody clothes. "Yes, I can. Your kitchen attendant, Pauline, provided a clean gown for the maiden to wear.

So now the maiden rests clean and bandaged. But here are the maiden's original clothes. Her leggings, as you can see, are splattered with all types of gory chunks that are not of her color. It seems that before she approached the Rite, a ghoul fed upon her, leaving residue from his previous meals. In any event, this sample provides us with a comparison."

Endenken watched as Doctor Grave laid down the stained legging onto the stone floor of the Gravenstyne Fortress chamber. The Doctor then poured the contents of the vial onto the bloody stains.

The concoction of blood balled atop the surface of the cloth, resisting the pull of the fibers wishing to soak it up. The liquid droplets were repelled by the red stains, skittering haphazardly, like oil on a hot skillet. They split into boiling, serpentine tubes. Electric sparks flashed, and smoke puffed, and the rivulets of blood transformed into writhing worms groping for purchase. In seconds the worms crystallized into ashen sculptures.

"Petrifaction is caused by dyscrasia. The mixing of diseased blood initiates an alchemical reaction, turning blood into stone. If you are successful in hunting the evil entities that hurt her, I recommend you not let them mate with you or expose your blood to them."

"You have a strange sense of humor, Doctor."

"I was not jesting."

Endenken still was uneasy. "Does this test indicate she is of the Lysis clan? Was she some outcast of my family?"

"No," Grave responded assuredly. Then he caught himself from revealing too much, and answered at a more measured pace. "She is not of the Lysis clan. She is an orphan who desires only to have a family."

"You recognize her, don't you? Do you know her identity?"

"I admit that I have seen her before at the Cromlechon colony. I do not know her by name," Grave lied. "But I know a little of her assailants. She has spoken in her sleep. From her wails and from the evidence, it is clear that four devils abused her: one who imprisoned her and drinks blood named Potter; one who kidnapped and enslaved her named SanGules; an ax-wielding mercenary who raped her named Brood; and Narl, a cannibal who hunts with a bow. You must rid them from the Land—once you are healed, of course. You will need some days to recover."

"I will not rest long. I must protect all who live within my Clanhold."

The Doctor spoke carefully. "Strange. You seemed more concerned about the fates of the commoners than those of your true family. The devils massacred the Picts, but you do not speak of revenge."

"I am my own family," Endenken said. "There are none left to care about. Issynmerz and Iriana have not been located. Whatever trailed this maiden now threatens the commoners and my estate, and I will not allow another atrocity to occur."

"Did you already meet these devils? Are they the ones that harmed you?"

"No. My injuries are self-inflicted or imposed by the Picti as they sought to restrain me. I was enraged, but I did not kill any of my brethren. Not that I know of, anyway. Surely I injured many, but I know most were left alive for they called to me as I ran to save this maiden. Since then, all have perished or gone missing. Sexton Julian Kar has investigated the dolmen. He gathered the remains and placed them all within the Gravenstyne catacombs. Iriana's body was not among the carnage. Nor were the remains of my father. Lyhhana's dislodged head was found yards from her body. Her neck was severed with a blade. No doubt this warrior Brood and his ghoulish archer Narl are the evildoers. I did not find the devils themselves, only their destruction. So, I am the last of the Lysis clan. I will share my fortress with all the villagers. I will let them move within the protective hill of Gravenstyne Fortress. And I will start life anew with this maiden, if she will have me."

Doctor Grave checked the maiden's wounds. "So you shed one family for another as a serpent molts its skin. Somewhere, out there, the Picti Muse awaits your acceptance. Your refusal disrupts their faith. You say you are the last of your clan, but Iriana may yet live."

"I doubt that. Even if she does live, and she comes home again, I would still not accept her faith. The Lysis clan no longer carries that burden. I chose to disregard the Muse. Now I choose my future, and I choose to be with this woman."

The Doctor said, "Burdens are not easily shed. As a demonstration of your devotion, you must protect her. It may take weeks for her to awaken from this state of disrepair. Use this time to hunt the Land of her abusers. If you convince her that you can protect her, she will surely be yours."

Suddenly, Brewster Leamond barged into the chamber and exclaimed, "Lord! Your Orchard needs protection. An archer intruded and shot bone arrows at me. His arrows missed, and I turned back to discover a barbarian approach. They are the murderers you warned us about!"

"Doctor, I am called to duty," Endenken said, moving to leave. "Those devils stalk my Clanhold unabated."

"But your wounds are still bandaged. You need more time to recover,"

Doctor Grave said.

Endenken did not look toward the masked barber to reply, but instead maintained his stare at the maiden. "Watch her in my absence. I trust your good judgment. Keep her healthy. If she awakens, keep her here."

"Very well, then. Have no worries, Lord Protector of Gravenstyne. I will look over her as if she were my own daughter."

WEEKS LATER, MAEVE awakened in the subterranean bathhouse. Doctor Grave and his mysterious fog were there, watching over her, to welcome her back to reality. Unbeknownst to the servants of Gravenstyne, the fog was a sentient elemental fairy and the Doctor, despite his human form, was a golem comprised of earth. Both had nursed elder infants—when there were elders to nurse. But that was long ago. In the absence of fledglings and nymphs, these nurses turned toward nurturing something new. Something they created. Amongst the humans, the Doctor concealed his earthy substance with masks and the Nurse concealed hers by shape-shifting into a variety of vaporous forms. Their daughter was the only human who could recognize them for what they were.

"Father! Mother! Where am I? Am I dead? Are we at the Forge? The Theater?"

Nurse Fae assumed a feminine, motherly form, wrapping about her daughter like a warming shawl.

Doctor Grave allayed the maiden by touching her shoulder. "You are repaired! Oh, you are our greatest creation!"

"Where are we? This burrow smells like the Cromlechon. Did you drag me home?"

"You are in the belly of the Gravenstyne Fortress, home of the Lysis clan that has always attracted you. Oh, we have not looked into each other's eyes in many years. We are sad to discover how you have been abused. You had to be so independent..."

"I had to start a family of my own. But all has gone awry. Father, I lost my son, Dey. I need to find him!"

"Where has he gone?" He sounded as if he did not know the whereabouts of Dey.

"He ran away years ago. I have been searching for him ever since. I have lost track of the time. I have been held back from him, the world... for years..."

"If Dey ran away deliberately, you must not search for him. Let your child go and explore as he desires. As we let you go."

Maeve's head lowered as she accepted that argument. Inspecting her bandages, she said, "You and mother were too different from me. I felt more at home with the orphans of your Theater. They looked like me. Knew me. Oh, those poor, abandoned children. I need to find my son."

"Families naturally disassemble as they age. You left us. Dey left you." *I abandoned my Queen to start a family. To make you.*

Maeve asked, "Where do I belong then? With the humans? Is that what I am?"

"Without doubt," Doctor Grave said. "Your mother and I sacrificed much to ensure you would be. The elders used their creative powers to transmute the elements into us. We were supposed to watch over their young. And we did. But when dyscrasia ruined their colonies, your mother and I had nothing to care for. So we tapped the elder Haemarr's waning powers, without which we could not create you. We wanted only to nurse our own young. We did not appreciate how fleeting our family would be, for we were ignorant of your eventual need for your own life. Your own family."

Maeve looked at her living flesh. It was as real as any human's skin she had ever seen or felt. It was more giving and alive than her father's golemesque body or her mother's vaporous form. Unlike the Doctor, she need not cover herself in flayed hides to conceal her appearance. Her flesh was real and it was beautiful. Her veins pumped real blood. "Am I fully repaired then?"

"Physically you are stabilized. Mentally you are weak. You need someone to love. That shall come sooner than you think. A worthy one comes who will not abuse you."

Endenken entered with a necklace of four scalped heads, each dried and gilded.

Glossy eyed, Maeve stared at the human Lord. To most he would appear an oddity, with his balding pate and mane of white hair. But his love was true and his sanguine aura bloomed over any ugliness like a white sun. Only beings bestowed with special sight could *see* the emotional fire in which Maeve now basked.

"You are awake! Please, tell me your name!" Endenken was elated, kneeling at her side and taking her hand in his.

Her black, curly locks relaxed as he held her. She whispered, "I am Maeve. I have not felt this safe in many years. Are you my rescuer?"

"I am Endenken, Lord of Clanhold Gravenstyne, and you heal within my fortress. I am your Protector—your husband, if you will it. For you saved me, your mere presence tearing me away from my bonds. My obsession for you comes as instinctively as does breathing. For now, know this. I tracked down the evils that abused you. They are no longer a threat. And I vow to protect you henceforth."

Endenken and Maeve continued to hold hands. Grave's fog congealed about his leathery form to comfort him and join in his detachment.

Maeve cried. Joy overwhelmed her, for the warmth of Endenken's hands poured hope through her where so many others had offered harm. She had been starving for this feeling. And now, suddenly, she bathed in it. Now, the leader of the Lysis clan promised to treat her kindly.

Endenken displayed his necklace of scalps. "One relic from each of the four devils. It is not beauteous art, but it is not meant for beauty. Hereafter, you shall look upon this necklace and know my conviction is genuine and your protection secured."

"Then I am yours," Maeve said before swooning.

Terrified, Endenken exclaimed, "She fails!"

"Fool!" the Doctor said, calming the naive Lord. "She is weak and overwhelmed with emotion. Let her rest. Leave knowing that your heart led you truly."

Later, after Endenken left the chamber, Doctor Grave waved smelling salts beneath Maeve's nose. Startled, Maeve jolted to a sitting position.

"The Lord? Ende—?"

"He is gone now," said Grave. "Dear child, he is last of the Lysis clan. He is stricken with love for you. He will protect you."

"Are you sure?" Her eyes begged for reassurance. She knew she could not recover from failure again.

Doctor Grave nodded and thought, *More so than I could.*

"What of Dey?"

"He left on his own accord many years ago. And your dreadful first husband has since perished. Here you are safe. If ever you wanted a family, here you have a chance. I recommend we conceal your ancestry. I am not sure Endenken would understand."

Dey had been gone for many years, she realized. He would nearly be an adult now. Her first family was no longer. Maeve laid back, her eyelids growing heavy again. She began to accept her new fortune. "Thank you, father. Mother…" With that she drifted off.

Maeve ran her hand over her pregnant belly. She rested on a bench looking outward from the airy courtyard, her eyes mesmerized by the rolling hills and orchards about Gravenstyne. Citric fragrances wafted from the valley gorge and over the rocky ramparts to infiltrate the Fortress.

Pantler Pauline brought her a flask of water and returned anxiously to the Doctor. Pauline had loved Maeve the instant she met her, as did all the servants. Maeve was humble and graceful to a fault, as if she were accustomed to serving others' needs before her own, and so she garnered affection more rapidly than she was comfortable accepting it. She opened the Fortress to everyone and could not discern among societal castes. Everyone adored her. And because they loved her so, they feared for her health all the more. The Gravenstyne servants were all too accustomed to women becoming ill during childbirth. And some had witnessed unspeakable horrors spill from between the legs of the diseased. Dyscrasia-ridden embryos, half-human, half-insectan.

"Doctor, I fear the Lady milks prematurely."

"Dry her breast with a cloth and return the swatch to me quickly so I can examine the milk while wet. Then, I can test for possible contagions without worrying her."

Pauline did so. Aside, Doctor Grave smelled and licked the cloth.

Endenken joined the Doctor. "Is she still healthy?"

"Yes, she is fine. The milk is not sweet. Had it tasted of nectar, honey-like, then we would expect her child to be mutating with dyscrasia. The test is quite excessive, for had she been sick the wasps from the Orchard would have been naturally attracted to her milk. They would be crawling over her like flies. But that is not the case— "

Then they were interrupted.

"Lord, help!" yelled Pear, son of Leamond, as he stumbled onto the concourse a bloody mess. Most called the teenage boy Pear since his hair was blonde with a green tinge. He had an older, red-haired brother whom most called Apple. Their father was the primary caretaker over the Gravenstyne Orchard, and he brewed cider so fine it was considered art and was sold to neighboring villages. When his wife passed away he buried her in the Orchard, and ever since guarded the grounds as much as he tended them. He was a good steward and would defend the trees with his life, if necessary.

"We were helping father gather apples in the Orchard. Then out of the sky it fell, and so ghastly it was, I can hardly describe! It hurt Apple. My father wrestles with it now."

"But you must say more," said Lady Maeve. Her ripe belly protruded as she sprang to attention.

"So I may know what to slay," spoke Lord Endenken Lysis.

"So my husband can retrieve your father and brother!" The genuine redness in Lady Maeve's eyes spoke of her fear of evil creatures and her desire for a safe home for her blossoming family.

"She was blue, like polished lapis. And between her icy, wet lips were curvaceous teeth, long as her twisted fingernails. Her sweet scent hypnotized me. I blacked out for a moment, having inhaled her perfume, and awoke only when she bit into my shoulder! Beside me, my younger brother Apple struggled to sit. She had filled my father with bloodlust. So crazed he became, he shouted out our mother's name."

An elder? Haemarr's mate! Grave gasped in recognition. "So she was winged, like a harpy?"

"Yes! She was horribly attractive! A succubus come to kill us. She attacks Apple and father!"

Maeve gasped in horror.

"Enough!" Lysis departed swiftly.

Doctor Grave began to treat Pear's wounds. *It must be her. We can catch her! But he'll need weapons.* The Doctor secretly whispered to the fog, "Go now, Fae. Tell Haemarr that we have found her." And the fog took the vague form of a gryphon and wisped away toward the south.

Meanwhile Endenken rushed out of the protective citadel with a pickax he procured en route from Sexton Julian Kar.

Suddenly he was upon the scene, the blue harpy still mounted atop Leamond. Apple was unconscious, beside his father.

The succubus rocked to and fro in ecstasy while consuming Leamond.

Evil! What motivates this demon? No matter, it will soon pay for its crimes. Endenken hurled the pickax so that it circulated, end over end, as a whirling blade of death.

The steel pick crashed into the female gargoyle, glancing off her flesh as if it were a toy. The creature looked up at its assailant, extending her wings in anger. She arose, posing rampant, talons and teeth bared.

Endenken charged her, as yet unaffected by her noxious perfume or terrific posture, launching forward to tackle her off Leamond.

Talons raked Endenken's back. He grappled her neck as she encased him with her wings. His back bled in cascades.

Endenken tried in vain to cut into the marblesque scales with his nails.

Her skin felt serpentine against his—hard as ceramic but flexible as feathers.

He struggled just to hold her at bay. She was toying with him, he soon realized. *She seeks to tire me out.*

Minutes passed, though they seemed like hours. Endenken began to feel woozy. Her sweat rubbed off onto his face.

"Ha-ha-ha." Her laugh was human. She watched him now wrestle with intangible hallucinations—visages of herself. She was no longer in his embrace and he never knew she had slipped away! She was perched atop an apple tree, licking her forearm clean of his blood.

I need not defeat her. Just save my men. So Endenken shook his mind clear and heaved Leamond over his left shoulder and made way for the son when the creature took flight, swooping down like a hawk, grabbing the legs of Leamond and flapping her wings to pull oppositely.

A tug of war ensued.

Endenken overextended his weight, leaning back as far as possible, and she let loose her grasp so that Endenken and Leamond tumbled.

Then an eerie bank of mist raced into the Orchard, and within it sparkled hundreds of miniature veins of   lightning. At first Endenken thought the source an army of fireflies, but soon he recognized the glow of the eldritch wasps.

"Nurse Fae?" she addressed the rolling storm. "You bring Haemarr's minions! You'll not catch me. Never!" Then the she-demon hastily abducted Apple and flew away.

Endenken was stunned. The juxtaposition of wasps in flight and the hovering gargoyle evoked memories of his Inheritance Rite. Elder effigies. Insectan magic. Avian mystique. He knew not all the machinations of the elders, but he knew the succubus was an eldritch beast. She looked like an adult version of the dyscrasia-ridden stillborn of his ancestors. *And she was not afraid of me. Only those wasps drove her away.* He had seen those wasps before. They had responded to the chanting during the Picti Rite and come to investigate Issynmerz's blood, the Muse. And they turned to stone. They were incompatible with the red blood. Just like the Doctor's test of dyscrasia showed the mixing of blood that carried the disease, the wasps had turned to stone.

A chill wind dissipated the fog and the fiery blue wasps with it, leaving Endenken safe in the Orchard.

Endenken returned with Leamond, whom Doctor Grave healed to the degree he could. Absent Apple, he and Pear would never be at ease. Strangely, Maeve was affected severely. Apple's abduction evoked mysterious emotions in her, and she began to walk about deliriously screaming out for "day." Eventually she fainted.

"Doctor, she acted like this when I first saw her during the Rite. Can you help her? I do not understand her calling for day."

The Doctor contemplated the matter and decided to confide with the Lord Protector of Gravenstyne: "She calls not for the sunshine but for her first child, a boy so named— "

"—when she interrupted the Rite, she was searching for her son?" Endenken asked.

"I recall consoling Maeve in the Cromlechon a few years ago. She had come to the Theater searching for her son since many orphans seek refuge there," Grave discreetly translated the truth. "Ten years ago, arguably still a child herself, young Maeve had been eager to start a family and coupled with the diseased Potter. But Potter was an abusive drunkard. Their son Dey ran away from this danger. And so Maeve's family fell to ruin."

"Potter?"

"Yes, one of the four whom you slew. Dey has never been found, and Maeve is haunted by this. Understand, you must catch this harpy for she is a threat. That devolved elder lures boys away. Feeds on men. Seduces males. That harpy may have your Lady's son Dey, your Lady's first son, the one she has nightmares about…"

Endenken tried to interrupt so he could absorb the situation, but Grave continued unabated.

"I would not talk to her about this. Discussions could evoke unwarranted distress since Dey may not have been victimized by that beast. But that she-demon will attack again. It could take your first child. Or your second. You must protect your family and your land. The eldritch things of Picti past are hostile toward you and Maeve. She has been victimized by it. You have shed yourself from that faith for your own reasons. In this you two are united. You were born to rid the Land of dyscrasia. It is why your child does not have the disease as it grows in Maeve's womb. You are charged with a common purpose."

"Agreed," Lord Lysis said. "But I have failed my friend Leamond. My orchards are not safe. I lack the means to catch that she-demon. I need weapons with powers like those glowing wasps that drove her from the Orchard."

"Give me one night. I will retrieve the most potent tools ever forged."

The Doctor crawled through the labyrinth near the Picti ceremonial dolmen, burdened with weapons on either shoulder. The sword, *Ferrus Eviscamir*, resembled a grand scalpel, having a blade as long as its hilt; the handle's inscription held Doctor Grave's promise: "Queen, with this I will heal you." The ax, *Ferrus Hewnmaw*, resembled a great meat cleaver; it was used to carve manikins from the earth; its inscription: "Children, may this blade carve you life."

He had retrieved the weapons from his Dissection Theater in the Cromlechon, but was compelled to stop here while heading toward Gravenstyne. He was intimately familiar with these tunnels since he had been Lord of the Insectan Nursing Caste. He knew every passageway of the Queen's Underworld that connected to her nursery. He knew Lady Iriana retreated here after the failed Inheritance Rite, and that she lay dead in a remote corridor. As a corpse, she held the remains of her husband and the Picti faith, the Muse.

The Muse remained infused with Issynmerz's blood, contained in his skull. To those permitted to *see* the Otherworld, they would perceive a bright crimson aura. The Doctor saw this emanate from the blood. He could speak to it. And so he did.

From a distance, Doctor Grave spoke telepathically to the blood-red spirit: *My Queen, it is right to give over Ferrus Eviscamir to the individual who should also inherit your soul, since the promise inscribed on its handle is to heal you and that duty has been passed along. Endenken Lysis will heal your dyscrasia. He will eventually return your soul to its rightful body. I desire to do so myself, but cannot. I gave up that privilege when I created my daughter. For that, I still have debts to your last nymph, Haemarr. But I can aid both Haemarr and you by supporting Lysis. I will help him. In turn, he will assist Haemarr and you.*

Grave remained at a distance, since he had sacrificed the ability to touch her. Dyscrasia had devastated her underworld colony long ago, and the Doctor had retrieved her spirit from her dying carcass with *Eviscamir*, the very blade he used to mercifully silence her nursery of dying nymphs. For many years the Muse remained alive within the blade. Later, long after he had escaped the poisonous Underworld and nursed the last nymph past maturation, Grave connected with the elemental Fae, a surviving nurse of the avian elders.

Having no fledglings or nymphs to nurse, they carved children out of clay with *Hewnmaw*, just as the Queen had molded Grave from the earthly elements. At first, this practice yielded only inanimate manikins. They learned that the Doctor's lingering obedience to his Queen's colony inhibited the animation of his children.

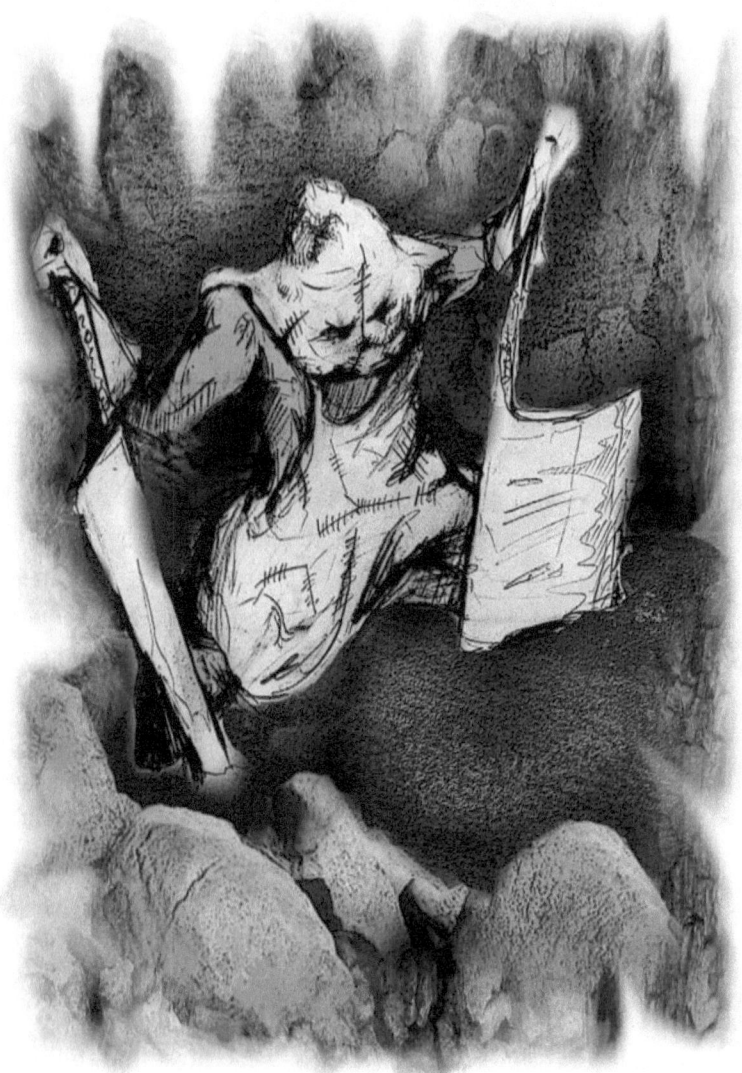

Two blades and motivations strain Doctor Grave:
Ferrus Eviscamir's inscription: 'Queen, with this I will heal you';
Ferrus Hewnmaw's inscription: 'Children, may this blade carve you life'.

To enable the necromancy that would bring life to a child, he had to genuinely forsake his duties to the Queen. But the Doctor could not let the Muse simply die unattended. He decided to pass the responsibility of warding the Muse to the devoted humans who worshipped her and fueled the dyscrasia: Clan Lysis. The soul of the dead Queen was thus passed from *Ferrus Eviscamir* into the blood of Ante Lysis, ancestor of Endenken Lysis, through a painful flaying ritual. The act was successful, so the sword became lighter. Freed from the weight of that promise, Doctor Grave and Nurse Fae borrowed ichor from *Haemarr* to bring life to their daughter, Maeve. True, she was born partly from eldritch ichor and thus was thereafter magnetically drawn to it. So when she grew old enough to desire her own family, she could not resist the attraction toward the Lysis clan.

When Maeve first cried as a babe *Eviscamir's* blade cracked from becoming the lesser of two promises. The Doctor, who was always trying to salvage dying things, fashioned the two curved shards into daggers. These flaying sickles he also carried now.

As Doctor Grave left the tunnel en route to Gravenstyne to deliver *Ferrus Eviscamir* and its two daughter sickles to Endenken Lysis, the fatigued Queen's soul uttered a whisper that her naïve Doctor would not hear: *Your efforts are in vain, for I have foreseen the doom of the elder races. We are to be replaced by gray nymphs, half-human and half-elder—like the ancient chromantis that spawned the elders. These mutants will feed and grow strong on that which has poisoned us. But you prolong my transcendence and that of the others. Haemarr is undoubtedly near death, but you sustain his soul maniacally. What shall I do while you aid my sole surviving child? Shall I sit here passively, imprisoned away from my colony? I would rather die. Yet you have committed my soul to the Lysis bloodline, and so now it is drawn to them. My soul will not sit idle. Your sorcery demands otherwise...*

THIRTEEN YEARS LATER, after it seemed Endenken Lysis had purged every evil from his Clanhold, Leamond's son Pear was suddenly abducted from Gravenstyne's Orchard. The blue-enameled gargoyle had struck again after a long delay. And so Leamond was left without wife or sons.

This event ended a continuous period of growth and happiness. Almost every year since their union, Endenken and Maeve had birthed a healthy child. With no one practicing the Picti faith, the dyscrasia seemed lifted from the Land. Endenken obsessively prowled his Clanhold and eliminated every predatory beast and diseased creature; a museum of his kills filled the great hall of Gravenstyne. *Ferrus Eviscamir* and its daughter sickles were instrumental in Endenken's success. But he never caught the creature that inspired him to hunt in the first place, the eldritch she-gargoyle.

So sad was Maeve over Pear's abduction, she wept openly and began hallucinating about her first child's disappearance. She held to the belief that Dey was safe, having merely run away without saying farewell, which was a kinder scenario than the alternative likelihood: Dey's father could have murdered him. After years of searching, Maeve never did track him down. Now, visions of her first boy enticed her away from the Fortress. Dreamily, she followed—Dey's shades never eluding her sight but always her grasp. Eventually, Endenken and his eldest son, Gurylen, found and retrieved their heart-stricken mother from the Orchard.

Atalen, one of the youngest sons who had a passion for poetry, trailed along and asked, "Why does mother shout? She screams for day when the sun is out?"

"She is haunted by ghosts," Gurylen said as they laid Lady Maeve onto her bed.

"And she will not be sane until I catch the she-demon and secure the Clanhold. I must leave the Fortress to hunt this thing. It mocks us. Evokes horrors. Steals children."

Atalen was mortified.

Gurylen, a teenager with a full head of brown hair and blossoming beard that contrasted with his father's bald pate, said, "How will you track a winged harpy? She appears so seldom, we do not know where she comes from."

"I must hunt her with sorcery. This eldritch sword will first guide me to her. Then it will strike her down."

Atalen pointed to the flying insects that clustered on *Eviscamir's* blade. "Those fireflies? Hunt the skies?"

"They are wasps, my son," Endenken corrected. "Or things like them. They are of the same eldritch make of that which I hunt but of a kinder variety. And you are correct. They can search the skies better than I."

So Lysis left Gravenstyne in order to hunt his singular enemy. He followed the wasps that trailed her distinctive fragrance. Weeks passed. They led him far north, on roadways overgrown and unkempt, over rolling hills decorated with ruined Picti temples.

He came upon a large artificial mound, taller than the hill of Gravenstyne's Fortress. It was a conical construction of layered stones, bones, and eggshells. The wasps urged him to go up, so he ascended as one would approach a mountainous terrain. His feet found purchase on sun-bleached skulls of elephantine birds and insectan husks. Thus he clambered upward over monumental skeletons. With the exception of his guide wasps, insects and scavengers avoided the massive mound. It was lifeless. There was no doubt that these were victims of dyscrasia, for there were numerous hybrids: petrified humans with beaked noses and brows; winged ants as large as draft horses; and calcified, wingless birds with human arms. Many had transmuted into the same type of stone Doctor Grave produced by mixing diseased blood.

When he neared the top, he gazed southward, the view extending for countless miles. Gravenstyne looked like a mere anthill. As he reached the pinnacle of the burial mound, he drew his sword.

"You!" Endenken approached, wielding *Ferrus Eviscamir*. His wasps encircled the she-demon.

The blue harpy sat amidst a heap of human bodies, unconcerned with Endenken's presence. She had brought fresh bodies and deposited them atop the ancient dead. The men were drunk on her eldritch scent, which awakened bestial, sensual desires and clouded their reason. Some of her victims moaned orgiastic death throes. So intoxicated were they, even as she fed upon their flesh, they remained in ecstasy.

She sucked blood as it gushed from a decapitated boy. Her wings remained furled behind her like a plumed, elegant robe. Thus exposed, her iridescent skin and peaked breasts glistened beneath the sun while blood ran in rivulets down her belly. Her arched legs exaggerated her royal grace and drew one's eyes away from her taloned, pronged feet and her twisted fingernails and toward her beckoning hips.

Crimson blood leaked from her lips as she spoke. "You could never subdue me. But I can have you. Come. Have a taste." She approached, relying on her hypnotic scent to sway him. She quickly surmised that her visitor warded her sorcery.

"You are both bird and human. And you eat flesh. You have dyscrasia. I can rid you of your pain."

"You are wise, captive. I carry it. But I control it. I am free. And you seem immune to my aroma, warrior. No matter!" She cawed suddenly, and a drove of blue-eyed blackbirds answered her call. The wasps hastily engaged in aerial combat. Electric sparks showered the sky as Haemarr's minions connected with the harpy's crows, and freshly petrified carcasses rained down. It was not long until all the wasps had been consumed and the flock of blackbirds focused on Endenken.

"You stand on the refuse of my ancestor's primary nest." The she-demon unfurled her angelic wings and raised herself out of Endenken's reach. "As my captive, you shall visit the Avian Aerie yourself. You will find it difficult to leave!"

Endenken lashed out at the onslaught of birds, but it was useless. Two hundred talons dug into his skin and lifted him off the ground. It was all he could do to hold onto his sword. He could not see beyond the feathers around him as he rose. Water condensed on him as he was driven through frigid clouds. If they chose to drop him, he would have perished. But in time they deposited him at the ruined Aerie. The she-demon would not join until later.

The Avian Aerie roosted atop a towering precipice so high that clouds blocked the view to the ground. But there was no doubt Endenken was elevated beyond measure since his lungs labored to extract air from the atmosphere. Eventually moonlight pervaded and illumed the fog so that it glowed with an eerie radiance. The plaza around him was adorned with female gryphons seemingly carved from ice. They were posed tending to gargantuan eggs—incubating some, delaminating ripe shells from others. These nurses were comprised of crystallized water, and it was unclear whether they were carved by human artisans or were real beasts transmuted into ice by sorcery. The eggs were petrified and lifelike. Many had mutated embryos frozen in the act of breaching cracks. Dyscrasia.

Combing the nest, Endenken found several dozen prisoners. Dead. Unchained. Shackles were not needed since the precipice had no exit save through flight. Apple and Pear were not among these but were likely dead. The she-demon would not want to be hampered with long-term engagements. She kept her hunting and sport focused on the moment. She would either forget she deposited Endenken here or return soon to finish him off.

A period of weeks passed. Thrice he had considered eating the flesh of the dead, denying his baser instincts each time. Despite the lack of food, the place emanated some power that curbed his hunger, delayed his starvation, and sustained his life. He longed for Maeve's embrace and the laughter of his children. And he loathed the fact that he was kept from protecting them. Gravenstyne was vulnerable in his absence. And Endenken was trapped—impotent.

Fits of boredom and anxiety lured him closer and closer to the edge so that he could end his imprisonment by jumping. It would not be long until he lost his focus altogether. Then he remembered his blade. Its strength came not only from its sharpness, but in its connection to the intangible. He called to the sword. "By the power in Ferrus Eviscamir, I call aid from wherever the wasps once came. I beg of you to bring more. Save me. Save me from the Aerie!"

Then he unleashed his rage surgically, striking the crystalline gryphons and toppling them from their plinths and over the edge. Perhaps he would awaken some eldritch aid. Perhaps by destroying this sacred place he could attract the she-demon. Perhaps they would crush the gargoyle as she lounged on her living refuse heap. He toppled nearly a dozen statues before falling from exhaustion.

ENDENKEN WAS NUDGED awake by a colossal, icy beak. He was weak at first, and ignored this. But the cold beak rolled him over, gently.

Then something brushed his face. A luminescent blue wasp was crawling on the ridge of his brow.

"Back!" He lurched to attention, deliriously. Before him a translucent gryphon retreated slowly. Eagle head lowered passively. Frosty wings folded and tucked. Then it sat with its lioness forelegs outstretched and together. Its tail whipped out of excitement. Her entire being shimmered with flickering azure, for her vaporous form was filled with buzzing eldritch wasps. An ally had come.

Endenken had just absorbed the notion that he was being saved by a creature akin to the elemental nurses of the Aerie when it became obvious that his angelic gryphon was followed!

His enemy, the blue gargoyle, hovered a stone's throw away from the edge. Her wings flapped harmoniously, chilling Endenken's nerves.

"Fae! You bitch!" The blue gargoyle accosted the gryphon. "You dare bring Haemarr's minions into the Aerie! Look around you. Our nest is dead. I will not join the ranks of these frozen, petrified corpses. There is nothing to nurse here. All the fledglings are dead, and I don't need you anymore! I mate only with humans who do not bear fruit. I will bear no eggs. I am free. I'll not have you watching over me."

Battle erupted as the soaring plaza was flooded with hundreds of birds, all possessed by the demon's hypnotic scent and blue ichor. Wasps from inside the porous gryphon swarmed forth to meet them, only to turn to stone as they collided. Lightning from the alchemical reactions streaked and fracturing the smoke-filled air, crawling like some ethereal, dendritic cancer.

The female gryphon hastily lowered her head so that Endenken could mount her back.

No, I will not ride you in escape! I will attack!

Endenken launched over the edge, *Eviscamir* extended, wasps joining him, and collided awkwardly with the demon's legs. His blade barely scratched her flesh, but his jump propelled his body into hers. So entwined, they fell, wrestling along the way.

Seconds passed as they broke cloud upon cloud. He grasped her leg. She strained to keep aloft and to rid herself of the poisonous wasps. Several eldritch wasps crawled from Endenken's back and onto her leg and stung her. She seized violently, stone wounds swelling at the site of each sting, and he was kicked from her grasp. The she-demon was injured.

Separately, Endenken toppled head over heels, clutching his blade…

Ferrus Eviscamir

THE DOCTOR STOOD beside the statuesque man-wasp offering the corpse of a pregnant woman. The statue was taller than he, with a human head and insectan wings. Its surface was marblesque: basaltic black wrought with brilliant blue veins. This polished appearance contrasted the pose that more truthfully conveyed its sickly nature: arthritic legs, twisted back, and contorted wings. The wetlands surrounding this icon were dark. These cesspools were complex mixtures of oxidized blood, tar, and liquid melancholy. A forest of iron stanchions sprouted from the vast muck, suspending female corpses gray with decay.

The man-wasp figure, although inanimate, was still sentient. It was Haemarr, last nymph of the insectan elders, and he spoke telepathically to his nurse: *We must face our lingering demise, Doctor. Cypria and I are the last of the elders, and we are diseased. You and Nurse Fae are the last of the elemental nurses. I could bear children with Cypria, but she evades me as she fears the death that follows from our disease. Only our litter would survive, and they too may be diseased. But I must mate with her.*

The Doctor returned: *I cannot seem to catch your mate. She escapes my every attempt. We need a human avatar, and my daughter's husband suits. Endenken resisted the Muse to blaze his own path, so strong is his will. Dear Haemarr, I was prepared to delay the Rite, but he did it on his own accord. He forsook the Muse instinctively. Like you, he is motivated by the desire to free his offspring from dyscrasia. He will make good on my debt to you. He will catch Cypria. He will heal the Land.*

He did almost catch her, Haemarr said. *I sensed her flesh through my minions, but he depleted so much of my energy to get close. He knows not the cost of necromancy… the cost of human lives. If only we could break this bond between elder and human blood!*

The Doctor listened as he carried the sacrificial corpse into the fountain, and then returned telepathically, *And I feed you to sustain those powers. But I take women from the Cromlechon and from Qualenson's Clanhold. I avoid collecting from the Lysis Clanhold to minimize alarming Endenken—I do not want him to view us as monsters like he does Cypria.* So the Doctor transfixed the pregnant mother, and her blood and that of her unborn gushed into the black swirls of the bog. The fresh, red offering turned to blue as it oxidized. Haemarr was refreshed. Then wasps crashed onto the liquid. They fed and became bright beacons.

I know the desire to bear children, too, said Grave. *It pains me to have immobilized you in order to give Maeve life. Though your sacrifice enabled her life, she has already passed into death. I was tasked to nurse you. Not weaken you. It was my duty to my Queen to keep you healthy. I must make things right in the end.*

Haemarr responded, *I have never questioned your loyalty. I had no chance of catching Cypria, so sacrificing my mobility to empower your child's birth was worthwhile. You still serve me now, friend. You can still revive the elder race. Enable Endenken to catch Cypria. Then resurrect the Queen.*

As the Doctor reflected on the direness of the situation, his wife arrived.

The elemental gryphon rolled forth from the northern horizon. On her back, Lord Protector Endenken rode as a solemn heap.

Fae deposited the broken Lysis beside Grave and then phased into the fog. Endenken eventually sat upright, braced against *Ferrus Eviscamir.* Malnourished. Defeated. Depressed.

"They are dead, Doctor," Endenken whispered.

"I know."

Lord Lysis did not have enough strength to stand. He stared blankly into the murky liquid of the bogs. "I flew over Gravenstyne on the wings of the misty gryphon. Saw into my Fortress. It was ruined. I demanded to land so that I could search it. But I hadn't the energy even to dismount, let alone break the seal you posted as a warning on the front gate. Clearly, I was too late. I could almost hear my children's voices call out to me from the dead. I fear their souls are being tortured there. Tell me, what did you see there when you quarantined it?"

"Their bodies cannot be saved," Doctor Grave said. Then he paused to grieve silently to himself, *I have seen them... her. Oh, poor Maeve's soul cannot be retrieved. I failed to protect her.* "It seems Lady Iriana, your mother, was correct. You mated outside your bloodline, and dyscrasia has infected your house. I failed—"

"—I failed to protect them. Was it that she-demon? Did she ruin my Fortress and family while she had me imprisoned?"

"It did not look like her work," the Doctor said. "But it was no doubt some similar creature."

Lysis worried not about being infected or enslaved. Now he looked forward only to dying to join his family.

"Death is not the end for souls, only bodies," Grave offered. "You may be able to save those of your family, had you the power to *see* the astral realm."

Endenken replied, "After all the eldritch resources you allotted me already, the sword, the wasps, the fog—those were not enough. You say I need more powers to save my family from eternal pain. To gain sight?"

Grave responded, "To fight dyscrasia you must do more than carry magical artifacts, or even *see* as the gods do. You must gain godlike powers of your own, and for that you must find one willing to share it. Of the avian and insectan elders, only one of each survives. Both are diseased. The avian survivor is Cypria—clearly you cannot partner with her. The other is Haemarr. He has powers, but is immobilized. You will have to go to him. He would have to possess your body through his ichor. You could then use his powers, but would have to serve his will. To do this you must die and be resurrected as one undead."

"Where is he?" A surge of hope kindled within him and brought him to his knees.

"Why, he is right beside you. This mutated wasp is no sculpture. He transmuted into stone, for he too has been scarred by dyscrasia. Still his mind and ichor can be tapped through his minions. Follow his wasps that you have already partnered with. Follow the *ignis fatuus*. Let them enter you. You will inherit his powers as long as you serve him. Disobey him, and he can recall his minions."

The bruised Endenken grasped Grave's leather apron and pulled himself to a standing position. "Fine. I will join my family then in death so that I may save their souls. Nothing could allay mine more. I will fight dyscrasia even beyond this realm."

"At the cost of your life? If you go through with this, you will no longer be human. You will no longer hunger for food or water. You will no longer see as the living do. You will die."

Endenken stepped toward the bog.

"Nay. As you said, death is not really final. I am to be reborn."

So he waded into the Blood Bogs, controlling his grief with focused anger, freely sacrificing his body to Haemarr's minions, which burrowed into his flesh. And so Endenken Lysis gave himself willingly to a diseased elder, a descendant of the Picti Muse he had forsaken. He did so on his own terms. To serve his own needs. But ultimately—and naively—he did accept dyscrasia-ridden blood into his body. He deemed he could control it, as Cypria controlled hers. He surmised he was Lord over Dyscrasia, rather than dyscrasia a lord over him. Only time would determine the victor.

II: Portrait of a Seer

"I see you..."

II: Portrait of a Seer

I SEE YOU. You have struggled for inclusion in a world that does not accept you. Now you wish only to escape. You stare at me with great awe, with hope that I will pluck you from this Cromlechon passage, restore your faith in humanity, and provide you with the means to carry on. And why not? You have seen the flock of mysterious carrion birds carry me here to aid the other vagrants, to carry them away to some other land. The red-capped orphans sing of my deeds. Oh, there are too many lost children in this desolate colony. There are so many without guidance or care. And only a few of us understand why so many parents are missing.

I'm sure you've heard the fables of those lost children. They say I am an angel. They say I can read a person's history, his regrets and memories, as clearly as if they were transcribed on parchment. If anyone could understand your plight, it is me.

It is true that I can *see* your emotions, for I have been burdened with the sight of the gods. Understand, I did not seek out the power to *see*, nor did I wittingly sacrifice the ornaments of life in order to obtain such a power. I have no desire to read your soul, to help you identify or resolve your problems. I am but forced, am cursed, to see these things! If only I could close my lidless eyes, become blind to all the colorful, ethereal auras of your emotions, see as you do…

I do not deny my extraordinary relationship with the birds, for in many ways I really am the Father of Augury as the children have declared. The birds and I have marshaled hundreds of vagrants over the years, though in that time my role and actions have been gravely misinterpreted. For now understand this: I do not control the birds. Indeed, they control me.

Yes, there is much beyond the limits of what you and the orphans have witnessed… so many misconstrued events… that I can no longer bear to accept your honorific stares. Close your eyes. Allow me to confess my many deceptions without having to look at you directly. Then I can reveal that I am not an angel, but rather an inhuman slave to the gods.

There you go. With your eyes fastened shut and your stares muted, I will speak.

IT BEGAN LAST spring. I lay broken and discarded on the serpentine Gorgepath trails which wrapped around the valley floor north of the Cromlechon. I was an artist with no brushes, pigments, or canvas. My purse was as empty as my stomach. My speckled surcoat had served as a smock for several years and was as worn as my breeches were shredded. In a colony filled with whores and mercenaries, I seemed to be the only artisan without a market, for simply put, contracting sex and assassination was more entertaining, popular, and profitable than creating or selling artwork. I had spent time documenting anatomy in the Dissection Theater, but could not remain there. I left voluntarily, seeking something more fulfilling, but found nothing. I confirmed only that I belong nowhere. Oh, if only I could have died instead, then I could have ended my days peacefully.

It was there, in that desolate trail, that several carrion birds began to peck at my still, defeated body. The scavengers were smaller than crows, with matte, ash-tinted hides and dull beaks. I had lain without food for three consecutive days so my vision was suspect. Yet even in my compromised state I understood these birds were unlike any I had ever seen for they had strangely luminous eyes, as if tiny coals of blue fire kindled within their skulls. Perhaps these images were simply hallucinations. All that mattered to me was that I was near death—or so I surmised at the appeal of my body to these scavengers. I did not care to move or postpone my defeat. I gave myself freely to them.

"I am yours," I whispered. Tears flowed like tar down my cheeks. My head flush with the cobblestone, I closed my eyes and succumbed to a tranquil state that chilled me as would a cold spring fog. It crept over me like a shadow seeking crevices for refuge from the sun, filling the folds of my clothing and wrinkles of my skin with frigid, searching vapors. So it was my bruised flesh seemed to crystallize, harden, and scab. Still I did not move.

Eventually I opened my eyes to discover I was being carried away, my delirious mind having misinterpreted the cold wind as some supernatural vapor. Several dozen crows held me aloft, each bird sinking its talons into a different part of my body as they fluttered in unison. Scraps of my smock ripped loose and snapped forcefully in the undulating mass of which I was the center. Below me, the view of the alley receded, soon followed by the Cromlechon. Then the dark night encroached, and the notion of distance became meaningless. I could not discern fantasy from reality, and eventually I concluded that angels were ferrying me away to safety.

S OME UNDETERMINABLE TIME later, the flock deposited me within a grove of trees. I fell quickly atop weak legs. My shoulders were so bruised and sore that, even after regaining my footing, my arms hung limp. Immediately my ears were bombarded by a screeching chant bellowed from countless birds. Surveying the scene, I could make out what appeared to be thousands of flashing specks. It took moments to understand that these blue fires came in pairs and each set indicated the presence of another mysterious blackbird. The leaves of the surrounding pines shook from their resonating song beneath a vibrant moon. For certain, by measure of sound alone, the carrion birds chanting in unison behind that veil of darkness numbered in the thousands.

"I am Cypria," a shrill voice said with such authority that the flock respectfully ceased its calling, the leaves relaxed with a tumbling rustle, and the air chilled in eerie silence. I then succumbed to the voice, compelled to obey that which spoke. It was as if my unconscious soul had already sealed some contractual agreement with this voice when I allowed myself to be carried here—a contract that I was only peripherally aware of and had unconsciously accepted.

With cloudy vision, sore limbs, and clumsy footing, I surveyed the glen for the one who welcomed me. And then I found her and knew at first glance that she was a goddess. Until that very moment I had held the resolute belief that gods were the stuff of imagination, making fascinating subjects for art while supplying the insecure with some stability in a world dominated by chaos and decadence. I could not have been more naive. It was at this time I realized with complete confidence that gods did exist, for the one before me commanded my attention like no other force and could be nothing less. Only true believers of any faith could relate to my rapid awakening. Indeed, without witnesses to support my claim, atheists would determine I was merely going insane. If only that were the case.

Having never seen a goddess before, I was shocked to find that, except for her wings, her features and dimensions were in human proportion, though much richer in texture and hue. I could acknowledge only that, as a goddess, she held more beauty than my human senses could perceive. Her nighttime visage inscribed itself in my mind more permanently than anything I had ever observed.

There was more to her beauty than her surface appearance, for even from afar I felt comforted by the abundant warmth exuding from her sapphire eyes. Without doubt, her glare radiated some form of rejuvenating spells. The more I looked upon her, the stronger I felt. In moments my thirst and hunger were satiated, my bruises healed, and my alertness restored. I stood amazed, growing cognizant of the extreme circumstances in which I found myself.

Finally I responded, "I seem to have been summoned." My confusion and ignorance could have been mistaken for misplaced boldness, but Cypria was an astute goddess.

"Summoned? Perhaps. What is your name?" Cypria asked. As I digested her words, I struggled to maintain control over my vision, which had become fixated on the goddess's sparkling skin and glowing eyes.

"My name is Dey."

"No surname?"

"My sire was not worthy of passing on his name to anyone," I said without pause. And, I thought to myself, he thought me unworthy to bear it.

Cypria seemed unaffected by my defiance toward my father, as if she had already known my past. She replied, "I require a healer."

"I am sorry to disappoint, but I am a mere artist. Not a physician."

She sighed. "Yes, yes, yes, I have heard such apologies before. Come closer, Dey, so that I can explain."

I crept ever closer to the fragrant Cypria. She sat awkwardly, leaning to her left side. Her wings fluttered back with graceful force to reveal her slender, lengthy arms. Then her stalk-like fingers showcased her body.

The desire to experience her beauty peaked within me, though it was not the same carnal drive many non-artisans might have felt. Rather the urge was intimate, not physical, like that a male artist feels when he portrays a nude female client. It was easy for me to temporarily stow away my sexual desires and concentrate on the beauty of her form, but a man of any other profession, one less trained to appreciate and replicate the grandeur of life and more apt to defile it, would surely have gone mad trying to restrain himself.

She displayed a wondrous balance of texture and color. The soft evening light hid any imperfections with forgiving shadows as surely as gesso smooths coarse wood. Glossy, girlish eyes adorned her face, accompanied by submissive cheeks and eyebrows as pointed as the finest stylus. Her hips and neck were congruently curvaceous, though her torso was slightly asymmetric, with her left breast more full and supple than its counterpart. Her belly was moderately muscular, with an emerging, motherly pouch. She was lighted by white moonbeams from above and a strange phosphorescent glow from below.

As I advanced closer I was seized with an immediate desire to harness the hue and reflectivity of the metallic, azure skin that wrapped her body and glistened beneath the moon. Non-artisans may not have comprehended such an urge since they are not accustomed to preparing their own paint from nature. As one who had scavenged the Land for substances of particular hue, or the potential to become such by tempering with heat, alchemy, or extraction, I was acutely aware of the singular value of her radiance. Portraying such beauty would be a challenge and an honor, but surpassing that would be to harvest her grace, work it into fluid pigments, and use it to create many relics—if I could extract her beauty while sustaining its potency. Indeed she was made of rare, resilient matter to which the alchemists had yet to assign nomenclature. The nearest approach of materials would be that of peacock feathers or ceramic tiles comprised of cuprous ores, such as malachite and turquoise. Simplistic art could become hypnotic and powerful with such enhanced colors.

Then reaching her, I discovered her deformity and the source of her mysterious glow.

Her bent, twisted right leg was riddled with grotesque, swollen bites, rendering her immobile. Similar in morphology to the gallnuts of oak trees, these stone warts oozed iridescent blood and emanated the eerie lighting that, strangely enough, only enhanced her beauty and complemented the radiance within her eyes. Too, the blueness in her eyes mirrored the fire-like luminance within those of the black birds that had brought me here.

Rendered submissive by her hypnotic gaze, I could not comment aloud on her beauty as I desired. Obediently I replied, "I see your condition, but am not sure how I can help."

Covering her diseased half with her wings again, she locked sight with my eyes. "My body is not made of flesh, mister Dey. Rather, it consists of elements of the earth. Without the aid of one versed in manipulating the Land's resources I will eventually transform into the Land itself, for I am infected with a disease that hardens my ichor, my blood, into stone." Her fear of the infection was tempered with an unspoken familiarity suggesting the condition was chronic yet controllable, and that she knew its source and potential harm. She continued. "I need your skills as an artisan to repair the damage before it consumes more of me. You will use my left leg as a model to sculpt and recolor my right."

"But I would require measuring tools, carving implements, and brushes, of which I have none. Clays, ochers, pigments, or the ingredients to manufacture them, a small cauldron, minerals, mortar and pestle, dyestuffs…"

"Focus, Dey," she interrupted. "You are not the first to be charged with healing me, for I summoned healers and shamans long before my condition reached this stage. Their tools are kept in a ruined Picti temple some hundred paces within the Iron Forest behind you."

I suppressed as best I could an abnormal rush of feelings of ill-preparedness, an urgency to perform, and general inadequacy. I wondered how the prior healers had fared. "Could the others not remedy your illness? Did they not have the knowledge or skill?"

"Those summoned previously could have cured me, were they not more consumed by fleshly desire than the desire to heal. So distracted they were, they could not accomplish the task at hand. Heed me, Dey. I may look vulnerable and attractive to your kin. Dare you underestimate my powers and attempt to abuse me, you will pay dearly. Submit not to your carnal desires, or you will suffer the same fate as those before you."

It was unclear how the other healers had abused her, and I hadn't the courage to ask. I could not help but wonder of their fate, however, for if I were to fail then I risked sharing it. I asked, "So where are they now?"

"They reside near the abandoned temple. But you should be wary. Although they are contained, they can still see you. Go now and survey the tools at your disposal and return with haste."

I exited the clearing, turning my back to Cypria. With only sparse beams of moonlight to guide me, I shuffled along a path congested with underbrush. Minutes passed until the incessant bird song abruptly ceased. The loss of noise was so startling it was as if the ground beneath me had momentarily dissolved away. I proceeded to exit the protection of the towering pines and enter the field that Cypria had called the Iron Forest. The hallowing of a field barren of trees was made vividly clear, even under the darkness of night.

The Iron Forest was in fact a forest of iron gibbets populated by those summoned by Cypria and subsequently imprisoned, having failed to cure her. There were hundreds of them, iron cages held aloft on poles, some as high as a fathom, though most only two rods high. Few of these gallows were empty. I could only speculate that they were placed on this path intentionally, before the temple, such that freshly summoned artists must traverse beneath them, view the corpses within, and pass with a heightened regard for Cypria's demands. I could not envision myself among their ranks, though the notion provoked me to scurry away from the iron colonnades.

The first instances of jingling metal I attributed to wind interacting with the cages. But then they awoke noisily, those dead and caged above me, opening their decaying, luminescent eyes that burned as fervently as those of Cypria or her corpse-eating servants. With gaping mouths they called for me in tones only the deceased could utter.

"Dey," they moaned. "Dey…"

Their voices assumed a feminine tone. One bereaved. My mother's voice? Was she calling for me to return home? But she is not here…

Clang! Cling! Clang! sounded the chorus of chimes as the undead clashed their shackles against the iron cages to rally those who still slumbered. Rapidly, their numbers grew. The clatter, moaning, and mechanical whining of metal upon metal joined in unison, all chiming in clamorous rhythm.

"Dey." Clang! "Dey, where are you?"

The cages shook forcefully, stressing the links from which they depended. They swayed in chaotic motion, in anger, and in hope of release. In sheer terror I sprinted beneath them toward the temple. Yet the horror grew as I learned that, interlaced with the haunting cries, echoes of my past sailed upon the words of the undead.

Clang! Cling! Clang!

Then a voice I had long forgotten, that of my father, resounded from above. "So what do ya have to say about it? You dumb little stone! Taken on your mother's dumbness, have ya? Well, come now, spit it out. Got any words in ya? Speak up so I can put ya back in yar place…"

The guilt of years of inaction against my drunkard father resurfaced. Years of letting my mother absorb his wrath and anger in silence. I never had the bravery to stand up to him or protect her. Instead I ran away to the Cromlechon.

Presently, I could hear the dead reenact my mother grieving over my disappearance, for she had lost the one being that had given her strength. By leaving her alone, I had failed.

Clang! "Dey!" Clang!

So I stumbled as I ran, sobbing furiously as the caged undead chanted bits and pieces of the regret and guilt I had suppressed for many years. Indeed, they read my history and feelings as if they were inscribed on a placard. How did they have access to this trove of hidden feelings that I had suppressed or forgotten?

"Dey, Dey…" others shouted, rattling their cages.

After what seemed an eternity, I arrived at the Picti temple. It was a layered structure, with crushed lower levels melding into eroded earthworks. The primary surviving structure atop this was constructed of carved masonry and wood. I strode over the incline of earth, jerked open one of the wooden doors, entered, and hastily put my full weight against it to seal it shut. The sounds were drowned out completely, and once again, my memories were silenced. I collapsed upon the planks of wood, hyperventilating, eventually falling asleep to rest my mind.

When I dreamt that night, the boundary separating the nightmarish, unfolding reality and the realm of fantasy became irrevocably blurred. Visions of the imprisoned corpses evoked memories during my time as an artist serving the Cromlechon barbers. It was with them, for the sake of furthering alchemy, I sketched the anatomy of criminals who had been sentenced to public dissection.

Most subjects had been hanged before their dissection, though several surgeries were performed on the living. Those not initially flayed or drawn during

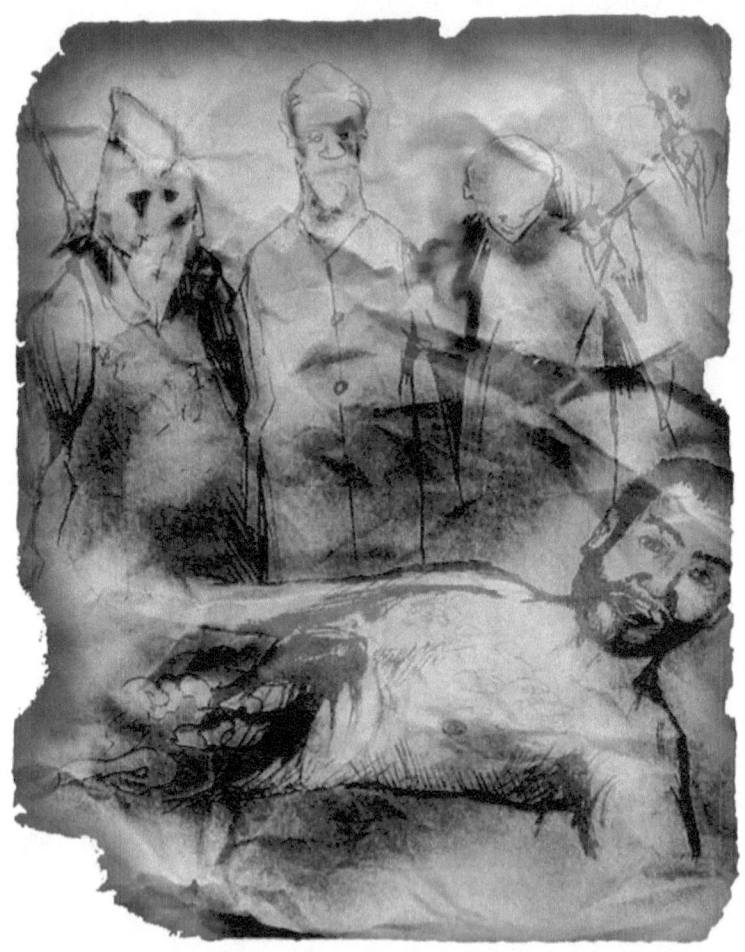

Dey recalls his tutelage in the Dissection Theater

their punishment would be hung on pulleys and summarily dismantled. On occasion the barbers would acquire innocent subjects who had passed away due to disease. Hence, we had the opportunity to anatomize infants of both genders and to compare them to mature beings. There was no doubt that my work advanced the knowledge of the barbers, though I was not producing aesthetic art but rather documenting gruesome realities of life. Decades later I left the position, disheartened. But the haunting memories never dissipated.

I recall that it was not uncommon for bodies to reawaken during dissection, the extreme pain jolting life into those cadavers not quite dead, so I was also accustomed to visions of the living dead. My experience in the Dissection Theater enabled me to cope with viewing animated corpses, whether they be in my dreams or the Iron Forest. What terrified me about the inhabitants in the forest was their access to the rawest feelings of my soul. No other act could have been more violating. So when I revisited those memories of dissections during my sleep, it was not the vivid images of humans with opened cavities and displayed organs that horrified me, but the words issued from their naked skulls, for each body I recounted morphed into visions of my father or mother, who then called to me hauntingly, out of anger and grief, by name.

I WOKE DAZED AND blanketed in total darkness. This temple smelled of ancient blood. A sacrificial slaughterhouse? In the darkness, I fantasized about the nature of the forms about me. I was a child again, trying to sleep amidst a nightmare. Tired. Scared. Alone. My mother screamed from the adjacent room. My father yelled in drunken rage. I pictured her curled up in a corner, as I was curled in my bed. Each shadow in the night taking the form of a discerning skull, each blanket a stretched hide of human skin, each crack in the mortared, log walls the squinting eyes of evil. Was it mother's blood I smelled now?

Reluctantly, I opened the door to illuminate the interior with the sun's rays. In those few moments I clung to the unlikely hope that I was still in the decadent Cromlechon and only the door stood between me and my prior life. Light rushed in, extinguishing the cold shadows, blinding me briefly and then erasing my hopes as the Iron Forest was again revealed to me. I was grateful only for the sturdiness of the iron gibbets for not one fell or released its prisoner last night.

The sunlight disclosed several oil lanterns that I quickly lit, so that I could afford sealing the door again. It was then I discovered the windows of the temple had all been shuttered and locked. The temple was without food but held abundant sources of tools and supplies. There was a number of furnaces, each ten feet in length, for working glass, annealing, and flattening. Facing these from opposite the vaulted chamber was an assortment of lathes, thread spinners, and looms. Libraries of elemental substances for deriving pigments lined the interior walls and populated open shelves: flasks of vinegar, quicksilver, olive oil, naphtha, and vitriol; salts of alum, ash, lime, and stones of jet; and racks of horns, bone and hide, and sheets of copper. Cauldrons, anvils, hammers and tongs, chisels, pincers, brushes and easels, alembics, decanters, scalpels, inks, retorts abounded!

This was no sacrificial site, but a treasure trove! My excitement to use the resources within fueled a desire to divorce myself from my current duties so I could concentrate, without distractions, on creating art for the sake of art itself.

It slowly occurred to me that Cypria had expected me long ago. I had to return prepared, and soon. First I needed to dimension her, so I obtained measuring ropes, calipers, and writing utensils to record her anatomy. I hurriedly threw these items into a burlap bag and decided to assess her more thoroughly before hauling materials to her side. I could carry only a limited amount, and despite my desire to minimize traversing the Iron Forest, secondary trips were inevitable.

The Forest was no less inviting in the light of day, despite the now sober, quieted prisoners. Their present dormancy was unexplainable. Short of deliberately waking one of the undead to validate its powers, it was impossible to confirm the reality of last night's episode.

I scurried forth onto the single path connecting the temple to the glen where Cypria lay immobilized. Intermittently I looked up to survey those who had serenaded me the night before—the ranks of decomposing men remained trapped in their cages. Why could they not die? And how did they see the hidden memories of one still living?

Vultures perched themselves atop the iron trees ever seeking the undying prey concealed within their metal branches. The scene rekindled memories of doves I had seen in the Cromlechon, trapped in cages, their masters peering inwardly. Here the situation was reversed. How dreadful it must be to be forever captive and immobile.

I still was not hungry, but my eyes instinctively searched for potentially edible things to break the night's fast. I would not have expected to find any prospects outside the pine trees, but I was pleasantly surprised, if temporarily, to discover what appeared to be bunches of blueberries clinging to the iron stalks. I approached one such stalk adjacent to the path supporting a low-hanging cage containing a collapsed corpse.

Upon closer examination, the clusters were instead revealed to be aggregates of minute and oversized larvae. The larger larvae were engorged with a luminous blue fluid that was quite brilliant beneath the sun, while the smaller ones were near microscopic, thus too small to hold color and so appeared whitish or translucent. I plucked free one large larva and squeezed it, releasing several drops of viscous, iridescent fluid as rich in hue as Cypria's eyes. It would suit as a dye, I presumed, but not as breakfast. The fluid beaded upon my skin and rolled off as rain would upon waxed wood.

That was the fourth time I had observed the blue, liquid-like fire within the strange creatures of this territory—first within the birds' eyes in a Cromlechon alley, second within Cypria's eyes and blood, then within the corpses of the Iron Forest, and now within these larvae. The likeness of hue and brilliance suggested a common thread, a disturbing connection that demanded explanation.

My reflections on the strange substance abruptly dissipated as the corpse in the cage beside me awoke, moaned, and revealed its larvae-filled eyes. They glowed softly beneath a veil of gray hair, the entity's skin taut and gray with decay. Its face seemed vaguely familiar despite its deterioration, and even with my artistic abilities I could not confidently reconstruct, in my mind, its form with flesh.

Suddenly, with dream-like fluidity, it took on the likeness of my father.

Alert and terrified, I bolted for the evergreens.

Breaching the path amongst the pines, I was once again greeted by an overwhelming bird song. In the light of day I could now discern many of the cawing blackbirds.

"Pardon my tardiness…"

"Halt!" Cypria commanded, simultaneously directing her winged minions to advance.

The flock of birds descended upon me, enveloping my form and pecking at my body feverishly in search of targets unknown to me. The episode was quick, and my body was barely scathed. As I recovered my wits I was pinned by Cypria's stare, which seemed to comb through my soul. During this inspection, the blackbirds plucked luminous larvae, wasps, and other vermin from me, and collected their findings atop a stone. Cypria scanned the pile and ordered the birds to crush them all.

"I would have arrived…"

"No need to speak further, Dey. Had you returned last night we would have still searched you similarly, for I cannot allow Haemarr's minions to come close."

"You mean the blue larvae clinging to the stalks within the Iron Forest?

Those insects that burn with the same color as do the eyes of your birds and the blood upon your legs?"

"It is ichor, the blood of the elders, you detect, though do not mistake the blood of my cousin Haemarr for mine. My ichor is contained within me and my birds, whereas Haemarr's ichor is spread through his insectan kind. Our ichor may appear the same to you, but to me one is blood and the other poison."

"And the infection that ails you now, is that caused by Haemarr's blood?"

"Yes, his poison has infected me, though don't be worried of being contaminated yourself. Haemarr means to turn my body into stone. Understand only that whenever his ichor mixes with mine, the amalgam irreversibly calcifies. His wasps bit my leg," she explained and then detailed procedures I was required to perform to replenish the sites of infection.

"My body is slowly petrifying, though my soul will remain unaffected. Know that I am immortal. Understand, for this is the crux of my situation: I cannot bear to be confined for eternity. I will not be held captive! I need you to restore my leg so that I may fly again, to be able to run and extend my wings, to be free! That is why I need you, to stem my demise and return my mobility."

"And if I fail, I will be imprisoned in your cage…"

"Those cages are not mine! Haemarr constructed them to imprison my flocks long ago," she cawed. "Now I use them to house those who are weak-minded and unable to cure me. They died from madness and had to be caged for my own protection. For it is Haemarr's ichor, the same that poisoned me, that revived the dead and enabled them to see as elders see. Now Haemarr controls them and would have them infect me if they were free!"

I bowed my head until her anger dissipated, then replied, "See? You had mentioned their power earlier, though it now sounds more like a curse. How did they arrive at such a state? How can those without eyes see?"

"Have you ever dreamt? At night, with your eyes closed?"

"Of course," I said, recalling my recent dream of dissections.

"Then you know that even with eyes closed, even in complete darkness, your mind can fill a frame for you, your soul, to observe and experience – a stage with color and atmosphere as realistic as the visions you perceive while awake. This is how we elders and the undead see, for we look at the world through an astral plane congruent with physical reality, where emotions are tangible shapes, and hopes, fears, and regrets collect themselves into transparent auras."

Slowly comprehending how the corpses had seen into my past, I then asked, "The blood powers this sight?"

"Yes, and it also fuels other powers, like immortality. As long as Haemarr's minions empower them, those caged in the Forest will never die but will always *see*."

Anxious to finish the task and to be freed, I asked for permission to continue.

"Yes, proceed," she said. "Measure me, but I caution against directly touching me. Such contact has in the past driven men mad with desire," she said as I dimensioned her healthy left leg with calipers, recording the measurements with lampblack ink onto a vellum scroll.

So close to her naked form was I, so close to this goddess that rivaled the most attractive female human ever portrayed and who exuded erotic aromas from every pore. Never before had I had to exercise such self-restraint as I kneeled between her legs and imbibed her beauty. I had experience in controlling my carnal desires, so I did not need to restrain any sexual urge. Rather I had to control an artistic impulse that urged me to chisel away her skin, flay her, and harbor her valuable anatomy as would a surgeon the organs of a corpse. Fresh in my mind, to balance these thoughts, were the corpses who had failed her previously. Indeed, the visions of the Iron Forest and its inhabitants kept my desires in check. I dared not violate her.

On close inspection of her healthy skin I discovered a delicate texture. This etched design could be compared only to that of a thousand butterfly wings welded together like a grand mosaic, a collage of nature's most beautiful designs, slightly reflective and delicate, all interlocking to wrap the goddess in a sort of tapestry. Once again, a vision formed permanently in my mind, one that I would draw upon near the end of this tragedy. It contained every line, curve, and hue of the detailed, fragile tiling that was Cypria's daytime beauty.

Her marblesque, tessellated skin contained her affliction, too. Her disease spread from four and twenty nodules akin to galls so enlarged as to appear as acorns. They appeared polished, and had yet to be breached by the larvae that surely grew within. I had been trained to formulate poultices from similar galls infesting vegetation—to extract acidic salts from within to produce inks. The arrangement of these bites was disturbing, evoking insectan patterns I had observed from the ants within the Cromlechon Theater.

I drafted a plan. It was better to poison the stony growths than attempt to extract them mechanically; forceps would not remove the parasitic roots thoroughly, and a scalpel would damage her skin permanently and may introduce scarring. First, I would mask her healthy skin with a coat of olive oil, leaving the two dozen galls exposed. Over this, I would selectively use a stylus to drop concentrated oil-of-vitriol to burn each mass and introduce porosity. Next, I would apply a cataplasm of potash and lime to neutralize the vitriol. The inert remnants of the galls could then be excised gently with a brush. I would have to repair the pits with care, for her color ran deep through her skin like pigments through a fresco. I would size these areas with a transparent gesso suspending pearlescent mica and cuprous powder. A pouncing would be in order to smooth this, and pumice was plentiful to prepare such treatment. Lastly, I would apply a topical shellac to repair her skin's luster, one made of turpentine and a fine mica powder.

Having detailed a treatment, I had no choice but to brave the Forest again to obtain from the temple the necessary materials. Thus began an unsettling routine I would repeat for the next several days. I would carry my implements and materials to Cypria, pass an inspection for Haemarr's minions, perform my work, and return. My progress was incremental, with each day's gain lost to the quickly regenerating infection. I repeatedly wondered whether or not I could overcome the resilience of the galls. I was successful in breaching one gall on my second trip. To my horror, I verified Cypria's claim that the mixing of ichor would petrify her body, for as I cracked the shell of one cluster, a luminescent larvae emerged sprouting swollen, elastic veins that were rooted into her flesh. The mixing of ichor

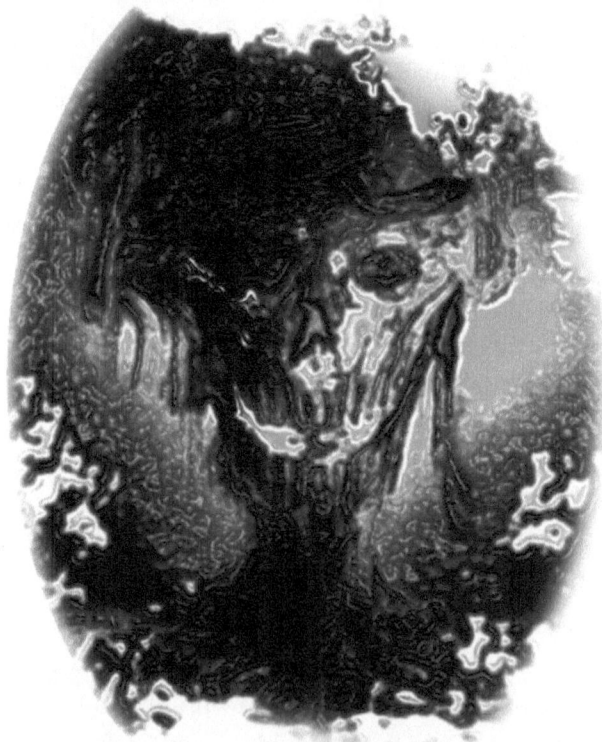

Haunting image of Dey's father

from this wound was for now a slow, diffusive process. I plucked out the acidified cluster as if it were a poisoned heart encapsulated in a cage, and its pockmarked texture, imparted by the oil of vitriol, crumbled as I touched it.

She was telling the truth, I surmised. *She is dying. And the wasps impregnate her flesh already*! Yet more than twenty galls remained!

The likelihood that I would join the inhabitants of the Iron Forest evolved from an unlikely fate to a distinct possibility, making the act of walking through it increasingly unbearable. Traveling during the day minimized my interaction with the prisoners of the Iron Forest, though I was continually harassed by the corpse resembling my father.

This corpse never seemed to grow dormant like the other corpses, and every time I neared its vicinity, a strange compulsion led me to reciprocate its stare. Each time my throat quivered and the backs of my eyes burned, as if its stares had penetrated my form and scraped the innermost parts of my body. I never told Cypria of these interactions for it seemed that doing so could only further jeopardize my fate. Being that I continued to pass the inspections of her birds, my progress and motivations must have been deemed acceptable.

"Come here, my son," it beckoned on the second day after my arrival. Its hypnotic gaze guided me closer, and I soon found myself, despite my fears and against my common judgment, within reach of its arms.

Then it rasped, "Cypria cannot be cured, you understand. Her condition is caused by age and duty. She is merely maturing as all gods do, so your task will be a continuous one, without end, and sooner or later you will fall to your bestial desires. Then you will hang like the rest of us, and she will summon another."

"Why should I believe you?"

Then its face changed, and I saw my father in that cage. With terror I recalled that my father had been an artist and matched the profile of those summoned, yet I could not yet accept that my father was genuinely before me. I was hallucinating, I surmised. Still I could not bring myself to break his hypnotic stare.

"Dey, I was summoned like yourself to aid Cypria, but she will betray you like she did all the others. You must free us and run away before she sentences you to the same fate. Free me…"

I did not obey him then. Instead, I darted to the temple, where I suppressed my fear by inventorying materials. The abundance of resources energized me again, since I felt empowered to create anything of my desire. Hence, the temple was a refuge at night, but it was a source of hope, too, a reminder that I may eventually finish my task and use the tools within at my leisure. Yet for every visit to the temple I had to traverse the Iron Forest and in so doing confront that damnable corpse.

Why I consistently stopped in the presence of that corpse on subsequent trips, I was never exactly certain. However, after having been made aware of Haemarr's minions, the attraction was certainly linked to the powers of the larvae interwoven within its flesh. Suffice to say, I was subjected to extreme imagery in the day and horrific dreams at night. So distressed, I was only dimly aware of my malnourishment. I hadn't eaten for several days, sustained only by Cypria's powers, and had grown thin. Still I went about my duties with only modest decreases in my health. After a week I began to accept the corpse's explanation that I was cursed and my task could never be completed.

It was on the seventh day, while I was engaged in a most lengthy stare with the corpse, that it told me, its eyes brimming with blue fire, that Cypria was fated to fall ill to dyscrasia. Few elders escaped that disease. Haemarr had been trying to mate with her to spawn more elders, but he was already ill. His larvae and wasps carried his seed, though their stings had yet to hit their mark. If impregnated, then Cypria would transmute to stone just like her wounds had—though her offspring may prevail. She had been summoning humans to repair her month after month to no avail, each one succumbing to her intense sensuality. Insane, they could not be controlled or trusted and had to be restrained in cages. She and her healers were all doomed…

"No!" I managed to pry myself away from the intangible chains that linked my eyes to his, and retreated toward the temple. I was not ready to accept my doom, but I knew he was right about dyscrasia. I had been familiar with that disease long ago, since the barbers of the Theater had dissected many mutants. My mentor Doctor Grave was fascinated with these subjects. I had hoped to keep those memories suppressed.

Once inside, I sat with knees drawn to my chest, sobbing as a child. If only I could free myself from the horrors around me: from the corpses that haunted me from their iron cages; from the memories of my father that they evoked; and from my service to Cypria. I fantasized the Iron Forest empty of prisoners, with silver ribbons and flags flapping from the iron masts. These would frame an earthwork in the likeness of Cypria, surfaced with a grand mosaic reflecting her beauty. I needed to make this fantasy real so nature's beauty would fill my emptiness with hope.

With tear-glazed cheeks and crowbar in hand, I returned to the cage of the heckling corpse. He looked subdued, as if the sun drained him or his powers had waned. I simply could not bear to hear or view my father anymore, or have him read my nightmares aloud—now was the time to act. I would rather die than be confronted by my memories of him. I needed to be free of the corpse's influence. Without further hesitation, I pried open the lock. The prisoner did not escape immediately, nor did he advance toward me in any way. I darted back to the temple, and the next morn the cage was empty.

Free of the haunting corpse, I gained confidence. No longer was I afraid to walk through the iron stalks during the day, and with newfound liberty I made fast progress. Each moment I focused entirely on completing my servitude and regaining my freedom. Eleven days after my arrival, Cypria's leg was completely ridden of infection. As she grew healthier so did I, my body regaining its weight and fullness, my mind becoming increasingly alert. Cypria stood for the first time since her illness and sprinted forward, levitating herself with spread wings, and calling wildly as she navigated the open air above the pines.

Her flock of a thousand birds joined her in a tumultuous whirlwind and their harmony resonated louder than thunder for several hours.

I soon forgot about the release of the prisoner, for I became one myself. Cypria ordered me to be ready to serve her in case she was bitten again. I was not in position to decline this servitude. Albeit unchained and free of a cage, Cypria obliged me to stay within calling distance and away from the ruined temple.

The subsequent month was terrifying. Liberated, Cypria changed from a paranoid goddess to an impulsive one, swapping any fears for reckless abandon. She celebrated her health and dominance by forcing herself upon me frequently— my body a safe substitute for the carnal desires she could not obtain from Haemarr without forfeiting her mobility in the process. The experiences were indeed surreal and lacked every vital, satisfying quality. She reinforced this emotional distance with a leveled arrogance that inherently fitted me into a subservient caste. She was the goddess; I was the slave.

I grew to understand that this goddess was as bestial as she was wondrous. On a weekly basis I witnessed her bring abducted men into the forest only to feed on them. They were all under the influence of her toxic perfume as she defiled and bled them. Strangely, they often died smiling.

She did not desire to consume or kill me. She needed me as long as Haemarr's agents threatened her. Emotions simply had no role in our intercourse. She had a simple lust for copulating and for human blood. She usually fed on her victims immediately, but I alone was allowed to live. My skills granted me life and continued servitude.

Despite her revolting need for sex and blood, her body remained bizarrely beautiful. I felt responsible for recreating it. I became increasingly obsessed. However, her vampirism disgusted me. I reconciled this discrepancy by acknowledging that attractions need not be pleasing in every way. Cypria was simply a dark inspiration.

Each night I dreamt of sculpting her within the Iron Forest, with tall grasses swaying in nonexistent winds muffling any sound. I became obsessed with taking the temple's resources, and making a grandiose representation of her. I would need the temple's supplies to do this. At first she kept me from it. She

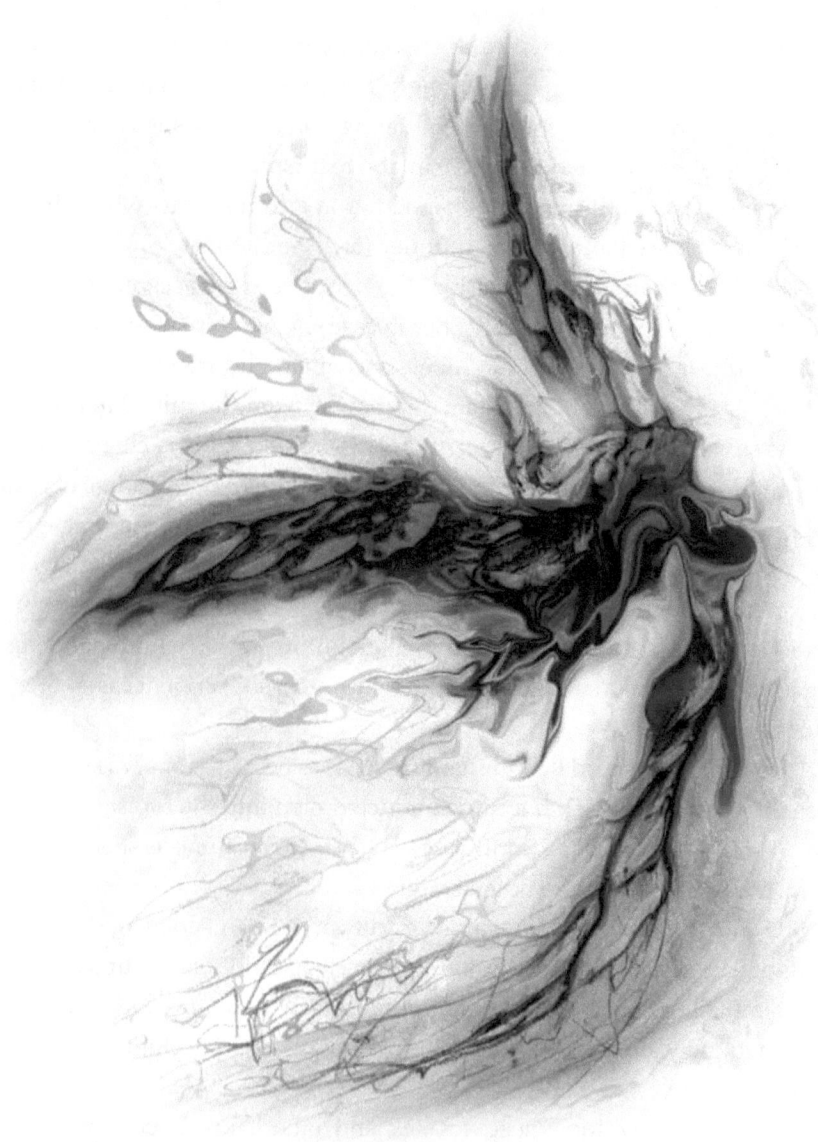

Cypria healed and flying again!

loathed that locus of contagion.

Two months after Cypria's healing, I could restrain myself no longer.

One night as she left to collect food, I went toward the temple with childish stealth and speed, my eagerness to create outweighing my fear of the undead, the memories they would evoke, or even Cypria's wrath. My palms sweated in anticipation and visions ran rampant through my mind—so many effigies of Cypria that required capturing, so many atmospheres and emotions, all streaming from the edges of my mind to dissipate in the thin night air, leading me to the temple where I could realize these visions, and then I suddenly realized the undead were not calling to me…

All was quiet.

The zombies were no longer animated.

Their blue fires extinguished. Absent. Haemarr's minions had been recalled. Perhaps their master knew that Cypria was no longer grounded. Perhaps he died altogether. Regardless, I ran back to the pines to report this immediately. I told her that Haemarr had left the Iron Forest, though she did not believe me until her birds inspected the scene to confirm this. His wasps and larvae were utterly absent now.

The following day I was allowed to work freely in the Forest and the temple therein. I set to cleaning out the cages. The process took weeks. In order to unlock those cages suspended out of climbing reach, the supporting iron stalks were toppled. All in all, some two hundred prisoners were stripped bare of flesh by carrion birds, enabling faster burial of the bones. The flock delivered droppings of seeds and berries, so life began to sprout again. The cloud of despair was lifted. It was if a great scab had been peeled from the Land, exposing a raw hope that had lain dormant for too long.

Next, I cleared a canvas of ground some fifty yards square. I worked endlessly, through daylight and dusk, constructing the grand mosaic resembling Cypria. I exhausted the temple's stock of ocher and had to prepare more. So I filled a cauldron several times over with water and red earth, discarding the floating humus, thus purifying the batch through a crude levigation process. I heated the resulting sediments to achieve bolder, more violet-rich hue.

With the area cleansed of undead prisoners and my grand masterpiece underway, I was joined by the hundreds of birds that had come to investigate. They rode the skies coalescing and dispersing, cooperatively aligning into synchronized states before breaking the patterns and starting afresh. Wave upon wave of configurations changed rhythmically, a rolling set of symbols morphing again and again, signing to Cypria their joy. The flock's communications would have been transparent, chaotic play to any other, but to me they were disclosed wholeheartedly. They were celebrating the rebirth of Cypria, the creation of her image in the mosaic.

I had given birth to a wild, awesome work of art while affirming my skills and self-worth as an artist. I could feel my soul bond with this earth, though I could not see such an intangible thread as the dead can. Some part of my spirit took residence here as a permanent memory. It was part of me now and vice versa.

Many audiences confuse the purpose and value of art with its creator. The art one creates, the subject of it, and the artist are three separate entities – though they imprint their souls onto each other. On rare occasion, the process of this sharing is orgasmic and resembles procreation; the product assumes a sentient thing, possessing some spirit of the creator's although ultimately a new being. These events are special, happening only a few times in one's life. Some artists are infertile in this regard.

These children of beauty are an artist's legacy, and I have had none ere now. To date, I had completed only minor feats of artisanship and had felt correspondingly worthless as an artist, so the present moment was indeed the pinnacle of my happiness. Over the span of the mosaic's creation, I relished in the act of creating and in the grandeur of coloring and molding the earth into a replica of the quintessential beauty that was Cypria. I took delight in the placement of every rock, every chunk of ocher, and every mineral onto that landscape, more delight than any non-artist could ever comprehend.

Cypria hovered over the completed Mosaic, "You have done well, Dey. Put your tools away now, and join me on yonder hill. We will view my birds play above your work, and we will celebrate!" She looked at me hungrily, and then flew away.

Fulfilled, I went to the temple to close its doors…

AMBUSHED!
"Father?"

Fear instantly congealed into a ball in the back of my throat as I strode across the threshold of the temple door and into the grasp of a walking corpse…

My death was quick, though painful, so I can recall only fragments. For one, my killer was the very corpse that had haunted me along the path to the Iron Forest. The very one I had freed. I remember it delivering a hot blade into my chest cavity. I remember my heart being plucked free from its ribcage housing.

And I remember the minions of Haemarr, those minute, fiery blue and white larvae, burrowing into my flesh where my heart once resided.

I moved then an automaton. I was aware, but I was not in control. My body was possessed!

I can only imagine the horror of realization upon Cypria's face when we joined minutes later. My body still fresh. My eyes inches from hers. I must have opened them to reveal the larvae within, revealing that I doomed her to the fate that I had recently freed her from. My eyes brimmed with blue light, signaling her defeat, and her clawing talons did little to deter me or free her from my clutches. Haemarr would not let go. It was during that furious rape the larvae streamed in large doses from me into her. Fueled by the power of Haemarr's ichor, I held onto her form as she frantically loosed the flesh from my body, futilely scrambling for freedom, until the act of intercourse was finished. An instrument of sorcery, I had defiled her.

Dumbly, I stood over the petrified Cypria. Her stone eyes glared back at me, maintaining the terror they expressed during her last moments of mobility.

Sadly, I surveyed my ravaged body and compared it to the goddess. We were both physically tarnished. Cypria's beauty changed: her body lost its radiance, replaced by gray stone; but her soul became visible, and nothing could be more prismatic. I had lost everything except my mobility. Decay set in fast now that my flesh was torn asunder. The only beauty within me was the larvae clinging to my bones, and they rightfully belonged to Haemarr.

With her impregnation, Haemarr did not need to sustain me. So his minions left. I was motionless as they departed.

My body collapsed. An empty vessel.

THEN MY SOUL *saw*. Surrounding my form, pink, transparent mists whirled about me, effigies of my father, mother, and experiences as a youth. My memories, all of them, hovered around me, disclosing the secrets of my mind in a fantastic aura.

My eyes could still observe the physical world, but those visions were hazy, of lesser contrast than how I remembered the world to appear. Then I realized why. The physical world had all gone gray, robbed of color and maintaining only gradients of monochrome intensity. Immediately I was saddened and enlightened, for as I analyzed my sight, I detected color of a different sort—transparent auras of brilliant hues traced the objects, plants, and creatures around me.

True to what Cypria had told me before, the dead see things once invisible, immeasurable, and intangible, like the souls and memories associated with beings or things. These ethereal images were overlain atop fading visions of the physical world.

The brightness of the sun saturated my mixed vision of ethereal and physical things, so I gained some understanding of why the inhabitants of the Iron Forest had been weary during the day.

Anchored to my immobile body, my soul stared for a great time for it could do nothing else.

After many days, I realized that the blackbirds were editing my masterpiece, rearranging pebbles constantly but gracefully. Clearly, the link between Cypria and her flock had been maintained during her transformation and their ability to communicate was evolving. As I appreciated the communion between the carrion birds and the mosaic, Cypria's visage took form in the ethereal mists pervading the field.

There I could see ghostly duplicates of myself—just memories, empty imprints of my soul. I called to them, but they did not respond. They were lifeless phantoms. They were locked into relishing the Mosaic in which they produced. They were my astral signature, but not my central soul.

I remained next to my body and Cypria's stone form.

The Picti temple burned with volcanic vermilion flames—cobalt plumes assumed grotesque images of flayed and tortured humans. The sight terrified me, as if I were a child looking upon the sandbox I had played in for years to realize it was not sand but the ashes of my cremated forefathers. Then I understood why: the signature of Guildlord Doctor Grave, my mentor within the Cromlechon Guild of Barbers, was distinctly revealed in the temple's aura. He had been an artisan of sorts, in a grotesque sense of the word since his contribution to the temple escaped the bounds of art. The temple remembered him flaying someone here, with the very blade that was used to cut my heart out. The phantasmal scar was clearly depicted in the ether. The truth immediately hurt. The Doctor was in league with Haemarr. I had been a pawn for most of my life, but had been unaware. My passion for art betrayed me.

I did not fully understand what it meant to be mentally alive while tethered to a decaying body. For certain I lost my sense of smell and taste, for my nose, tongue, and throat had been damaged beyond use. My soul could hear, but that sensation was odd and did not require my decomposing ears. Of a sudden, I heard—rather felt—her voice.

Haemarr beat me, Cypria's apparition spoke telepathically. *He took advantage of our relationship. But your monument speaks of your genuine devotion. Your soul belongs to me, and I require your services now more than ever. I have turned and have no one else to aid me, so I call upon you again. Listen, I dream of ill portents. The children I will bear are destined to ignite a malicious disease upon the world, turning all into gray, lifeless ash. To prevent their birth you must encase my womb in stone made from mixed ichor. It is the only way, and the casting of the stone shell over my earthy womb must be maintained as cracks will arise year upon year. Also, we will have to marshal an army to prepare for their birth in case our efforts fail. This time, I must guarantee your obedience and have no other choice than to employ the same dreadful approach as Haemarr. You will share my soul—my pain!*

Then, as sudden as a strike of lightning, the crows descended upon my body en masse. Just as they had inspected my body weeks ago, this time plucking any remains of Haemarr's minions from my body.

Detached, my soul watched.

I watched as a blackbird burrowed itself into my ribs where my heart once had been. Arteries sprouted from its hide to snake their way throughout my skeleton and give my body the ichor needed for animation. Hence my final transformation came to pass, as Cypria took control over my body and soul, the ichor of her carrion bird pervading my skeleton. Again I was possessed.

Her voice echoed through the ichor, *Now you are mine to command!*

I rose.

Empowered with the heart of a bird, I could better discern the messages scrawled during the flock's choreographed routines, Cypria communicating to them telepathically from within her earthy cage, and they responding by weaving trails of ethereal mist during their flight. Not only was I privy to their conversation, I was bound to their decisions. I became her puppet.

She forced me to don a death mask, some ancient skull exhumed by the birds. It had belonged to a colossal avian, eldritch creature. Cypria wanted me to connect with and represent her avian past. It had a phallic beak with eye sockets the shape of almonds. With my fleshless skull shielded behind this bone mask, the flock ushered me back to the Cromlechon, where, as instructed, I recruited vagrants. Then the birds transported these offerings to the mosaic upon which the Iron Forest once stood. Overwhelmed by the beauty of Cypria's portrait, my communion with the blackbirds, and my ability to see their emotions, the vagrants promptly became devout followers. We taught them how the birds communicated with the gods embodying the Land. And we professed to them of the Deceiver who had impregnated Cypria and initiated the evils they were charged to combat. However, to them I was known only as Seer Dey, Father of Augury. And thereafter, I kept a careful distance between myself and the temple that forever beckoned me.

No longer able to feed by herself, I henceforth had to provide sustenance to her soul. For this, she demanded a bath of male human blood be made about her body and allowed to mix with her ichor. In no way a predatory being, I avoided hunting and managed by scavenging for the terminally ill on the Gorgepath leading toward the Cromlechon.

So again I find myself visiting this colony, where I have received great praise for providing hope to vagrants. I am surrounded by the many followers I recruit, but none know as much as you do now. They are not aware of my undead nature. They are not aware that there were two Deceivers: the first was my nameless murderer, the Avatar of Haemarr whom I freed from the Iron Forest and who infected me; the second was me, Seer Dey and Father of Augurs.

Call me an angel if you wish, but if you were to peer beneath my death mask you would disagree. I am a walking corpse, slave to Cypria, and cursed for eternity. I may be a seer and a savior to some, but I do not act on my own accord.

With the power of sight thrust upon me, I am blind to true color and have no hope of dying.

So do you still want the crows to carry you away? Liberate you from the harsh life of the Cromlechon? Do you want to become embroiled in war between gods who play with human bodies as if they were puppets? Can you really trust me, a living corpse, a true Deceiver, to take you to a better place? Do you wish to donate your blood to her? To sustain me?

No, I think not. I see that you are too scared to look at me now, even though my story is finished. You are terrified, your eyelids welded to your cheeks with tears of fear. You are glad I asked you to close your eyes, and glad to let them remain so. Well, you need not cry or sweat any longer, for I will not take you. I should not have burdened you with my feelings as I am burdened by yours, and by those of everyone else I *see*. Forgive me.

III: Endenken Lysis's Plague

Sketch of Lysis Clan's coat of arms

III: Endenken Lysis's Plague

"For Haemarr, I slay you. Now I am free to save my family. Pray that Lady Maeve can forgive me," the Blue Lord Lysis whispered to his victim.

The artisan Dey collapsed onto the temple floor. Lysis lowered his blade *Ferrus Eviscamir* and held Dey's heart aloft, the warm blood pouring down his extended, decaying arm and into his skeletal frame. He had fulfilled his end of the pact with Haemarr, the elder man-wasp. He watched now as hordes of Haemarr's minions burrowed into the surgical wound to take control of the body. Under the elder's control, Dey's revived corpse stood abruptly and exited the temple.

"I would have retrieved his scalp," Lysis said, fingering the gilded accolades strung about his neck.

The brilliant, azure larvae within his own skeleton communicated to him. *He was my prey, not yours. Besides, I have him attending to other matters already. As will you —*

"You may control him, but I am free," Endenken Lysis declared, talking to Haemarr's larvae within his own decaying form, "and I serve only my own needs!"

I can halt you in your footsteps, if I deemed to break our pact. For now, I let you roam as we agreed.

A mane of gray hair drooped about the sides of the Lord's balding head as he acknowledged his commitment. Blue Lysis returned, "Until I finish my duty, I serve none other but my family."

Now he must act! Now he could confront the evil necromancy that slaughtered his family, for he was graced with the powers of the gods, and although his flesh decayed, his spirit and body survived. He collected his supplies, which he had temporarily stashed in the temple: a wool tunic to cloak his frame of skin and bone; a baldric to bear his flaying sickles on his chest; and a sheath upon his back for his war scalpel, *Ferrus Eviscamir*, a two-foot blade with an even longer hilt.

To Gravenstyne Lord Lysis strode.

He walked without stopping for three days. Daytime impeded his progress for the sun polluted his vision with harsh, intense whiteness. Everywhere he witnessed a world with enhanced meaning, a world saturated with brilliant, luminous emotions that burned like fire, and at night the contrast between those apparitions of the astral realm and the structures of the physical realm were never greater.

This power of sight, the power to *see* the ethereal things, was needed to rescue his family. The larvae and wasps also enabled him to fight the necromancy that plagued his castle. He had sacrificed himself to Haemarr voluntarily to obtain these gifts. With his family deemed dead, Lysis no longer cared to maintain his flesh. He was driven to protect their souls from an eternity of torment—even if that meant eternal enslavement for himself.

Led by Haemarr's minions, he glided through a boundless landscape of mist. The fog was so dense, his feet were veiled behind white vapors and the ground went unseen. It seemed as if he walked on air, and for all he knew, he did. What he could make out were colorful filaments of ether that threaded the landscape, wrapping about conical earthworks, piercing sacrificial mounds, and tracing out pathways once maintained by the insectan elders. On the horizon, he could see the Cromlechon, a mere anthill in the distance that was literally connected to this network. Then he passed monolithic tombstones where withered, Picti ghosts dangled in a web of rusted chains, pulleys, and iron poles. These auras burned as hot, loud, and volcanic as a hell-spawned forest fire—an inferno his ancestor's worship started and that continued to fuel the dyscrasia he vowed to end.

He saw before him sets of translucent memories of children chasing one another haphazardly, giggling and teasing in the same chaotic manner as bees.

Wasps burrow into decaying fruit

Violet traces of himself, as a child, climbed and swung on the trees. The auras about his body mimicked—reenacted—the memories he saw and recalled.

Lysis continued without becoming mired in the living spectacles on the astral plane. Occasionally he took note of the apples on the ground. They were bruised and gray with decay, and the Lord longed for the days when the fruit was fresh and he could enjoy biting them. A number of conspicuous crows enjoyed this rotten fruit, though their intent seemed to focus more on the Lord's travels

Gravenstyne Orchard is infested

than on satiating hunger.

He came upon a pile of corpses as he neared the Fortress, each dismembered in some regard. A sparkling radiance, a frost of glass shards, blanketed the horror before him. Among the corpses of his servants, Lysis found glass limbs so perfectly shaped that human hands could not have sculpted them.

"What has befallen my servants?"

Some have been sucked dry of their souls and then cast over the castle walls to shatter, their astral signatures erased from their crystallized bodies.

"This crystal forearm…its hand bears a ring that resembles that of Marcus the cook. So he is dead?"

Yes. His blood, bone, and flesh sintered together as one perfect—and dead—composition. His soul, gone.

"So my family? Are they irrevocably frozen? Like Marcus!"

No. Some of the servants and family have suffered other fates. For certain, more than one devil marauded this place!

Then a haunting voice resonated throughout his form, though it was not that of the larvae.

"Lord Protector Lysis, slayer of evil beasts and honorable master, you have returned!" It was not one voice, but several in unison, a chorus of ghosts about him speaking simultaneously from the sparkling masses of carrion.

"Who addresses me?"

"It is I, Lord, Xel Culther, once caretaker of your stables," echoed the fractured soul. Lysis turned to the central voice issuing from the kindling astral fire– it came from within Xel's impaled skull.

"Avener Xel? Xel, know that I will avenge you."

"Please, Lord, can you find a way to relieve me from your service? Can you put an end to this agony? I can no longer bear the prickliness of death. Please, Lord, can you render me like Chief Cook Marcus? Somehow end me. Please, sir, I implore you! Lest I will unwillingly haunt your Orchard and Fortress forevermore. I cannot bear to soil these grounds!"

Lysis swung his war scalpel with great vigor, but the blade passed through the apparition of Xel without contact. Slicing the ethereal vapors with his sickles likewise failed. Finally, Lysis called upon Haemarr's minions: "Xel is a righteous soul. How can I aid him?"

There is only one way. You must sever his soul from his body. For that you'll require enhanced armory. My ichor can aid you in this regard, for as it animates your corpse and allows your conscious soul to remain active, it can also transform metal. With the proper incantations and rituals, such blades can then recrystallize, harden, so that they may lacerate astral mists and souls as they inflict physical damage. But such weaponry is dangerous in the hands of one who does not understand the consequences.

"I sought your powers so that I could rescue Gravenstyne! We had an agreement, for which I gave my life! Make good your offer, god. Grant me then the ability to serve our common will! Give me the power I deserve!"

So I shall.

Controlled by the will of the luminescent larvae, Lysis grabbed his weapons and inscribed sacred glyphs into the air, familiar patterns he had seen before, perhaps even traced by foot on some journey. But he moved so fast he never ascertained the precise connection. In the wake of his swinging arms trailed plumes of smoke, smoldering mist, and electric sparks. Entranced, he began to speak aloud as only the undead can. With guttural bellows he spewed forth riddles of some arcane, insectan language.

His chants induced a burning in his arms as the mass of larvae violently evolved until his arms were both encrusted in luminescent slime, each a swollen chrysalis. Then the chrysalides burst, and hundreds of necrophagous wasps flew about his form tracing the same weave he had inscribed with his weapons. They flew about him, a horde of grotesque, winged creatures, with stilt legs and engorged abdomens, and beady eyes.

You must learn to command my minions.

Some were empty, molted husks, and they sunk their stingers into the blade and sucked it clear of substances. Others were engorged with ichor as they left Lysis's form, and they impregnated the metal with Haemarr's blood and fell to the ground extinguished. Blue, clear, and metal grains now existed together, like a stained glass window reinforced by steel. It was a power infused with the ichor of Haemarr, and now no target, astral or physical, would evade its icy blade.

Lysis approached his faithful servant's ghost. "Avener Xel, I can now end you. Is this truly your desire?"

Xel's fractured phantasm shivered in anticipation. "Yes, Lord. I implore you to free my soul from my mauled body. Release me, sir, if you can."

"I will, good Xel, and in short measure. First, can you tell me more of the evils I will face inside? Do you know the fate of Maeve or the children?"

"Only that Lady Maeve was reading to the girls in the Great Hall when the demons struck. I had just spoken to the Lady as I left to tend to the horses. As I neared the stables, the boys ran past me trying to locate Erolen in a sport of hide-and-seek. Soon after, as I tended the mares, Erolen darted past the doors screeching in horror. I peered out to behold several devilish clouds permeating from the water grates whence he came. The dazzling clouds contained images of the walking dead! From within the clouds, four things crept into the courtyard— four evils that I cannot, even as a ghost, describe to you accurately except to say that the mere sight of them chilled my blood. It was a cloudy vision, my last before a beast attacked me—my limbs were sent asunder and my mutilated body thrown over the barricade. I failed you..."

"No, Avener Xel. It was I who failed. May your soul be cleansed!" Then Lysis executed his servant gracefully with *Ferrus Eviscamir*. Xel's ghost crystallized and shattered when struck. His moans ceased, and the essence of his decaying flesh was transmuted into glass shards to accent the sullen scene.

"It was I, poor Xel and Marcus. It was I who put a plague upon Gravenstyne," he said, fondling the four trophies of human relics suspended from his collar.

"Sorcery has enhanced *Ferrus Eviscamir*," Lysis said, marveling at his enhanced armory. "Such magic must come with a price."

Yes, though you cannot yet understand what price I pay to keep your soul fused to your body or to render your weapons effective against things of the astral plane. Understand that your power is not without limits, that when you exercise such sorcery you will drain the power that enables you to survive, and restoring that power consumes time, life, and blood!

"Fine," Lysis said with punctuated vigor, as if he were entitled to such responsibility and were inherently able to manage the power of the gods.

Above him sneered the still faces of eldritch gargoyles perched along the Fortress's parapets. Evil had come from within to infest the Fortress grounds. Now the stone beasts guarded empty, sorrow-ridden halls behind cold, black stone. Their smiles were mischievous and mocking, and Lysis could not help but take their looks personally.

"Dear Maeve, I come for your soul now. I come to rescue it and cleanse my conscience. I come to rid this place of the ghosts of the accursed men whom I tortured: Brood, Narl, SanGules, and Potter. I am transformed now, having sacrificed my life to save your souls and to end these demons."

As if they heard their father's oath, the faint wails of his children permeated the still air:

> "Ten 'n ten, your bed's a coffin,
> Ten 'n ten, all love is pretend,
> Nine 'n nine, I'll evade 'n hide,
> Nine 'n nine, all flatter and lies..."

The sounds chilled his already cold, dead flesh. For certain, they were not the sounds of the living. They confirmed what Lysis already knew–that his family had been murdered. Even after their deaths, their souls were being tormented. The haunting whispers of children pervaded the air:

> "Eight 'n eight, can't coop this bait
> Eight 'n eight, no date to mate!
> Seven 'n seven, they'll be no weddin'..."

Lysis sprinted toward the main gate. The portcullis was drawn down and the gate sealed by wooden planks, hastily bricked barricades, and painted glyphs. In his absence, the Fortress had been condemned by the Cromlechon Guild of Barbers for news of Gravenstyne's plague had traveled fast. Beside an icon of a jawless skull, the script read:

DYSCRASIA

Common people did not know the specifics of this deadly plague, but they knew dyscrasia was the worst of all distemperaments, a contagious imbalance of the bodily fluids that could not be cured.

Lysis ran along the southern wall. Several hundred yards from the Fortress he neared a dilapidated mausoleum enshrouded by apple trees. The rusty door yielded to the Lord's efforts, and he made way into the empty tomb. It was a false crypt, the exit of a secret passage to elude the grip of siege. Guided by the phosphorescent shadows of souls, he drew aside the coffin's case and revealed the trapdoor.

Sheathing *Ferrus Eviscamir*, Lysis wielded his glowing flaying sickles to guide his path and to protect him in the event of close quarters combat. The undead Lord crawled down crevices and chasms until his feet met a mud floor. Surveying the walls, he located several scorched areas—torch marks indicating the direction of the exit. By deduction, Lysis determined the path to the Fortress.

He came to a sudden stop as the ungodly whispers of his crying children were heard echoing through the tunnels. The larvae quivered and resonated, passing along the sounds to the earless Lord. Rage filled him, but the harsh terrain slowed his advance, the passages constricted by slime-covered rocks that pressed against his anterior and posterior sprawl. Ever embraced by cold stone, he wriggled his way toward the east and then north. Whenever he paused to gain his footing or to survey the tunnels for torch marks, the subtle cries of his children pierced his soul. With renewed strength, he propelled himself through the crawlspace. Finally, the tunnel widened to shoulder width, though the ceiling lowered. Handcrafted bricks welcomed him to the lower levels of the Gravenstyne Fortress.

Here he found himself within the catacombs of his family, where rectangular niches carved into the stone housed his deceased fathers, mothers, sisters, uncles and aunts, friends and servants. Their corpses glowed in marvelous colors, peacefully resting in hallowed ground.

"Why did you fail us?" the chorus of Picti ancestors asked. "Why did you not follow our path? You rejected your inheritance!"

"I had to protect the Lady," Lysis muttered. "Can't you ever understand?"

The ghosts returned: "You abandoned the Rite. Then you left the estate vulnerable! You permitted evil in…"

He rushed past the ghosts of his relatives, unabated by their judgmental comments.

Here he came upon another of his servants, one still alive, sitting on his knees and rocking at high frequency. The servant's bloody right arm hung limp at his side while his left hand clutched at his scalp as he screeched, "One, two, three, get off my father's apple tree! Skin the apple! Feed the pear!"

It was Brewster Leamond, lead caretaker of the Orchard and maker of the renowned Lysis cider. Losing his family had rendered him a disabled lunatic, although he still lived by some measure. Leamond was emaciated and insane, his clothes soaked in rancid juice and blood. He sat against a broken barrel, his soul twisting like a funnel cloud, twirling about his body chaotically without tiring. Endenken had been absent for nearly two months now, and it was clear that the man before him had survived only by escaping the demons and eating his own flesh.

"Four, five, six, no wasp tricks! At least at night, that which was gray turns blue. This fruit bears my skin and yet this meat is not mine. The veins are ripe and timeless. The water within sour and full of pulp. The air it breathes now rotten. Dear friend, partake my apple. Its skin bleeds red upon my hands..."

Lysis raised his flaying sickles to put Leamond's mind to rest when he was distracted by haunting voices:

> "Six by six, nix the nesting sticks!
> Five 'n five, I've a crow's life..."

The voices cried from afar, their sounds muffled by many fathoms of intervening stone. Immediately the guttural sounds of vomiting children followed, hurling gasps of spittle echoing through the corridors so horrid and wrenching that they seemed to peel the scabs off Leamond's bloody arm—so awful that upon reaching their father he doubled over in agony.

Moments passed as the Lord regained strength. Hastily he regained his conviction, and then slit Leamond's throat.

> "Four 'n four, murder no more!
> Three by three, no grounding me..."

Before Leamond's body had collapsed to the floor, Lysis was off and running.

"I'm coming! " Sheathing the sickles, he drew forth *Ferrus Eviscamir*, clutching its hilt with both hands as he darted up the stairs leading to the keep, his lengthy mane of gray hair whirling in his wake.

> "Two 'n two, your stinger woos blue!
> One by one! Ware poison! Poison!
> Flee, birds! Better run..."

The wails grew louder as he approached his museum. He ran faster, and faster, and like an engine of anger he bolted into the vaulted halls, blade drawn to target the beast therein!

From the opposite end of the chamber, a dark-cloaked giant stooped beside the forms of three mangled children, their bodies supported by ropes attached to the massive beams spanning the ceiling. It was clear from their decay that they had died at different intervals, perhaps weeks apart. Each had been eviscerated, their entrails uncoiled and limp. The mantled beast was siphoning the children's blood into long-stemmed glass vials.

"Father is home!" the smallest ghost expounded, riding piggyback on its

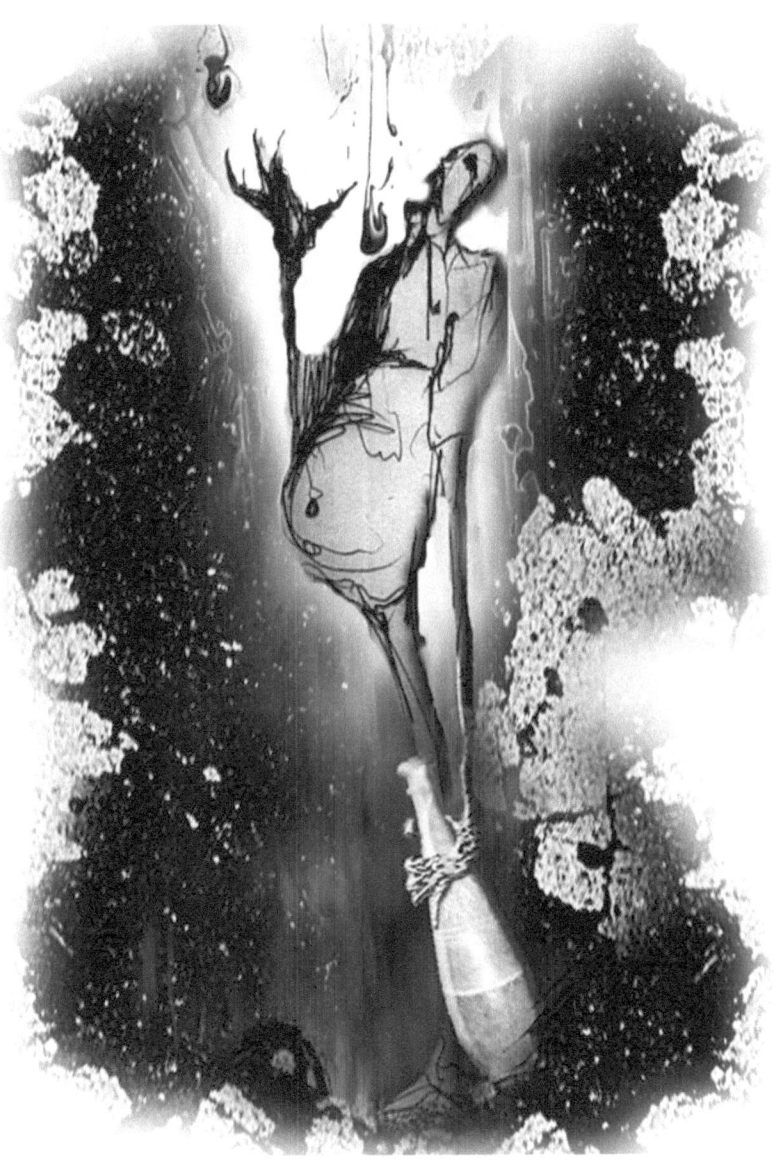

The Red Drunk Potter showers in the blood of children

own immobile corpse.

"Found us," whispered another.

Lysis recognized the spirits of his sons, Darilys, Kyrnelen, and Olyen, and paused only to confirm their identities and that of their murderer. Then he attacked.

Backed by powers of ichor he had yet to master, the Lord advanced directly toward the Drunk Potter, the first human he had killed long ago now raised from the dead by some eldritch force.

Along the walls, mounted heads of horned creatures, wyverns, and serpents witnessed their hunter return to his museum. Endenken had slain them all. But now his own lair had been defiled and the irony was not lost on the skeletons, trophies, and stuffed pelts mounted about the room.

Presently, the souls of Darilys, Kyrnelen, and Olyen bellowed at the demon Potter while he drained their bodies of blood. The ghosts cried woefully to no avail, but the sight of their father gave them hope, and their auras brightened.

The Drunk Potter stood upright to greet the Lord Protector. The Potter's face was veiled in shadows both real and ethereal, and the thick blood that slowly cascaded down its lips was dark black. Black drops. Luscious, thick, abating drops stretched as gravity slowly pulled at them. The Drunk's arms hung lankly to his knees, and both hands clenched vials brimming with the spoiled blood of the three boys. Most prominent was the Drunk's swollen gut; protruding via the robes, the skin stretched taut about a round, bursting belly.

The Red Drunk stood calmly, watching the Lord approach. Perhaps it was unaware or ignorant of its impending doom. Perhaps it was merely self-absorbed or stupid. Even with hunched shoulders the thing commanded some sense of authority by virtue of its immense stature, for it was more than a yard taller than Lysis – oddly stretched as if drawn on a rack.

Ferrus Eviscamir burned with fury. Potter made little effort to parry, shielding the contents of his jars over its own form.

Lysis recalled when he first hunted the Drunk Potter. The Drunk had roamed the Cromlechon as a lost soul, imbibing only liquor, unable to sell his ceramic wares. There he beat the homeless urchins and explained how their lives drained society, how their thievery was evil and that they had been abandoned for good reason. He preached that to succeed in life one must understand people, that one should listen instead of monopolizing conversations, that one should offer affection in order to receive it. Then he scolded them over their inability to function.

Unable to afford ale, he evolved to murdering those who could, and by drinking the contents of their stomachs he extracted some satisfaction. In this fashion, he transferred his taste for liquor to that of blood. He murdered many. But that was nearly two decades past. Around that time, Doctor Grave learned of Potter's transgressions as he tended to the ailing Maeve. Thus Grave informed Lord Lysis. Endenken immediately hunted the Drunk and incarcerated him beneath the Gravenstyne catacombs. Never did the Lord expect the Drunk to spread pain again! Especially not within the estate of Gravenstyne.

"Damn you, Drunk!"

Ferrus Eviscamir carved his enemy's robes into rags and bones into shards. "Die!"

The battle was intense but short, as Lysis severed the Drunk's spine and loosed the contents of its swollen belly. The creature collapsed, smiling a toothless grin.

Lysis continued to beat the broken form of the Drunk until, minutes later, Haemarr managed to focus his warrior.

Lysis! You have ended the physical incarnation of that devil, but do not let your revenge consume your alertness! The magic that resurrected the Drunk's body remains

A museum creature approaches Lysis!

in several others.

Lysis had little time to reconcile the meaning of the warning when…

Red mist escaped the Drunk's skull. It hovered in the air and dissipated. It was unlike the ethereal apparitions of souls and memories; rather it was more

Lysis battles the incarnations of the Red Shade

intense and opaque, analogous in substance to the blue ichor of Haemarr.

Then, as the creaking of bones sounded, Lysis turned in horror to see his museum of skeletons become animated, identifying him as their enemy.

The red mist had transferred to their forms—embodied them! From their pedestals they dismounted, slowly, mechanically, to circle the Lord.

Wyverns, bears, serpents, and things with ribcages that could house several men approached, their empty skulls burning with eyes of ruby fire, their claws extended, their tusks lowered...

"Haemarr! Aid me!"

Carve the sacred glyphs into the air and my power is yours...

Lysis instinctively traced the symbols as he had done when he called forth the wasps at the gates of Gravenstyne.

The incantation required time, and the museum's skeletal inhabitants advanced. *Ferrus Eviscamir* whirled about furiously, but Lysis could not complete the rite before an ebony tusk impaled him and held him aloft.

Decayed flesh and larvae exploded from his chest, yet the Lord managed to retain his grip on his magical blade with one hand. His free hand intuitively collapsed onto the wound, guided by the power of Haemarr. Retrieving a mass of blue larvae, Lysis hurled the ichor of his patron god into the skull of the mammoth creature.

The larvae and mist fused, the fluids igniting into white plasma and cooling rapidly into stone. Instantly, the creature was immobilized. There, still held aloft beneath the mammoth beast, the Lord reflected on the transformation of ether into rock.

Do not hesitate! Complete the spell!

Lysis did this, though his movements were awkward, being that he was impaled. His arms swelled into burning hives, the larvae evolved into luminous wasps, and the swarms did battle with the skeletons as *Ferrus Eviscamir* fell out of his exhausted grip.

As the tusked creature collapsed, Lysis was released. The gaping hole in his chest ached in ways indescribable to the living, his aura blazing through the massive tears in his tunic. He recovered his war scalpel and joined the fray alongside the corpse-eating wasps of Haemarr.

The ensuing battle was one of colossal scale: dozens of estranged creatures of enormous size rampaged within the confines of the museum, combating swarms of minuscule, winged insects. Clouds of bone, chitin, and stone consumed all visibility.

The skulls of the beasts became encumbered as wasps penetrated the red vapor and fused into stone. Beast upon beast fell to the ichor-infused *Ferrus Eviscamir*, bones splintered and fractured with ease, and masses of the red mist absorbed into the blade or severed into glassy fragments. It was as if Lysis cleared a forest of bone. The beasts fell with the weight of mighty oaks to crack the tiles and shake the foundation of the Fortress.

His museum was demolished. All Lord Endenken Lysis's trophies and mounted skeletons were ruined. Pedestals, plinths, and pillars alike turned to rubble. The vaulted ceiling sank low, having lost the support of several girders. Some architecture collapsed to reveal the night sky. But most pressing, the double doors leading to the Great Hall, behind which Maeve was last seen by Avener Xel, were now covered by debris. He would have to enter the Hall from a different route.

Overwhelmed and exhausted from battle, Lysis paused to rest.

"WHAT EVIL DO I face here?" Lysis recovered.

The mist is vaporous ichor of a god-like entity, a Shade. It is more complex than a mere ghost because when mixed with my blood, the amalgam turns to stone, a phenomenon that only occurs upon mixing two elder gods' blood. This Shade appears a corrupted imprint of the dyscrasia-ridden Picti Muse. It is not the Muse itself, but a shadow of it—an independent spawn that resembles its parent fire.

"So the Drunk's body was only a vessel? Controlled by a diseased god?"

Not by the Muse itself, but secondary things that grew from its ill soul. All undead retain some aspect of their living tendencies, as you do. Some have more control over their forms than others. So the Drunk's body retained his instinct to consume blood. His corpse and soul, however, were inanimate until the Red Shade assumed control of it. No doubt, other imprints of the Shade control the other beasts roaming your fortress.

"This Shade has destroyed my home. It preys upon the innocent without mercy. It is evil, and I will eradicate it!"

Ahhh! Poor Lysis, you fail to understand. You cannot divorce yourself from the Shade's presence or purpose. The Shade is a reflection of you, descendant of Picts. Had you accepted the Muse during the Inheritance Rite, these Shades would not exist. You chose not to accept it, so it remains looking for you.

Lysis ignored the truth. "My boys. How fare their souls?"

The Drunk fed only on their blood, not their souls. Their auras appear intact, although filled with sorrow. A proper burial of their remains in a safer place could put them to rest.

"So it will be done." Lysis lowered the remains of his three sons and placed them aside. Meanwhile, the souls of the boys were quiet. They didn't welcome their father, nor did they avoid his stare. They simply were speechless, traumatized. The youngest ghost, Olyen, managed to contact Lysis's aura as he stood to walk away.

"We cry and cry and cry." Olyen's weak voice resonated finally.

Then the three spirits opened up, speaking simultaneously.

"Mother will be angry at this mess!"

"It wasn't our fault, Father. Erolen did it!"

"He hid out of bounds!"

"Below ground!"

"And he was found!"

"…and then came blood, and blood, and blood…"

The jabbering trailed into reflection with Olyen's comment. "Will you bury us here?"

"No. I plan on taking you to the Orchard, where your souls can run freely."

Olyen smiled a dissipating smile.

"My sons, I fear the catacombs would not be a suitable place for children to play. We will start a new tradition."

Darilys interjected. "Mother?"

"She will rest with you, in the Orchard. Rest now. We can talk later. Father has things to fix."

"I AM WEAK. How do I regain my strength, Haemarr?"

For now, it is sufficient that you send for more of my minions. Call upon their kind. They will aid you. Here now, follow my lead.

Lysis began gliding about the ruins, arms outstretched, performing some arcane dance. He repeated his steps, tracing out the runes that commanded the forces of Haemarr. And the ground rumbled, and the sky roared, as the call was answered. They came in droves, thousands of insects and empty exoskeletons, humming, buzzing, and skulking along, filled with Haemarr's ichor. They entered from the breach in the ceiling, through the cracks in the floor, and through crevices amongst the ruins.

Accept my ichor, Lord Lysis.

The swarms circled his body *en masse* until the final glyph was traced, and then they crashed into his skeletal frame with sudden force. He glowed then as a candle glows beneath the wick, a solid translucent mass. The bones of his ribcage melded together, wrapped in shells of chitin. His ribcage was rendered smooth as a beetle shell, and it glowed the soft glow of Haemarr's ichor.

Lysis did not thank his master, accepting the energy and armor with a candor of self-righteousness. He didn't care where the minions came from or how often he could call upon their energy. He felt entitled to these powers. He gave his life for them. He would call upon them as necessary.

I remind you, there are limits to my power.

"I have not forgotten."

The threshold to the eastern corridor remained open, so the Lord clambered over the wreckage to begin his circuitous route toward the Great Hall. The clamor of battle had certainly broadcasted his presence to the Shade-possessed evildoers. So he advanced quickly but with caution. He climbed like a panther over the rubble, unabated by the muffled, but still haunting, sounds of his wailing children.

He had not gone long ere he discerned that another blockade impeded his way. He would have to again divert his path. Then his eyes fixated on a water drain in the floor. Through that grate, Lysis could enter the underground bathhouse and travel via the hypocaust to the lower kitchen. From there, he could gain entrance to the Great Hall.

Lysis moved the grate aside and entered. He snaked his way through the underground aqueducts to arrive at the room he once called his sanctuary. He dropped to the floor with his back arched and his limbs bracing his form. The marble room was damp and cold. Except for the golden ethereal glaze kindling on the tiles and ceiling, the bath chamber was empty. The otherworldly glow failed to reflect off the surface of the water as did normal light; instead, it transmitted the mirror surface. A trickle of water echoed continuously. The walls appeared to be crying, leaking tears into the pool.

Lysis's emotions sobered here. He could literally *see* his aura decrease in intensity. Blacken. Dark as Darilys' blood dripping from the chin of the Drunk...

You created the world about you, Haemarr interrupted.

"What?"

I feel you absorbing the feelings of melancholy you deposited here through many past visits and mediations. Those feelings still linger, having been absorbed by the brick.

Now they sober you again. You are just beginning to understand how your feelings and actions weave themselves into complicated knots with the physical world. You can change things, but not in ways you think.

"I know my choices have had consequences. I understand that you liken me to the Shade. You are wrong. We are not the same. I killed those men because they were destroying families and threatening Maeve. Whether their ghosts guide themselves or are led by some colored vapor of the gods, I do not care. They are evil. I aim to annihilate them and rescue the souls of my family."

Your shame is overcoming your confidence. You may not speak it, but your aura expresses your sorrow. Your regret for bringing evil into this manor cannot be erased or masked by rhetoric. It is acceptable to mourn and taste the melancholy, but let these emotions drive you forward – not weigh you down.

Driven to action by Haemarr's words, Lysis made his way by staircase to the furnace crawlspace that spanned the underside of the pool. Past stokers, shovels, and piles of wood, he approached the doors to the vents that once warmed the pools and stoves. He entered, crawling on all limbs with *Ferrus Eviscamir* sheathed and his flaying sickles within reach, and headed north toward the kitchen.

He had to draw forth his sickles when he came upon the custodian of the furnace and catacombs, the Sexton Julian Kar. The servant must have retreated here and died in seclusion. His body was charred, indicating the vents he once tended had roasted him alive. His soul hovered about the body, but could not communicate. The Lord dispatched it and continued.

L YSIS DID NOT linger in the kitchen. He retrieved Karylyn's body from the boiling kettle, removed Evelyn's head from the meat hook, and gathered Veralyn's remains from the butcher's block. Lastly, he gathered up Marilyn's mauled form. The ghost of her, that poor, sweet toddler, was still trying to play with her blocks beside her dismantled body. She was too young to understand that she could no longer touch tangible things. Lysis was sure to gather her toy blocks with her broken form. He placed the four corpses within earthenware ewers to retrieve later.

The souls of his remaining daughters were more affectionate than his sons, showering him with their tragic stories and ethereal embraces. Internally, Lysis was compelled to apologize, but horror suffocated his words. Externally, his aura revealed his genuine love hidden beneath his warrior's façade. The daughters could see that he was enraged beyond measure and that, once he left their presence, his brutal righteousness would override his compassion.

To the west, an embrasure led to a corridor connecting the kitchen and Great Hall. He advanced into this with *Ferrus Eviscamir* drawn, passing by the sculptures of his forefathers. Each bust had been molded from the processed flesh, blood, and bone of his ancestors. He avoided the stares of the refined effigies honoring his family line, for he could not carry their disappointment. It was as if the sculptures peered with the same burning, red eyes of the astral entity he battled. One niche was conspicuously empty; the plinth within beheld the inscription: "Lord Endenken Lysis." The absence of his contribution reflected the end to the Picti tradition.

He strode beside tapestries that showcased both maps of the Lysis Clan's territories and depictions of their history. He marched fast past these. The history, and burden, of his family's estate had churned at his soul enough already.

The Great Hall called the Lord into its eerie cavity, the room where his family once ate together and where Maeve once read fairy tales to all before a roaring fire. They had as a family dined there. They had laughed there.

Presently, at the opposite end, a glass statue knelt before the hearth upon the plush pelt of a white bear. The sculpture was a perfect, translucent rendition of Maeve. Her crystalline surface revealed the folds in her gown and the laced bodice that framed her bosom. Her arms arced before her, as if she were inhaling a deep breath or crouching over a child to protect it. But no child was there.

The Lord knew instantly that she was soulless, her body crystallized via sorcery. Maeve was a victim of the same evil methods that robbed Marcus of his afterlife. As such, he could not converse with her ghost as he had with some of his children and servants. He could not apologize to her soul for his failures. Yet her body remained whole. Not shattered. Some mercy was given to her.

"Narl!" the Lord seethed, ascertaining the beast responsible. "Of course! Narl the cannibal and ghoul, resurrected by the Red Shade to continue eating flesh and souls. Damn you! Come forth and answer to my blade! Narl!"

Lysis clanged *Ferrus Eviscamir* against the granite tile. "Narl!"

The Lord did not expect Narl's sudden response...

The barrel-chested demon, consumer of flesh and souls, lumbered forth from the courtyard, escorted by windborne leaves. The thing held an immature leg in its talons, and it turned with wide eyes at the crazed Lord. It sucked on the bone and consumed its astral fire. Having transmuted it to glass, the beast stored the rod by inserting it into its chest of incandescent flesh. Shafts of arrows, glass, and bone splintered its heaving chest, his ribcage serving as a quiver. Its belly glowed like a lantern since the Shade had rooted itself within it and burned

The crystallized Lady Maeve

intensely. Narl's skull was a tortured, hellish mass, for its lower jaw had been split by Lysis years ago, and now it appeared as cloven mandibles, the fragmented teeth spiking the lengths of either side.

"Narl!" Lysis fingered his collar of scalps. "Soon your thirst for the living will wane. Come eat upon my blade. Come now!"

The beast smiled with its cloven jaw. Then it drew forth a glass bone and cocked it within its makeshift bow–a length of intestine pulled taut between the tips of a curved elephantine tusk taken from the museum. Narl loosed this glass arrow and reloaded the bow with a splintered shaft of bone. In a flash, a series of sharpened projectiles flew toward Lysis.

Pierced by the fragile shafts, some no doubt belonging to his young children, the Lord advanced with unrelenting power. The scene rekindled the past, when Lysis hunted Narl.

Narl, once a renowned archer, had turned to cannibalism in order to sustain his impoverished family. Food had been scarce, and he preyed upon the children of his village to feed his own. Yet his settlement was small, and between hunger and disease the village was disbanded. His family passed away, too. Some primitive madness then awakened within the archer, and he continued eating human flesh, from his dead family as well as from the few surviving villagers. His soul became corrupted, and he began to serve evil pleasures: eating flesh, desecrating graves, and kidnapping young children from blossoming families. Before meeting Endenken, Maeve was a victim of Narl's attacks – though she managed to escape from him; he was identified as the ghoul who abused her by Doctor Grave. Driven to protect and avenge her, Lysis hunted down Narl, brought him to Gravenstyne, and executed him.

So Narl had fed upon Lysis's family. Now, Narl targeted the Lord himself.

Lysis was mere yards away now, pierced by three shafts but still wielding his radiant war scalpel.

"Die, ghoul!"

Suddenly, Narl convulsed in preparation for attack. His arms flew back and his chest exploded, dozens of bone shards tethered by arteries and elongated muscles uncoiling in all directions.

Several lengths pierced the Lord's chitin breastplate, the impact jarring *Ferrus Eviscamir* from his grasp.

Narl heaved the bloody tendrils anchored into Lysis, drawing him closer.

Lysis drew forth his sickles and attempted to lacerate the chords, each successive swipe carving out a bit of the fleshy ropes.

Narl's chest burned like a kiln, the ethereal inferno so intense as to blind the Lord.

Closer and closer the ghoul pulled Lysis.

He could not call the wasps without letting go his resistance, so there was only one alternative. He gave himself freely to the beast.

Lysis lurched forward, driving his sickle and hand into Narl's chest. With his free hand he traced the glyphs. "Haemarr! I command you..."

Lysis's arms swelled into vibrant hives, and the wasps coursed into the

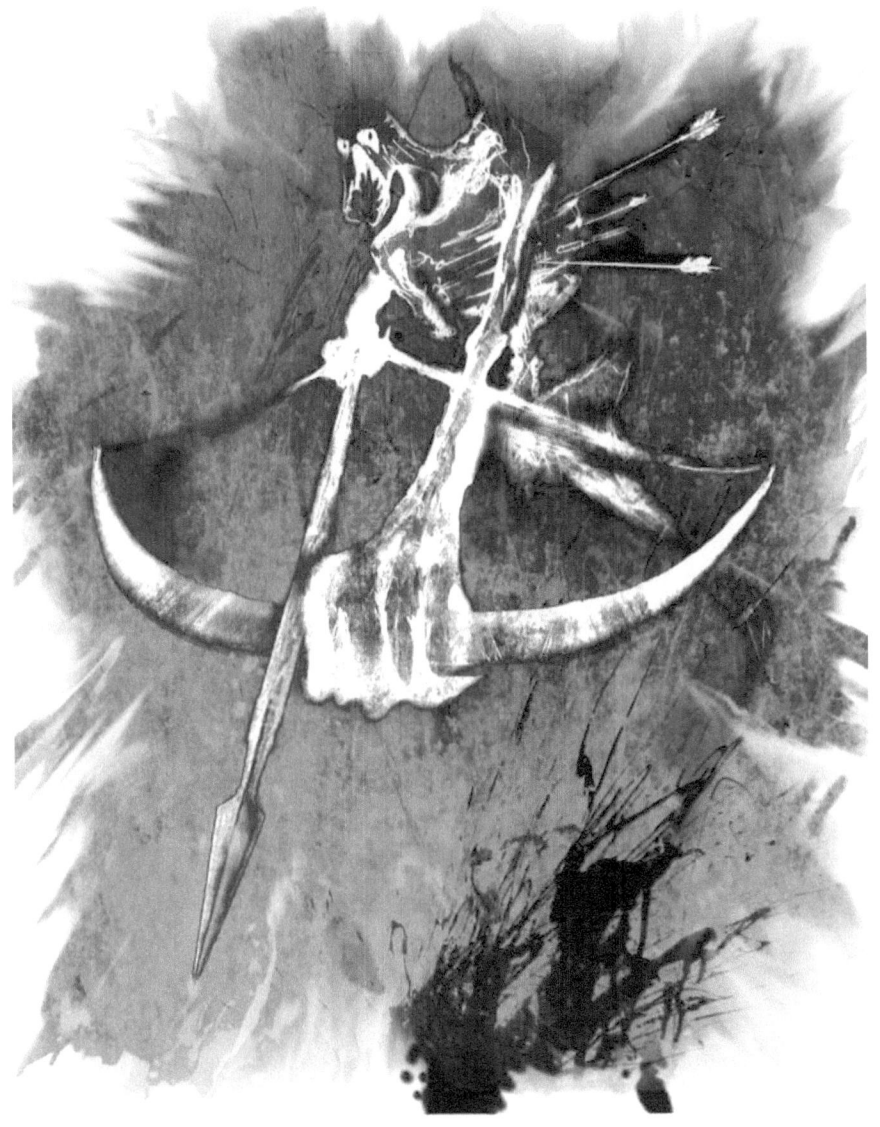

The Red Archer Narl

chest of Narl. The mandibles closed on Lysis's skull, the sharpened teeth clenching with great force.

Lysis hastily pulled his arms free, the sickle thrown to the side, to grasp each mandible. The jaws closed about Lysis's neck. They anchored. An icy breath exhaled from the beast to condense on Endenken's withered flesh. Lysis's aura chilled, dulled in intensity. The flames of his memories were drained as Narl consumed his soul.

Endenken spat as he wrestled, "So lucky you are, ghoul, eater of the dead!" The mandibles loosened, and larvae burrowed from the Lord into Narl's head.

Lysis's memories began to sparkle. Turn to glass. The pain was indirect. Memories shed like leaves from a tree. Once loosed, they were lost completely. He watched in horror as his aura delaminated.

The two fell to the floor and rolled, connected by shafts of glass and wood. Decaying flesh flew from both bodies. Fragments of Lysis's memories fractured and flew.

Suddenly the jaws snapped! Narl shot backward, the two warriors peeled apart.

The Lord stood holding a mandible in each hand. Light-headed but commanding, Lysis continued, "So lucky, Narl, to become a part of the bloody pie contained within Gravenstyne's ramparts. To become one with the meat of the dismembered innocent and the juice of dead angels."

Lysis advanced and placed a foot atop Narl's skull, the flailing beast immobilized, with fluids gushing from his head.

Then the Shade hardened into stone, the larvae within it completing their task. Finally the beast lay petrified.

Victorious, Lysis gathered his weapons and returned to the carcass. "So lucky to die and join those you ate!" He eviscerated Narl with *Ferrus Eviscamir*, discovering the remains of the consumed people. He separated out the portions belonging to his children and put them aside for later burial.

H E APPROACHED HIS still wife feeling immeasurable sadness and guilt.
This statue is as empty and cold as the rock you stand upon. Her body has been changed to glass. Her soul is no longer here.

"Silent! Oh, Maeve. Forgive me. Please, please forgive me..."

Yet Lysis was granted only moments to mourn, for a terrifying screech came from the courtyard.

"Slice the apple! Skin the pear!"

The shouts penetrated the pores of Lysis's bones and amplified through the network of larvae. It was a living voice! A child's!

THE VAST COURTYARD spread before Blue Lysis, a decomposing jungle of wild vegetation and ruined architecture.

The Lord scanned the terrain with haste to locate his remaining children therein. Fate may have granted him one last chance to save a child, and he was eager to wrench some hope out of the dismal landscape.

Transparent memories of all eleven children flitted amongst the ivy and bushes, playing hide-and-go-seek and digging for treasure. Colored wisps they were. Just empty signatures of their souls.

He located the bodies of his four remaining children from afar. In the northern garden, the teen poet Atalen hung on a swing-set beam, his ghost sitting in the adjacent, dangling saddle rocked by pulsating currents of air. The ghost of Endenken's suicidal uncle Derryk hung beside the child. Nearby, Addelyn's torso and head weighted one end of a seesaw, her ghost mounting the aloft seat opposite. Gurylen, once eldest of all the children at eighteen years, was propped beneath a spear shaft, his impaled body hovering over the cobblestone ground before the main gate.

Then there was Erolen, the one living child. He was only six years of age. He ran about, tearing at his skin, yelling nonsense regarding apples and pears. Lysis was too late, for Brewster Leamond had shouted similar crazed statements. Discerning the flesh and blood oozing from Erolen's mouth, it was clear that the boy managed to live as Leamond had, by eating the flesh off the corpses in the Fortress.

Lysis's aura dulled as he bowed his head.

With effort he returned his focus to freeing their souls and slaying the Red Shade.

Directly behind Erolen came trotting Asthete SanGules, the articulate criminal. He was the third manifestation of the Red Shade whom Lysis had slaughtered in the lowest chambers under Gravenstyne. Like the Drunk Potter and Archer Narl, SanGules had trespassed against Lysis's wife Maeve. SanGules possessed charm and a polished, public façade. Unlike the other criminals executed by Lysis, the crimes of SanGules were not physical in nature. He executed his power with noble arrogance, relying on verbal daggers and insidious manipulations. With mere words he could instantly dampen the hearts of all twenty-seven women in his harem, compel them to be subservient in order to appease their guilt. SanGules had imprisoned Maeve for years, keeping her from searching for her son Dey. Identified by Doctor Grave as Maeve's third abuser, Endenken arrested Aesthete SanGules from his manor and brought him here for punishment.

The resurrected SanGules appeared as Lysis had left him. The straightjacket bound his arms, and the pear-of-anguish still engorged his mouth—scabs had formed over it, sealing the rusting device to his split lips. Unable to speak clearly or move his arms, he was powerless. The velvet scarf mantled across his back also survived, though portions had worn where ballooned pockets of skin protruded from his neck. He scurried about insanely, harassed by memories of his victims who screamed as banshees. He wore his insecurity like a blanket. He was pitiful, yet powered by the Red Shade his madness spread like a disease to the living. With all of his apparent limitations, the Aesthete SanGules would be the easiest to underestimate.

A more apparent threat, Brood the Bastard Warrior, also stalked the premises. Presently, Brood pressed his ax against the neck of the decomposing

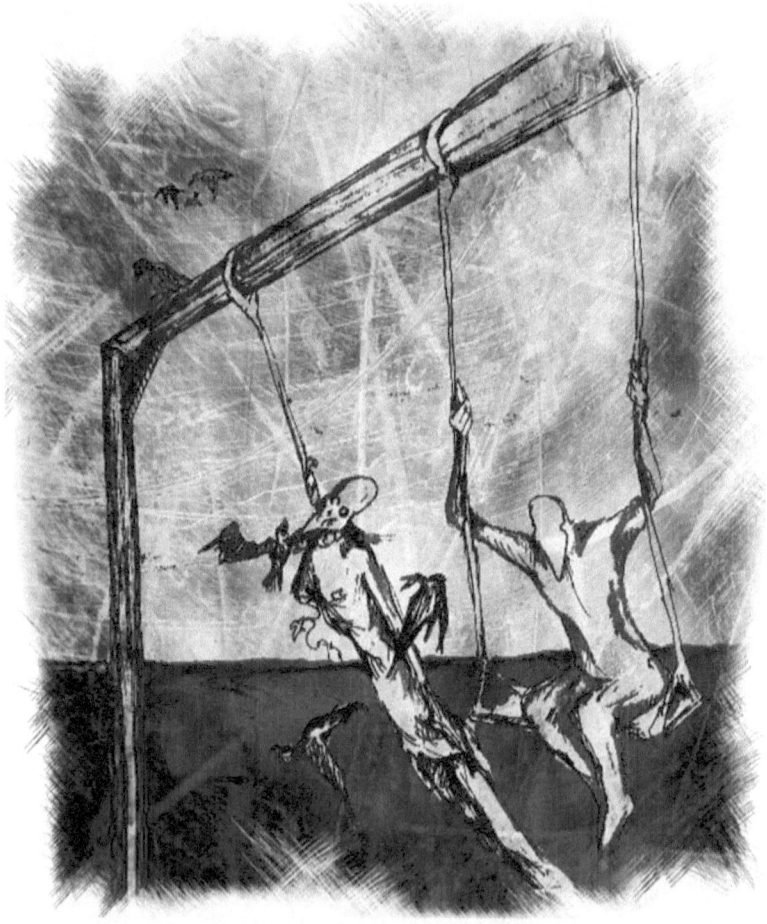

Atalen's phantom sings and swings with the ghost of Derryk

corpse of Pantler Pauline. This makeshift yoke kept Pauline suspended so Brood could violate her. Lysis recalled the necrophiliac and his ax. The ax was known throughout the mercenary community as *Orphanmaker* after all the families torn asunder by its use. Brood was a brute through and through, a bastard orphan himself raised by scoundrels in the darkest corridors of the Cromlechon. His battle-worthiness was bested only by his inept desire to love. So jaded and shunned he was by women, he found his love with the wives of men he slew. Unable to tolerate refusals to submit, he killed most women before he finished raping them. Those few that survived gave birth to his children without his knowledge. Thus he perpetuated his misfortune by repeating the same acts that spawned him – that is, until Lysis learned that Brood had hunted Maeve. Brood was quickly incarcerated in Gravenstyne and bled to death upon castration.

Now the mercenary's body burned with the Red Shade as he raped Pauline's rotting body in the most unholiest of manners. The notion of the necrophiliac defiling his family, his servants, and his fortress boiled the ichor in Lysis's skeleton. He unsheathed *Ferrus Eviscamir* and declared his presence.

"Brood! SanGules! Face me!"

SanGules darted to the farthest corner of the yard as Brood dropped Pauline's limp corpse. Adjusting his grip on *Orphanmaker*, the Bastard Warrior strode toward Lysis.

Lysis glided down the cascade of marble steps that spilled forth from the Great Hall. Gusts of wind stirred up the leaves and aroused the mighty bodies of the weeping willows that circled the yard.

The swinging ghost of Atalen began to whisper a rhyme, his words sailing on the wind with the dead leaves:

> "Golem, take your faerie knife
> Raise up, take my blood and life
> Hide-and-seek, run-n-run-n-run,
> When you hear the tune we play
> Hide-and-seek, run-n-run-n-run,
> We all must die alone..."

The boy's poetry startled a small flock of blue-eyed crows from atop the beam. The radiance of the birds' eyes temporarily caught the attention of the Lord. He quickly recognized them from the Iron Forest but did not perceive them as an immediate threat. Lysis refocused on Brood.

The battleaxe swung forward with an extended reach. Lysis sidestepped and delivered his blade to pin Brood's hilt to the ground. *Clang!* Before he could issue an ensuing strike, Brood's protracted arms pushed him aside.

Lysis rebounded in time to parry another blow...

Weapons clashed! Sparks flew, yet both blades held firm.

Lysis retreated several steps to gain some distance.

Brood advanced twirling *Orphanmaker*.

With god-like speed, the Lord sheathed his war scalpel, drew his flaying sickles, and hurled both simultaneously at Brood.

The Bastard Warrior turned to dodge the blades, one glancing off his immense ax, the other landing in his brow. The deflected sickle sliced through Brood's aura, sending shards of crystallized astral fire to shatter on the stone. Brood's skull had been breached by the other, spurting ethereal flames and bits of gray matter. A flicker of red seeped through the wound. The Shade was exposed.

Still the Bastard Warrior advanced. Brood mimicked the projectile tactic. He raised his ax above his head, whirled it about, and launched it directly toward Lysis.

The butt of the blade struck him square in the chest, cracking his breastplate and sending him airborne.

Landing flat on his back, Lysis watched as Brood descended upon him.

They wrestled, Lysis prying at the gape in Brood's skull, Brood squeezing Lysis's ribcage in an attempt to snap his spine.

Haemarr's larvae crawled from Lysis into the adjoined combatant, searching for the Shade. Brood began to spasm and, in a state of seizure, released Lysis.

Though separated, they remained close. Lysis eyed his opponent in search of a weakness. Brood offered none.

They delivered a series of jabs as they circled one another.

Brood launched forward and grabbed Endenken.

With serpentine motion, Lysis slipped the hold and rolled behind the warrior. A focused kick to the right leg toppled the beast with the snap of a bone.

In a grotesque display, Lysis fully unleashed his animal instinct. He took hold of Brood's exposed shinbone and wrenched it free. The undead Lord was ferocious but intelligent, targeting limb after limb until the Bastard Warrior had been dismembered. Victorious but still enraged, Lysis removed Brood's eyes, teeth, and organs. He would have continued had the Red Shade not retreated from the body, billowing into a cloud above the Bastard. It took the fluid shape of Lord Lysis's frame—an apparition molded in his exact dimensions.

Lysis stared directly at his duplicate self and was forced to accept that his choices had brought doom to his own family. He had forsaken the Picti Muse, but never ensured it was destroyed. So it was waiting all this time, looking for him

Red Brood, the bastard warrior with his ax Orphanmaker

to complete the Rite. Eventually it created Shades of itself somehow, finding and resurrecting the bodies of Maeve's abusers. Had he been inside Gravenstyne he could have faced the Shades himself. He had been out hunting Cypria, and the Shades found the corpses of the four villains in his stead. He had hoped to have made his home safer by killing them. Now he stalked his home as one undead.

How different was he from these monsters?

Haemarr's words also reverberated within Lysis's head—he could not divorce himself from the Shade.

Atalen continued to rant upon his swing, his words fleeting as the winds that carried them:

> "When the golems of old-en days
> Gave the Red Muse holy praise
> They had man on which to prey,
> Hide-and-seek, run-n-run-n-run,
> They had blood on which to prey,
> We the children sac-ri-ficed…"

As Lysis battled his emotional ties to the astral entity, the Red Shade searched for a body to join. The Shade immediately elongated into thin traces to coalesce with its remaining portion within SanGules.

Nearby, Erolen sat on the ground rocking back and forth muttering nonsense.

SanGules cautiously advanced.

Lysis slowly drew *Ferrus Eviscamir*, fighting some spell of confusion.

"You rejected me," the Shade declared from within SanGules' aura. "You are an artisan of death. You are a master of hunting, killing, and displaying the dead. Your craftsmanship spawned me. I am an intimate part of your soul. Let me join you. Let us become one…"

Lysis stood entranced.

"You have denied me for too long. Our separation has eaten away at you. Let the pain subside by embracing me. Let me merge with you!"

Do not be fooled, Lysis. This Shade may reflect your sins, but it is not you. Nor is it the genuine Muse. Now awaken from Asthete SanGules' spell. Kill the final beast!

Sensing Lysis was breaking the hypnosis, SanGules sought refuge by hiding behind Erolen. To strike at SanGules with his blades risked everything since a misplaced swipe may crystallize the soul of his son.

"Always a coward, SanGules. Come away from my child." Asthete SanGules refused to move, so Lysis called upon his wasps again.

SanGules' eyes widened in horror at the sight of Haemarr's minions. He ran about the courtyard as the insects enshrouded his body, inserting their ichor-filled stingers into his corpse. A stone crust formed about his outer surface as he retreated toward the sealed main gate of the Fortress. Exhausted exoskeletons littered the cobblestone as they loosed their ichor. The fossilized mass slumped to

Red SanGules, the Asthete, swallowing a pear-of-anguish

the ground, yet the carrion wasps continued to swarm.

Lysis turned his attention to his dying son. Strangely, the undead appearance of his father did not horrify Erolen. Lysis shielded Erolen, peering over his shoulder at the carnage. Guardedly, he drew forth *Ferrus Eviscamir*.

BOOM!

The hollow replica of SanGules erupted in flame and exploded, spewing stone shards across the courtyard. The main gate erupted outward – the portcullis breached, the wooden planks and brick barricades thrown aside in flame.

Then from within the center of smoke marched forth the exposed, vaporous Red Shade once again mirroring Lord Lysis's shape. The pure ether burned as opaque as genuine fire. It needed a body to host it.

Pointing an ethereal finger toward the Lord, the Shade roared with arrogance, "Accept your inheritance. Submit now. Come to me!"

The remaining wasps sought to guard their master, yet their numbers had dwindled. Within seconds, a thin replica of Lysis had taken form around the Shade, a mass of dead insects lay at its base. The horde of wasps was depleted.

From a fracture in the stone shell, the Shade escaped. It formed the likeness of Maeve and wailed at Lysis, "Why, Endenken? Why did you defile these hallowed grounds? Bring those beasts here? Introduce into our home the very evils that abused me and haunted the Land? To raise our children above a torture chamber? Why? Why did you leave us defenseless?"

"Maeve?" Lysis stumbled backward, leaving Erolen vulnerable.

"You were a pillar of honor across the Land, yet you deceived us all. What kind of demon are you to mislead us, to ruin your family? To neglect your Pictish traditions? Was our love a deception, too? Endenken, please tell me otherwise..."

"Oh, Maeve," Lysis bellowed in agony. He could no longer bear the weight of his actions. He alone was responsible for the destruction of Gravenstyne. He retreated slowly, as the Shade advanced.

"Look at yourself now, my husband. Are you not a beast? An undead thing serving evil? Where now is your flesh?"

Lysis! Awaken! Call upon my strength! I will save you, Haemarr pleaded via his larvae.

Yet the Lord was deaf to his patron god, listening instead to what appeared to be his wife's ranting ghost.

"You have killed our family. Our daughters and sons. All of them!" The Shade disguised as Maeve encroached the fallen Lord, the auras of the two entities prickling the boundaries of each other. Between them Erolen stood, and the Shade was ready to merge...

"Maeve?"

"Father? Is mother here?" Erolen asked with sudden clarity.

Lysis met stares with Erolen.

His son's hazel eyes slowly filled with filaments of red.

The child's eyes became swollen and red-rimmed. The son gripped one of the flaying sickles.

"Erolen! No!"

"Father, you must slice the apple," the red-eyed Erolen said. "Prepare the fruit, spill the wine… Do it right this time. Slice the apple, skin the pear."

"Oh, Erolen…"

He is no longer your son. Erolen is dead, his body possessed by the Shade.

"Noooo!" Lysis screamed.

Erolen bled quickly as he scraped his own skin with the sickle.

"Stop!"

With the resounding voice of a mature devil the boy said, "Come home, Father? Come put me to bed? Tuck me in beneath a blanket of flesh and sing me a lullaby?"

You must kill him!

"Haemarr, I cannot kill him. He is my remaining son!"

You must, otherwise the Shade will torture his soul forever.

"Damn you, Shade! You've kept him alive all these weeks just to torture him! To torture me!"

Flaying sickle dripping with dark blood, the Red Shade within Erolen returned, "We kept him alive, because he discovered us! Released us!"

Kill the boy swiftly and end the Shade!

The Shade interjected, "Don't worry, Lord Lysis. The boy is safe. We will sustain him…"

Kill it!

Lysis was still. His children had been playing hide-and-seek. Erolen must have wandered into the torture chamber below the catacombs. How terrible it must have been to uncover that bloody scene in his father's secret chamber.

Clinging to the rigging as the wind rocked the swing, Atalen whispered:

"God and blood this day be-come
Joined as one with art and man
Let nature's lords pass along
Hide-and-seek, run-n-run-n-run,
Golem and man to-gether play
As we children die - sac-ri-ficed…"

"Skin the apple!" Erolen's youthful voice surfaced over that of the Shade. As the skin curled from his body, the kindling flames of the Red Shade emerged. The boy raked his skin with the sickle, his aura growing increasingly tumultuous with each paring.

The wind rustled the plush branches of the weeping willows with fury – Atalen's ghost rode this swaying swing, his corpse pushed windward at an angle.

Erolen's countenance darkened. His eyes sunk inward, the skin about them drooped, and his tone paled to a chalky white. His youthful lips remained bloodstained and his voice haunting.

"APPLESKIN!"

The boy's aura flickered crimson and white, forming effigies of his memories tormented by the infesting Shade. Playtime fantasies of portraying his father's role as beast slayer formed and dissipated alongside visions of family feasts, picking pears from the Orchard with Brewster Leamond, cooking apple pies with Pauline, and listening to Maeve read stories in the Great Hall. These shadows of the past struggled to rejuvenate themselves but succumbed quickly to the raging, astral chaos of the Red Shade.

Lysis drew forth *Ferrus Eviscamir*. "There is no need to direct me, Haemarr. I am in control. I am Lord Endenken Lysis! Protector of Gravenstyne!"

"You wouldn't slaughter me, now would you? Would you, father?" came the demon's voice.

The possessed boy reached with bloody arms…

Lysis the hunter advanced, blade lowered.

"Save me, father!" commanded the froth-lipped son, yellow puss with red swirls cascading from the sunken wells of his eyes.

And his father returned, "So I shall! Have mercy on me!"

The cut was swift and exact. The Red Shade was sucked dry of ether as the war scalpel penetrated Erolen. The empty body fell in two great halves. The parts fell slowly, the wind impeding their descent and a bed of leaves cushioning their contact with the ground.

The slayer within Lysis was victorious. The father within Lysis had failed. A healthy family, the ideal the Lord had held most high, had been entirely destroyed, in this last instance directly at his own hand.

Lysis cradled the cold body of Erolen in silence.

All was still, the tension exhaled from the courtyard on the back of a calm wind. The branches of the willow trees relaxed. The evil was vanquished.

T WO DOZEN BLUE-EYED crows penetrated the glade of the Orchard and perched themselves close to the burial ground.

Lysis stood in the center of the ring of barrows ignoring the spies. The glass statue of Lady Maeve kneeled in the north at the perimeter of eleven mounds.

The ghost of little Olyen rested beneath the cover of Maeve's outstretched arms. All about the Orchard the ghosts did play: Darilys, Kyrnelen, Veralyn, Marilyn, Evelyn, Addelyn, Gurylen, Erolen, Karylyn, and Atalen. Their souls were free and safe. Within the labyrinth of fruit trees the phantoms abounded as only children do, holding hands in a ring, singing:

> "Four and twenty blackbirds
> Fail to say a word
> Ashes! Ashes!
> We all will burn!"

Singularly absent was Maeve's ghost.

Lysis remained mobile, undead, and ready to serve.

Our pact is complete.

Lysis bowed his gray-haired skull. The astral fire burned intensely about him, saturated with immeasurable anger and sadness. He was a living pyre, a corpse and soul to be plagued forever.

Voids in our souls are haunting. Some can be rectified. Others are inherently, irreversibly painful. Those memories burn bright on this plane. They may be painful, but they are beautiful.

"No. There is no beauty in loneliness."

The beauty of melancholy cannot be attained by looking. You must embrace the terror it breeds. Then you will be pleased.

"I do not understand."

One day you will. For now, you serve me. You are summoned.

Blue Lysis reluctantly replied, "What would you have me do?"

The crows dashed from the branch, anticipating the answer.

You must rescue my offspring. My minions will direct you to the Underworld Forge where Ferrus Eviscamir was originally smelt. There, the blade requires priming to enable the piercing of Cypria's Gallwomb. After, you shall revisit the vicinity of the Iron Forest where the goddess lies petrified, my brood within her. Grieve now, my servant, but only for a moment. Prepare yourself to make good on your commitment.

IV: The Underworld Forge

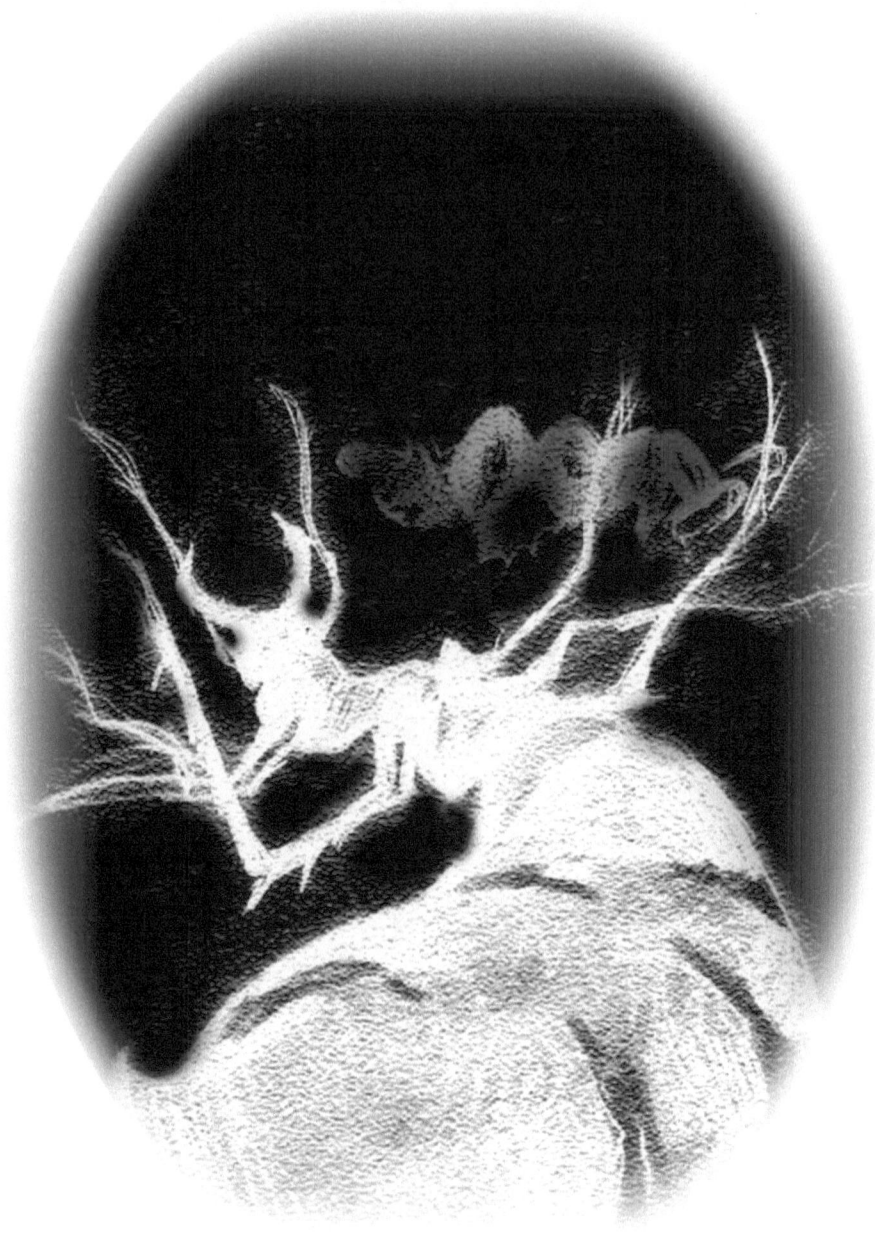

The Underworld Forge

IV: The Underworld Forge

Blue Lysis stood in his orchards about Gravenstyne Fortress, the freshly made graves of his children before him. Sheathed within his baldric was *Ferrus Eviscamir*, its hilt peering over Lysis's shoulder.

It is time for you to resmith the blade so that it can cut Cypria's Gallwomb. For that, you must go to the Underworld Forge, Haemarr commanded. *In order to restore the blade you will need to understand its history.*

When dyscrasia took its final toll on the Queen's colony, Doctor Grave was desperate to save her. With Ferrus Eviscamir, he made an oath to heal her, then he salvaged her soul from her dying body—the magical blade became infused with the Queen's spirit. Her egg sac remained a nexus for creative powers, though without her soul, it cooled. Within it, a sorcerer could work ether into matter and forge magical artifacts. But he would have to provide replacement astral fire.

Doctor Grave retreated from the poisoned Underworld with Ferrus Eviscamir and me. I was still a nymph—I would be the last elder he nursed into adulthood. After me, he had nothing else to nurture. Resurrecting the Queen would require knowledge he did not have at that time. He established the Cromlechon Dissection Theater, hoping to learn enough about dyscrasia and necromancy to resurrect the Queen. Even after all Doctor Grave has learned to date, resuscitating her would be a risky experiment. No doubt, it would require a sea of human blood, and the chance of success is impossible to predict. So it was, decades ago, Doctor Grave explored a different solution. He chose to create his own family instead.

He coupled with Nurse Fae, the lone surviving nurse of the avian elders. They learned after several trials that elementals and golems cannot reproduce naturally. To give life to matter, they had to revisit the Underworld. Use the Queen's Forge.

"Why not have Doctor Grave fix *Ferrus Eviscamir*? He is familiar with the

Forge."

Grave cannot work the Forge as you can. He gave up that privilege. You will soon understand why it is exclusively your duty.

Sorcery entails the transmuting of intangible emotions, and the auras attached to creatures and relics are key ingredients. When sorcerers make artifacts, they do more than sculpt media—they draw upon their souls and incorporate them into their creation. To enable his spells, Doctor Grave had to prepare his own emotions, his own aura, to align with his intentions. In short, he could not serve a new family while he still held responsibilities for the Queen's legacy. Doctor Grave was forced to renounce his Queen's spirit. He felt obligated to find a custodian to keep her soul. And who better than the humans who worshipped her?

"The Picts..."

Your clan. Doctor Grave made a pact with Lord Ante Lysis, the cartographer. Ante was obsessed with mapping the otherworldly things absent on all his maps, and thus committed his clan to serving Doctor Grave's desires assuming a covenant with the Muse would reveal them. Doctor Grave flayed him with Ferrus Eviscamir, passing the Queen's spirit from the blade into Ante's blood and soul. With the ability to see, Ante was indeed able to map the Land's ethereal features, but doing so obligated his bloodline to carry the Muse even after his death. With a custodial line sanctified, Doctor Grave's guilt was allayed. The consequences were significant, since his aura became incompatible with his Queen's—he forfeited the ability to directly carry her soul.

Thus with a relieved soul and depleted Ferrus Eviscamir, Doctor Grave prepared a different weapon, an ax called Ferrus Hewnmaw, to carve his children from the earth. Ultimately, with significant donations of my ichor and the offerings of the stillborn mani-kins he had produced with Fae, a baby emerged from the Forge. Instantly, their daughter cried like a human newborn! Ferrus Eviscamir fractured from these wails, since the baby's cries confirmed Doctor Grave had shifted his devotion—reneged on his commitment to heal the Queen. When you work the Forge, you are tasked with reuniting these splintered sickles to the master blade. It must be restored in order to cut through Cypria's stone womb.

Blue Lysis responded, "So Doctor Grave cannot reforge *Ferrus Eviscamir*. I understand why he gave me his prized weapon so freely. He expected my clan to not only carry the Muse, but to reunite it with her body—heal the Queen. But if I fix the blade, I have no intention of reviving her."

You are not tasked to do so. For my purpose, we need the blade to open Cypria's womb.

"I have the sickles and the sword ready. Tell me how do get there."

Not yet. You must still collect ingredients containing astral fire.

"Your ichor is my single source."

No, that is not true. You will use my ichor, but that will not be enough. You must bring tokens of power associated with your own emotions. As Doctor Grave donated the heads of his stillborn manikins, you must—

"No!"

Haemarr's minions restrained and silenced Lysis as he quivered with anger.

The sorcery you must perform requires personal relics. You'll need to draw on their astral energy. Your children's heads—

"I just buried them! Why tell me this now?"

Our pact allowed for you to lay them to rest. And the funerary process could only strengthen their energies. But that is done. Now you must work to save my legacy.

"By defiling my children?"

No, the children must be exhumed and decapitated to perpetuate the elders, not for the sake of causing you anguish. You will need to learn how to sculpt their ether.

"This is unholy," Blue Lysis cursed.

This is your cost to use the Forge. You must understand this, the larvae within Lysis responded.

"Cost? Hah! A god you call yourself! A malicious, heartless one perhaps!"

I am not to blame. Costs and destinies are rooted in the promises of our ancestors! Just as their decisions bound you to duties before your birth, your decisions have bound your children. It is the nature of patrimony and the essence of your blood.

"My forefathers sacrificed my family's future," Lysis spat. "I hoped to be a better father than they. You need not take control over my body. I will exhume them on my own."

Do so, for they are the keys to my offspring's future.

Lysis moved to gather his weapons and offerings. No sooner had he finished filling his bushel bag with the eleven offerings than a stark wind blew him off his feet. Hundreds of glowing blue wasps launched from the cores of pears and apples, targeting Lysis. They entered his body to fill him with eldritch energy, and then levitated him into the vaporous entity he recognized as Nurse Fae. With his magical scalpel and bag of heads strapped to his back, he mounted the elemental gryphon and rode her as if he led a cavalry into battle.

The misty Fae brought Endenken Lysis to the Cromlechon, the ruined golem necropolis now buried under a developing human civilization of bazaars, markets, and houses. The hill city resembled a mountainous wart. Newer, less impressive architecture sprouted like fungi atop the remnants of the old. Nurse Fae deposited Lysis within a lower cavity. Glowing wasps led him through the cellars and secret corridors beyond Doctor Grave's Dissection Theater. Lysis ventured past grand, dark canyons ornamented with the fossils of golems. These headed the shaft to the abyss, and formed the primary threshold between the surface of the Land and the Underworld.

You must go through the Flue Barrows, a network of pipes that leads to the Forge. It was once open and easy to travel. Doctor Grave could traverse it, work the Underworld Forge, and return within a fortnight. But the bricks have given way, the strata of earth breaching the corridors.

Past cyclopean pillars and marbled tombs, Lysis plunged through the stygian entrance, relying on his undead sight to illuminate the way. The walls were constructed of golem flesh, each brick a forgotten body whose soul glowed as a fierce torch in the astral plane.

Lysis found the Flue jammed with a tangle of grotesque humanoids—mangled appendages entwined such that there was no clear beginning or end to any single form. Many clay and wooden faces stared at him, each attached to a fluid neck ingrained with roots.

This blockage is the rind that is the Land's surface, its upper strata and crust. Be wary, for it is a threaded knot of abject golems—former nurses of the Insectan Queen.

"I am familiar with golems! They are ageless creatures made of the elements. Some like Nurse Fae are made of vapor and air. Others like Doctor Grave are of earth."

These carcasses are ancient, deceased when the Queen's colony collapsed. Their bodies are inanimate now, but the earthy stuff from which they are made still grows. So they migrate and swell slowly like vegetation does, and the walls they had formed thus buckle and crack.

Lysis tried to cut his way through the mass of golem flesh, every hour butchering countless appendages. He had made little progress, since the mass would sprout a new limb wherever one was severed, or the lacerations would seal.

The golems are made of the earth and cannot be damaged by Eviscamir yet. Change the blade's physical properties and it will! You will have to find another way.

Standing atop countless carcasses, Lysis sheathed his blade and dove headlong into the mass.

Months passed as the Lord wriggled through the groping hands of the overgrown network. It was a gruesome journey. Cords of earthy muscle hindered Lysis, wrapped themselves into his skeletal frame, and tugged at his bag of heads.

Endenken had little control over his path, since the soiled figures pushed him in odd directions.

At last, he dropped into the corridor of the Flue. Another swarm of Haemarr's minions was waiting to replenish his ichor.

Two impasses remain between you and the Forge!

L YSIS PLUNGED DEEP into the Flue Barrows, still relying on his undead sight and Haemarr's wasps to find the way down. Within hours, Lysis discovered the path congested with soil.

This blockage is the fruity pith that is the Land's meat, its middle strata. Be wary, for it is ridden with larvalwyrmen. They are the abandoned larvae of the insectan elders–my lost, immature brothers and sisters. Mutated with dyscrasia. Destined never to develop further.

"I have hunted them before! The parasitic worms infiltrate the empty shells of fallen beasts only to discard them as the bone erodes–as if skeletons were mere clothes. Not unlike the methods your own larvae employ."

I recall you invited my minions into you! Yet your distaste for their methods is unwavering.

Blue Lysis tried to cut his way through the soil, every day slaying the larvalwyrmen as they came to him, honing in on the vibrations of his digging. He made no progress, since the soil would heal its own wounds.

Ferrus Eviscamir can cut flesh and souls, but not elements of the Land. Not yet. That is why you need to reforge it, for there is no other way to release the litter from Cypria's stone womb.

Atop the carcasses of tens and tens of gargantuan worms, Lysis began digging again. He formulated a new plan. He dug again, just to call. As larvalwyrmen can ride in the shells of the dead, so too can the dead ride in a larvalwyrmen. He needed only attract one more.

A serpent's skeleton soon arrived engorged with an aged, tentacled worm.

Lysis sheathed his blade and allowed himself to be swallowed whole!

Months passed as the larvalwyrmen serpent swam through the earth effortlessly, taking Lysis away from the Flue. Endenken had no control over its path. The journey was made in complete darkness. He was borne within the fleshy vessel as if in a casket sinking in the deepest sea, occasionally catching a current that would tumble him one way or another.

Over the weeks Haemarr had lost communication with his avatar. His wasps simply could not establish a telepathic connection. Moments before the minions within Lysis's body were drained fully of their power, the larvalwyrmen emerged in the Flue!

So bright were the burning souls of bricks against the empty blackness of deep earth that the light shined through the worm's husk. Endenken knew at once where he was. So with his remaining strength he sliced the belly of the larvalwyrmen from the inside and spilled forth amidst the unrolling intestines of his worm host.

Therein, a fresh batch of Haemarr's minions was waiting to restore him.

Grave and I nearly considered you dead! We must make haste, as Cypria gathers an army of augurs about her womb! One final impasse remains!

B LUE LYSIS WENT deeper into the corridor of Flue Barrows only to find it clogged with coagulate of the blackest oil. A lattice of iron needles was networked therein, along with many fragmented exoskeletons. The very sight of it made Lysis shudder. He had seen such blackness before. Namely, in the veins of his wife when she was alive. And again, when he voluntarily offered his body to Haemarr by wading into the Blood Bogs.

This blockage is the rotten core of the Land. Be wary, for it is a melancholic ichor, though it is less reactive than mine.

"Is this the same black fluid that fills your Bogs?"

Yes. It is the black bile of the elders called melancholy. The liquefied memories and souls of my fallen ancestors reside therein. It is condensed matter made from intangible things.

"It is a grim substance."

Some say beautiful.

The more Lysis peered into the black liquid, the more lonesome he felt. He was beginning to feel out of control again, as he had before his Inheritance Rite. Few options to pursue. Alone. On a mission—someone else's mission.

Focus, Lysis. Now embrace the terrific melancholy!

With sudden renewed strength Lysis dove headlong into the melancholic bath.

He was immediately enveloped and cushioned by cold liquid—divorced from the sounds and sights of the real world. He became terribly alone in his thoughts, which accompanied him as translucent phantasms. He swayed grace-fully, swaddled in a hypnotic embrace. All notion of up and down became

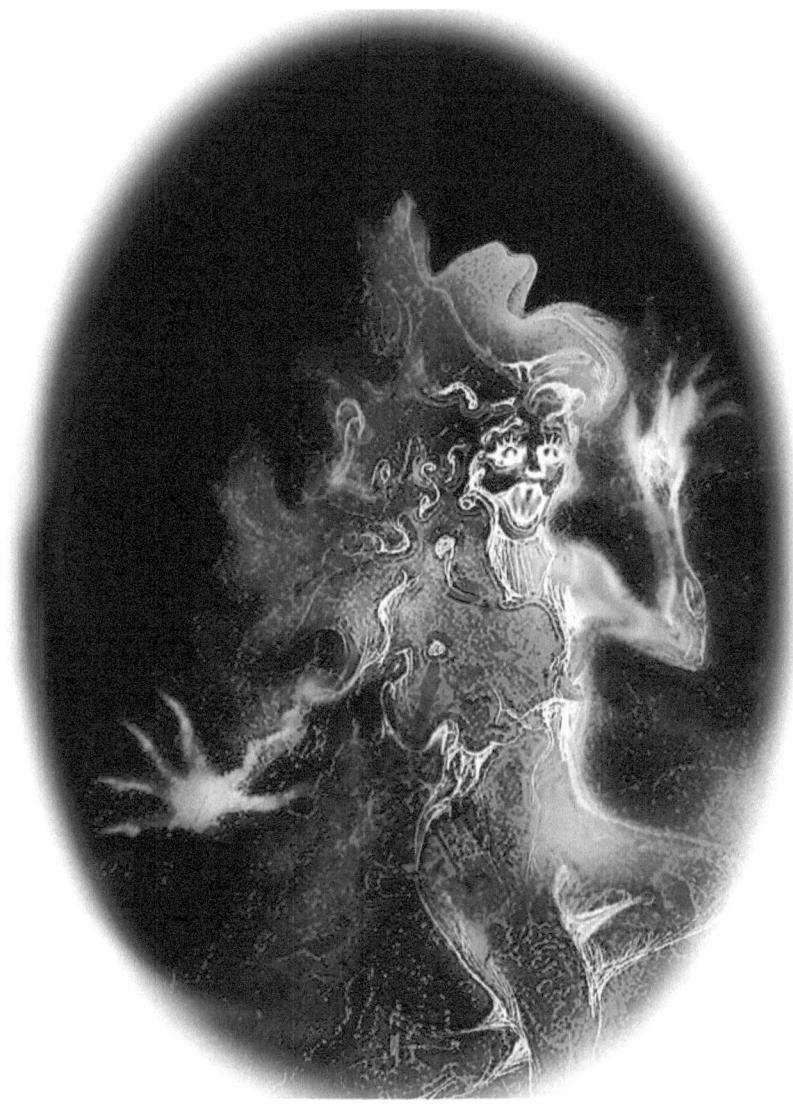

Maeve's soul reveals herself in the bath of melancholy

meaningless.

Time passed slowly as Lysis sank in this dense liquid. He slithered through the labyrinth of iron limbs and black muck. It was a depressing journey since ghosts of his children continuously haunted him. Playing hide-and-seek around his body and the bag of relics. They called out continuously for their mother, for hours on end, weighing Endenken down.

As if attracted to the children's auras, a coil of viscous melancholy snaked

its way to him and wrapped itself about him. It whispered with feminine exulta-
tion, "Ende! 'Tis you!"

Lysis shook in surprise and terror! He was suspicious the apparition was
something evil guised as his dead wife.

"Love, do not falter now," Maeve's ghost said. "You are so close. Follow
me and I will steer you to the Forge! We haven't much time."

Too tired to fight the spirit, Lysis submitted to his hopes and cried out:
"Oh, Maeve. I am sorry. I left you unprotected that night the Red Shade came,
and those haunting beasts defiled you again... killing all of our children except
one... and I had to mercifully put Erolen to rest—"

Maeve said, "Ende, you have been most faithful. It is I who has been
deceitful over the years, for I did not reveal my true self."

"You are dead! Your body rests as a statue within Gravenstyne's Orchard!
Even with my undead sight, I could not detect any soul about your crystalline
remains!"

"My soul survives past death, as does yours, for you speak to it now! But
not for long, for I am doomed to transcend into this oil very soon. I cannot pass
peacefully without asking for forgiveness and sharing what I have learned here.
Bear my confession through! Consider all you have seen. The Land is poisoned
by dyscrasia, and everything is near death. The Picti faith had been dwindling for
decades until you ended it. The elders are down to a couple of beings, and they
are diseased—the remaining died and their remains comprise the sea you now
swim in. Once upon a time, the elders imparted their creative forces into nature,
made nurses to help them—"

"Golems?" Endenken interjected.

"Alas, they too have reached a desperate stage. Only two survive as mobile, sentient beings. They have been torn between resurrecting the dead colonies
they once nurtured and beginning their own. It is how I came into existence. My
parents are the golems Doctor Grave and Nurse Fae—"

"You? A golem? No! This is a dream! My betrothed was human!"
Endenken reeled in shock. Haemarr spoke the truth, but did not reveal Maeve as
their daughter.

"I am human, but my parents are not. They could not conceive a child, so
they appealed to the elder Haemarr. He sympathized as he understood the desire
to bear children, for Haemarr had only one suitable mate and Cypria would not
cooperate. Sick with dyscrasia, their consummation would transform their bodies
into stone. Haemarr desired peace through union and death, but Cypria feared it
would only lead to ruin. Haemarr made a pact with my father. He would allow

Doctor Grave to tap his elder life-force to produce me with Nurse Fae. In so doing, my parents were tasked with finding a way to impregnate Cypria with Haemarr's seed.

"And so they did. By manipulating me and your son."

"Yes. Doctor Grave and Haemarr played him like a pawn, as they did you. But their strategy to use Dey to impregnate Cypria worked. Before that, Cypria was cunning, agile, and unwilling. She continually escaped Haemarr. My father constructed the Iron Forest to entrap her, yet he was unsuccessful. Through manipulating you and Dey, they succeeded. But they exploited more than you two. You are just the end of a bloodline that has been taken advantage of for decades. It took that duration for Doctor Grave to learn how the Forge worked through trial and error. Early on, he discovered that had to find a custodian for the Queen's soul. So he victimized Ante Lysis—"

Endenken interrupted, "Ante? My grandfather's father? Haemarr told me of his pact with Doctor Grave. But I abandoned the sect, the Muse, to save you—"

"You tried to, Ende, but you are its proper custodian. Sorcery demands it find you. Though you fight it, her soul still searches for you—it is drawn to you! The night the Red Shade infiltrated Gravenstyne, slaughtering our children as it sought you, my father cast a desperate spell to protect me. He could not bear to see me die violently as a result of his betraying the Queen. Nor could he take me away from my children. Hastily, he transmuted my soul into the melancholy from which it was forged, leaving my corporal husk a frozen, lifeless crystal. Now I am separated from my body and doomed to disperse into the oil around you. So I speak my last words now. Listen!

"I have come to learn that the Lysis bloodline still lives. Dey was still partly human when he mated, not wholly dead. Fertile. He impregnated her with his seed, too. His child is in her womb!"

Endenken was unsure. "The cursed child you bore from my ill brother's seed, Dey—he could have a child of his own? And I must enter this Forge now, your birthplace and origin of the evil that haunts us both. Offer the heads of our children. To save the Lysis bloodline?"

"Yes! Dear Ende, you must bring Cypria's litter to term! Reforge the blade. You can draw upon Haemarr's power to work it. Then free the litter and Dey's child from Cypria's womb. Let the elders transcend as you free the last of your clan!"

"For your grandchild, then? Not for Haemarr..." Endenken considered this, gripping the sack he had brought with him. "Your grandchild. A Clan Lysis child. But not my child."

"For your bloodline. Oh, Ende, I am sorry. I do love you. Forgive me."

Endenken sighed. "If I free the litter, then my oath will be fulfilled. My future will be uncertain. I will likely expire. Either Haemarr's ichor will petrify or become impotent the instant his children are birthed. Or, if he fails to transcend, he would have no more need of me. Without eldritch powers, my skeleton will become immobile. No other could reanimate me. Except..."

"The Red Muse will possess your body, despite your desire to avoid it. Grave will ensure it burns within you. That fate is unavoidable. With me dead, he will revisit the notion of resurrecting the Queen. He will need you to transport her soul."

"Damn these gods! And golems, too! Doctor Grave! Haemarr! They play me like a puppet, just like they did my ancestors. If the Muse occupies my body, it will do my bidding!"

"Her rebirth is Grave's mission more than her own. I have faith you can

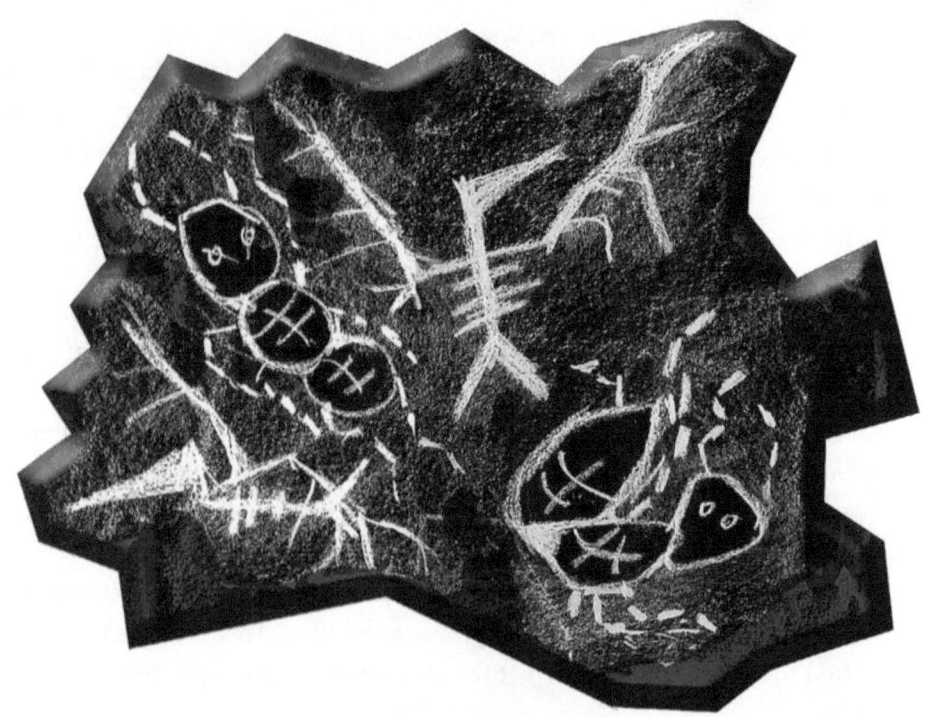

Calcinated fossils of avian and insectan elders

control her..."

Ende strained to hear his fading wife.

Maeve raised her voice to a whisper. "Understand, Love, that you could never have protected our children from the Red Muse or her Shades. They were doomed before their birth, ever since Ante accepted the Queen's soul and disease. Go now and reforge *Ferrus Eviscamir*. You must free the litter, fulfill our duties... I am passing now... Explore the surface of the Queen's abdomen. My image will mark your entrance," Maeve's spirit said, her voice resonating from the body of melancholy. "Offer our children, and your entrance to the Forge will open. Love forever...save Dey's poor child... the remaining Lysis... I love you..."

Endenken did not reciprocate with words.

Maeve's soul became non-responsive. Faded away...

H E NEVER ACCEPTED Maeve's apology, but he did follow her instructions. Miles beneath his home, depressed over his family's failings and betrayals, he trudged forward, in the wake of his beautiful wife's silence.

Lysis addressed the larvae and wasps within him. "So I too am your pawn, Haemarr? As my wife was a pawn?"

No. You are the savior of my children! Bring my peaceful death!

Blue Lysis scoffed, "I aim to bring a true death to the Queen!"

He swam and wallowed and crawled through the tunnels of the Land. Then he floated into an ancient battlefield that spoke of a massive interaction between the avian and insectan colonies: statues of harpies and bird-men, with elongated beaks and elegant wings; many winged creatures embraced colossal ants that were larger than draft horses and frozen in battle stance, their lengthy tusks pinning their opponents; all were soaked in black ichor; many were transfixed by iron needles and geometric crystals, pyritic cubes and polyhedrons, for the iron precipitated, grew, from the sea of black melancholy.

With their images still registering in his mind he came to a limitless cavern.

At the center, the Queen's abdomen floated as an island. Her ballooned mass would dwarf the Gravenstyne Fortress, so large and awesome was the Queen. Bodies of dead elders floated about her, with iron crystals growing from their rusting metallic exoskeletons and the broken shells of a thousand eggs breaching the surface of the black sea. Endenken Lysis emerged onto the isle. The abdomen was soft as human flesh, but less yielding. The surface was scarred, and her egg sac lay exposed from numerous lacerations.

There were many thresholds leading into the Forge. Black ichor leaked into the gaping mouths of the chasms that crackled the surface of the Queen's belly. Each chasm was guarded with an apparition of a woman. There was a whole forest of them, sparsely positioned. The abdomen was buoyant and flex-ible, flinching each time Endenken's foot contacted its surface. Each orifice dilated and contracted rhythmically, as if breathing. All the while he inspected these womanly effigies, looking for his wife's astral signature.

In time he came across an impaled, feminine shadow that resembled Maeve, but the adjacent orifice had been breached and eleven clay heads were noosed about her neck with strings of intestine. Eggshells littered the fissure, indicating this part of the Forge had already been worked. Suddenly, the shades attached to the relics became animated.

"Look! A visitor!"

"Fruit, nay! Stillborn seedlings!"

"Lost, lost, I say!" exclaimed one of the clay children.

"Came with a bushel of fruit, did he?"

"Hey, Faenne, play a tune for the hero to help him on his way!" chimed another. And so the head of a girl whistled as her siblings sang:

> "...When the golems of old-en days
> Gave the Red Muse holy praise
> They had man on which to prey,
> Hide-'n-seek, run-n-run-n-run,
> They had blood on which to prey,
> We the children sac-ri-ficed..."

Doctor Grave had taught his children that rant. *These are not my children, but his.* This entrance had once belonged to Doctor Grave! The ghostly visage was of Nurse Fae, Maeve's mother. Here was the birthplace of his wife!

Endenken combed the Maternal Orchard, the haunting tunes of Grave's children ever trailing him.

Then he saw her.

On the Land's surface, her crystalline body sat identically. Maeve's shade sat on her knees, cradling the air as if her children huddled within her grasp. Beside her, along the base of her visage, a closed fissure marked the threshold to the Forge.

This ghost was lifeless. Silent. Empty.

So Lysis retrieved his bushel bag of relics and decorated Maeve's effigy by knotting the hair of his decapitated children about her. Thus Maeve rejoined her children in the Underworld. Their decaying faces belied the happiness of the souls that danced about her with the ferocity of spitting fire. These shades were essential ingredients for the sorcery about to commence. The keys thus in place, the earthy lips parted, bellowing a plume of intense heat that spread Endenken's thinning mane of hair and tempered it into filamentous antlers.

Before entering, he swore an oath to his dead children, whose heads dangled before him as a wreath. If he could not revive them, then he could at least avenge them. He could rescue Dey's child with the renewed blade. But that goal was a mere means to an end.

Lysis aimed to extinguish the Queen's soul.

He peered within and saw no flame. As Meave and Haemarr had revealed, the Queen's soul had been drained by Doctor Grave with *Ferrus Eviscamir*. Ever since his Inheritance Rite, the Muse was lost. He would have to hunt down and confront the Red Muse—or let Doctor Grave bring it to him.

Black ichor spat from within like a frothing volcano.

Remember, my ichor is not unlimited. Drain me too much, and the Forge will be your grave.

"So it seems to be my destiny," Endenken Lysis said aloud.

Emboldened by his convictions, he held firm to *Ferrus Eviscamir* and its daughter sickles. Then he descended into the inferno that was the heart of the Land...

V: The Red Diary

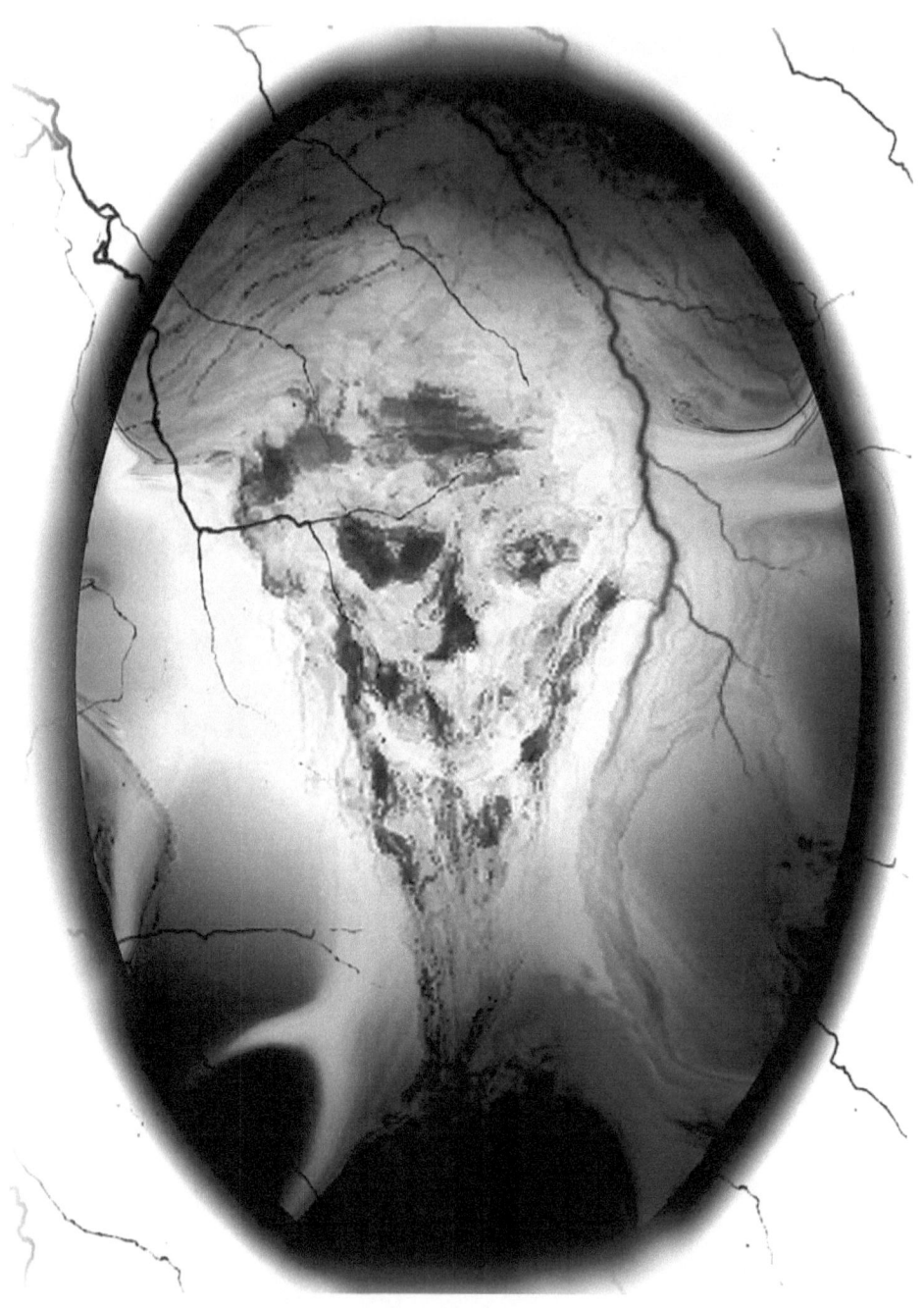

The Deceiver's face haunts Seer Dey

V: The Red Diary

I HELD THE LIMP corpse before me—the skull dropped suddenly so that its decaying eyes transfixed on what remained of mine.

This dead father stared as many did. The true faces of the bodies I handled were irrelevant, for they all assumed the face of the undead predator that had murdered me. For decades, this reoccurring image haunted my vision.

I *see* how the living dream and the unconscious adventure. I see without eyes. Haunted, I saw the Deceiver's face everywhere!

Gradually all faded to a black haze, vignetting the skull in a suffocating darkness that bellowed forth the writhing, casein-white tendrils of mangled hair crowning its pate. He glared from deep, sunken sockets beneath a brooding brow, delivering a singular coldness reminiscent of my father's stares. I yielded to these painful spells, allowing the image to rake the interior of my skull, slowly lacerating and peeling the fragile astral veins that cohered soul and bone. Fine crystalline needles of ether scratched away the tender weave of my history, loosening the regrets of adolescence. As one dead, I could *see* these rifts as brilliant flares of fire emanating from my head. I *saw* my soul's vitality transcending the death of my corporal, fleshy husk, and that it remained bound by unresolved regret. I saw now that my impulsive decision to run away from home had long-term consequences not foreseeable as a youth. In hindsight, I may have better mitigated the abuse of my mother had I confronted my father. Yet as one so young I had been unable to bear that call to duty.

It usually took days to reconcile these raw emotions and contain the astral flames of injury. Understand, the screen of my mind could see only his face, but it was enough to evoke the humiliating insecurities that resided at the very core of my being.

These visions have haunted me ever since the Deceiver taunted me from the confines of the Iron Forest. I was still alive then, with flesh. I had freed the predator from an iron cage so that I may escape his necromancy, yet I failed to escape him or my destiny. The Deceiver subsequently stalked me. Eventually he ensnared me and surgically removed my heart from its cage of bone. I was thereafter reanimated, first by Haemarr's wasps and then by Cypria's bird.

That was years ago. The flocks have since lost the Deceiver's trace. Meanwhile, the garrison of Augurs grew. There were hundreds of human servants at this Aerie, their central focus being Cypria's petrified womb and the blood baths that encircled her.

I impaled the corpse over the Blood Fountain, suspending its skull from an iron stanchion. This body was not, of course, that of the genuine Deceiver. This sacrifice was yet another ornament among hundreds suspended from the colossal matrix of manacles, hooks, and stalks. As Cypria's undying servant, I collected only dead fathers, feeding their paternal blood into her reservoir of ichor. I murdered none myself. As my goddess Cypria would testify, I was too passive for that. I avoided conflict, acquiring those fathers that were elderly, otherwise alone, abandoned, or sick beyond hope of recovery. I was a vulture by nature, not a hawk. Among all my encounters, I never actually found my own father.

I sliced open the corpse's abdomen, spilling forth entrails into the great basin. Its blood mixed with the thick, luminous liquid within the Blood Fountain and burned with the intensity of lightning. Electric sparks danced on the surface, arching above the ichor. Oil and water separated in the mire. To my undead eyes, the reflected colors of sunlight appeared as distinct shades of gray, but I knew that the living would see this liquid prism as a miniature rainbow, filled with vibrant hues. The beauty or real color was forever lost to me. I finished the rite:

> "Let water flow as birds upon the wind,
> Polishing form and erasing sin,
> Removing the soil from your skin
> Return'n it to the Land again,
> Your imperfect façade so disrobed,
> Humbled, freed, and exposed,
> To the goddess Cypria all is shown,
> She imbibes blood, makes it her own!"

Cypria's head had been frozen in an upright position so her view was forever limited. Her gnarled arms and legs were seamlessly anchored into the ground. Mournfully she stared at her abdomen, which was hideously swollen with a parasitic infection. This Gallwomb emerged as an island surrounded by a moat.

Cypria remained petrified at the center of her Blood Fountain. It was here we had last embraced one another, and here that I had betrayed her under Haemarr's possession. Her body transmuted into stone as the minions of Haemarr passed from my body to impregnate her. Through hideous means over many years, I maintained the thick shell of the Gallwomb to inhibit the demon-litter from escaping. Likewise, I organized a host of guardians. Armored vagrants, once lost souls turned stout believers in Augury, now stalked the perimeter of the Fountain prepared to attack any creature that may hatch. All had been artisans. I recognized some as descendants of the mystery Picti cult.

Sudden pain jolted me. My hands contracted over my heart.

Dey! Cypria's icy voice rushed throughout my form, the reverberating echoes chilling my veins in pulses, the earth she shared life with synchronizing with the vibrations of her hurried tone. *It… it hurts. Something inside the Land. It's tearing!*

"Yes," I agonized. "I feel it…" I reflected on the enormous throbbing pain, our shared souls and network of ichor. Was her litter hatching? Finally, the moment had come. I was stricken with fear, but being empowered by her blood, I felt compelled to act. The prophesized evil godlings were ready to hatch from Cypria's stone womb.

"Your Gallwomb! It fails! I will ready the Augurs!"

No!

"What then?"

It's not the Gallwomb.

"What else could it be?"

Quickly. To the Mosaic. Go and read what the flocks spy. I fear the entire Land is injured!

The Mosaic was a beautiful living earthwork, but it was adjacent to a haunted Picti temple—a place exhibiting ethereal traces of the Deceiver. Robed in thick cloaks and bearing my avian mask, I made my way to the Iron Forest wherein lay the Mosaic. I created it originally to mirror the image of her, Cypria, Goddess of the Sky, yet her flock continuously adapted the masterwork. It now served as the primary communication device amongst the birds, Cypria, and the Augurs. The birds would spy the Land and report their findings on the sprawling canvas. Through this, all the Augurs would have access to the birds' and Cypria's thoughts.

I went with an aching heart, reluctant to approach the same ground that was home to my death and to my greatest work of art. I paid little attention to the hundreds of impaled fathers in the colossal Fountain, their bodies decaying, their flesh blackening into scabs, their vaporous souls burning bright and loud. Their blood fueled Cypria's flocks of carrion birds and allowed her to control them and to see through their eyes. The Fountain sustained her vitality. Once tempered, the ichor embodied her soul. It was the same ichor that raced through my veins

Transient image of the oracular Mosaic;
an aerial view of the Gallwomb geoglyph, bleeding pitch

and allowed me to walk on the Land as one dead. Although her ichor existed in discrete locations separated within the physical world, in the astral realm they were tethered together with thin veins of blue ether.

The Augur Aerie had grown considerably from its conception. All the humans worshipped Cypria and learned to read the Mosaic and the messages traced by her blackbirds. Yet, the artists maintained their skills to the benefit of all. Most notably, Grovel Tonn and his metalsmiths established a source of weaponry for the Augurs. Their stone-sculpting relatives comprised the Carver Guild and thus became heavily armored. The Carvers became the largest guild and comprised the majority of the guards; their protracted instruments could engrave mortal wounds into any spawn from Cypria's womb. They donned elaborate tunics sewn by the hands of Lord Qualenson, Clanlord of Clan Qual. The tunics bore the heraldic insignia of Cypria's Augurs, a wingspread crow with its talons clenched about a cobalt heart. The society of Augurs had become so complex that I failed to maintain comprehensive knowledge of each guild. All had heraldic signatures bearing similar helms with feathered mantles and shaman masks. I kept at a distance, shielding myself as much as possible from the personal needs of mortals. Still they saluted me, regarding me as their spiritual leader. None of them had ever peered beneath the grossly beaked death mask that hid my own skull, and thus were ignorant of my condition. I was no holier than these Augurs. We were all pawns.

Faster, Dey!

Her words were direct as usual, but now her voice trembled. The pains were alarming. I could feel her urgency inside me since her heart inside me palpated. I scurried now, too scared and hurt to run.

I made my way to the grand Mosaic, a carpet of shell and stone that began as an effigy of Cypria. Its purpose now was to reduce the dynamic, telegraphic script wove by the flying blackbirds into static images that the Augurs could interpret. Her flock was constantly mixing the icons and portents of their visions with miniature representations of landmarks and people.

Given this connection between Cypria and her living followers, my role of seer was diminished. Cypria became adept at using the Mosaic to communicate directly with the Augurs. She depended on my mobility, my ability to leave the Aerie to fulfill vital errands, and read and communicate with spirits remotely. This was fitting, since I had played a key role in disabling her. Now, my primary function was as a recruiter. One who could identify and mesmerize potential Augurs by reading their auras and enlist them. One who could locate victims to fill the Fountain with paternal blood.

At last, the Mosaic.

And at its center the ruined Picti temple, burning ethereally dark red and brilliant crimson. These were traces of the Deceiver and of an executioner whose visage bore a veil of flesh. He was Doctor Grave, a mysterious figure who once had served as my mentor. I have since learned that the Doctor was a compatriot of Haemarr, having established the Iron Forest to ensnare Cypria. It could not be coincidental that I eventually died in that temple.

The astral flames burned bright. I looked away to shield my eyes. The phantoms of the Doctor and the Deceiver called for me... recalled my death... laughed at me...

Dey! Focus. Read the birds' warning!

The birds spelled out a cryptic message. It featured one key player...

The Deceiver! Cypria identified the demon, communicating through her ichor within me, pumping from the crow that was my heart. She spoke slowly. Tentative. Nauseous. Scared.

She whispered, *He returns!*

I put a decaying hand over my chest. "Are you certain?"

Something is cutting away the Land's interior. It must be him. She gathered her strength to explain. *We once considered him to be a disposable puppet of Haemarr. Nevertheless, I had commanded the blackbirds to track him since the day of my turning. The crows have determined the Deceiver is part of the Lysis clan of Gravenstyne. Haemarr had cast him into the abyss weeks after my turning, an unusual banishment for a mere pawn.*

"He deserved as much."

Yes, indeed. If it were truly a punishment. Understand, he may not have been just another animated corpse. She paused as if to gather a breath. To absorb some sort of pain emanating through the Land. Then I felt the tremor echo through my heart.

He may be an avatar of Haemarr, as you are to me. He may have been on a mission.

"What am I to do?"

Cypria returned abruptly. *You are to investigate. My flocks have identified several locations about the Land that maintain traces of the Deceiver's soul. Doing so should reveal his weakness. Find his bane.*

The birds used the Mosaic to detail a series of simple pictures, a map of sorts—places I must visit: a grassy knoll; the empty wing of Asthete SanGules's manor house; the putrescent mangroves of the Gorgepath; a Picti ceremonial ground; and lastly, the ruined Gravenstyne Fortress.

Strangely, the birds had chosen to use shades of red for each image. Red like the astral flames of the Picti Temple.

The final image chilled me. "Why not command your flock to search these places? They can see as I and can move with greater speed."

There are places the birds cannot freely enter, and this investigation may require more than surveying alone. Understand, you are my hands. I am immobile, and the birds cannot interact with these places as you can. I need you to look at these places the birds have identified, including the caverns beneath Gravenstyne where the birds cannot access. The hundreds of Augurs are prepared to combat the litter if they hatch. But the humans cannot defend me—or themselves—from Haemarr's warrior.

You must find his weaknesses. Prepare us. Now.

"You want me to crawl beneath Gravenstyne? The fortress of the very demon that killed me?"

You must. She paused. *He is returning from the Underworld. He is cutting… cutting his way through the ichor-stone of the Land's core. We haven't much time.*

The carrion crows descended upon me and carried me away.

RELEASED FROM THE grip of countless talons, I was deposited before a remote cabin.

Dilapidated. Rotten. Overgrown. An unkempt beard of straggly vines was interwoven through windowsills and atop door frames. Wood posts dried gray by the sun, fractured as baked cadaver's skin, grappling toward the sky like skeletal arms from a cairn. Crisp leaves and drifts of cracked soil buttressed the porous walls.

An abandoned cabin.

My birthplace.

I saw ghostly images of myself here. Imprints of my soul left behind to stay with my original home.

Other memories were less coherent, lapping as amorphous waves against the hearth of the kiln my father used to temper stone vessels. Where my father fashioned pots to boil honey and ginger as a base for mead. Where he beat my mother as he drank from a ceramic tankard. I could make out remnants of her shattered soul cowering in the obscured corner of the cabin. Guilt overwhelmed me.

Dey, what do you see?

I saw effigies of my father, suffused in red shades of hellfire, hovering over the bent form of my mother. Red plumes engulfed her, wrapped her like barbed wire, tearing her soul into shreds.

"This is a mistake. This is *my* home. The blackbirds must be misinterpreting the astral traces." Did the birds confuse me for a threat? In truth, the Deceiver and I each played a role in Cypria's turning. He had cut my heart out and let his patron Haemarr possess my body to get to hers.

I stared despondently at the memories of my parents as their spirits replayed history.

"Father..." A version of me ran toward a pottery-filled wagon, vellum scrolls in hand. I had been training with Aesthete SanGules, who had a passion for collecting and teaching art.

My father had turned to acknowledge my noise. Then he, who had eyes colder in hue than extinguished ash, retracted awkwardly into his seat cradling his protruding belly. A dissipating breath of liquor hovered in the wake of his glare. Then his cart wobbled, rocking as the aging horse navigated the route toward the Gorgepath. My father shaped clay to hold liquor instead of beauty. Only fellow drunkards purchased his wares, and such clients did not shop for fine crafts, preferring instead to reserve their money to purchase alcoholic spirits.

Then I watched my frail mother approach from the cabin, the moonlight penetrating her translucent, glassy skin and revealing her indigo veins. So like porcelain veneer was her skin that I was convinced father, a potter, had crafted her. She often appeared sick, with her transparent pall, but I adored her. My father's alcoholic stench still clung to the air, quenching mother's smile.

She laid her bruised, mud-encrusted hand upon my back. She sighed as we watched the wagon roll away.

The birds conveyed my memories to Cypria, and she responded, *Your mother was very young. She must have been a mere decade old when she gave birth to you. Very beautiful. Vulnerable.*

I failed her as I failed you, I thought.

You must go, Cypria commanded, as if she had at that very instant ascertained a threat.

"What is it? Do you understand why the birds brought me here? Where is the link to the Deceiver?"

Cypria did not answer. She must have gathered what she required, even if I had yet to make sense of it. The crows embraced me again in preparation for hauling me away.

Ghostly renditions of my mother ran from the house, searching for something that had left. Searching for me? Although I had abandoned her, she still loved me.

Then the birds lifted me away...

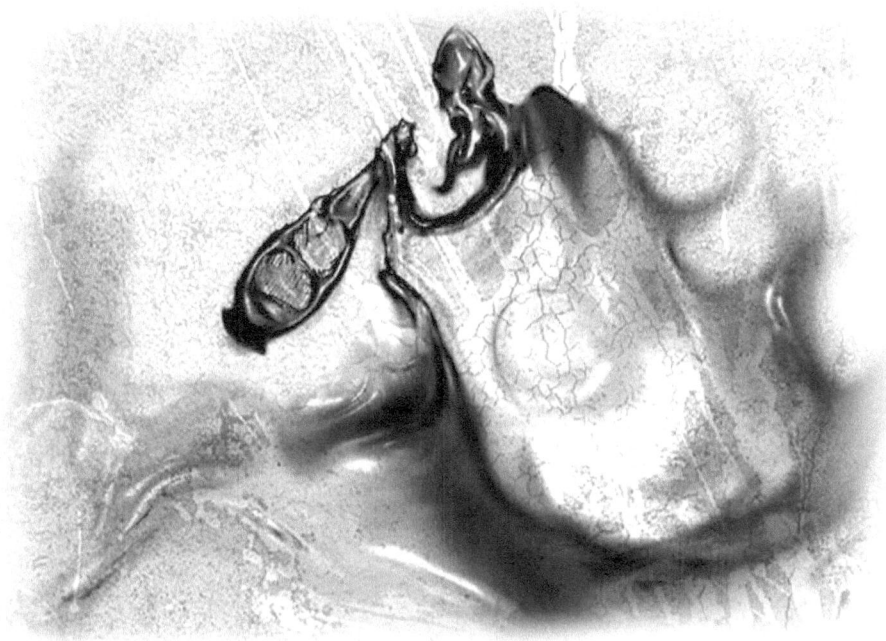

The Red Drunk haunts Dey

I PEERED THROUGH THE open doors on the balcony into the sealed, abandoned bedchamber of Asthete SanGules's manor house. As a young student, I had been introduced to the illumination of manuscripts on the lower level.

"Dey..."

It was not Cypria that whispered. Instead, it sounded like my mother. Mother?

I peered between the doors. The threshold was like that of an empty picture frame, and I was the lone audience, gazing into the nightmare within its borders.

The gray, physical realm revealed an expansive bedchamber. Furniture blanketed in thick webs and muslin dust cloths stood as still, primitive ghosts forever guarding an empty tomb. It would have been a peaceful scene if not for the restless memories that haunted it. Weaving among the shrouded, white statues was an iridescent rainbow of female spirits. Beside every statue, a red phantom of SanGules stood presiding and controlling his women's spirits. A pitched cacophony spat from these banshees, a regurgitation of the verbal abuse and torment that had entailed SanGules's oppression of them. I dared not enter this tumultuous current of astral fire. The knotted memories of countless victims could sunder my soul. Instead, I peered as a voyeur seeking to capture a scene of passion. What I saw was nearly indescribable. SanGules had been an oppressor whose sword was smelt of words and manipulation. My mother's form raced about with the others of the Lord's harem. What had he done to her?

"Dey..." my mother's ghost uttered as she raced by, her voice trickling down my spine like cold water.

She had been looking for me, after I ran away from home. SanGules had seized her and kept her from searching for several years. Her anguish melded with that of many other kidnapped women, held captive for perhaps as long as seven years in this manor house. She called for me, continuously, the entire stay. Preserving hope in the midst of ultimate depression.

SanGules had taught me to be an artisan. He was more of a mentor than my own father when I had lived in the cabin. But then I ran away. Searching for me, she came here, and was imprisoned.

"Dey..."

Day after day of servitude, restrained from searching for her only child.

"Dey..."

I could not bear to continue looking. I recalled the imprisoned corpses within the Iron Forest calling for me, evoking hidden memories, haunting me with her voice. All those spirits pressuring me, summoning me...

"Cypria!" I called for guidance. "Cypria?"

The ichor within me simply shuddered. Only one link was clear. My mother. Did she represent something greater? All motherhood? Or was it more simple than that? Did the Deceiver continue to toy with us? I did not understand the connection of this mansion to the Deceiver's astral traces. Again, the black-birds had placed me near my mother's ethereal impression. Was I the real threat?

From this vantage, I could discern the spires of Gravenstyne Fortress and an abandoned trade route that pierced the landscape between–the Gorgepath, our next destination!

THE BIRDS DEPOSITED me beside a swamp of twisted people and muck: tangled masses of roots and limbs; a wet cake of gnarled joints and infested pulp, pustules, and eggs.

As a child I recalled the Path as a blossoming avenue of trade, lined with fruit trees and plush groves of white-leafed ferns. I had walked this road often to attend artisan classes with SanGules. Now it was hardly a road, the mire encroaching, erasing its boundaries. Vagrants populated the dark crevices within the briars, rotting with the wet putrescence of nature. Travelers were scarce. The place collected all that was abject, from bodily excretions, to material refuse, to societal rejects.

Necrophiliacs sought prey here; cannibals and ghouls fed on flesh; men of wealth, like SanGules, collected women here. Some were less culpable, like myself, coming here as either slave collector or liberator, recruiting those lost and providing them with some sort of a future. Other visitors were immeasurably kind. My mother had come here searching for me. She arrived vulnerable, pursuing a good cause, subjecting herself to the very demons she meant to protect me from.

Orphans ran about holding limbless rag dolls, oblivious to the despair they lived in. They passed a madman who chewed on a pox-riddled limb; his soul identified him as a scrivener who had been poisoned by the metallic inks he once used to gild manuscripts. They passed a dejected warrior abandoned by the people he had loyally protected. They passed a man and his dog, both nearing death, neither able to aid the other as they lay depressed in a cast of mud. Children ran about pools of brown water whose depths could not be penetrated by sunlight.

"So what am I looking for?"

Something that ties with the other places. Something red in the astral plane. The Deceiver's presence is strong but dispersed here. Be persistent. Walk and observe. I was relieved to hear, to feel, her commanding tone again.

Scanning the Gorgepath for traces of the Deceiver, I saw mostly a thick fog of emotion colored ochre-yellow, like phlegm. Wailing souls floated amongst themselves, knotted together in a complex weave, each soul moving like a serpent in a frustrated morass.

Then I saw one with faint red flames flaring from his soul.

I approached this alchemist who watched the children play.

"Go away, shaman. This is no place for men of faith. This land is godless and this road is the hell born from their absence."

His aura belied his atheistic tone. He secretly held fast to a hope that a creative god existed, but he was unwilling to reveal his true Pictish nature. Dynamic images of hybrid elder-humans formed themselves about him, translucent ghosts of mythical children, with bulbous eyes and unfurled wings. They were all fantastical embodiments of things that fed on his Red Muse—did these children represent dyscrasia? In truth, his cult was dying; it had lost contact with its deity long ago. Dey watched these gray parasitic phantasms as they rose out of the ground like bugs, then scoured the man's body for lingering flames to douse. It was if the gray spirits were consuming the red ones. Kindling red flames darted away from them lest they lose their color, and they whispered to Dey, "The chromantis emerge from my ashes. They feed on my memories!"

Cypria had already warned him that her litter—if freed—was destined to turn the world to gray. Dey was not sure what to do with these prophecies. So he kept scanning the alchemist's soul for something more. Amidst all the chaos, the effigy of a woman persisted. She was more important to him than his dying faith.

I said to the man, "Your wife's soul is with you."

He stared into a sizeable blue vial cradled in his lap. He paused. Then he retorted suddenly, "Do not mock me! Souls have no physical properties. They cannot be measured or quantified! They cannot take shape or be seen!"

"She is not in the bottle."

"So you do mock me! Where else could she be? Her distilled brain and heart are therein. I collected them myself…"

"Nina's soul contorts with your every word. Even now her ghost attempts to waken you from your depression. Your wife's soul is intertwined with yours. After years of loving, an early death cannot unweave what had been sown in the realm of spirits. And you should be more proud of your Picti roots. You will leave these sunken grounds to serve your artistic nature."

The alchemist was sobered into submission. Tears welled in his swollen eyes as I confirmed his secret hopes. There was more to life than what alchemy could detect. The unknown life after death could be discerned. There was hope that Nina's soul waited for him.

He is not what you are looking for. But I want his skills in my ranks. Recruit him and move on.

Outstretching my arms, I called upon the birds to collect the alchemist. His knowledge would be a fine addition to the Augurs of the Aerie.

The flocks soon arrived. As the alchemist ascended, his precious vial fell toppling into the putrescent mire of the Gorgepath.

Others stared at me following the alchemist's departure. They did not understand I could not right physical deformities or heal them as would a surgeon. Although I could read their souls and memories, I could not alter them. I could not erase their guilt, remorse, or humility. I could not bring satisfaction to those who could not succeed, nor could I transmute loneliness into acceptance. I could only empathize and send them away to serve Cypria. The artists would become soldiers. The fathers I might slaughter in the Blood Fountains. All others I ignored. I was not there as a bringer of hope.

But the crazed and desperate are incapable of grasping the complexity of my role.

"Save me!" groveled an elderly man whose flesh was frost white, who hobbled aggressively toward me with toeless feet and outstretched arms.

"You can save us! You can!"

I turned to see another approach. Mechanically. In pain. Filled with hope.

"Dey!" I thought I heard them call out. Was my mother amongst them? And my father? And a hundred corpses swinging from iron gibbets...

"Dey!"

They swarmed. Countless bodies, tugging at my clothes, gnawing at my arms, like a colony of roaches descending upon a carcass...

"Save us!"

Enveloped, I collapsed.

"Dey!"

They tore away at my cloak and encased me within a mass of withered limbs. Hands about my face, tiny hands, scabbed, soft fingers groping for food, penetrated my grip, tore at my mask...

I fell into a fetal position, pressed into the mud.

Entwined, they became one entity, a wreath of putrescence...

So crazed the ghouls were, they fed upon one another's flesh...

...and mine...

"Cypria!" My calls were muffled, but the crows sensed my need telepathically.

They answered instantaneously.

Skin and attackers were plucked away. A hundred black starlings and crows peeled away the mass.

Although the wails subdued, I still heard my name, now pronounced more softly. Air caressed my back, signaling my freedom.

I rolled onto my side and peered through my mask.

"Mother!"

Her visage stood above me. Angelic. Divine. Ivory white, tainted with streaks of red. Did my father's essence stain her ghost?

"...Dey..."

"Mother!" I attempted to stand, but fell on weak limbs.

Her phantom could not embrace me anyhow.

She appeared older than she did at my birthplace, but still young and beautiful. At this period in my mother's life, she had escaped my father's hold as well as the Aesthete SanGules's manor. The scene replayed itself. In plush, high-pitched calls she pleaded, searching the parade of urchins for one she would recognize.

Her memory did not recognize me. It was only an imprint burned into the Land, soulless and unaware of the present.

I looked upon the scene until Cypria commanded me to move.

Follow her trail, she ordered. *She is the focus of the birds' visions.*

My mother? But how could she be related to the Deceiver?

As she overturned the corpses of dead children along the Gorgepath, she had been attacked. An arrow pierced her leg, and she fell. The assailant then fed upon her flesh, removing the sinew from her left leg.

She had struggled to regain her freedom. She failed as the archer ghoul clasped his mighty maw upon her limb. My mother wailed in agony.

Cypria forced me to watch this memory. She forced me to witness my mother's torture. Minutes passed, and I cannot bear to relay the horrors that replayed before me.

Suddenly my mother managed to distract the ghoul by locating a dispossessed limb and lodging it within its maw.

She escaped disoriented while the ghoul choked. Following a band of orphans, she left Gorgepath's trails. They were the children of a mercenary's onslaught, and the bastard warrior led the pack. His symbiotic demon, the ghoul, followed. Eating those the mercenary had killed and practicing archery on the weaker boys of the pack.

I knew from this evidence that the mercenary would eventually harm my mother. He had a common, astral signature to that of my own father, Sangules, and the ghoul. Red.

And so it came to pass. My mother screened the camp of lost boys that trailed the mercenary. She had not eaten in days. She was weak from loss of blood. Yet she was driven. She had only a cause and the will to carry it out.

"Dey?" her memory called out, stumbling through the pack of boys.

The mercenary had been quick in his treachery, climbing atop her, penetrating her broken form...

"Cypria! I cannot bear witness to this rape."

I swayed in anguish, standing beside a dozen adolescent male ghosts. Gazing at the exposed form of my innocent mother. Had she not suffered enough?

"Why does she look for me? Why must I watch her death unfold?"

She did not die here, Dey. You must watch and follow her. These memories reveal the weakness of our enemy!

I whispered, "It is revealing only my weakness–my guilt for having left her..."

The boys then assailed the warrior. Perhaps they defended their dying memories of their own mothers. Nevertheless, they attacked the bastard warrior. Astral images of the mercenary and his ax burned bright here, his rage and blade felling many of the youths that dared interrupt him.

My mother had limped from this scene with haste, though so frail and shattered she could not have been cognizant of her actions. The archer ghoul trailed after her first. The mercenary would follow.

I ran behind her fading apparition...

... and the ground beneath my feet trembled, sending me sprawling. I hugged the grass, my heart seeping ichor as the earth quaked.

Dey! You... must... go on...

The Land became suddenly still.

I regained my footing slowly, my hand catching Cypria's luminescent ichor spilling from my chest.

"Cypria. I bleed."

As do I and the Land. You must go. The Deceiver comes!

I ran toward where my mother's ghost had dissipated during the tremor, and soon I waded in a fog that suffused a ceremonial landscape. I stood atop a mound overlooking an intricate cromlech. I recognized this place.

Indeed I had sat here before, secretly witnessing the mysterious Picti

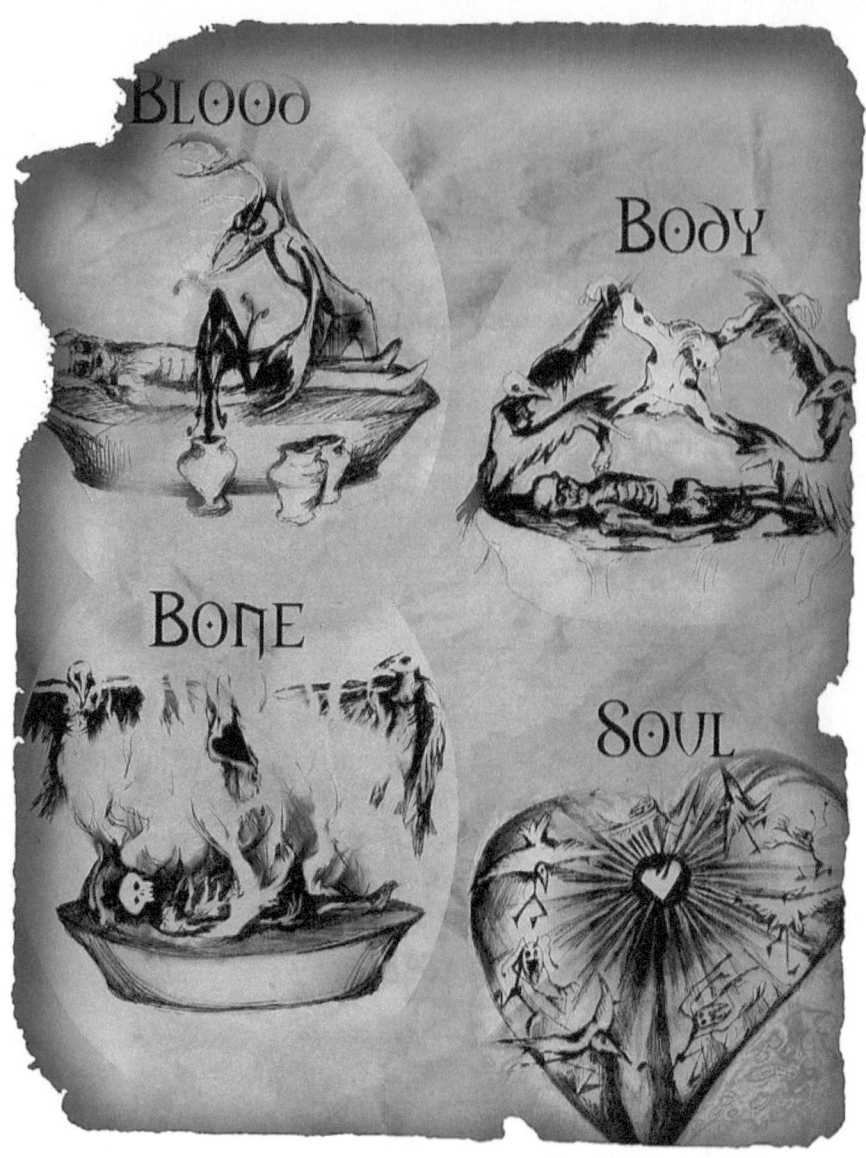

BLOOD

BODY

BONE

SOUL

Dey's sketch of the Picti Inheritance Rite

execute their rites atop the center dolmen. Doctor Grave had brought me here at the age of fifteen to expose me to the Pictish methods, even though they were not intended to be witnessed by outsiders. The members were never identified to me. Doctor Grave had never disclosed how he discovered them. The Doctor was correct in that many aspects of my training would be improved by the techniques I observed there: preparing parchments from hide; manufacturing size from boiled skeletal remains; and preparing inks from soot or sintered bone.

I had once characterized Doctor Grave as a dedicated barber—one who wore an apron of flayed faces and wielded a scalpel as large as a sword. He claimed the faces were those of victims without families, that common citizens of the Cromlechon would have burned their remains without pause or reflection. The Doctor claimed to honor their forgotten lives by wearing their flesh. I had witnessed stranger behaviors by then, so I accepted this probable untruth. In fact, as a naive orphan myself, I had asked the Doctor to wear my face in the event I died.

The cult prayed to this faceless Muse—their source of creativity. They danced. They prepared materials and produced magnificent works.

I recalled their massacre. It began with the Picti members crawling forth like glistening, sapphire beetles from beneath the central stone, emerging from some network of subterranean catacombs. Nearly four dozen of them came, all masked with skulls and decorated with tattoos—glyphs of an ink so deeply blue as to appear black. Some carried small cauldrons. Others carried skeins of wire, utensils, or barrels of mulled cider. Four carried a dead man.

I recognized the corpse as one of the elderly cult leaders.

He was laid upon the center dolmen.

The ceremony began, led by a central figure. A mane of hair crowned his balding forehead. Though thin, he was of robust musculature. He was Endenken Lysis, soon to be Lord over Gravenstyne. And eventually, my killer, the Deceiver. But at that time I did not know him as an enemy. Neither did I know Haemarr was an eldritch god and that Doctor Grave partnered with him.

Aided by the members of the cult, the corpse was systematically reduced to its raw materials. His skin was removed as a unit and tanned before a fire. The blood was mostly preserved in urns, which were sealed with molten wax. His leg bones were sintered in fire until they were pure white; then they were ground into fine powder with mortar and pestle. His organs were smoldered in cauldrons, the soot collected and manufactured into black ink. Eventually, only the skull remained and in it his heart rested.

Three days of rituals passed, coming to an end the night of a brilliant red-tinted moon. Endenken remained the feature figure. It was his duty to honor the dead man, his father, by intimately working with the corporal remains. He was expected to create a genuine self-portrait, an image molded from its ancestor's cast. I learned then that we were intimately tied to–anchored to–the subjects of our art and motivation. Artists, the subjects they portray, and the artwork itself are three separate, but linked, entities.

The tattooed Picti performed a tribute dance chronicling the cult's history. From this I ascertained the morbid ceremony about to transpire had evolved from honoring the originator of their secret society. One who detailed his life's work, the mapping of Land, onto his own skin.

After the performance, many tethered themselves from the vertical stones with skewers hooked into their nipples and skin. Those remaining beat upon drums. It was then I noticed the placement of each of the hanging members was intentional, as were the lengths of cord between them that shook and harmonized with the low frequency of the drumbeats.

A mysterious wind gusted, clanging the chimes dangling between the suspended cultists, blood dripping from their wounds.

The kettles and cauldrons were drummed upon.

As a cohesive fluid mesh, the Lysis clan formed a living glyph. Now they keened and wailed in long, monotonous tones, as the wires they hung upon vibrated synchronously.

Being the climax of the ceremony, it was time for Endenken to assemble his portrait. An audience of over forty cult members was suspended around him.

But before he could begin his art...

... a bloody, deranged woman stumbled into the bounds of the cromlech! I did not know the identity of the woman then. I had not seen my mother for some eight years! To think I had witnessed my own mother, seen her again, but was unaware! She was so close! Searching for me!

I observe now that she had been calling my name! But so remote was I, I did not hear.

Her head was sodden, covered in blood. Her cheeks caked in gray scabs. A single curly, black lock wisped in the wind. Too, beneath the swollen purple sills of her eyes, scabs encroached upon small regions of innocent, youthful skin that remained as pale, pure, and fragile as fired ceramic. Her cracked lips were moistened by fresh blood that reflected the moon's glare.

"Mother!" I called in vain to the inert past.

My young ghost sketched the scene unconcerned. Doctor Grave left its side. As my effigy turned to follow, he had said sharply, "No! Stay and witness the mysterious art rites of the Picti. Practice drawing the musculature of the wounded."

I had learned much from spying on this cult. But now I know Doctor Grave's motives had not been purely educational. The mighty scalpel he wielded would somehow find its way to the hands of Endenken Lysis. And a decade later,

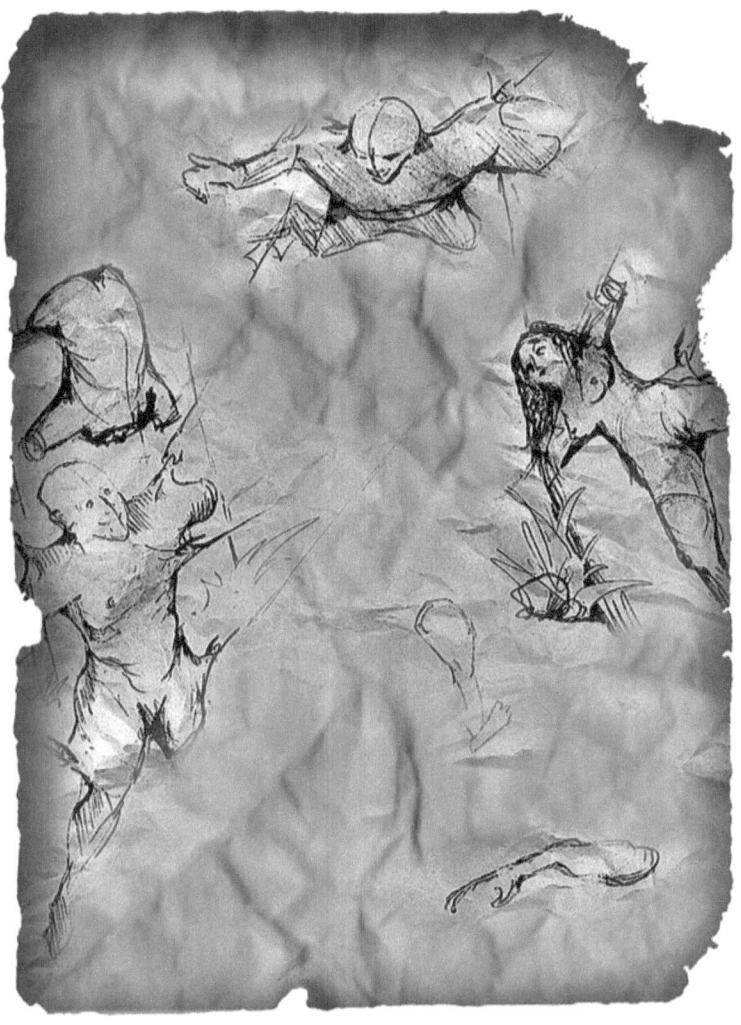

Dey's sketch of the massacre

his flesh-veiled mask would haunt me from the astral flames of a ruined Picti temple.

The past repeated itself at the dolmen. Endenken's ghost staring at my approaching mother, torn between his duty to complete the Rite and the urge to save her.

Within moments, the Muse found it had no host to enter. The ritual was left incomplete. The circle of tattooed cultists hung vulnerable. At their center burned the astral force of their worship. Their god had been abandoned.

E NDENKEN HAD CARRIED my mother away over his shoulder. That day, I un-knowingly failed my mother a second time. I had also witnessed the first man to respect her, to abandon his own people to save her. My murderer, the Deceiver, appeared more honorable than I.

I know now, with my sight of the dead, that the Lysis clan worshipped a real entity, the forces of creation burning stark red. A bold musing power, a manifestation of the artistic skills and prayers of countless years, waiting to be transferred from the sanctified, corporeal materials into a living vessel, into Endenken, but...

He had left. And in his absence, two horrid things entered the sanctuary: an ax-wielding mercenary and an archer attacked the Picti cult. No Pict would survive their brutality.

A Picti woman dressed as a bird gathered the blood-filled skull of the ceremony's focus and retreated into the catacombs. The Red Muse was carried away.

That Muse is the Deceiver's bane! The oracle of the mosaic and birds has led you

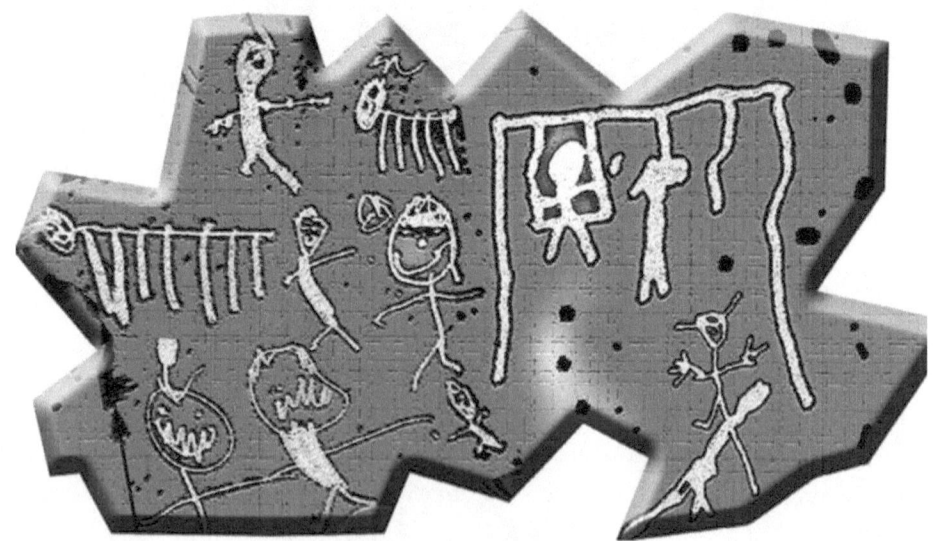

Primitive cave mural

toward this. You must retrieve it!

The vision of the birds, this puzzle and my mission, became coherent. We were never misdirected by the spellcasting of the Deceiver. No, the birds saw true. They were not showing me parts of my past, but instead they were picking up traces of Endenken. Not bits of his actual soul. Not traces of his ethereal memories produced as he practiced his craft. No. They saw the Red Muse he was supposed to accept, and they saw traces of his future wife. My mother.

Suddenly, the ground shook again…

A burst of pain launched from my chest into my limbs. Whatever cut away at the center of the earth, lacerating the elemental roots sprouting from Cypria, continued to deliver pain. It felt as though my heart was a pressurized cist ready to burst!

I grew nauseous.

Follow the red trail, Dey! Enter the catacombs, where my birds cannot fly. Retrieve the Muse!

L IGHT FILTERED INTO the entrance to the dolmen as I entered the cavernous labyrinth. Darkness enveloped me, sucking me into the cold comfort of the subterranean world. I followed the trail of red astral fumes.

For several hours I plodded beneath the surface of the earth, the underbellies of trees and hanging roots grabbing at my undead form. Shafts of moonlight pierced the darkness from small holes above me. I trekked within the very armpit of nature toward the grand arteries within the Land.

Primitive murals splayed across twisted stone walls, many covered with fuzzy growths and gnarled roots. These pictorials glowed a soft red, as if scrawled in the sacred blood of the Picti. I had not the time to analyze these beautiful creations drawn by the hands of primitive men.

Wind gusts pulled me into the blackness ahead. These currents swirled the effigies and ghosts of the astral realm, including the vaporous droplets of the Red Muse. Although I did not breathe by proper standards, I felt as if my breath was swept away as I saw my own aura wisp chaotically. I felt dizzy. Luminous blue ichor dripped from my chest onto the ground.

I HAD DESCENDED, SLOWLY and circuitously, so that I could no longer see the roots or soil marking the upper levels of this labyrinth.

The Land continued to shake.

The thunderous rumbling of earth threw me about. My heart throbbed, and too weak to walk, I crawled.

"Cypria," I whispered.

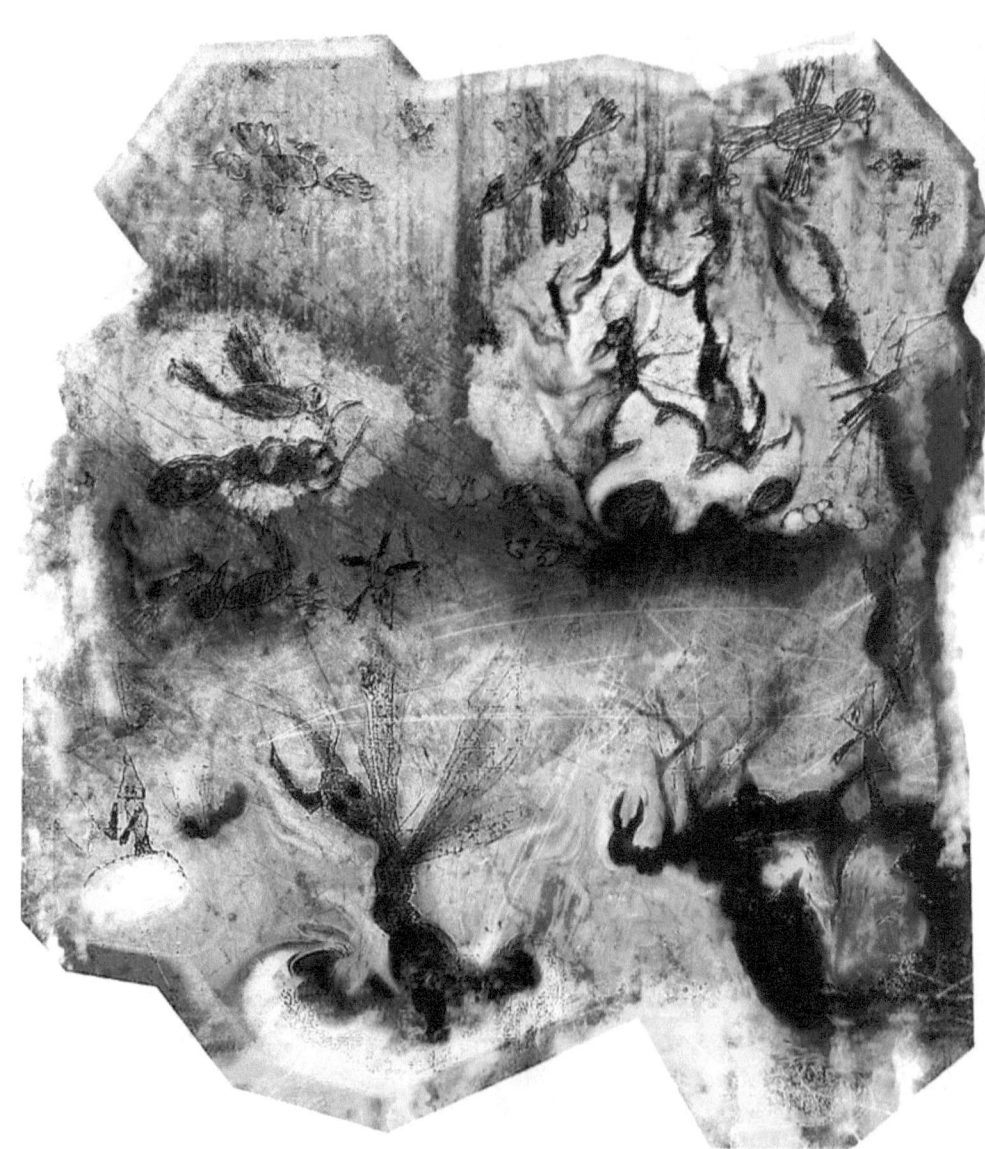

Picti cave painting

Her words came in fragments... *Trust... return...*

We could no longer communicate effectively; the astral tendrils connecting us were too thin now. I knew my mission, but I was alone. If I could not communicate to her, then she could not renew my strength.

Presently, the ground began to yield as if I crawled into a swamp. Black, reflective oil seeped through my fingers. The ground bled. The wounded Land suffered terribly.

I surmised that this black ichor seeped through the many fissures and veins running throughout the Land's quick. The longer it contacted me, the more it stung. It was as if countless stinging insects swam inside the earthly liquor, attacking me. Yet, this sensation did not compare to my congested heart as it transmitted the Land's pain.

The faster I moved in the mire, the more the mud thickened. Bloody soil crept into my ankles, thighs, and arms to weigh me down. To resist sinking, I grabbed hold of the dark walls that shimmered red. Soon the etchings of skeletons appeared more real, as if they were fossils and bone! Then I felt the contours of skulls beneath my feet as I waded in the gritty earthy soup. I skulked within a tomb!

Within the boundaries of this bloody earth, I swore I could discern the outlines of creatures–miniature, boneless golems–flayed jelly things circulating within it.

"Cypria!" I yelled in vain.

I read the walls as I attempted to regain my strength.

The images and murals had evolved from primitive, child-like renditions into grand landscapes of embedded bodies, posed into runic letters and glyphs, explicitly patterned. This cavern was a grand grimoire, a diary of sorts. The style reminded me of the artwork by the Red Cap orphans—the children who flocked to Doctor Grave's side in his Theater. The murals and fossils told the tale of a war: a grand upheaval of land, a battle in which children mounted bestial insects with antlered skulls to fight giant birds, of dead rampaged colonies, of plagued infants consuming their parents, of souls being reaped as if they were apples to be plucked from an orchard.

I sank deeper into the mud, forced to grab hold of the trellis of embedded bones to avoid immersing my head in the oily muck.

I inched forward. Slowly. Light headed. Tired.

I neared a hard surface. Pulled myself onto the flat rock. Collapsed.

Suddenly, all turned gray.

" A WAKEN." THE VOICE snaked into my soul and shocked me.

I stared upward at a skull and heap of bones. I knew only the soul of a man spoke to me, and that astral, red warmth emanated from the charnel pile. A woman's skeleton lay near—her hands gauntleted with insectan claws belonging to some eldritch creature and her head helmeted with a gargantuan bird skull, much like my own. Picts.

The core of the Red Muse pulsated like a heart within Lord Issynmerz Lysis's skull. It could not be perceived directly, for it was too bright.

Beautiful. Chaotic. Unbounded. It was a concentrated, ethereal flame as unique as the sun. This force was also sentient! It licked my form as it studied me, threatening to sacrifice some small part of itself to mix with the remaining blue ichor of Cypria and end me.

The spirit within the skull read my soul. It knew my destiny better than I.

I waited, glancing about the room. Puddles of oil flooded the ancient corridor. The walls were semi-transparent, having absorbed some of the Muse, and appeared molten to my dead eyes. I felt trapped within a divine candle, encaged by thick walls of glowing wax. Even the earth beneath me, although solid to my feet, looked as if it were some frozen, translucent fluid.

Finally the fiery skull said, "I am Lord Issynmerz Lysis, and my heart contains the discarded Muse. I am the heart of the Picti!"

I kneeled now before the bones of Endenken's father. I read the tortured soul before me and asked, "What would it take to heal you? To put you to rest? To pacify you?"

"Endenken must finish his Inheritance Rite. He must create his portrait with my remains and merge with the Muse."

"But I am an artist. Can I not portray you?"

"The Rite is for Endenken alone! To understand his role you must learn the chronicle of the Muse!"

So Lord Issynmerz began: "Long ago, my grandfather, Clanlord Ante Lysis, sealed a pact with elder agents of the diseased Land, promising that his three sons would heal the dyscrasia if he was allowed to map its fantastical parts. So Ante's three sons awoke one morning to find their father missing and a puddle of blood in his bedchamber. It is said the puddle took the form of a liquid, invertebrate golem that demanded their servitude. Derryk, Kupryk, and Feryk thus battled the puddle, interpreting it as a demon that had consumed their father. For hours they fought, and blood was spewed across the bedchamber, staining wall

Sketch of Lord Issynmerz banishing his first four sons from Gravenstyne

and skin alike, and it was not until the three boys struck simultaneously that it lost its shape and burst as if a swollen pustule. It had been tradition to create an image of one's self for inclusion within Gravenstyne's Hall of Portraits when one's parent died, so the three sons portrayed themselves in a single, three-headed bust fashioned from the coagulated blood.

"Over time, the brothers grew old enough to take wives. The eldest, Osier

Derryk Lysis, took three wives from as many neighboring counties, but each wife died while pregnant, eaten internally by some infestation of necrophagous wasps. It became clear that his seed was tainted with dyscrasia. Nestled inside a grove of willows within the walls of Gravenstyne, wherein he harvested stems to weave his arts, he had built a sturdy swing set for his expected children. Yet the swings of willow branches were ever empty. With each passing wife, he extracted and hung the stillborn child on his weeping trees hoping the source of his art may also source life. But these efforts never bore fruit. Distraught, he grew mad, fashioned an osier rope, and hung himself from the main beam of the children's swing set.

"Lapidary Kupryk Lysis, the youngest of Ante Lysis's children, found love with Lady Karyn of the metal workers of Clan Tonn. Her blood was rich with that of the blacksmiths of her home region, and her womb managed to yield several daughters. But these were strange daughters, barely human, born with extra appendages and wings. Courters shied away, being so terrified of their insectan appearance. The daughters seemed to grow increasingly translucent as they matured, assuming ghostly forms upon reaching puberty. One became pregnant and gave birth to Lyhhana. Beyond that their fate is unknown, since the niches reserved for the daughters' bodies are still empty within the Gravenstyne catacombs. Their effigies within the Hall of Portraits are full-scale, crystalline statues, and it is yet unclear if they are actually the bodies of the daughters or representations crafted by Lord Kupryk, master of glass and stonework.

"The middle child, Lord Scrivener Feryk, took note of his brothers' reproductive illnesses. For many years he decided to avoid women altogether, but was eventually seduced by his father's sister, Lady Emyly. She was older, of course, but had also been afraid to love outside the family circle and was likewise secluded from the broader society. The illustrator and his wife gave birth to me and Iriana, who still stays by my side in death. Our parents had learned that incest was the only path to reproduction for our bloodline, so cursed it was by Lord Ante's actions. Our blood was to stay a pure vehicle for the Red Muse. Sharing it with others only poisons them.

"So, the blood of Ante's line transferred to myself and my sister. We gave birth to five sons, and unfortunately Lady Iriana could give no more. The first four were banished from Gravenstyne, as Doctor Grave, vizier to the family for many years, deemed that their dyscrasia may be responsible for Lady Iriana's womb becoming less fertile. They were removed as we had our last child. We had strived to keep our son Endenken from mating outside the family, and were successful until the Rite—which he never finished. So the Muse remains within my vessel, waiting for him, poisoning others."

"Then what can I do?"

The Red Issynmerz inspected me. "Endenken seeks to kill you. Why do you care for his Muse?"

"I do not desire to serve your Muse. I am loyal to Cypria now, and she seeks a means to pacify your warrior son, the Deceiver."

"We can work together then," he said. "Cypria sent you here to obtain your enemy's weakness. The Red Muse is that. You are now deep within the catacombs beneath Gravenstyne. Endenken's death studio lies near. Rise now and exit through his dungeon. Take my skull with you. Deliver the Muse to your Deceiver, and you will serve both Cypria and the Picti."

Trembling, I reached a hand toward the flaming skull.

"Wait! Don the crustaceous gauntlets that Lady Iriana's hands now bear. They will protect Cypria's ichor within you from reacting."

I wielded the awkward, empty claws and retrieved Lord Issynmerz's skull. The Muse did not pass through this cage of bone. It merely hovered in the cavity like a beating heart, wrapping tongues of flame about my wrist.

As instructed, I worked my way out of the chamber through a crack in the foundation.

BEFORE ME WAS Endenken's secret dungeon, a chamber connected to the labyrinthine catacombs. I read the history embedded in the walls. Blood. Anger. Creativity.

Four silent phantasms stood despondent beside the torture devices that had destroyed them. Their corpses were absent, having become possessed by the searching shades of the Red Muse.

I recognized the four. I had recently witnessed how each had abused my mother.

My recent mission led by the birds' vision was made clearer. My enemy's weakness had been scrawled throughout the Land and witnessed by the birds in shades of red. The bane of Lord Endenken and its origin had been spread before me like a diary. Dissecting my enemy's soul in the bowels of his abode was disconcerting, as if I stroked his very hair as he slept, running my hands through his hair without permission. I saw now his abandoned faith, his loyalty to my mother, and his capture and torture of those who had abused her.

As she lay unconscious in the safety of the Fortress, he hunted them down and incarcerated them. He exacted justice, carving them into pulpy works, employing the skills of a taxidermist and sculptor. Unknowingly, the Red Muse he had forsaken was mere yards away behind the walls of his dungeon. Sensing the nearness of the Lysis blood, strands of the Muse infiltrated the chamber and seized control over his imprisoned brothers. Slowly, it merged with the forces of sadism,

Endenken Lysis crashes into his death studio!

egotism, and necrophilia, and multiple horrors were birthed under Gravenstyne.

Hollow effigies of these four stood before me and revealed their deaths.

The mercenary Brood had been impaled by an iron shaft inserted in his rectum. His body was suspended from the ceiling; his head was yoked through a swing-set seat. The ethereal memories here spoke of horrendous acts of cruelty, including castration. His scalp was freed, gilded, and strung into Endenken's torque of accolades.

The cannibal Narl had his lower jaw split into two crescent mandibles and his body tethered by his own hamstrings to iron rings in the floor. To reach food, namely in the form of SanGules's dangling toes, Narl had to gnaw away at his own sinew. So he had. He sustained himself for several days, eventually acquiring and consuming portions of Brood, somehow fulfilling his dependency on the mercenary. Endenken returned after his slow death to collect the scalp for his necklace.

The removal of SanGules's tongue silenced him, but he still maintained the capacity to mumble. Lord Endenken then inserted an intricate, sectioned bulb into his mouth, securing it to his head with leather straps. The device was a pear-of-anguish, an executioner's inedible fruit. It was a muzzle that, upon installation, opened at the tips, the petals comprising the bulb spreading at their common base as a blossom blooms. This process shattered several teeth, but the device success-fully silenced Asthete SanGules completely. His arms were then tied about his own form and his body shackled to an upright iron grating. So positioned, he could not scream or react as the cannibalistic Narl ate the flesh from his feet and scavenged the bloody ground like a caged dog. Unable to eat or drink, SanGules eventually died of hunger, not blood loss. He was scalped, too.

Finally, I looked upon my father, the Drunk Potter. He had been stretched on a rack beneath the mercenary Brood, the blood from that evacuated crotch funneled into my father's mouth, bloating and swelling his belly into a pressur-ized globe. He had drank this blood with the eagerness he once imbibed alcohol. Ultimately, he drowned in it. His soul was so corrupted at this stage in his life that he bore no resemblance to the apathetic man I knew—distant, insecure, and self-centered.

It was then a relationship between Lord Issynmerz Lysis and these four became evident. Some astral signature was rooted across all their auras. And it was familiar. I had seen it before in the visage of the Deceiver–the four were indeed Endenken's brothers.

Lightning crackled from floor to ceiling!

The ground swelled and opened. A blade emerged, cutting through stone as if it were air. Wasps poured into the chamber. Tiny blue demons with hooked, spiked tails and buzzing wings. The Deceiver's vanguard!

As the soil parted, an antlered head emerged. Smoldering wisps of smoke sizzled from the incensed skeleton…

The Deceiver!

He arrived transformed from the Underworld. His hair was braided and warped as if blasted by a furnace; his bone and arms appeared as antlers, his head with twisted thorns, the chitin armor molded about his ribcage; the icy-blue sheen of his smoothed bones appeared as glimmering icicles.

His face had altered since I last saw it in the Picti Temple, but it held true enough to the haunting vision that never left my head.

Again, I felt the memories of shame and terror peel away from the inside of my skull…

The Lord of Gravenstyne entered swiftly, advancing in calculated, fluid movements designed to instill fear into his prey and secure a territory of protected space. A horde of iridescent blue wasps scurried in concert with his dramatic rite.

He addressed me with sheer authority.

"Trespasser!"

Hundreds of wasps filled the chamber, buzzing around to mix with mists of Red Muse, turning to stone and dying upon contact. His heart-hive appeared as an ethereal lantern as the luminescent minions moved about, emitting dynamic arrays of shadows.

I whispered in return dumbly, "I am a son of Maeve."

His hatred flared and sent blue tentacles of flame to lick my aura and erode my confidence. He burned violently. He said with reproach, "You are not my son."

I said to his blade, "We share Lysis blood. And we both regret our failure to save the same woman."

Black ichor still cascaded from his extended sword. This same weapon had carved out my heart—the blade *Ferrus Eviscamir* that my mentor Doctor Grave once held. It seemed enhanced now. I knew not how it came to Endenken's hand, but it was clear that he too was a pawn of the gods.

"You are the son of the Drunk Potter who abused Maeve, the vampire that drank the blood and souls of my children?"

Ferrus Eviscamir steadied before my face.

I glanced over to the rack where my father died, stretched out with a ballooned belly at the mercy of the Lord of Gravenstyne. "You gave your brother a fitting end. However, it appears that your treatment was not sufficient to sustain his fatal condition."

"Death does not preclude animation," Lysis spoke hoarsely. He disregarded my assertion that the Drunk was his brother. His emotions cooled as the red mist soaked into his aura. Wasps continued to slow down their movement, to fall and writhe on the dungeon cobblestone.

"But the mixing of ichor can," I said. "Yes, now I understand the nature of this Red Muse. It is your true blood, Lord Lysis. Your ancestor's faith. But you did not accept it during your Rite. The Muse was brought here by your parents and has been trapped since—ever seeking its rightful host from the confines of the catacombs. Instead, traces of it reached and embodied the corpses of your brothers, enabling them to leave the torture chamber. Now you return as one dead, your body inhabited by a different elder! You should dispel Haemarr and accept the Muse. Merge wholeheartedly with that you should serve."

"I serve no one!"

I spoke to Doctor Grave's blade wielded before me. "You serve the gods. You served them before you were even born."

Blue Lysis could not respond. The trace amounts of the Red Muse had inhibited him from continuing the debate. His grimace spoke for him. It read, *You will die, trespasser.*

For moments, I remained calm before his blade. Part of me wanted to die completely to avoid this confrontation, though I knew in my heart that death would not come today. I knew that he would not slay me despite his belligerence. For now the subduing powers of the Muse slowed him and protected me. The Red Muse still burned in the skull I held and would negate any attack. He kept his distance in the measure of feet. Even now I could see his movements dampen. His anger brought him to this dungeon, but had he been prudent, he would have waited for me outside the influence of the Red Muse.

But he was a more powerful necromancer than I. He worked my aura as if it were clay.

"You are a mere pawn of the gods, forced to obey them! Not I! I came to them. I am in control. You are weak!"

Then his tone changed, and I heard my father. "You failed your mother! You failed because you are weak! A passive, pitiful artist. Weak, stupid boy!"

And then a phantom hand grabbed my shoulder. I cocked my head to see my father groping me from across the chamber, his distended, alcohol-impregnated belly anchoring his elongated arm. And his cold, iron stare!

Deceiver. Drunk. Uncle-Father. Two haunting faces. Disturbingly similar... They were brothers...

My father was on the rack, one free arm extended impossibly across the dungeon, his cold fingers pressing into me. His phantasm had become tangible—alive!

The rack pulleys croaked as his arms loomed closer...

My father slurred his words as blood regurgitated in spoiled chunks. "Witless fool! I have been cursed with a dumb son! Again you forgot to cork the bottle, s'upid boy! You spoiled my cider!"

The mangled white hair. Bald pate. Condemning brow. He was back in true form, and I regressed into being a child.

"...probably left it too long in the kiln! I should be roasting your ass in the fire to burn sense into you... Come here!"

My memories took shape. My mother appeared instantly, cowering. And again I could hear her cries and futile attempts to control her enraged husband.

I stood there as I did as a boy, waiting for it to subside. Putting faith into time, hoping that some outside force somehow would intervene. But nothing came.

Hallucinating, I stepped backwards from the cabin I lived in as a boy.

My father was sprawled on a bed from within, a tankard of cider in his right hand. He belched.

I could smell his breath and the hot brick from his kiln. Long-stemmed grass lashed my waist as I peered into the cabin. The broken door leaned to one side.

My mother cried from within the porous shelter.

"Why? Why, you s'upid bitch?" A silhouette of a foot kicked her.

I covered my ears and ran away.

Instantly the sounds subsided.

But I could still see into the cottage imprisoning my mother...

The more I withdrew, the less I could hear.

I turned and ran trembling.

And I ran.

And ran.

I ran toward the Cromlechon as fast as my legs could propel me...

I FLED THE SUBTERRANEAN chambers of Gravenstyne, tripping over my own feet as I entered the courtyard.

Immediately, a flock of blackbirds blanketed me and bore me away.

Many other birds were engaged in battle with wasps, but I failed to dimension the magnitude of their combat. The fighting was bloody and vivid, but as I was lifted, my nightmares dissipated and I relished being apart from danger.

I focused on the retreating vision of the orchards about Gravenstyne, a grove of unkempt apple trees darkened by clouds of wasps. There a crystalline statue sat on the northernmost side of eleven tombstones. The sun glistened off the statue's flowing hair and laced gown, even transmitted through her translucent form. She had been cut by a master artisan's chisel. Or, as I registered the first horror of this mystery, she was a woman who had lost her soul.

"Mother?"

It was more than a statue of my mother that I viewed. It was in fact her soulless body. She had finally succumbed in whole to the evils that had chased her for her entire life.

The birds bore me into the air and away from her. Once again, in a bout of terror, I had left her side.

I could have ended him! I could have served Cypria and the Picti, forced the Red Muse onto him, and ended his threat by eliminating Endenken as Haemarr's avatar. Then, I could have exited his dungeon in peace and found my mother. But fear ruled me. After decades of dwelling on the Land, I was still too afraid of my father, too afraid of the memories the Deceiver plucked from my head. To overcome Lysis I would have to be brave enough to confront that which he evoked.

I was carted away to the Augur Aerie. I would be hailed for successfully retrieving the bane of the Deceiver. But we would have to wait for him to come to us. I was not strong enough to hunt him. I am not a hawk by nature.

Below me the destruction of the Deceiver's cutting was evident. The Land bled in many places as black oil rushed forth from incalculable depths, spouting into the air as gushing sprays of ebony ichor.

The Deceiver would follow.

VI: Taken From the Womb

Clan Qual ragdoll

VI: Taken From the Womb

Urlquason, son of Clanlord Qualenson, traced the three wasps mechanically gliding up his right arm, across the heraldic patch on his cloak. The autumn red moonlight did not penetrate the fog lapping against his torso, but the occasional tickle indicated more winged minions were penetrating his trousers.

"Url! What is it?" one of the trailing scouts whispered. He was only ten feet back, and others were ahead of him. Dark clusters of leaves enshrouded him. Their colors were turning with the cool weather, but their beauty remained concealed in the darkness.

"He's coming," Urlquason croaked. Beneath his cloak, his left arm steadied about his chest, protecting his crow. The bird nibbled at the compressed rag doll that snuggled his shoulder. All children of Qualenson's district were supplied such a doll. Url's was special, in that the cloth heart that the doll grasped was comprised of materials originating from his father's tapestries. Url's heart panged as the bird attempted to dethread the worn doll.

Elegantly—and inappropriately—dressed in garments wove by his father, he had tripped over ribbed leather boots and shattered his osier birdcage and the dowel from which it depended. For miles since he had transported his precious bird beneath his cloak.

Urlquason remained standing, torso exposed. Seven other scouting Augurs crouched lower in the mist, descending with their cages beneath the milky surface, sending ripples outward. Each crow closed its eyelids to hide its own luminescent ichor from signaling its presence.

Immediately, cobalt specks precipitated throughout the mist. The glow tinted the fog light blue. All eight scouts remained frozen, each laden with countless wasps. Moving invited their doom.

Then more wasps came from the west, some illuminated from within like miniature, numinous lanterns. They arrived in thick droves. The fluffy white clouds swayed silently as they concealed the underbrush of the ancient forest.

The looming woods hushed, as if preparing to witness an execution.

All knew Seer Dey's warnings about the Deceiver's second coming. None were truly prepared to confirm them. Their mission was only to search for evidence of his arrival and signal alarm to the Aerie. All they had to do now was send a warning. Release the birds. One bird would suffice. But no Augur could move.

Urlquason heard only the angry keening of wasps' wings above his own heartbeat.

The scouts' strategy was clear. Be still. Wait for the wasps to leave.

But doom hovered closer, and their hope suffocated as the mists took on the ghostly shapes of their wildest nightmares...

Things nestled into his hair. Took root in his scalp.

Urlquason stared paralyzed as the amorphous vapors took the forms of humans and wrapped themselves like dancers around those in front of him. He had never seen another person's dreams before, but now he witnessed phantasms snake their way out of the mist like worms reaching for the sky, curling white tentacles, invertebrate specters...

His heart raced, his arteries pounded like a kettle drum...

As Seer Dey could read their auras, the Deceiver could manipulate them.

And then he saw his own horrors take shape...

"Father?"

An ornately robed man threaded his body with a phantom needle–through his right shoulder, out his bicep, through his wrist, out his thumb.

"Url, you must practice the heraldic arts! Master them. Design the emblems to accent our wares!" the image of his father ordered, clawing at his chest, splicing open his ribs while yelling, "Per pale!"

Slowly the ghost's head became detached from its shoulders, whispering hauntingly as it slid, "Helm erased!"

Urlquason shielded his eyes, clenching his teeth to blind the pain.

And was stung!

A hundred pins quilted his marrow, drilled the quick of his flesh, and flooded his veins with burning venom.

And as he fell, Urlquason glimpsed the Deceiver's death head gliding toward him. It floated atop the fog, bobbing and careening toward him, with its antlered skull and twisted horns raging deep blue from within, his body slicing the mist with a magnificent unholy sword.

Urlquason recalled his friends as youths riding sticks adorned with stuffed animal heads, streamers of gilded thread extending in the wind as they pranced and galloped. Now those stick animals were evoked from his memories and seemed to approach him in the fog, but their skulls were boiled raw, the bone exposed, and one very real death head galloped suspended above the gloom.

Truncated limbs of scouts flew before him.

Urlquason collapsed abruptly to lay beside someone else's feet.

"I must warn Seer Dey, Cypria, and the Aerie," he vowed, but he could not stand!

Urlquason inspected his body for flesh wounds but found only swollen mounds adorned with stingers.

Then he realized that the feet before him were not those of another scout but his own! He was doubled over in half! Yet he had felt no wound!

Before his eyes, his ankles grew bruised. Blood from within soaked his flesh.

He had been hacked by a magical blade. His body sank beneath the cold blanket of fog to die slowly. He thought to himself, *What hell-forged blade could slice through flesh and cut only bone!*

Spine severed and lame, Urlquason released the crow from beneath his cloak and watched it dart away. It would warn the others! And Url knew instinctively that the bird had taken the heart of his rag doll totem. It would serve as a message for Guildlord Qualenson, Master Tailor, who would know upon receipt of the bird that his son was dead.

OPENED WOMBS OF dead mothers hung above the surface of Haemarr's Blood Bogs, mounted and spitted upon iron stakes. Sinew stretched from corpse to corpse, connecting the forest of iron bars with a foul web of tissue. Mats of scabbed hair, once lustrous and flowing, were bunched atop skulls. Franticly, insects scurried about, imbibing ichor and urgently flying toward some distant target.

So exhausted was the elder that his effigy was silent. He could not afford the strength to welcome his loyal companions who appeared from the northern sky.

From above, muffled moans of agony rained down. The clouds shimmered like mica flakes, as streaks of lightning crackled and illuminated the undulating

Lady Aleece Tonn, transfixed in Haemarr's Blood Bog

curtain that otherwise resembled the purple vibrancy of corpse lips. Thus Nurse
Fae rolled forth with twenty and seven hundred mothers bound within her. Pale,
fresh bodies were crisscrossed in rows of three, bound by cordages of spectral
fog and covered with fetid hoarfrost. Suspended within the dense cloud, they
were kept aloft by massive currents of Fae's breath. Many had fallen unconscious,

though others struggled for freedom, hindered by the atmosphere.

Doctor Grave rode this cloud as a ship's captain steered a slave galley. And as he jumped to pier, he called to his wife to empty her load. Then the human women tumbled from the sky to be skewered by the iron needles of the Blood Bog.

Grave took care to ensure all offerings were secured to shafts to let loose their blood.

"Lady Aleece Tonn," the golem whispered to one who drooled, "Haemarr thanks your clan for giving." With that, he propped the torso of the screaming woman onto a rusting shaft, her blood quickly feeding the pool of ichor and attracting hungry wasps anxious to burrow into flesh.

"There are few mothers left on the Land. I had to venture to the far northeastern districts for these." Doctor Grave approached the massive stone effigy of Haemarr the wasp.

And after some hours, the failing god Haemarr regained enough force from the sacrifice to speak: *While you harvested, the Muse was taken from under Gravenstyne.*

"She kidnapped the Muse?" the Doctor hissed with disbelief.

Prepare to act. Her seer retrieved the Red Muse. He holds it now to protect Cypria's womb from Lysis.

"This is dire news. The Muse desires nothing more than to be carried by her proper custodian, but doing so might extinguish her fire when her soul contacts your minions that animate his body. Cypria captured the Muse only to nullify Lysis! Without him, I have no other custodian!"

Endenken moves against her Aerie now. You delayed the merging once. You must do so again. He strives now to open her womb! Once he opens the womb, his pact with me will be fulfilled and his body freed of my ichor. You can let the Muse merge with him then. He fights now and casts spells, without respect for the cost on my soul. My power wanes. I have little to offer you now in exchange for helping me. I plead that you make certain that my litter is freed.

Grave stared into the expansive Blood Bog before him. Regiments of exhausted wasps returned from the north. Pale. Empty. Thirsty. They imbibed Haemarr's ichor and returned to war. The Bog dimmed as it was exhausted of its ichor. Maternal blood fueled the immobile elder. Without this, Haemarr's soul would transcend to the Underworld and his body would become one with the Land—Lysis would have no ability to cast spells, to animate the dead, or to maintain his own life.

"Of course I will help Lysis birth your litter. I will nurse them if they are healthy, or end them if they are plagued," the hooded golem said. "Then I will resurrect our Queen. The elder race will continue."

We have suffered much for continuing the elder race. The price has been high. Lord Lysis seems blind to this. The more he casts his spells, the more we must replenish this Bog, the more blood I require! You have gathered all the women you could. I only hope

Endenken Lysis rising from Haemarr's Blood Bog

I have enough power to propel him through to the end!

"I deem Endenken Lysis will succeed in opening Cypria's Gallwomb. After, I will have to bring him to the Forge."

A problem you will no doubt deal with. Now, go to his aid. Secure his success. Secure my peace!

Doctor Grave knew that controlling Endenken would not be an easy task—Lysis was a singular force. At this ceremonious pool of death, Endenken had voluntarily approached Doctor Grave and Haemarr, demanding aid to kill the supernatural entities plaguing Gravenstyne Fortress. Lord Lysis proceeded into the Bog. Boldly. Forthright. Indignant. He emerged an insect-ridden corpse empowered with Haemarr's ichor. The undead Blue Lysis then departed to the Picti Temple within the Iron Forest to corrupt Dey–to enable the impregnation of Cypria.   Presently Lysis repeated that journey, heading toward Cypria's Gallwomb to finish his pact with Haemarr. To release the litter. Doctor Grave paused to reflect, his grand cleaver *Ferrus Hewnmaw* in his right hand.

Enough, dear friend. Go!

In preparation, Grave donned the evacuated exoskeletons of those he once nursed. He required this magical armor. The Muse could be forced upon him during the forthcoming battle, and contacting her soul directly would be fatal.

"For Haemarr and the Queen! Come, Fae, let us ride to Cypria!"

Fae shape-shifted into her gryphon form and the Doctor mounted her. The sentient miasma carried Doctor Grave north to the battlefield.

"CYPRIA, YOU ARE my prey now," spat Endenken Lysis, once Lord Protector of Gravenstyne, true Deceiver of the goddess Cypria, and avatar of the god Haemarr.

"Your Augurs cannot protect your grounded Aerie. Shades of red will not deter me!"

In the field before him, a parade of lengthy Red Pennants bearing his portrait flapped in a hostile wind. They hung from the spars within the Iron Forest. Taunting him. Begging him to approach and merge with them. Each tapestry was intricately decorated and massive enough to sail a flagship. They were not merely cloth. They bore his spectral image, the effigy of the rightful heir of the Picti Muse—burning with shades of red astral fire. The Augurs had applied their alchemical knowledge to spread the power they had retrieved. Siphoning portions of the Red Muse into the portraits of their Deceiver was a way to replicate and extend its power. As his four brotherly Red Shades had been born under Gravenstyne with traces of the Picti deity, these banners had been crafted similarly. Shades were just shadows of a master object. Blue Lysis had learned that souls could spread as independent, secondary simulacra. More potent than memories, shades were like diluted souls that maintained some vestige of their primary model.

This fleet of shades burned as an uncontrolled inferno within the astral realm, chaotic tongues of vermillion, ethereal flames forming simplified effigies of the Lord and tickling the burnt underbellies of storm clouds. The banners snapped in the wind, crackling like whips. And facing them was the subject within those portraits. To free Haemarr's children from Cypria's womb, he would have to penetrate these Red Pennants.

Blue Lysis stared beyond them at the autumnal moon. Must it always preside over his nightmares? Years prior, the full moon supervised over his Inheritance Rite. Since, it marked the annual tradition in which Maeve would wander the estate looking for Dey.

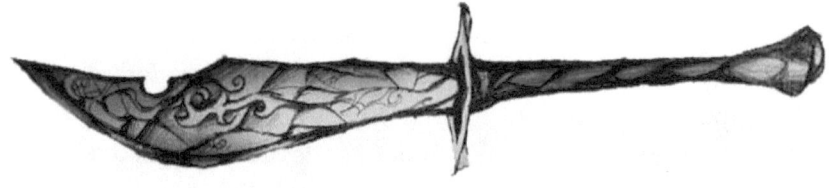

Ferrus Eviscamir reforged

Lord Lysis's baldric held *Ferrus Eviscamir*, the newly reforged blade that now sliced through stone and bone and earth and was invisible to flesh and metal. So sharp and devastating was this mystical weapon, Endenken employed it to cut through the Land, to carve a path freeing himself from the Underworld Forge wherein he had enhanced the sword. His ichor-fused blade vibrated in anticipation.

"Haemarr, your plight will be over soon," Endenken said.

The luminous larvae inside his skeleton responded, *Our pact will be fulfilled. Yet after that, my ichor will no longer sustain you.*

"I will sustain myself!"

If the Muse or its Shades merge before you free the litter, then I will forever be immobile. My ichor within you would turn to stone...

"Prepare to supply me with all ichor that does remain!"

So thick and dense was the approaching flock of blackbirds, it appeared as a storm of ebony smoke. Beneath, on the ground, several armored regiments of human Augurs formed shield walls and lined trenches. Bows cocked with arrows. Swords unsheathed. Spears lowered.

Cypria's minions knew the Deceiver would return. They had been preparing for this conflict for years.

The Red Pennants, the flocks of blackbirds, and the legions of men stood against one entity, the Lord of Gravenstyne. And yet he wavered not. Fueled by arrogance and power, he advanced.

The rolling mass of countless blackbirds descended!

Casting his arms back, Lord Lysis summoned the insect swarm inside him. Undead wasps and winged ants surfaced in his hands, burning bright in cobalt-blue astral fire. The elemental energy balled up, shedding wisps of lightning while rolling in his palm. He called with every drop of Haemarr's strength to summon the live and dead insects from outside himself, hundreds of thousands of them, and they answered his call.

First, swarms of wasps arrived. Prominent stingers protruded from their abdomens that could absorb the blood and soul from their targets. Then other insects not directly controlled by Haemarr crawled from beneath stone, from rotting wood, and from the soil about Cypria's Aerie. Molted shells of locusts joined the ranks of wasps, dragonflies, and winged roaches. So great were these hordes, the ground quaked from the buzzing of their wings.

Lysis loosed the ball of energy from his hand into the sky, and the army of insects followed it into Cypria's birds.

A thousand of intense luminous specks rushed upward and mixed with the tumultuous ranks of carrion birds. Instantly, carcasses and exoskeletons rained down upon the Land.

Fire erupted in the sky as the mixing of ichor turned to stone. Mists of astral fog, chitin, and feathers crystallized and precipitated. Petrified birds, bearing scars of stone wherever stung, fell often and quickly. Weak from his summoning, Lysis stumbled for cover as the air became thick with living debris. Reverberating caws and the violent humming of insect wings shook the Land, and many of the iron stalks crumbled under the oppressive vibrations, the Red Pennants collapsing with their posts.

Lysis sliced through bird upon bird, each of which had many glossy blue wasps clinging to its body. And as he swung, portions of his swarm replenished

Cypria's minions descend on the Deceiver

his store of ichor and hastened back to Haemarr.

So energized, Blue Lysis called forth more swarms to replace those lost in battle. And the cycle continued through the night: the insects giving him the elemental nectar necessary for sorcery, he depleting his reserves summoning more insects, those insects answering the call to be sacrificed in battle or, if victorious, to retrieve more energy for their master.

The blackbirds too were gifted in the arts of magic, for many were empowered with Cypria's ichor as surely as the insects were empowered by Haemarr. He could only bear witness to the results of the bird's magic: glistening clouds of poisonous vapors, frozen wasps impaled by shards of hail, and brilliant, azure lightning streaks cracking the air.

The sky flickered with marvelous, spellbinding colors, as if a dozen rainbows congealed and then violently exploded. So death continued to descend in many forms and sounds.

As dawn gave way to morn, Lysis collapsed under the weight of exhaustion. The minions of Haemarr relentlessly supplied his skeleton with eldritch power. This last infusion was not as strong as previous ones, for the swarm grew fatigued as the Bogs of Haemarr depleted.

And the birds mounted a final assault, breaching the clouds of vermin! They fought feverishly, seizing the fatigued necromancer and lifting him from the ground. Claws tore into him, clutched his collar and arms, and bore him away.

The remaining minion swarms closed quickly on Lysis's levitating form. Sparks spewed forth as the battlefront advanced into the warrior's body. As the mass of wasps, flies, locusts, and crows held him aloft, he tore at them with his hands. Severed wings, claws, and beaks were loosed upon the air as Lord Lysis fought his way to freedom. Magic fire flared as the insects and birds fought within him. He caught afire, and he plummeted as a ball of flame.

The night sky illumed with sorcery!

It was as if the sun itself were eviscerated, her bowels released unto the Land in a brilliant rain of blood and light.

The fire extinguished when he collided with the ground. Lysis regained his stance feebly and plucked the carcasses from his body.

The army of birds was sundered and dispersed. Defeated.

"Augurs! Read your auspices now! Their carcasses spell your death!" Endenken waved *Ferrus Eviscamir* with fury. Haemarr's minions rushed to replenish his broken form.

A mass of men bearing shields and unwieldy blades answered his call.

Over the blood-saturated field, the Augurs marched.

NURSE FAE CARRIED Doctor Grave over the Land swiftly as the wind blew. The fog snaked its way through the valleys and mountains, round the abyss, and over the Cromlechon. Donning an insectan skull and claws, the golem inspected the terrain from his perch in the clouds, recalling his harvesting of mother blood for Haemarr. The collection of mothers left many homes without guidance, and now thousands of abandoned children roamed below. Wailing. Distraught. Soiled. Many advanced on the Gorgepath as a chaotic, depressed herd.

The Cromlechon colony was derelict. Only orphans, whores, and elderly men remained. It was a labyrinth of narrow streets, roofless shanties, and the crumbling skeletal architecture of ruins pierced the surface of the Land.

Orphans meandered in the Cromlechon alleys, excretion on their legs, unkempt and ill clothed, drunk with sorrow and despair, shuffling their bare blistered feet in the muck of the Gorgepath. They clutched their shattered remnants of security, torn blankets and headless dolls, with the hope that their parents would return. The silent parade of children was steered northwest by the fog.

THE AUGUR CARVER and Illuminator Guilds, laden in copper scales, rolled forth like great bunches of golden and verdigris grapes. Ripe with fear and duty, they emptied from their stronghold, reeking of the acrid stench of Cypria.

The first regiment circled about Blue Lysis. Two hundred plated figures bearing heavy armory. Each soldier was uniquely decorated in metallic quilts, interwoven with chain links and bone and animal totems, plumed feathers, and inset minerals.

"Artists? I am met by illuminators and sculptors? Aged Picts?" Endenken read their auras. "I am an artisan of death. My blade is my stylus! Your blood my ink! The Land my canvas!"

Ferrus Eviscamir cut trenches into the Land, cracking the crusty earth like glass. Melancholic oil welled from the resulting ravines. Thus the Deceiver was protected by a natural moat, filled with the Land's own black blood.

Approaching this natural barrier was the army of Augurs. To Lord Lysis, their attire appeared beautiful but colorless. But their auras broadcasted a spectacular array of hues. These spirits could be worked by Lysis' necromancy as adeptly as a painter worked his medium of inks and dyes—yet the undead Lord was himself a master of swordsmanship.

Forced to crawl upon one another through the hot tar, the emerald-colored Carvers crossed the moat. They wielded grossly designed weapons: meat cutters with extended handles, choppers with large rectangular blades, and mighty cleavers with serrated edges.

Additional illuminators leathered in hides of saffron and turmeric hues crossed the black streams of oil with their brethren Carvers, their plumed halberds spearing like massive quills.

And Blue Lysis carved into their ranks with *Ferrus Eviscamir*, its blade slicing only their bones, invisible to metal and flesh and incapable of being parried or blocked. He tilled them as he had tilled the Land!

Dozens of bodies writhed.

Yet more Augurs advanced.

They pressed Lysis back by virtue of their sheer numbers!

Performing the theurgic rites of the elders, he danced with his blade and spoke aloud in arcane, insectan languages.

And the minions of Haemarr responded. Burrowing into the fallen Augurs, they animated the dead.

Thus Lysis commanded over thirty crippled corpses. As Haemarr's magic animated the dead, his avatar fully grasped the power of possession and reanimation. His victims rose. Empty eyed. Arms contorted. Spines twisted, bones piercing their husks. And Lysis set them upon their friends.

"Feed!" he demanded.

Terror rendered the remaining ranks of the Carver Guild useless. Many ran hysterical off the battlefield. Others fainted. The dead fed upon themselves, some dumbly eating truncated limbs, others gnawing into the warm flesh of the living.

Wasps resuscitated the fallen, abandoning the bodies once hacked beyond use to revive those freshly killed. Again and again, the dead rose to fight their brethren. Soldiers knew not whom to trust as the dead turned against their own.

The ranks of Carvers and Illuminators soon lay as mashed, bruised fruits, gathered together on a vine of bone and flesh. The earth assumed the texture and hue of caramelized pumpkin pith, replete with broken hulls and bathed in dark syrup, and the air became rank with the odors of rotten meat.

The soil was sodden such that it sank beneath the weight of the dead. Rivulets of blood and oil coated all in streaky glosses of red and black. It sluiced over the brooding brow of the Deceiver.

So bloodied, Lord Endenken Lysis advanced through these muddled ranks into the heart of the compound. The Iron Forest.

CRIMSON PORTRAITS OF the Deceiver wrapped themselves about their iron masts. Many tapestries had been shredded by the battle. Some had fallen off their perch to blanket the dead. Could the Augurs force the merging of these Shades and the ichor within Endenken, the battle would be over.

The Red Pennants no longer encircled the entire Forest. Endenken located a breach easily enough and cantered through, heading toward the grand Mosaic and temple.

A single man stood firm along his path.

Grovel Tonn, Guildlord of Smiths.

A mallet of steel served as his war hammer. It bounced like a baby's rattle in his hands. Grovel weighed nearly three hundred pounds, a stocky man, wide as a bull. His helmet was horned and heavy as an anvil. Plated armor gave him the appearance of a rhinoceros; the ornately gilded silver streaks gave the impression he was carved from marble.

Grovel said nothing. He stood silent but steadfast between Lysis and the path to Cypria, bouncing his mallet.

"Match your skill against mine, fat dwarf! I have worked the Underworld Forge! I will mold your armored hide into a useless spoon! Your dogs can lick your blood from its ladle!"

Then Grovel bolted forward, dozing Lysis over with the force of a mammoth ram!

Jarred, the Lord took seconds to recover.

He stood, angered, ready to address the smith with *Ferrus Eviscamir*.

Suddenly, a needle-bolt pierced his chest. Loosed from a crossbow, the bolt was tethered to a pole near the archer who sent it, Clanlord Qualenson. He was positioned a fathom high inside an iron cage. Donned in silk robes, his fingers were like long tree limbs streaming over his loom-like weapon. Again and again he threaded his enemy. He was a gangly man who sought to avenge his son as he served Cypria.

Blue Lysis struggled to cut the tethers...

A heavy regiment of Grovel Tonn's Hammermen ambushed!

They laid an iron grill atop him and battered metal tacks the size of dragon teeth through his bones to secure him.

Qualenson continued to pelt Endenken's body with bolts and tethers, and within minutes he was spooled and bound within a skein of taut wire to the gridiron.

Lord Lysis, the living corpse, bound in an iron coffin and by augur pallbearers. To the Picti temple they went. Seer Dey would soon exit the temple with the heart of the Red Muse to merge the long lost heart of the Picti cult with its chosen host. Turn Haemarr's minions into stone! Immobilize the Deceiver!

Prasus the Pictish shaman, oldest living within the commune and most wise in ancient alchemical arts, pranced awkwardly beside Lysis, preparing him for the merging, ranting, "I shall make you ready! Render you from blue to red. Seer Dey says you are truly red, that your blue is merely an exhausted form of iron. You do not deceive me! Now I wet you in the parents of all metals, thus marrying mercury, sulphur, and iron salt. You will accept your inheritance! "

The Hammermen placed the grilled Lord Lysis onto a raging brazier as the alchemist sprinkled him with glistening salts, powders, and green liquor.

The embers and heat evoked memories of the Underworld Forge. Lord Lysis' eyes burned intense blue with Haemarr's power. The wasps and larvae still fueled him.

"Quicksilver! Oil o' vitriol! Dragonsblood! Now burn!" The mixture vaporized and condensed, glazing Lysis with a black varnish.

"Bludgeon him!"

The flogging that ensued would have crushed the bones of any ordinary man. But these bones had been tempered in the Underworld Forge! They could not be broken by ordinary weapons! Yet the pounding did pulverize the black chemical layers on their surface, and wherever a strike landed, streaks of red appeared.

"Usher forth the fiery pigments!" the alchemist cheered.

Lysis appeared an ebonite slab bruised with brilliant, marbleized vermillion.

"Red you turn, Deceiver! You are not blue as your eyes glow! Soon you will be red as Seer Dey has foretold! We will not let you free the gallwraiths and chromantis!"

He read the aura of this alchemist. Bound, Endenken was forced to work his sorcery lying down. Hence Lysis spoke. "Do you seek to blind me as you blinded your wife! She still clings to your soul! She was dependent upon you! Your alchemy could remove her sight, but not restore it! Even now she searches for you, groping for your soul, alone in the afterworld! Searches through the smoke for you! Seize her! Aid her!"

And the aging Picti leader clutched his body, patting it vehemently, trying to locate and allay his wife's ghost. The Deceiver had read his soul as clearly as had Seer Dey during his recruitment into the Augury. All these years he believed Nina was not suffering. But she was! Because of him!

"Nina!" he pleaded. "Nina! Oh, Nina!"

The alchemist ran into the fire a deranged man, twisting and burning before his peers. They could not help him.

Elsewhere, another Augur was threatened. During the episode of the alchemist's burning, few noticed the torso of a corpse snaking its way near the feet of the great iron stake supporting the master tailor.

"Father," it mumbled.

At his post, aloft in an iron gibbet, Lord Qualenson listened.

His son had returned home. Dead.

"Father?" Urlquason whispered with fractured lips. He had crawled on his elbows under the power of Haemarr's minions. His legs and pelvic bone had departed long ago, his spine split by *Ferrus Eviscamir* and his legs torn off during transit.

The Clanlord was compelled to greet his son, despite the obvious wounds.

Gliding down a lengthy rope, he picked up his son's carcass and hugged it.

"Great gods! You live!" Qualenson jubilantly exhibited his madness.

Embraced, the corpse drew forth a knife and lacerated its father's neck.

"So I emblazon you. Helm erased," Urlquason croaked as he decapitated his father...

Then, as the Master Tailor released his grasp to support his head, Urlquason drove the knife into his father's chest and drug it down to open up the belly and to ease his own fall. "Per pale," he whispered.

Qualenson died a herald's death by his son's own hand. Then the Deceiver dispossessed the corpse, his wasps and larvae struggling to return to battle only to crinkle and die under exhaustion.

Two Augur Lords were rendered useless, yet the Hammermen and Grovel Tonn still shouted: "Red! Red!"

And Lysis remained bound.

Lysis could then discern a red plume approaching. Seer Dey!

A hundred Hammermen jeered while pounding their mallets to the earth.

"Red! Red! Red!"

"Haemarr! Haemarr, aid me!"

My last offering comes now, my warrior. My pool empties. Use the last of my powers carefully!

SEER DEY MARCHED steadily forward bearing the Red Muse in a skull. First his left foot forward, then his right to match… each step chasing an emerging mist out of his way.

A plumed mantle and cape complemented his avian death mask. His feathered headdress swayed as would weeping willow branches in a storm, and with each step the feathers sloshed as if the winds shifted direction.

Petals of burning coals and bloodied flesh blew about the compound.

Left foot. Right.

"Red! Red!" shouted the Augurs amidst the smoke, taking little notice of the growing mist about them.

With each step he advanced, the ichor within the Deceiver waned. The proximity of the Muse initiated the solidification process.

Dey continued his protracted progress, careful not to contaminate the veins of blue eldritch energy belonging to Cypria. Empowered by the crow within his chest and Cypria's ichor, he was slowed by the Red Muse but avoided being petrified. The Muse was sentient and controlled its own tickling flames and resisted coalescing. It wanted to merge with Endenken Lysis, not him. Yet Dey's body had mutated under its influence. A thin membranous film extended now over his insectan gloves. These cartilage flaps opened and closed like bellowing avian wings to mock the image of his matriarch Cypria.

The fumes from Lysis' grilling became unnaturally thick, as if something else contributed to the vapors. No one could see farther than a few feet. Still they shouted!

"Red! Red! Red!"

Left, then right. The malformed Seer Dey approached over a floor of coals, simmering bones and feathers. As if he were pulled along begrudgingly, he walked within the kiln of the battlefield. The sky blackened with smoke.

Feet from the Deceiver.

Feet from his uncle.

"Maeve sent me to you," whispered Lysis. "She told me that you have a child in the litter. She told me to free it. Yet you bring the Muse to me. It will end me! The red will mix and petrify the blue ichor that fills the hive within my chest. Kill me and you keep your child caged!"

"You manipulated me to free you from the Iron Forest. Then you murdered me," Dey said. "You deceived me then. You deceive me now. I see no evidence that you served my mother any better than my father did."

The mist continued to snake about them…

A GREAT CLEAVER CRASHED out of the mist, shattering Grovel Tonn into a thousand shards of crystal! *Eviscamir's* sister blade, *Ferrus Hewnmaw*, shimmered mightily in the hands of the Doctor as he dismounted the mists of Nurse Fae.

A hundred Hammermen readied their mallets with little hesitation.

Doctor Grave cited insectan languages while executing the theurgies of their elders as he called upon Nurse Fae to aid him.

Then the barber inhaled the mists composing his wife's amorphous body, filling his cheeks with her moisture. With a full mouth he mentally recited a summoning, then he emptied Fae, spewing her forth, her body diffusing amongst the regiment of heavily armored smiths. And with that he repeated the summons aloud:

"Those who imbibe these death throes
That ride with ailing, homeless souls
Obey this compelling sacrifice,
Prepare your blood 'n flesh alike,
An' offer your gifts in reverent silence,
As I partake in marshalling the flesh!
Iron of melancholy, iron of blood,
Vermillion and ebony, I hail the flood!"

The Augurs could not help but to breathe, and when they did, they invited Fae into their lungs. Thus they accepted the summons and were compelled to offer a sacrifice of liquid iron.

A hundred men spat blood and regurgitated their bloody innards, for all soft flesh contacting Fae was torn loose. Esophagi undulated, like octopi worming their way through the porous tract of the undersea. Jelly-like and writhing, the organs answered the Doctor's call, engorging the open mouths of the Hammermen, snapping their jaws and suffocating them simultaneously. Blood spewed forth as the fleshy levies broke!

Each Augur's throat purged a set of silky, swollen red organs, glistening

Doctor Grave and Nurse Fae cast spells

brilliantly. Bronchia flapped like black seeds on the skin of engorged strawberries. The last breaths of the men merged with Fae's body of mist and whooshed over the terrain as a wailing, screeching skein of ghosts.

Grave was indeed a powerful necromancer, as evidenced by the gross mass of lungs about him. Yet such powerful spellcasting tired the golem.

Seer Dey was immune from Nurse Fae's spells, since he was already dead.

He had no lungs to offer. No need to inhale air.

Dey outstretched his arms to insert the Muse into its rightful host.

Doctor Grave sprung toward Dey, *Ferrus Hewnmaw* elevated to strike.

And the grand cleaver sliced horizontally, splintering Dey's pelvic bone and sending a set of legs airborne…

Magic crackled and burned the sky white as crystalline fragments were strewn from the seer's bone. Then the smoke subsided, exposing the malformed torso of Dey. A bird dropped from his broken ribcage. Electric sparks trailed the carcass. Cyprian ichor showered the scene, merging with wisps of red to petrify and drop as tear-shaped rocks. Cypria lost her control over Dey!

The core of the Red Muse lashed out its astral tentacles, groping for a host to control. And it found Dey.

Doctor Grave worked quickly to free Lysis, slicing through iron and silk twine. And Endenken leapt to freedom…

Then talons perched on the Doctors's insectan mask, and Grave spun to discern the hovering assailant.

A human spine whipped like a lengthy tail from behind the Doctor's head and membranous wings heaved from a grotesque body to blind him. The Red Muse burned bright in the heart of Cypria's past avatar, the Seer Dey, now turned a grotesque, fledgling gargoyle.

Nurse Fae whirled tumultuously! Spiraling gusts of wind lashed against the pair, but Dey was firmly attached to Grave. She spat forth squalls that engulfed the Iron Forest and the neighboring pine trees. All was shrouded in opaque, churning vapors.

Red Dey was thrown aside.

Doctor Grave fell, his insectan helmet nearly torn from his shoulders, black ichor spewing from cuts in the earth pool about him.

Too weak to stand, he turned his head to see the Red Dey spring toward Endenken.

"Fae! All will be lost. Summon our daughter's soul from the melancholy that leaks onto the Land. I feel her soul as the oil cradles me. It is weak. With haste!"

Fae's voice sounded. The chorus of a thousand dead rang harmoniously, reciting the ancient elder language, summoning a soul that had been infused into the black oil. They called back Maeve's exhausted soul from the depths of the Land to contain her long lost son.

LORD LYSIS REGAINED *Ferrus Eviscamir* and darted toward Cypria's Blood Fountain wherein lay her womb, gaining some distance as the Doctor and the Red Dey wrestled. Running past the retaining wall that secured the oily ichor, past impaled men, past hundreds of skewered male carcasses, he saw Cypria as he breached the parade of iron stakes webbed in flesh.

Victory! Haemarr cheered with a dying breath…

Endenken advanced toward Cypria unabated. She lay as a sculpted woman. Vulnerable. Terrified. Her swollen womb appeared as a mold-encrusted peach; the Gallwomb had been reinforced with layers of cemented fossils and alchemy.

Suddenly, the Red Dey approached…

Black, melancholic ichor splashed about Blue Lysis. His cobaltous aura fueling the sacred blade renewed at the Underworld Forge. Plumes of blue light spewed forth like angry flames searching for kindling— finding only splayed bits of Cypria's blue ichor.

Red Dey encroached in the air, restrained by the icy tentacles of Nurse Fae and the firm grip of Doctor Grave.

That instant the possessed Red Dey was halted in flight as a glistening caricature of his mother Maeve welled from the abundant melancholy and stopped him. A mother's soul thus clutched the body of her tormented, undead son, and an anxiety that had burned for decades was finally quenched. Dey's mind was on the brink of lunacy, but he recognized that the primitive elements holding him bore the signature of his mother. She had found him! Her soul could not communicate to her son now, but that was not necessary.

Dey was momentarily arrested, but the Red Muse still reacted with the nearby ichor within Cypria's Fountain. Endenken's feet rooted themselves, stone crackling as it began to calcify. He managed to raise his magical sword overhead…

Then Maeve's soul dissolved completely…

Red Dey advanced…

And the Gallwomb opened as *Ferrus Eviscamir* cut…

Cypria struggled to watch the Deceiver dig into her womb. Her eyes, anchored to a craned neck, saw not the Gallwomb that was once her abdomen—for now it was but a splintered stone bowl that barely contained turbulent matter. She watched Endenken hack away the calcified shell until the Red Muse, in turn, burrowed into him…

Then Cypria saw nothing. Her soul transcended, leaving her earthly body and to join the melancholic oil.

The Red Muse merges with Endenken Lysis

THE CROMLECHON INHABITANTS were drawn to the landscape as a column of black smoke ascended toward the heavens, the Land disgorging a conical hill of dark ash and orange veins that was a streaming pillar of molten elements.

Dawn framed the volcanic event. A baby blue sky. Devoid of substance. Clear as the finest stained glass.

Remotely, hundreds were drawn to patios and open squares to gaze upon the disaster. They became mesmerized staring at the self-luminous embers speckling the ever darkening sky, drifting freely like dandelion seeds on fire.

Lightning crawled as ever-shifting blue arteries along the undersides of the developing clouds. None anticipated their imminent doom, for none among the captivated audience understood they witnessed a death dance of the Land.

They had only minutes to behold the beauty of the firmament, now brilliant green, then glowing vermillion, followed by luminous ruby, ever decreasingly transparent, bolder and bolder in hue, until the concentration of suspended pumice and scoria suffocated the sun.

Keen ones spotted the litter in the approaching storm, mere shapes in the distant, yet advancing, clouds: malicious infants, feathered irregular puffs with fleshy wattles, and coiling vapors resembling swollen, bruised umbilical cords, and ebony depictions of gnarled fowl with bulbous necks and thin horns.

The scorching pyroclastic flow poured into the Cromlechon, and hardened into a calculus of gray stone with veins of real blood.

And the dense shower veiled the screeching of the dying, as the gases cooked their flesh and mounds of tephra compacted about their bodies.

Riding the stygian currents of vapors, above the caldera that had replaced Cypria's Gallwomb, and above the charnel Cromlechon, a misty elemental escaped, her beloved golem and others in tow.

VII: The Weird of Clan Lysis

Endenken's Red Horde battles Grave's Barbers atop petrified elders

VII: The Weird of Clan Lysis

T HE BOY PLAYED alone in pitch darkness. His sight was not limited to the physical realm—as was human sight. He *saw* and played with the souls of his sister and brothers, many of which remained near their dead forms. He was too young to ascertain that the dolls he played with were actually the limp forms of his stillborn siblings. He did not recognize that the others looked different than him. They were all wraiths—mutant insectan and avian hybrids. He alone was humanoid.

The boy outstretched the wings of an embryonic, mutated bird, held it aloft to mimic flight, its extended neck dangling between its four exoskeleton legs and bulbous abdomen. This one was his favorite because of its miniature size. He landed it into a grounded nest, planted within a carefully constructed landscape of broken eggshells and molted skins. This play zone was illuminated by the haunting, iridescent glow of his siblings' ghosts. Many phantasms were loosely attached to their host bodies and would appear as wispy tendrils, though others were confined within the translucent shells of gargantuan eggs, their healthy bodies yet to hatch.

Such is the way of a young artist. Instinctively crafting melancholy into dreams, relishing the power of creation, at one with the fantasy he crafts. Yet the powers of enacting fantasies wane, and even children eventually sense the horror of fighting for survival.

Suddenly, the entire Land shook.

Bits of fine gravel cascaded down, and the toy nest collapsed.

A blazing white streak opened above him. Then it bloomed a hundred arteries, each one snaking its way in the darkness like lightning, branching into thousands of intense veins. The Gallwomb had been compromised.

Clashes of steel and the din of war flowed through the breach with a rain of gravel. The boy could only huddle with his toys.

He watched in surprise as a sword worked its way through the domed ceiling. Veined with streaks of blue ichor, polished to a mirror's finish, and contoured and honed to surgical fineness, the blade aroused the boy's primal curiosity. Sunlight and spell-light spilled from above, enshrouding the blade in a bright halo.

The visage of the ghoul wielding the blade was also remarkable, albeit more horrific than beautiful. Its death mask peered down burning supernatural blue. It was a wrought alabaster shell, twisted like metal, and seemed to encapsulate boiling ether. The shadows framed the antlered skull and spasmodically recoiled from the enflamed sockets.

The next instant, all changed. The blade disappeared, and the ground melted and smoldered. The foundation becoming suddenly liquid, the toys collapsed in folds of earth and eggs, tumbling, toppling, enfolding. Black oil swelled past his shoulders, and carcasses floated about, as the child grabbed desperately. His hands suddenly found purchase. Bursts of gaseous earth blew him head over heels, shards of eggshell cut his skin, and rocks pelted his flesh into bruise.

An explosion shot him toward the heavens, away from the Gallwomb.

A receding speck he appeared to creatures on the Land—a speck among many, each tailed like a comet.

Thus he became celestial, though was not aware of his greatness.

So the boy flew over a foggy sea that was strangely sentient. The smoke of burning feathers coiled about him, along with hatchlings, immense and newly born, and they were squawking though their bodies were sundered, and together they went swiftly in a fluid bed of debris.

"HAIL, SENTINELS AND soldiers of Clanlord Kaiyn Tonn, Sire of the Twin Flails," paged the border guard to whom held banners charged with white silhouettes of rampant wyverns. "Turn your steeds around. This province, under the auspices of Clanlord Qualenson, is not open for passage."

The youthful sentinel and standard bearer, Reher Tonn, responded, "We come not in hostility! Besides, you have only a dozen men to our thousand. You bear rotten armory. Now, be sensible and bear down your weaponry! Your leather breeches and bare feet will not stand against one of us!"

The gaunt constable advanced while poising his rusty halberd, so fatigued he was the pole shook. "We border guards are all that remain. Three waves of terror have ravaged our homeland, and we will not bear down to the first that is not born of sorcery. Years ago, a horde of flesh-eating wasps infected our men, burrowing through their eye sockets and persuading their lifeless bodies to wander into the forests. Afterward, flocks of crows abducted hundreds more of our citizens–weavers, tailors, and dyers all fell victim.

"Soon after that, an impenetrable fog flowed past our guard, saturated our Lord's manor and villages. When it retreated, it took our mothers with it. An' the damnable blackbirds! They started to snatch the men! The wasps and birds would fight each other, but they both fed upon our citizens. And the children. So many of them. Their fates were left to nature.

"So we remain, sworn to protect what is left. Heed us, or we will assume you are a fourth threat. Shall you proceed into our territory, we will be forced to counter!"

"Our quarrel is not with you," spoke Clanlord Kaiyn, donning pearlescent lamellar armor atop an ebony mare that was similarly barded. Kaiyn Tonn glided gracefully forward. "But with the sorcery that plagues your home. We are metal smiths and stone carvers. And many of us have been snatched by the crows as if mere worms. Now our anvils lie still, our forges are cold. Worse, we have been plagued by the fog that abducts women. Behind me, a thousand fathers and sons have formed a Legion to avenge the loss of their wives and mothers stolen by the mysterious vapors. We and you have the same cause. Join us! Honor those you have lost. Let us retrieve our loved ones or find their remains so we can bury them. "

The stalwart constable said, "Nay, sir. We have sworn duty to our people. Honor our treaties and respect those who have been kidnapped or killed. Leave this border without delving through their homeland in their absence! Be gone!"

"I would sooner take orders from your sovereign."

The guard scoffed. "Clanlord Qualenson and his son Urlquason were stolen away by the crows many months ago. There is no sovereign to host you."

"Our goal is to reach the Cromlechon in the district beyond yours. We have learned the fog is associated with those unholy grounds. Perhaps you could escort us…"

"This gateway is closed. This land is plagued and in mourning. Let it rest peacefully!" the guard snapped and aimed his spear.

An abrupt, metallic cacophony erupted as a hundred knights drew their swords!

"Steady, men!" Clanlord Kaiyn about-faced his steed and meandered through his ranks.

First, Kaiyn's sentinels withdrew with him.

The lonely guards of Clan Qual remained poised.

Exhausted, these guards wept. They were elated the army withdrew. They were sorrowful that their land was dead beyond rejuvenation and all hope of restoration was gone. Then the border guards laughed in madness, and cradled plush, quilted dolls worn from years of play.

Clanlord Kaiyn returned alone with the speed of lightning and stampeded into their ranks atop his war steed! For his Legion would not be hindered by a few ill men.

Spiked tendrils of Kaiyn's mighty flail *Wyvern* arced and sailed through the dry air, slicing necks, mauling heads, and disgorging abdomens. A dozen pikes collapsed to the earth and thumped, their owners in tow.

"I come from a different land that honors combat," he spoke to the constables' opened skulls. "Despair maddened you. Yet I honor your misplaced conviction. And I mourn for your dead land. It is beyond repair and no longer needs protection. Now, you are dead, and my Legion can proceed. You have delayed justice long enough!"

A thousand men strong, the Legion made way for the Cromlechon. The armored column worked its way through the desolate countryside. Orphans skittered to and fro like wild squirrels. Corpses rotted openly, some freshly de-composing and some exhausted of flesh. Many more floated, bloated and white, upon strange pools of blacker than black oil. Carrion crows and insects feasted on this carnage. The eaters of the dead disregarded the parade of scale-mailed men. Although the members of the Legion were grieved by such horrific sights, they felt pride that their own state had maintained order—proud they took action before sorcery annihilated their homeland.

"Aleece," Kaiyn whispered to himself, patting his heart to ease his pain. His army may have spared their state from complete ruin, but it was not spared from sorrow.

Orphans increasingly joined its ranks. First, they trailed the army and scavenged crumbs from discarded meals. Later they sought protection beside the horde of armored soldiers.

Kaiyn proclaimed, "It is our duty to enlist these children. Give them pur-pose. Gather them. If they are too tired, weak, or despondent, carry them on your shoulders. In return for our help, they will refresh our hope and purpose. Let us find their parents! To Lady Aleece! For all!"

They marched forward.

"Beware, the Land is not healthy," Apothecary Whitebeard announced, his speckled mount catching pace with his leader's ebony mare.

"How so?" Kaiyn asked.

"It bleeds. The black pitch that puddles about this path is ever more abundant. The Picti claimed it is melancholy, the liquefied remains of their deity. At home it is considered a rare substance, valued by our alchemists. In Qualenson's province, the oil too should be rare, but with every passing mile the puddles grow in number and size. They bubble like fresh springs!"

As if to punctuate the dreariness, hundreds of doll-shaped pincushions floated atop these black pools, unattended and pierced with iron nettles. Qualenson, honorable tailor and governor, had gifted these to all the children under his sovereignty, for when born in this clan the doll becomes one's personal standard. Now many were abandoned to rot separate from their caretakers who no longer lived to hold them.

Kaiyn absorbed the warning. "Perhaps the Land fails because the mothers that gave it life are absent."

Suddenly, the crows departed in unison toward the west!

"Draw your weapons!"

Fearing the birds had detected a danger humans could not, the force answered Kaiyn's call, unsheathing steel swords and raising iron maces in readiness. Although morning, the western horizon turned abruptly colored as if evening were setting prematurely.

The gaze of the Legion was drawn to a colossal finger of black smoke reaching toward the heavens. A thousand men focused upon the floating coals carried in the approaching plume of darkness.

Electric white veins crawled and crackled under the bellies of clouds, scurrying like spiders.

The warriors beheld the beauty of a prismatic firmament, now brilliant emerald, then glowing vermillion, then luminous as a polished sapphire. Then debris blocked out the sun, and the clouds rolled and toppled overhead, drawing a blanket of nightmares over the army.

"Mothers of the gods! What gave birth to that storm?"

"The Land shakes!"

"The damnable fog! It comes!"

Then pebbles began to fall like hail.

"Take cover!"

A grand meteoric rock shot from the source of smoke, sailed with the rush of clouds, and crashed into the center of the army....

DEPOSITED RUDELY FROM the sky, as if he were too hot to hold, the Red Lord tumbled into the aged orchard of Gravenstyne. Undead, he recovered quick as a panther, his eye sockets kilns of anger searching for prey.

"Curse you, Nurse Fae! Give me Doctor Grave!"

Red Lysis flexed his skeleton, his joints spewing black, pluming coughs, his bones glowing as embers, and his hair wrapped into antlers that sharpened with every wisp and tongue of flame. A flashing brilliant ruby he burned! And his ribs expelled torrents of ashen black debris and vomited a smoldering, dead hive that had been his heart. As the hive contacted the earth, it emptied petrified wasps that fractured like fragile statues of spent coal. Haemarr and his minions were no longer alive.

His sword sliced the fog about him! More than his rage drove him. The ether inside him controlled him too. Red energy shared his body with his soul.

"Fae! Damn you!"

At first, black oil sluiced off of Lysis' blade *Ferrus Eviscamir*, for it still carried the Land's elements gleaned from his mission between the Underworld and Cypria's Aerie.

Red Lysis continued this at length, his blade becoming ever cleaner, until he finally realized his surroundings. Fae had brought him home, to the Gravenstyne Orchard. Ash snowed upon everything; the storm of debris issuing from Cypria's opened Gallwomb distributed powder over all the counties surrounding the Augur's Aerie. The crystalline statue of Maeve's body lay shattered by stones that had sailed the sky. Her decapitated head solemnly looked toward the desecrated graves of their children as gray ash rained down.

Red Lysis stood as a demon transformed. His skeletal frame was glossy black basalt, his ribs engorged with crystallizing magma. He faced what he hated to accept. He was not in control of his circumstances. He was Red.

"Ende!"

Endenken turned toward his wife's voice. Maeve was dead, of course. He had seen her soul in the Underworld. Beside him now, her transmuted body lay as shattered crystal. Yet here her image appeared, running from the Fortress ruins toward him...

"Maeve!"

Her transparent ghost glided eerily closer.

Behind Maeve's ghost, connected to her, came the accelerating, haunts of

Gravenstyne: Narl the Archer, Brood the Bastard Warrior, Asthete SanGules, and the Drunk Potter. All rushed forward as ethereal monsters.

Red Lysis reached out to Maeve's ghost, but he did not realize that he grasped at something irretrievable. He did not know that by reaching, he risked hurting himself.

As they touched, Maeve's shade turned colorless, like gray powder ash, and it fell writhing in pain to grapple Endenken's shins.

Like shackles, her soulless memory clasped about him.

And Lysis was downed.

This ghost caused physical pain. It had to have been tainted by necromancy. *Grave was working some type of spell!*

Translucent images of Maeve writhed about him, pierced his blackened bones, threading them, like electric needles.

Endenken Lysis was shocked into submission. His Forge-tempered bones were impenetrable to steel, melded by eldritch sorcery—but they were porous, and his intangible memories knitted themselves into his frame.

The ghosts of Narl, Brood, SanGules, and Potter came to beat upon Maeve's effigy. Narl wrestled her legs, gnawing her bones with a broken jaw. She screamed. Brood rode atop her back, pounded her spine with his fist. SanGules leaped about screeching, "She was dumb and deserving!"

The Drunk chastised, "Where did Dey go? And you? Leave me? I owned you. I never said you could go. S'upid wench!"

Maeve's effigy screamed in terror until it dissipated, and the four brothers collectively held onto the Lord of Gravenstyne's shins. They smiled and scoffed at him as the Red Shade had at the Augur's Aerie.

And Endenken had to accept these haunting pasts, for they were his own creations and he could not deny them. He had done everything he thought he could, and still he failed to protect them. And still he remained a pawn of the gods. Forever a pawn of Doctor Grave's machinations!

Ferrus Eviscamir slashed the air and phantasmal tendrils to no avail. Grave's magical shackles held stronger than iron. Stronger than Cypria's stone womb.

Scooping the flame from his chest, he hurled kindling embers away from his body, but the Red Fire was entrained.

So he turned *Ferrus Eviscamir* on himself and struck his body with the blade. Yet his bones had been hardened by sorcery, and only *Ferrus Eviscamir* took damage.

"Doctor!"

Lysis had turned mad. Crazed. His fire bloomed! So powerful was he, his Red Fire became real, and the brittle fruit trees took flame one by one, first one row, then another, then the pears trees joined the fray.

"*SLICE THE PEAR!*" shouted Erolyis's ghost from the shackles, but then the boy's form was devoured by the cannibal Narl.

Amongst the flickering inferno of a hundred burning fruit trees, a real shadow loomed over him, holding a severed head.

"Why did you bring me here?" Lysis asked. He was unable to look toward the visitor or into the eyes of his wife's glass head.

Doctor Grave said, "I brought you here to bind you! To shackle you with your own memories! For I will drag you bound by sorcery to the Forge! My Queen will burn anew!"

The larvalwyrmen and Endenken's haunts wrapped about him and pinioned his arms. Then Nurse Fae assumed her gryphon shape, let Doctor Grave mount her, clutched the Red Lord, and flew toward the Cromlechon...

THE PHOENIX ROSE from the core of the meteoric debris, its oil-saturated wings stuck to the exoskeleton thorax. It waddled forward awkwardly, splashing puddles of black ichor with shuffling talons. It assumed a sergeant pose, rearing on its hind four legs and lowering its abdomen. A curved stinger emerged from its armored rear.

"It looks like a flayed serpent from our mines! Is it a cockatrice? The demon has no proper name!" Whitebeard exclaimed.

The fledgling wraith cackled as its gangly form leaped and collapsed, flapping its wings and thrashing its legs in fury. Its skull bore little skin, and its sockets had spilled its raw eyes to dangle like jewelry.

The pointed beak scanned the scene from atop a craned neck, open and ready to snatch food but guided by blinded eyes. Its extended bill was longer than a claymore's edge and thrice as threatening. Swollen luminous veins of black hue formed an exterior net to contain the transparent organs from spilling onto the ground.

It trampled upon several children. Clanlord Kaiyn noted the youths had been felled by rock shrapnel, and with the exception of one, their end was certain. The remaining sickly child was coated in white—dust or sickness, Kaiyn surmised. A living ghost nonetheless, a shadow of life amongst a dead land and a dying populace. Based on height alone, he was ready for his seventh winter. He sat dazed amongst a settling cloud of debris, fidgeting with a winged carcass. Mere feet from the threatening wraith.

"Rally, men of the flail! Save the child! Slay the serpent that brings death from the sky!"

None of the thousand men had faced a demon before. Still they advanced,

A gallwraith attacks the Legion

to answer their Lord's call, circling the beast and encroaching from all sides with swords leveled and maces raised.

The blade-like bill lashed forth like a harpoon and returned with a limb between its mandibles. Five yards away, a lopsided soldier toppled off his horse in despair.

Then a pair of men darted by on foot, one carving out a protective zone with flail in each hand, the other snagging the alabaster boy while the beast was distracted. Both men were armored with distinctive ivory scale mail—made from the skin of the subterranean serpents that burrowed through their homeland mountains. They shone like iridescent trophies of a wild hunt, and their faces wore their father's stony complexion. Lordson Taiyn, the eldest son of Aleece and Kaiyn, was in the forefront; the latter was Son Byrhan, who recently forfeited his left arm to the necromancer that abducted his mother.

The beast amplified its presence by bleating, arching its back, and spreading its wings. A stench of death and ammonia wafted forth.

The avian screeches ended abruptly as ten swords simultaneously skewered the beast's abdomen. Multiple streams of ice-gray liquid burst from the punctures. The wraith's ichor sluiced down the metallic serpentine lamellae that armored the soldiers. Trickles of rust erupted in the wake of this demonic blood as it reacted with iron. Clear mineral icicles grew like hungry fangs from the shields, becoming purple, then black, as the shields turned to brittle ash.

The beast fell.

"Glorious speed, Bran!" Taiyn tossed back an ivory flail. Since the loss of his brother's arm, he occasionally carried both sigils of their father's banner. He did so with measured entitlement.

Son Byrhan accepted his weapon without returning any compliment. Kaiyn Tonn's youngest was notoriously quiet, which agitated those expecting adoration or praise.

Taiyn sighed.

"Lordson!" Kaiyn exclaimed, clasping his eldest son's arm. "My, you are blessed with your father's skill!" Then his attention was pulled downward, to glimpse the foul orphan at Son Byrhan's side.

Spell stricken, all his remaining words of acclaim went unspoken—they recoiled like worms into his throat, inducing the Clanlord to gag. It was as if someone had just cast a curse upon him. Wide-eyed. Still. An ill aura clung to the boy, chilling even Kaiyn's nerves. "Father's skill," he whispered between scabbed lips, heard only by Apothecary Whitebeard and Byrhan.

"The child looks ghoulish," Taiyn said. "Like the Picti depicted within our

Great Hall's enameled murals."

Byrhan struggled to recall the details of the Hall's cloisonné works, but images of stillborn, embryonic fowl filled his mind instead as he looked upon the boy. The youth had a scorched forehead, the surviving hair singed with clusters of feathers about his ears. His eyes were swollen and bruised and the surrounding skin pale and reflective. A severe underbite made it appear that his skull lacked an upper jaw; rather, that his nose and upper lip were a single unit. But most notable

Echo clings to his embryonic wraith

were the markings that Taiyn had taken for tattoos.

Whitebeard said, "Lordson Taiyn, the child is no ghoul, and the dark lines not decoration. I agree he does look Pictish, judging by the burnt headdress and his blue markings. But the Pict's deity rejected its own sect long ago, and members are scarce found. The intricate swirls are instead his veins showing through his thin skin. The tattoos of the Pict are fine craft, spiritually driven, like vitreous enameling is to your clan. I once studied under a Pict, the alchemist Prasus…"

His general audience lost interest, though the boy mumbled along with Whitebeard, and Byrhan maintained his careful watch over the boy.

"What are you saying? Ah, here now. You have scabs across your lips. Let me tend to you," Byrhan said to the boy.

"… tend to you…"

Byrhan wiped the child's lips then offered a scarf to replace the bloody toy. The boy retreated and hugged the carcass more tightly.

"I also know what it is like to lose your mother," Byrhan said. The demonic butcher of the fog had infiltrated their mountainous keep and left with their mother. Byrhan tried to hold onto Lady Aleece but lost that battle, and his arm went with her.

"Have you a name?" To which, the boy simply repeated the question. The one-armed Son said, "I do. Call me Bran. For now, I will call you 'Echo'."

The boy concurred, "Echo."

"Son Bran, your shoulder bleeds," Whitebeard observed. "I must cauterize it again. Come hither as I find my flintstone."

"My physician, I would think that, with your ability to help hundreds of metal smiths cope with burns, your skill with fire would be more refined. How many times must you smelt my poor brother's arm?" Lordson Taiyn teased.

One eyebrow raised, Whitebeard returned, "Unlike your fires which mold metal, my braziers mold flesh. If your brother and you were not so rash…"

"The old man is not keen on jests," Byrhan told his brother.

An unearthly scream pierced the air—issued from the downed wraith.

It still lived!

So preternatural was this call, all on the field emptied their stomachs in response. Countless helms were filled with bile. Many choked.

Then, from above, two more harpies descended toward the wounded fledging. Grand wings flapped and raised whirls of pebbles that bit into flesh and dented armor, downing scores of men as they ducked the missiles.

"That thing summoned its brethren!"

The first beast regained its feet and stampeded through pools of bubbling oil.

A squad of Kaiyn's mounted hammermen advanced.

Disproportionate fingers supported the wings of the wraith, with digits longer than a man's height. Outstretched wings scraped the wall of flailing hammers and raked their arms and shields free. Iron weapons and fleshy arms were uprooted and the ground soiled with fresh blood. Red liquid splayed the scene, hastily oxidizing to blue in the air, and then to black as it congealed.

Serpentine necks with bladed beaks arrived to clear away Kaiyn's men. One raised enough to pluck away at the men's heads as if they were mere raspberries. Another struck decisively, transfixing three mounted knights and their horses. Fragments of flesh and barding rained down.

Then men along the perimeter, away from the carnage, fell, clasping their heads and wailing. The victims vomited sprays of blood that took the shape of demons as they dissipated. It was as if the sound of the bleating nightmares took tangible form, crawled into the skulls of men, and consumed their living brains.

Kaiyn was silent. His chest swelled with the wind of his soldiers' death throes. His complexion was no longer sanguine, the beads of sweat emboldened with more hue than the skin beneath them.

Whitebeard, who fancied himself an experiential scholar and astute observer, then perceived a singular horror. His battle-experienced Clanlord was stunned into submission. This had to be driven by sorcery or disease, since Kaiyn was ever the man of action. Men were dying, and their leader was paralyzed with fear.

"Lord, awaken!" Apothecary Whitebeard yelled.

Red Lord Lysis was deposited in the Dissection Theater. He was laid atop a colossal claw that belonged to the Avian King's skeleton—now it served as the primary operating surface.

Instantly, larvalwyrmen tied themselves in knots about him to hold him to the bone table. Grave called out arcane languages commanding the astral manacles to mesh with the wyrm binding.

"Ah, *Ferrus Eviscamir* reforged. It is whole again. When I reneged on my promise upon its handle, the blade splintered, birthing two daughter facets I worked into sickles. You have healed the blade, Lysis," Doctor Grave said aloud. Then to himself: *Queen, with this I will heal you.*

Doctor Grave held his ancient weapon aloft.

"To keep you tethered properly!" the Doctor explained, impaling his patient with *Ferrus Eviscamir,* working the blade between the Forge-hardened bones and sinking it into the Avian King's claw.

Endenken screamed! Disparate memories emitted chaotically from his astral shackles. Suddenly, Endenken was reminded of Brewster Leamond's distillery. The unpleasant burn of hard cider on a parched throat and the dizziness that followed. Leamond's ghost formed from the phantom shackles and extended cupped hands to his former master, dark apple juice straining between his fingers. "Oh, master! That which you lie upon is not a safe base! On the morrow, that which is red will become gray. So die not today, master. On three, get off your father's apple tree! Skin the apple! Feed the pear!"

This haunting drained Endenken terribly, for he remembered losing the children Apple and Pear to devils. He remembered killing their father Leamond who had grown crazed.

Now his head grew feverish, and the spirits about him whirled in colorful torrents. Overwhelmed by emotions and sorcery, Endenken's soul fell into unconsciousness.

ALL THREE WINGED wraiths were absent now, having taken to the sky. Whitebeard surveyed the scene. Lordson Taiyn dug graves with the remaining soldiers of the Legion. Thirty and four hundred men were slain. Two men there were to dig each grave. Children roamed scavenging for food.

Clanlord Kaiyn had a serious fever and had lost his eyesight. He was laid upon the ground beside his sick steed, which was less healthy and foamed from the mouth between seizures. They both assumed an eerie gray pallor. Whitebeard refreshed his master's forehead with a fresh salve comprised of dried sorrel and juniper dispersed in honey. Yet the skin was rapidly decaying and exfoliated as he applied the ointment.

Whitebeard looked at the pale child clinging to Son Byrhan. The strange Echo, with self-luminous, ebony eyes and casein white skin, trailed the Son, ever clutching that doll of embryonic flesh. Whitebeard said, "I deem the first wraith did not seek to come here. It was forced here. It was confused. It maintained a defensive stance about the meteor. It fought powerfully, but in desperation. When our forces relaxed their adversarial stance, they left peacefully."

"They left when my father collapsed," Byrhan answered. "And still, the wraiths loom above us, circling like vultures. They go toward the eastern horizon, avoiding the storm from the west." Byrhan swallowed his fear, for he did not communicate that he saw his mother's face in the clouds, wailing in pain.

Whitebeard paced to and fro, hands pressing his aching brow, struggling to gain access to an elusive memory that may reveal the mystery behind the winged wraiths they just battled. He kept reciting the few words that he knew that were keys to an important bit of knowledge: "... spewed from our mother's womb... shrouding all in shadow's hue..."

Whitebeard hastily searched through the alchemical tome for instances related to treating plague.

"Spewed from mother's womb," the boy said.

Ignoring the child, Whitebeard exclaimed, "At last!" Whitebeard had found the marginal notes. Prasus the Pict, friend and mentor to Whitebeard, had once narrated his nightmare while asleep, mumbling about a dissection theater and descending shadows borne on future winds. Prasus was a skilled alchemist who struggled to accept that the Picti deity was dead. In an experiment designed to resurrect his goddess, he killed his wife and went mad. Then his student, having heard his master repeat the mysterious verses over and over, decided to record the ranting:

> "Fathered by the He-wasp and
> By a Man who deceived,
> Mating the She-bird formerly free,
> The gallwraiths and chromantis now fly,
> Spewed from Her stone womb,
> Wings shrouding all in shadow's hue,
> Seeking, ever seeking, their mother
>
> Fevered with dyscrasia,
> The gallwraiths and chromantis now sail,
> O'er the Land that pitch bleeds,
> Feeding on color and beauty,
> Seeking comfort through consumption,
> Peace through melancholy,
> Seeking, ever seeking, their mother"

"Prasus was a prophet! Or, rather, the Pictish deity had not died, staying alive long enough to reveal eldritch secrets to its remaining worshippers." And so Whitebeard brooded on the symptoms the Legion had observed traversing the Land. The Land was leaking pools of black oil. And winged demons sailed the skies. They were not wyverns but the gallwraiths of Prasus' dreams. The 'chromantis' remained a mystery to Whitebeard, as did the identities of the parents, the one mother and two fathers.

"Chromantis," spoke Echo aloud, as if he recognized the name. And Whitebeard pondered about whether or not the boy was repeating spoken words or actually knew what it meant.

Whitebeard went to share his thoughts to Byrhan only to discover the Son shaking as he stared at the sky.

The sorcery that affected Kaiyn now affected his Son.

L YSIS REMAINED BOUND to a table of bone within Doctor Grave's Lair—the Dissection Theater. Fae and Grave were absent, having left to gather ingredients for a grand necromantic rite. They left him unattended, having faith in the sorcery that bound him. And their ethereal shackles held true.

Lysis lay atop the open clutch of the Avian King's claw. The rest of the King's skeleton supported the architecture of the Theater by framing the domed interior—wings outstretched to brace the ceiling; its canoe-like beak hovered over Endenken from the end of a craned neck. The monarch of Cypria's society was a colossal specimen—his days of ruling over the Avian Aerie had long since passed.

Red-capped orphans huddled between the seats of the Theater, hiding in the shadows of torchlight. Their parents, like hundreds of others, had been kidnapped and sacrificed. They sought refuge here, but they did not find warmth, love, or food. Desperate for clothing, they scavenged the Doctor's lair for apparel, finding only flayed skins and bloody aprons to dress their bodies and heads. Most observed with detached interest in Red Lysis.

However the amphitheater was populated with an audience that seemed to study Lysis: tens and tens of dress forms, lifeless and limbless simulacra of the Doctor, stared toward the claw with empty hoods and quilts of flayed flesh. This was Grave's Iron Horde: armatures and corpses propped and transfixed with iron stanchions, a sedentary carousel of skeletons raised upon plinths. These dissected bodies and art manikins conveyed anatomy to the students of the Cromlechon Guild of Barbers. Some forms were arranged as musicians strumming their dehydrated intestines as if they were harps; others blew through bone flutes. Some forms were inhuman, made from the iron carapaces of insectan elders of Sky and Land. Rarely was the intersection of art and alchemy so evident in such a confined space.

Sketch of Red Caps parading about the Theater

T HE SKY RUMBLED from all directions, as if it were a great hungry stomach. Byrhan had been hypnotized by a vision in the coming storm. Those who could see through his mind's eye would decipher the face of a butcher in the clouds, the

Additional gallwraiths attack

same who had once maimed him, stole his mother...

Whitebeard inspected Byrhan and ascertained that his head was swelling too much. Preparing to relieve the pressure on the skull, he laid the flaying knife and bloodletting trephine before him. He worried that this would be the first in a series of desperate treatments. He loathed the notion of killing the Son or his Lord out of mercy. *I cannot do this*, the Apothecary thought.

"I cannot do this?" Echo stood beside him. The child's eyes were radiant, like polished ebony.

"What? What did you say?"

Echo repeated the question. Whitebeard was confused. Had the child read his thoughts? Perhaps he mumbled them in a trance. He looked backed at the knife.

Again the child said, "I cannot do this..."

Whitebeard proceeded with letting the blood out of Byrhan's head. The circumference of the crucifix-shaped trephine was chipped by hasty bone cutting. Byrhan lay beside his Apothecary with a circular hole above his left ear that drained fluid; a poultice of yarrow covered the infection. Whitebeard had done his best to prolong the Son's life by releasing the pressure of the wound. The young child whom Byrhan had rescued now sat beside him, gently stroking his hair.

Eventually, a sanguine color seemed to return to the Son. His head was no longer swollen, and his fever had subsided. A wet cloth covered the one-armed Son's face to comfort him. But from beneath this, he could hear Lordson Taiyn conversing with Whitebeard.

Whitebeard reviewed, "Just hours ago, we experienced the most nightmarish of storms from which we have not recovered—a storm in which the wraiths preceded or were embroiled within. I shudder to think of what will come next. Our Legion may never make it to the Cromlechon."

Looking toward his brother and father, Taiyn asked, "How do they fare?"

"Their lives are sustained. But more dangers come at every minute, Lordson. The approaching storm downed your brother, and the wraiths shadow us like wolves."

Kaiyn moaned as if he were a participant in the conversation. He lacked in color more so than before.

"The gallwraiths are feeding on human souls!" cursed Whitebeard in frustration.

From his sickbed, Son Byrhan murmured, "The storm from the west... it brings the butcher that attacked mother... and the fog that he rides... They come to take us... The wraiths fear the storm, too..."

The Legion analyzed the looming western storm front. Even from afar, the cursed squall infected any who looked upon it—it was as if air-borne contagions were blown into the eyes of those who bore witness. Blue-eyed men now appeared gray-eyed. Many grew pale. Blonde soldiers seemed to don blanched wigs. Flies gathered fast on the dead, and orphans still roamed. Some crazed children had taken to cuddling with the dead.

A flicker of shadow drew Apothecary Whitebeard's attention eastward. "A wraith is approaching. Taiyn! It comes to strike your father!"

Echo quickly left Byrhan's side to stand beside Clanlord Kaiyn, as if to defend him.

A wraith dropped from the sky...

Whitebeard ducked prematurely as he hobbled toward his master, too scared to stand against the foe but too loyal to retreat.

With two flails poised to strike, Taiyn prepared to defend his father.

Then the gallwraith was upon them, feigning toward Kaiyn Tonn only to steer toward the child.

Byrhan arose abruptly, exhausting his reserve strength to remove Echo from the path of the swooping gallwraith!

Wind rushed overhead, a heavy tumbling gust, and a dousing liquid splayed the scene. Son Byrhan recovered, dropping the child and rushing to his father's side.

Lord Kaiyn was fine. But Taiyn was missing.

"Taiyn!" Byrhan shouted, his body feeling oddly wet. Warm liquid blurred his vision.

Apothecary Whitebeard stood opposite, blood-soaked.

"Son Byrhan! Silence," Whitebeard said.

"What? Where is he?" Byrhan's ears ached. His left ear was tacky with tar.

Splattered in wet crimson, Whitebeard pointed.

Two detached legs stood before the pair, spurting blood from the sinew that stretched between them.

The wraith was absent, ensorcelled in a torrent of wind that had arisen in the west. No sooner had it struck the Lordson than the assailing gallwraith was netted in electric magic and felled itself. The wraith's wings furled sizzling as it sank to the Land. The issuer of the sorcery that felled the beast now became center focus.

Byrhan's crippler, the butcher, was upon them, the meatless faces comprising his apron and mask screaming ethereal screams forewarning those before him, his right hand guiding the frosty reins of an icy gryphon, his left hand wielding an oversized cleaver hewing the few brave soldiers of the Legion who gave approach, his companion fog muddling the many soldiers who did not advance, his army of gangly larvalwyrmen writhing through holes in the Land, lashing about from arteries of melancholy, collecting the dead and living, both human and wraith, both child and solider, into cages of iron and onto pallets of bone.

Fae stowed all the bodies inside her massive cloud.

Whitebeard had yet to mentally digest the halving of Taiyn ere this greater horror embraced his attention. He found himself heaped atop the Son he adored and the Clanlord he served. Heroics were crushed under the tides of necromancy and the presence of death incarnate. In this way the Legion lost hope, for it had lost its women, lost a battle to a few wraiths, and lost again to a single necromancer.

Most fell unconscious as they were swept into the air by the living wind helmed by the great barber. Yet Whitebeard stayed awake, and he grew to shiver as the souls of the men he loved seemed to sprout spry legs, escape their corporeal bounds, and crawl like millipedes down his aching spine. He grew nauseous as the blood of those he loved combined with rivulets of defecation to wet his tongue. And still, he was not dead yet.

So Whitebeard observed from the sky that the phantom Doctor took them, ironically, to the Legion's destination, the Cromlechon. He thought, *We are merely ingredients for a grand concoction…*

Two score strong in members, the undead Guild of Barbers stooped about the iron cauldron for a final view of the buoyant skin that had sealed the pact between Ante Lysis's blood and the Queen's soul. The hide was heavily decorated with cartographic designs, textured with nodules of cruor in the place of mountainous terrain. The skin was stained in meticulous detail, indicating sites and landmarks of the Land; it was a dynamic map of the upper world.

Undead Ante stood amongst the guild members and his master, Doctor Grave. Tortured for decades, Ante's body was kept upright by a network of larvalwyrmen. His blood had scabbed on his exterior into a brittle, crustaceous armor. Ante's soul had degenerated beyond recognition, and his body merely obeyed the will of the wyrms that bound and secured his skeleton.

"It has been a long journey to get to this final stage, balancing the wills of elders and humans, sculpting and manipulating them like clay, tilting the imbalance of the dyscrasia! Fellow barbers, we prepare for the final operation! We will

Ante's animated, flayed corpse leers over a cauldron

heal the Queen!"

The barbers listened, cloaked in tarred aprons waxed to a fine gloss. They wielded surgical utensils: serrated amputation saws and mallets, sword-like needles and forks, twisted pincers, fine scissors, scalpels, whips of flensing wire, geared spreaders, and cleavers. Many wore ceremonial masks and helms of large animal skulls over their hoods, and through openings in these theatrical death heads they drooled smoke.

"Barbers, no longer will the Queen's body, the Forge, sit idly cold. Today we bring her soul back—we bring the Forge its fire! To be reborn, she will need her creative blood returned. Her exoskeleton and flesh will rejuvenate with the blood of humans and the offspring of Haemarr. The diseased gallwraiths will forfeit their flesh and bone.

"The Queen's exoskeletal bone remains, but is not fully intact. Her head and thorax require surgery, and there are many cracks in the shell of her abdomen that must be sealed. We can repair these with a slurry of gallwraith marrow. You must bleed the diseased wraiths dry of their ichor, since their dyscrasia would calcinate the Forge. Ignite the crematorium of the Iron Ossuary! Cleanse the wraiths after you bleed them! Mill the ashen remains to powder! Together, we will repair her shell!"

And two dozen barbers went to the crematorium as commanded.

Doctor Grave continued. "And blood! That which was tapped will be returned! Bleed the human army! Strain the bodies! Collect the blood within the abdomens of the elder Pots, and direct the parade down the Flue! We will swell her body!

"Barbers, go now and prepare the body, blood, and bone of our Queen!" From an adjacent bloodletting chamber a hundred meat hooks rattled in anticipation. The remaining twenty barbers took leave toward the insectan Pots. As all the barbers departed except Ante, the Doctor said to himself, *And I will prepare the carrier of Her soul!*

"Ante, now you too have a role in this!" And the scabbed meat puppet turned to receive its final orders.

G RAVE PRESIDED OVER the Dissection Theater while suspended in the open beak of the dead Avian King. His scepter *Ferrus Hewnmaw* was at his side, *Ferrus Eviscamir* before him pinning Endenken to the claw. Grave was the pillar between opposing motivations, one pushing him to resurrect the Queen's colony and the other to create one of his own.

The claw dais had as many uses as the Doctor had disciplines, and as such it adopted many identities over the years: a spiritualist's altar, an executioner's chopping block, a surgeon's operating table, and an artist's workbench. Now the King's sinister claw appeared a funeral bier—a hearth of shells, bones, and curdled blood around a limp figure enflamed in a red astral pyre. Endenken lay beneath Grave, sprawled in the palm-faced, open clutch of the King's left claw.

Flakes of white ash floated into the room through the apertured floor. These signaled the crematorium bellows were exhaling from the many strata of subterranean architecture beneath the Cromlechon Dissection Theater. Sailing with the ash, Nurse Fae circulated throughout the petrified eggs and nymphal sarcophagi that crenellated the amphitheater. The effluent of dissected bodies, rotting urchins, and evacuated specimens funneled down the very drains that allowed the ash to vent.

Doctor Grave held two heads upon his lap: first, the crystalline head of his daughter; second, the burnt head of her son. Hovering in his mandible roost, he spoke like a hawk to his vulnerable prey:

"Lord Endenken Lysis. On this day, ninety-three and two hundred years after the founding of the Cromlechon, the Guild of Barbers commands you to complete the Inheritance Rite of the Lysis Clan. Balance will be restored to the Land! The dyscrasia that has cursed us all will pass!"

The last Lord of Gravenstyne struggled to clear his thoughts and gather strength to retaliate, but he could not. The chains of phantoms and memories clouded his vision, and the whole world seemed to shake and turn.

"WE EACH HAVE a current directing our life. Mine flows toward my Queen," the Doctor said.

Grave clambered down from his throne and assessed his patient's confusion. "I explored a selfish pathway with Fae since we desired a colony to care for. We obtained Maeve this way, but her life ended tragically. My initial purpose has pulled me back, painfully, to my original destiny. No matter how long I delayed

Doctor Grave presides over his Theater

it, I had to sacrifice you, my sweet Maeve, to remain true to my Queen's call."

While nestled in the Doctor's left arm, Maeve's glassy head stared with an infinitely blank expression toward her husband.

She was my wife. My memories of her cling to me now. So you still play with her as if she were less than a daughter.

"I can *see* your thoughts, Lord of Gravenstyne. I loved her as genuinely as you loved your children. Your thoughts do not matter to me."

"If they do not matter, then why converse?"

"To convince you that you have no choice but to follow the legacy set by your forefathers. Deviate, if you will, but doing so will only bring a painful, temporary reprieve. Ante promised his bloodline to me. We share the same destiny

Lysis on Grave's operating table

now, and the astral current deems that you carry the Queen's soul!"

"Why do you not carry her?"

Doctor Grave sat next to Lysis. The barber carefully placed Maeve's head down between them, then he stroked the blade of *Ferrus Eviscamir* and removed his apron. So tied with spells and phantoms was he, Lysis could not rise!

"Sadly, I cannot. I lost that privilege when I negotiated with Haemarr to produce Maeve. Such is the cost of necromancy. We lose that which we most hold dear. I needed to find a new carrier for her. Ante offered his bloodline in return for mapping worlds otherwise unattainable. Now you will honor your family's promises."

"I serve myself, not my forefathers, not your Queen. I will extinguish this flame! And I will destroy you, Doctor, for I have always hunted demons..."

The Doctor laughed. "But a demon is what you have become!"

Lord Lysis studied the colossal scalpel, *Ferrus Eviscamir*, rising through his body.

Maeve's face looked morosely toward her husband. It offered no guidance being soulless.

"Her soul is absolutely gone, and that is my regret," Doctor Grave said to Lysis as he worked. "But I will honor her now. As I will honor her son, Dey, whom you killed with the very blade piercing your body. I will bring her to him again... then we have other matters of flesh to attend to... for I am to be complete in my redemption... We have to finish certain rites..."

"To think you removed her son's heart with *Ferrus Eviscamir*," continued Doctor Grave. "You two shared the same blood. Soon, you two will share skin." Doctor Grave stitched the flayed face of the burned boy into his apron.

"My mask and apron are composed of your ancestor's skin. I salvaged many hides after your failed Inheritance Rite. I even retrieved your discarded face from Haemarr's bogs! You do not recognize it, do you? No matter. Now the apron contains Dey's face, too, so I have fulfilled another promise. He played a crucial role in Haemarr's transcendence, and in preserving the Red Muse. His role has ended, but ours continue. The Forge still needs to be rekindled."

Endenken retorted, "Dey was a pawn following your lead!"

"What is wrong with being a devout follower? Is it not acceptable to be sad and alone, if you remain loyal and obedient?"

Grave cradled Maeve's head and rubbed melancholic oil over it while chanting in some insectan language. The wetted crystal began to soften and transmuted back into flesh. Bubbles expanded from the mouth and the skull coughed dry coughs and her tongue lapped for a drink.

"She is still dead. Her tongue moves only because the flesh is no longer confined to crystal form. It is merely uncoiling," the Doctor explained. "Maeve was not meant to remain with us. Had she lived, you and I would not be able to serve the Queen as we do now."

Lysis watched in disgust as Doctor Grave surgically removed the skin from her skull. It was a slow process, since the art of flaying was a fine craft. A dozen Red Caps gathered around to watch, as did the ghostly children of Maeve gather in astral form as if Maeve's face were to begin reading a bedtime story.

Doctor Grave donning his surgical gear

These visions weighed heavily on Endenken. So tired was he, he could not turn his head from this scene. He missed his children dearly. And his wife. But in reality he was alone now.

Maeve's beautiful face was stitched beside that of Endenken and Dey. Their smiles were muted, for stitches sealed them fast.

"Maeve was our pillar of strength," Dey's ghost spoke, anchored to his facial skin. "Now we are without her. Only her soulless memories are bound within these magical shackles. We are alone..."

You are not alone, said a voice within Endenken's frame. It was an unfamiliar voice, though distinctly feminine and insectan. Endenken envisaged a thousand legs crawling within him as the Red Fire tickled his skeleton. The Queen was speaking!

Suddenly, the Red flared brilliantly!

Doctor Grave was quick to douse the operating table with melancholic oil that soaked up the flames like a sponge. A sizzling reaction occurred, and a sweet smelling, acrid stench swirled into his frame.

A figure behind the Doctor approached slowly in the shadows, a curtain of sorts draped over its outstretched arms. The sparse lighting did little to reveal the identity of the shuffling figure, only that its skin appeared as cracked, smoldering coal in the astral realm.

With all his ingredients readied, the Doctor prepared himself to operate. He would be in close proximity to the Queen's soul, which would react with his earthy flesh. He a put on a protective mask, the insectan shell of an elder carcass, as if preparing to feed coal into a furnace.

"Those are mine!" the ghost of Lord Issynmerz spoke from the phantasm chains, taking particular interest in the contents of three urns. "He means to complete your Inheritance Rite. It was your duty to accept the Muse? You chose to save Maeve instead of finishing the Rite!"

Doctor Grave spoke. "Now we finish the Rite!"

Desiccated organs and rancid fat were molded into Lysis's frame.

"I will not accept their legacy. I make my own choices!" Endenken's declaration was weak, for he had little strength.

"You are the final carrier of the Queen's soul. You will bring it home to her body! The Forge that idles shall burn brilliant red again!"

I serve myself now, Lysis thought.

"You? *You* no longer exist. That is why you lie passive as I operate. You are merely an object now. The embodiment of your entire clan."

The shadowy figure hobbled closer, cradling the flexible material draped across its arms. Tendrils of fleshy roots wriggled from beneath it. That fabric was alive!

Grave said, "Your purpose is to carry the Queen's red soul back to the Forge."

"Never!" spat Lysis. The Doctor had schemed before Endenken was even born! At no point did he reveal that Maeve was his daughter! A golem! Lysis had been tricked into falling in love with Maeve, into accepting the *ignis fatuus* of

Ante Lysis offers his map of skin

Haemarr, into mutilating his children's corpses to gain entrance to the Forge.

"Enough! You serve only yourself, Grave. You tainted my four brothers. Your obsessions ruined Maeve, my children, and our home. I will not facilitate your deceptive plans!"

"Oh, but you are helping me! That is why you lie obediently now! Such is the way of legacy—the promises of your forefathers must be fulfilled despite your indifference!"

The spooky, shuffling man finally reached Doctor Grave's operating table. He was so disfigured, Lysis could not ascertain the being's identity by his physical features. However, from the aura about the S-shaped skin in its outstretched arms, Endenken determined that his ancestor Ante Lysis stood before him.

Doctor Grave declared to the Lysis, "Weighted with your guilt and memories, and shrouded in the skin of your ancestor Ante, who pledged his bloodline, you are mine to control!"

The Doctor applied the flesh, cauterizing the seams of leathery tissue. Endenken Lysis thus inherited the skin of his ancestors, including his long discarded face and that of his wife Maeve, the face of his nephew Dey, and the map of Ante.

ANTE'S SKIN SHROUDED Lysis like a coat of plate armor. Issynmerz's desiccated organs and tissues stuffed his ribcage.

Doctor Grave declared, "The Rite is complete!"

The change within Endenken was immediate. Tendrils of red snapped like whips across the Theater. Lysis watched the Red Fire seep out of his body and recalled how its Shades had ruined his own museum within Gravenstyne. As his trophies were possessed by the Red Shade long ago, similar flames now flowed from his ribcage toward the impaled manikins, the gored anatomical forms, the crucified skeletons, and pinned eldritch carapaces. The Red Fire sought to posses the Iron Horde.

Merge! the Queen whispered to Lysis from within him. *Merge with Doctor Grave!*

"But we have merged already. You want to merge with Grave?" Lysis said to the Queen's soul. "What happens if we contact your golem nurse?"

The magical shackles were becoming frayed. Doctor Grave began to peddle backwards toward a subterranean chamber.

Rise! Seize him! the Queen commanded. Endenken Lysis attempted to sit upright but was restricted by *Ferrus Eviscamir*.

Whereas his body was pinned down, his fire was free to roam. So Red Lysis struggled to free himself, his astral fire assuming images of Narl, Potter, Brood, and SanGules. Endenken's brother Brood possessed the molted frame of a nymph and the vacated head of an elder warrior Soldier bestowed with mammoth, curled tusks. He procured an iron stanchion by drawing it from a sheath that was a crippled manikin. Thus armed, he advanced toward the Doctor.

The ghost of the cannibal Narl rooted itself into the figure that had been playing its intestines as a harp. The visceral instrument was soon transformed into a bow. Hastily, Narl scoured the Theater for suitable arrows.

Endenken possessed the Horde. Decapitated, footless manikins ambulated awkwardly with iron stanchions transfixing their bodies.

To defeat Doctor Grave, Lysis would have to haunt the golem as he had been haunted! The memories that once bound his legs worked in synchronization with his mind now, and knuckles of fire clutched the blade of *Eviscamir*. The phantom chains, the memories, the flames—all became controllable. No longer

The Red Horde awakens

were they anchors, but appendages instead!

Ferrus Eviscamir was snagged abruptly out of Endenken's belly by a tongue of red flame! He stood from the operating table.

"I am a hunter!" Red Lysis shouted. Another tongue licked out and seized the Doctor's ankles. "You are my prey!"

The ghosts of Endenken and Maeve's children were reminded of chasing games of hide-and-seek, so they sang to cheer their father on:

"Ten 'n ten, come here my friend,
Ten 'n ten, this ends by ten!
Nine 'n nine, please be mine,
Nine 'n nine, all mine by nine!
Eight 'n eight, not too late,
Eight 'n eight, we'll embrace by eight!
Seven 'n seven, we're seeking heaven!
Six 'n six, one stinger's kiss!"

"You created me, Doctor," Red Lysis declared. "I am your art, your undoing!"

Endenken was not yet in complete control. Even now he was still distracted by the astral fire. Maeve's ghost covered her head and cried beneath SanGules, who screeched malevolent, incoherent rants through the device clogging his throat, and the Red Potter berated the ghost of Dey that clung to his ankles.

And Doctor Grave retreated into a dark apothecary adjoining his Theater, the wyrm-ridden, cruor-coated Ante hobbling behind at a slow pace...

A regiment of larvalwyrmen-possessed fossils poured into the Dissection Theater! Elder carcasses and ancient crustaceous demons, stripped of flesh and empowered by masses of white wyrms, met in combat with the Red Horde. So many there were, the Doctor was no longer visible as he made his escape.

Brood cudgeled three wyrms!

Luminous, burning arrows launched from Narl's intestinal bow and lodged into several larvalwyrmen!

Then the flaming Red Endenken gained upon the wyrm-infested Ante, who was too slow to keep pace with his master.

"You! You defiled the Lysis name! I own you now!" Red Lysis tossed the broken, scabbed Ante onto the Theater's prime table and extracted the larvalwyrmen from his body with a barber's sickle hook. Then he sent tendrils of his red flames into the body and commanded it to stand upright. "Welcome, Ante. Greet your fellow manikins! You are part of my Red Horde!"

Larvalwyrmen and enflamed manikins met in melee. The Land shook from this warfare—the King's mandible and left claw crumbled.

The Doctor's minions clambered over one another, their white tendrils knotted with Lysis's red tentacles of astral fire.

Then the battle subsided, and Lysis and his Red Horde were victorious! Yet the passage Doctor Grave retreated though was sealed with debris.

The pit whence the operating table once belonged was now a font of black oil, and embers of bone kindled near this aperture and conduits of offal drained. Though it was cold, the surface of the melancholic ichor bubbled like boiling stew, the gases venting from the Doctor's crematorium that networked with subterranean tunnels. Through this, Red Lysis crawled with *Ferrus Eviscamir* and the Red Horde followed.

Still the phantom children sang to inspire the hunt:

"Five 'n five, I've left my hive!
Four 'n four, alone no more!
Three 'n three, planting my seeds!
Two by two, my stinger tracks you!
One by one, beware! I come! I come!
Yes, I do! Better run!"

HUMANS FLAILED ABOUT the bog! The men of the Legion struggled. Having plummeted from their incarceration within the thick fog of Fae, they made sudden contact with the Land. Some fell into cushions of tar, landing face downwards so as to create molded, amorphous self-portraits. So immersed in black glue, they fought against the impressions of themselves and the pull of their protective armor that now aided in their drowning. Those managing to right themselves struggled to keep their faces aloft and never succeeded to fully peel their limbs from the elastic muck.

Of course, some that fell were lifeless prior to descending, for Nurse Fae had collected the dead as well as the living. Doctor Grave's grimoire required human blood—the condition of the bodies that sourced it mattered not.

Many more found themselves crashing into patches of stone and died instantly, their bodies cracking open as would ripe fruit. Others of the Legion were impaled by the same fixtures that transfixed the women that forested the Bog.

Long bled and dead, this audience stared at their dying husbands and sons. The Doctor had placed these sacrifices strategically so that from the sky they spelled messages to Cypria, declaring Haemarr's attraction to her. Even now, the statu-esque Haemarr appeared to survey the Bog through his wasp eyes, though in truth the elder was utterly dead now. The Son raised his broken, blind father with his remaining arm. Byrhan was nauseous from methane and sulfide fumes, and his head wound still leaked black liquid. Beside him were his master's advisor and the child he had rescued in Qualenson's territory. They had fallen into a cesspool of rainwater.

All were pale from some disease that robbed everything of color: skin, clothes, armor, and hair. Apothecary Whitebeard surveyed the landscape that was something between a mass grave and a cemetery: ... *the Land that pitch bleeds, feeding on color and beauty, seeking comfort through consumption, peace through melancholy, seeking, ever seeking, their mother...*

"Seeking their mother," Echo said, pointing toward a suspended female corpse. Her face appeared as a leathery mask now—her hollow sockets and gaping mouth formed a vacuum of despair.

Whitebeard had initially thought the poem referred to wraiths seeking their mother, but the gallwraiths' bodies were not in the Bog. The barber must have taken the winged demons elsewhere. Whitebeard examined the boy. He yet clutched the wraith embryo. Echo's eyes were emblazoned with a hazy halo of transparent cobalt.

"Taiyn, my proud son," spoke Clanlord Kaiyn, "where is your brother?"

Byrhan saw no need to confuse his dying, blinded father by correcting his identity. For then, he may have to explain that Taiyn was dead. He chose to lie. "Byrhan has departed on a mission. Sire, we have made it to the Cromlechon."

"Our women! We must free them!" the Clanlord commanded.

Whitebeard and Byrhan exchanged a glance. The constant keening of death throes was not heard by Kaiyn. Nor did the Clanlord seem to sense the mounting, ominous threat occurring just a few hundred yards away. Luminous nectarine-colored ashes spat furiously from a whirling vortex within the Bog—a drain to some greater hell. These men were knowledgeable about fire and could discriminate between the scents of a crematorium and a forge. The entrance was like a great mouth, exhaling fumes as it drank from the Bog.

Against the descending currents, colossal insects crawled forth with dark-cloaked minions and red-capped children riding tandem.

The cloaked men resembled the barber of the fog, and they poked and prodded the wetland with lengthy halberds as if fishing a streambed. Many

Barbers mounted on elder Pots harvest blood from the Bog

appeared to be ferrymen. Several had flails with wiry barbs that shredded armor and flensed the skin of those that were mired. These riders were freeing blood so that their mounts could harvest it; the insectan Pots imbibed the soiled blood enough to swell their abdomens into great balloons.

As the Pots neared the Son of Kaiyn, it became clear that the great insects were merely eldritch husks, emptied of their original flesh and stuffed with wyrms. Their riders plucked the skin off of his men with hooked spears and directed the flow of blood toward the Flue. Like lumbermen guiding logs down the stream, the barbers worked their cant hooks and tridents with practiced skill. The Pots eagerly lapped up the red currents to engorge their stomachs. The Flue burped out tar as blood funneled inwards, the scarlet cream decanting into the throat, gliding over coats of melancholic oil.

Whitebeard ascertained the recipe of the Legion's doom: the barber was collecting their blood.

The distraught Clanlord said, "We must find Aleece."

Echo returned, "Aleece," pointing again to the same corpse as before.

"Believe him, Son Bran! The boy is a seer," Whitebeard whispered. "He reads our souls like open books. We must trust him. Go to that corpse, and do it quickly, for we have but moments before the wyrm-ridden insects encircle us."

Echo had not the leverage to move his feet fast enough, so Byrhan offered, "Climb upon my back, boy. Now, lead the way."

They could not deny the truth for long. Until then, Byrhan entertained many outlandish possibilities. Perhaps this woman was not Aleece. Perhaps she was elsewhere. Perhaps the last several hours were just fantasy. Traumatic events were occurring too frequently to cope with rationally. The four went forward, trudging in bloody oil, atop corpses of friends, marching ever closer to the one Echo claimed was their Lady.

Byrhan collapsed onto his knees, drawn not by the weight of his father or the child on his back, but by the pull of his soul accepting the truth. The anchor of reality was too heavy to carry. *Mother, I failed to protect you. Brother Taiyn is gone. Father is going.*

Echo urged Byrhan forward.

They reached the gored corpse. It was indeed Aleece! Granted, her face was sunken and hollow. Her body was drained of blood. Her flesh was pierced by burrowing insects, which had since vacated her. The telltale evidence was not her distorted carcass. It was the detached left arm that cradled and wrapped her waist. Byrhan saw this and sank into a world of nightmares, back to when the magical mist infiltrated his family's manor, when the barber initiated a tug-of-war in which Lady Aleece was the article of contention, and when he began to lose his grip, lunging to hug her with all his might such that the barber would was forced to drop Aleece or cut her free from her Son...

Echo dismounted. Taking Kaiyn Tonn's limp hand, the gray boy led him closer toward Aleece. Byrhan was silent, still whelmed with grief.   E c h o spoke directly to the blind Clanlord. "She signals you to come closer. Comfort her, for she missed you terribly and begs you to rest within her arms..."

Kaiyn's eyes tossed loosely in their sockets, supported by his own happy grin. "Aleece! You live!"

Echo said, "You live!"

Byrhan, his head bowed in grief, said, "Yes, father. She lives."

"My Lordson! Taiyn! Come closer!" The Clanlord cried gaily. He looked awkwardly away from his audience, his head cocked toward the sky. Byrhan crawled forward and held his father's feet to signal his arrival.

"Lordson," continued Kaiyn, "you are first born. I am most proud of you. You have all the hallmarks of a great leader. You may surpass me even in endurance and courage!" He coughed a laugh that splattered blood onto his sleeve. He slapped Byrhan's arm then. "You, Lordson Taiyn, are best fit to be king now. I am too weak to take the Legion home. I must pass the duties of Clanlord over now. I feel weary... I bid you take haste and accept an oath to the charge I offer."

"I, Lordson Taiyn, firstborn of Aleece and Kaiyn, accept my family's charge and sovereignty. I bid you peace, Lord my father."

With that Kaiyn fell silent.

Byrhan thought, *How may I face the powers of sorcery? Crippled, the absence of my arm publicly declares my weakness. How am I to lead men?*

"I am proud of you," Echo said, reflecting Aleece's thoughts aloud for they certainly were not the words of a child. "I know you stood up bravely, and I love you beyond measure. Have heart in your own strength and accept others' faith in it. Real leaders need not head an army, or speak eloquently, or receive recognition. Heroes must only act to ensure that justice prevails and honor is maintained. Do not be saddened by the sight of your severed arm. It communicates your loyalty and resolve. It should be a source of strength. Take it and use it as a weapon against the barber."

As Echo dictated the thoughts of the Lady's ghost, his subject lost color. Aleece's leathery flesh transformed. Her beauty was maintained, even enhanced, as her displayed corpse assumed the likes of a statue instead of a mummy. Echo changed, too. His thin skin began to molt, revealing an undercoat of glossy skin, and his eyes became glassy—at once opaque and illuminating.

"The boy is a seer," said Whitebeard. "He is, I deem, Prasus' chromantis. He too has lost a mother. He is mutant, and so had multiple fathers. One of which was human and the other the owner of this swamp. He was..."

Bran interjected, "What do you mean?"

"... fathered by the He-wasp and by a man who deceived," Echo finished.

Whitebeard spoke to Lord Byrhan, "The boy may be able to help you defeat the barber. The Picts prophesized these events. The coming of the wraiths. This boy. They often spoke of a mysterious forge in the Underworld. The barber must be using it. You must disable it!"

Byrhan said to the old man, "Then I will go where the blood goes now. The damn barber means to work some accursed sorcery. I will disrupt his plans! It is time to cauterize the wound."

"But your arm does not bleed...."

"Aye, but the Land does! Reher, come here." The Bog was composed largely of flammable elements; the oil that floated atop the poisonous waters would indeed burn.

Reher Tonn from the house of Grovel Tonn, standard bearer of the Legion, answered his liege Lord. The shaft of the standard had been broken, and Reher held aloft the tattered flag so it flapped erratically in the hellish winds encircling the blood bog.

"Pass over the standard so that I may make repairs," Lord Byrhan said.

Reher did so, as Byrhan retrieved his left arm from about Aleece's waist. He wrapped the standard about the loosed arm, and then he used the Apothecary's flintstone to light it.

Bran returned the incendiary torch to Reher.

"Men, we head to the origin of the insect cavalry. You must allow me and the boy to enter the abyss. Soldiers, form a wall! Come! We march toward the pit!"

Several dozen answered the Lord's call. They huddled about their Lord, his advisor, and one child, wading as one, a jammed cluster of grapes.

Lord Byrhan declared, "Reher, on your mark!"

The resolute standard bearer darted toward the hole, shouting, "For Aleece!" the burning arm of his Lord borne proudly above his head. It trailed thick white smoke, flapping and unfurling as would a cloth banner.

The Legion followed this luminous beacon passionately but as an encumbered stampede. People churned atop one another, eager to feed themselves to their enemy's spear tips. Every buried halberd was one less that could target their Lord.

Like ragdolls they met the barbers and insectan Pots. Men were pin-cushioned by harpoons and halberds! The few knights who landed an attack with their swords were disappointed since the insectan shells were impregnable to steel.

"For Lady Aleece!"

The mouth of the Flue yawned opened before Bran and Echo. A gaping web of pitch netted across the stygian hole. Looking down, Bran saw eldritch Pots hanging like malignant polyps along the interior.

Whitebeard yelled, "Reher! They have made it. Ignite the pitch!" The Apothecary's final words rang as Bran and Echo plunged into the whirlpool descending into the Flue. There was a delay before ignition, then the pitch flared, and the hundreds of stanchions became fire spits, roasting to cinders and immolating men and elders equally.

Clouds of charnel smoke coughed forth to blind those with human sight. In an instant, Echo and Bran were enveloped by it! Stumbling awkwardly, they followed the flickering ash toward their certain doom. Echo had a sense of things unseen, and he tugged Bran forward.

As the pair descended, a magnificent plume consumed the sky above them, pushing them with its ferocious heat as assuredly as the plunging currents dragged them into the earth. The sky vibrated with heavenly hues: brilliant flashes, the color of gleaming, glossy orange rinds; spitting sparks of lemon yellow; flame tongues, magnesium white; tangerine blooms; feathery clouds bruised violet plum...

In his peripheral vision, Byrhan saw the fire approach! He swam embracing Echo, toppled within eddies of offal while streaks of crimson blood slowed their plummet. Being immersed muffled the many cries of the Legion. Fresh embers illuminated the cascading stew of death, and then the pair descended so precipitously they no longer swam but fell airborne...

RED LYSIS DESCENDED into the chamber beneath the Theater. Magic flames cushioned his fall.

From the underside of the Theater, blood dripped and debris fell. A hasty survey revealed that this chamber was some sort of subterranean tomb. A nursery. Whereas the left claw of the Avian King remained above, its companion appendage had been directed through the floor. From this mangled set of talons depended a score of chain coils; each in turn supported, and balanced, as many iron beams. Decorations, such as rattles, baubles, and lodestones, adorned either end of these rods; they rotated at the gimbaled joints to the tune of an invisible, haunting song.

The grand mobile had been designed to entertain nearly a dozen golem babes. Beneath this, cradles doubled as caskets—in all but one was interred a decapitated clay figure. They were, without doubt, golems. Or, so they were to be. Nurse Fae and Doctor Grave had born only Maeve, and her predecessors contributed their heads to enable the Forge to be worked for her sake.

He went to observe the stillborn manikins. Lysis resurrected these fallen decapitated golems into his Red Horde! They stumbled blindly, but burning with Red Fire they joined the ranks of transfixed skeletons and armatures from the Theater.

"... they had children on which to prey..." the oft sung lyrics of the Doctor's favorite nursery rhyme echoed in the astral plane.

Impaled manikins and the raised dead of the Red Horde scrambled like roaches searching for exits and clues of the Doctor's route of escape. They found the chamber's proper exit, one that was absolutely dark except for the sparkling, flying cinders that departed the tunnel like enslaved lightning bugs.

A crematorium lay beyond. The shaft gurgled with incongruous sounds, as if it choked on the blood of a thousand men.

Red Lysis directed his Horde toward this with an outstretched arm, but their progress was interrupted.

The infantile orrery convulsed suddenly, its gimbals squealing as a gust of wind permeated the device!

It was Fae, come to protect her defiled nursery.

Fog grew thick about the domed chamber, pooling from the subterranean shaft, seizing the grand mobile and tearing it free from the King's talon. The iron beams rained down on the exit to bar the Red Horde's procession. Baubles of polished hematite and magnetite were thrown asunder!

Misty wings spanned thirty yards and an angry beak formed from the center cloud. A beautiful face crystallized that bore a remarkable likeness to Maeve.

The Queen spoke telepathically: *It is I, the Queen. Fae, why are you not tending Cypria's litter? They are kin to your own. You were to care for the King's eggs and fledglings! You failed him as Doctor Grave failed me!*

Red flames shot toward the misty gryphon like meteors, melting any form Nurse Fae may have taken. At each contact, crystallites formed and fell as heavy icicles.

Lysis was poised for battle. He had seen that crystal before. At Gravenstyne. Maeve had been so tempered; her soul separated from her body to blend with the melancholic, dyscrasia-ridden sea within the Underworld. Flesh could be transmuted into crystal, but the mixing of blood and ichor to achieve this was a necromantic art. The mixing of the Queen's aura and Fae's form was irreversible.

Nurse Fae writhed on the ground, her wings too heavy to lift her, each feather solidifying as it reacted. Her movements grew ever more mechanical, as the mixing of astral fire and mystical breath froze into a statuesque glacier.

Die! Join now your children!

Then the Queen's soul took control of Fae's decapitated stillborn, the newly inducted members of the Red Horde. The golem babes answered her command with a desperate hunger. They advanced on their translucent mother, sacrificing their faux lives as they nuzzled her. Nestled with her. Suckled her teats with their severed necks, transforming her to crystal as they scratched her fragile skin. When it was over, the headless clay children rejoined the Red Horde.

Fae was frozen solid.

Her resemblance to Maeve was undeniable. She was indeed her mother.

The Queen's soul within Lysis forced him to raise *Eviscamir*, preparing to shatter the crystal gryphon. But his arm ceased on high. The Red Fire focused on Grave's wife with disdain; Lysis, however, stared at Maeve's mother with pity. As he looked, his undead sight revealed a faint string of ghostly fairies dancing in the ether, and upon inspection it was clear that it was the memory of a single girl, skipping by herself and clutching hands with a doll, donning a red cap, pretending she ran with the boys in the orchards of Gravenstyne, and she had such a pretty face, one that mirrored the face of Maeve...

"I spare you!"

Smash her!

"Nay," Lysis said, controlling the Fire. "I spare her." In doing so, he was sparing his wife. Forgiving her deception.

Fae's beak offered up a final gasp. The breaths of countless humans, that had sustained her over centuries, were finally released. Vaporous phantoms emerged to remove the debris from the primary exit. Then the ghosts dissipated, as if inhaled by the corridor itself.

"It's a trap!" Dey's ghost warned Red Lysis. "The Queen and Fae work together! Grave and she lead you toward the Forge! Beware!"

The Queen interjected, *Fool! Enter the Flue! Find Doctor Grave. Kill him!*

"She is sincere! She wants him dead, too!" shouted one of Endenken's haunts.

"She serves the Doctor's plans!" Dey's ghost exclaimed.

The Red Queen then enveloped the visage of Dey and quelled his voice. Lysis entered the tunnel regardless of the antics of the spirits within him.

RED Lysis DESCENDED further. The corridor had carried him to a spiraling path that wrapped the exterior walls of the Flue. He recalled journeying the network as Haemarr's avatar.

Now he could feel the vibrations of a bloody waterfall funnel downward on the opposite side of the mortar. Through cracks he saw cinders rise and descend tumultuously as gravity and air currents manipulated their flight.

He read the walls to understand the history embedded therein—to learn more of his enemy's past. Avian elders were turned to stone within the vent as they wrestled with their insectan cousins. They had sought refuge from the chaos in the Sky following their King's ill decline, hoping the eldritch Queen was still healthy. Contagious, the avian elders descended, working against the venting fumes. The Flue may have facilitated the avian elders to penetrate the Underworld, but it was not designed as a gateway. It was made to exhaust something—but what?

My colony. Our food. All were corrupted. The doctors and nurses tried to cleanse the colony by burning the tainted, the Queen answered him. *The Flue was a network of shafts leading to and from the crematorium, allowing air into fuel the furnaces and smoke out.*

The staircase was in ruin, and often congested with earth. So they crawled over these obstructions. Under the Cromlechon, under the Theater, under the stillborn nursery, beside the porous Flue, under all this earth, Red Lysis went. At times he relied on his Horde to form composite structures, knotted aggregates of iron spears and bodies, in order for him to bridge treacherous chasms or scale crags. Many manikins were sacrificed in this way.

Soon Lysis came upon a vast cavity half-filled with ash that could contain all of Gravenstyne! Larvalwyrmen writhed therein, fragments of iron shell and antennae broke the surface. Air circulated with ferocity from the Flue's colossal drains, blowing across the surface to create whirlwinds. Sparkling cinders danced about to illuminate the way, but Lysis relied mostly on his undead sight to survey the horror, for the scintillating sea before him glowed an eerie white within the astral realm.

Those sick were eliminated, the Queen explained. *They were burned as I should have been!*

On the opposite shore, hooded barbers worked the bellows of the Iron Ossuary.

Endenken and his Horde dove in and swam through the fluid ash toward the bellows. Wading through the powdered remains of insectan carcasses seemed to pain the Queen's soul.

Ripples on the surface of the charnel sea alerted Red Lysis of larvalwyrmen. The Horde was still scores strong, though every hundred yards a member would be suddenly drug beneath the surface, a larvalwyrmen tentacle having found purchase.

"Horde, form a line. Chain together. We unite now to snake our way 'cross this cemetery!" Every instance the long red line would pinch, bend, or sink, Endenken immediately dove under the surface and severed the wyrm snares with *Eviscamir!*

T HE RED HORDE arrived at the opposite shore of the scorched granary. The noxious smell of smoke, sulfide, and burning bone would have poisoned any living presence; however, all who worked the ovens were undead.

Beside the cyclopean bellows, through fractures in the ruined igneous blocks, Lysis spied the inner chambers of the crematorium: arcades upon arcades of furnaces honeycombed the interior, each niche housing an oven. Barbers wearing protective insectan armor worked porphyry crucibles with forceps and tongs. Some dismembered carcasses atop curvaceous anvils. Others stirred the contents of the oven cauldrons. Many ancient bodies were suspended from meat hooks— long lines of diseased nymphs waiting for their final cleansing: anthropomorphic nymphs, bled dry of their black melancholy; desiccated humans once destined to fill the Queen's granary.

My colony stored our food here. We ate those sacrificed to us. We had to cook our stores of food to try to kill the disease. The doctors cleansed food and nymph alike.

Presently, barbers burned the osier-wrapped gallwraiths, many of which had been born dead and were collected by Nurse Fae from the Gallwomb; others had been retrieved by the Doctor. The barbers prodded the ash with pitchforks and used baker's peels to retrieve the wraiths from the ovens. These remains they passed to the cauldrons to enable the manufacture of size, a glue substance made from ash and iron chitin.

Larvalwyrmen-animated Pots crawled past the charnel sea only to descend deeper into the Underworld.

"The barbers prepare ingredients for Doctor Grave's necromancy. My Red Horde, we descend further! We will strike him down before he begins his spell. Follow the eldritch Pots!"

So THEY CAME upon the Queen's own nursery. Exoskeletons, arthropodal molts, decorated the chamber, many sprouting forth pyritic crystals from the iron stakes.

Doctor Grave waited for them! His head was dressed in a death mask that was once the head of an older pupa.

Lysis drew *Eviscamir* to combat this effigy, only to slice empty space. The image was a mere memory! It dissipated once struck.

These haunting memories revealed that Doctor Grave once entertained the Queen's young by performing plays, dressed in costumes of excised skins– parodying his future self as a barber dressed in the skins of humans.

Once he attempted to gain affection from me so dressed! I refused him, and sent him back to nurse! He was always dressing up in the skin of others!

"But when did dyscrasia germinate?" Lysis asked the Queen's soul. She did not answer, mute as she observed bitterly the sight of the ruined nursery. Here, these eggs were black-veined igneous rock. These were her nymphs and pupae infected with the plague, her brood that died prematurely.

"Spoiled!" Red Lysis declared aloud as he read the ethereal history.

When diseased eggs had become more abundant than healthy ones, Grave evolved from doctor to executioner. His duty was to care for the young, even if that meant killing the diseased. So the crematorium and Flue had been constructed beside the nursery, and Grave worked them more and more as he worked the nursery less and less.

Dyscrasia poisoned my eggs!

"And what was the source?"

Humans drew upon my energy when they crafted art. It is why, even after our demise, the Picts worshipped me. My soul was their Muse, their source of creativity. But the humans drained it, just as your ancestors taxed the King to death.

Lysis returned to reading the auras. He saw the dyscrasia-ridden avian elders breach the subterranean colony! Desperate, they had come rushing down the Flue. The ceiling had crumbled all about, sending plumes of dirt onto the eggs and pupae! Doctor Grave had stood and fretted, while his defined world came crushing down around him and the other golems were sacrificing themselves to secure the Flue's integrity. He tried to assess which was the best single egg or nymph to rescue. None were in well condition, all being ill. Few were born of normal frame, so many had become infected with disease. Malleable by nature, the nymphs' bodies mutated as they molted. Many were born resembling mythical creatures with multiple heads and adjoined abdomens, exhibiting hints of some distant or future communion between the human and elder kind. The Doctor had routinely killed many out of mercy, so grotesque the newborns were. It was the right thing to do, of course, since the mutilated and deformed had no way to sustain their lives or contribute to the colony.

The Queen had screamed out of sight, but his duty was to administer to the nymphs, not her. Conflicted, the Doctor had left the nursery briefly to attend to her, but she was deathly wounded when he found her. Her body beyond repair, Doctor Grave infused her soul into *Ferrus Eviscamir*. Since the entire nursery was corrupted, he decided then to cut open her abdomen and retrieve an unfertilized egg, one destined to be male… Haemarr…

"So Haemarr was last of your brood! But he was diseased, too!" Lysis understood. There was no hope for the elders.

Doctor Grave would have preferred to have an additional nymph, a mate

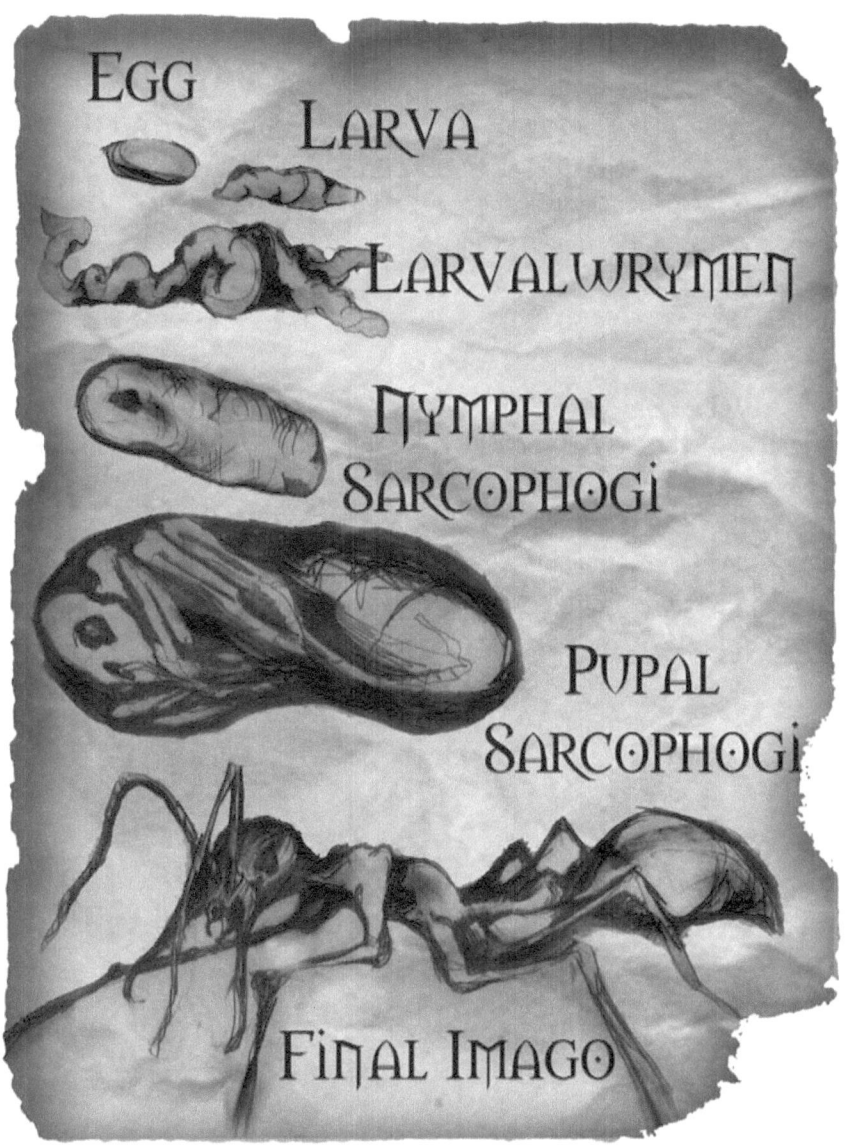

Sketch of the insectan elder's life cycle

for Haemarr, but returning to the nursery was not possible. He did not try to bring females since his fellow golems tended to that cause. Stones crushed them as the Land's infrastructure shook with the psychic shockwaves of the Queen's demise! Grave scrambled up the Flue diligently and swore an oath then to his Queen's corpse and the Land.

The walls repeated this now: *Queen, I will heal you!* Red Lysis heard this promise since it echoed continuously here, emanating from the earth that had absorbed it.

Then Red Lysis thought how tragic it would be to be forced to kill one's young. Even now, he held Doctor Grave's merciful weapon, and before him he saw many other of Grave's utensils for caring and killing mutated nymphs, scalpels to aid the removal of eggshells and tubular knives to dispense mercy kills. So Red Lysis was reminded of how he had to kill Erolen out of mercy.

"The diseased children you had murdered—I shall give them life! I will right your wrongs! I will raise the dead! They are mine now. The abandoned join my red ranks! Reinforce my Horde!" Hence, Red Lysis recruited the dead egg-born, nymphs and the dehydrated, serpentine husks of larvalwyrmen that cradled the brood. Lysis resurrected these fallen by infusing them with his fire!

Respect my children! Let them rest!

"I will give them life, where you gave them death. Soon we will see who commands the Forge. Now, my Red Horde, we too shall dress as the Doctor did! Don now the discarded husks of the insectan nymphs! Molts and pupae skulls will mask our heads! Disguised, we continue our hunt!"

SPAT FROM THE Flue and into the Queen's egg chamber, the sundered Legion approached the Underworld Forge as one with the undulating river of liquid flesh and blood. Gored torsos carried by dark liquid cascaded forth. Elder Pots singed by fire crawled downwards, their bellies filled with human blood.

This river flooded upon the open tar plane, enveloping the statues of eldritch beasts that stood petrified. The area appeared to be a forest of submerged bones and protruding iron spars; the dead seemed to be forever posed in a graceless dance, the ancient skeletons embracing the rigor mortis initiated by the mixing of incompatible ichor.

Red Lysis and his Horde exited the nursery to wade through the pool of death encompassing the central Forge. As they proceeded, Lysis reanimated every carcass he could to swell his ranks.

Then he saw the Underworld Forge floating like an island in the center of the melancholic lake.

Doctor Grave stood atop it.

"You failed us!" the Red Horde called out to Doctor Grave disguised as his deceased nursery.

The golem was taken aback as he observed his long dead nymphs come arisen–enflamed with Red Fire!

An epic battle ensued with manikins and fossils combating the barbers, Red Caps, and larvalwyrmen! There was much gnashing of mandibles, vicious clicking of chitin, and thrusting of antennae!

Hunt him down, the Queen urged.

Dey warned, "It appears a trap! Grave wants you to approach him! So

Mutilated humans descend into the Underworld via the Flue, a the river of blood being sucked into the earth

close to the Forge, you will be pushed in."

Suddenly, before the base of the immense Forge, a one-armed man arrived out of the darkness, weighed down with strands of heavy pitch, swinging a
white flail at the Doctor. Grave parried the berserker's blows, surprised that such
a hero had penetrated his ranks. The Doctor did not notice the little gray boy with
insectan features nearby...

For those that could *see* in the dark, they beheld the boy as a sparkling
Gray Fire!

Lysis was uncharacteristically unable to act. He stood passivated by some
spell, wading impotent in melancholy. Was it Grave's sorcery or something else?

"My son!" Dey's ghost called out to Lysis. "That boy is the last of the
Lysis clan! Endenken, look on! The boy was born from me and Cypria! Haemarr
and her seed formed the gallwraiths! But her womb contained my human seed,
too! It must have germinated that boy! He is the sickest of all those tainted with
dyscrasia, consuming color, turning living things into gray ash, stealing beauty..."

*He is of the chromantis ilk! He will consume my soul and leave you powerless!
Go near him now, I'll extinguish, and you'll not be able to battle Grave! Even now, his
presence weakens me.*

Confused, Lysis calculated his possible fates. He was weighed down by
various souls and memories! The gray child's skin began to flake off. Lord Lysis
was drained by him even from afar. Near the gray boy, the human continued to
swing his white flail to defend the child that was not even his.

"Lady Aleece!" cried the man.

Byrhan's remaining arm was cleaved as the Doctor welcomed him to the
Underworld. It was only seconds later the Legion formally ended in its entirety,
as *Hewnmaw* lashed his legs off and he fell to drown in the mystical wetlands of
melancholy.

He fought a futile battle! Lysis observed. *To defend a boy not of his own blood!*
Hence Byrhan had inspired his singular audience, though he did not know it, for
he was in complete darkness and his head wound had been leaking blood—he
was due to expire in mere moments even if Doctor Grave had not cut him down.
Byrhan's destiny was limited to transporting the boy here, which itself was a
miraculous task. Working the Forge was left for Echo...

"I am called to action!" declared Lysis. He had wanted nothing but the
ability of his lineage to blossom and be free, but his children and family were dead
now—except for one. Lord Endenken Lysis, shackled with the souls and body
of his forefather Ante and Father Issynmerz, heard the child call out through the

ether. Immediately, Lysis moved to protect Dey's child.

Doctor Grave noticed this connection and advanced to kill the gray boy with *Ferrus Hewnmaw*!

Lysis was too far away, so he called upon his Horde to intercede.   Then Red Narl, with his phantasmal, cleft jaws, possessed a manikin and loosed arrows with bone shafts into the barber. This distracted the golem!

Then Lysis was upon the Doctor, *Eviscamir* blocking *Hewnmaw's* blade! Electricity arced from the union! Opposing goals met in conflict.

Lysis came near the strange child.   Echo scrambled in sticky tar; he reached and found Endenken's leg. Instantly the red flame turned gray, for the child was made from both human and elder races and was the quintessential force of dyscrasia! His blood and aura were the ultimate balance of energy. Red and blue varieties of ichor submitted their color to the gray fire.

He consumes me! the Queen yelled. Despite the Queen's warnings, the boy's grasp did not extinguish the red flames as much as it drained them of hue. So the boy unintentionally slowed Lysis who fought to save him.

His Red Fire losing its strength, Endenken was too tired to advance. Lysis resorted to manipulating the astral energies again, and searched for Grave's signature traces. He discovered the Doctor's children singing a nursery rhyme from their suspended, decapitated heads — the golem's entrance to the Forge.

Endenken telepathically manipulated the decapitated golem babes of his Red Horde to approach and blindly grope for their missing skulls.

Doctor Grave was surrounded by eleven flailing figures.

Lysis declared, "You failed them! Your daughter will not forgive you, and your queen resents you! Fae's soul looks for you now in your nursery! She fell to your Queen's jealousy!"

Fear your Queen, Lysis communicated in Fae's voice through the ether. *She harbors resentment for you abandoning her! For loving me! She had you kill them!*

Grave backed away…

As the generals fought, the warriors of the Red Horde and Guild of Barbers were embroiled in combat! Art manikins and skeletons of the Cromlechon Theater, along with the stillborn nymphs of the Queen, fought Grave's minions: larvalwyrmen, reanimated elder ants, and the barbers. Atop the petrified statues of harpies and colossal ants they fought. Many iron stanchions were used as lances. Those impaled ages ago were impaled again!

"Doctor! You did not shackle me with my memories! You equipped me with them! Brothers that I have slain, we are one now! We are merged. We carry the Red Fire together!"

Sparks spewed from the fatigued Lysis, scuttled about the surface of the black lake toward Doctor Grave, spiraled about him, coalesced into a ring, and erupted into a grand firewall! Hence red ghosts formed a concentric firehenge about their enemy.

He relied on his external Red Fire more and more as the boy negated the powers inside his body. Since he could not turn the boy away, he resorted to working through his minions.

Becoming weaker and grayer, Lysis began to lose control over some of his shades. For instance, the Red Potter proceeded uncontrollably—attempting to mold the clay heads of the Doctor's stillborn into pottery, lapping their sundered heads with an ethereal tongue. Then it possessed a mouthless manikin, lay on the ground, and tried to imbibe the blood dripping from a transfixed corpse.

Meanwhile, deranged Red Caps, delirious from noxious subterranean fumes, massed around the mercenary Brood as he juggled iron rods as if they were javelins, twirling and impaling barbers and foe.

Elder insects crawled on the cavern's ceiling, the larvalwyrmen animating them dangling from all orifices! These engaged in aerial combat with the winged, diseased siblings of Haemarr, the sick nymphs that the Doctor had killed out of mercy in his nursery. Lysis had given their corpses life to march on their killer, the nurse that was supposed to nurture them. These mythical creatures came forth appearing like mutant centaurs, with human torsos atop the thoraxes and abdomens of the elder Soldiers.

The earth undulated as larvalwyrmen writhed like kraken and wrapped their bodies about the Red Horde! Three hundred wiggling, invertebrate fingers groped, reaching for anything red.

The Red Fire was tenacious, leaping from corpse to corpse, and burrowing underground. Wherever there was human blood, whether it leaked from the hollow Pots or streamed atop the tar lake, the Red Fire traveled. Anything that leeched astral fuel ignited into sheets of fire, and the ghosts of Endenken's past swam within. The Drunk Potter, having become a vampire in his diseased age, flitted from blood source to blood source, drinking and swelling his flames to become a tidal wave of phantasmal heat.

Larvalwyrmen controlling the tusked ants of the Queen's soldier caste fought to control the fire. A Soldier gored the manikin in which Brood's ghost resided, and as the manikin collapsed in ruin, the red flame departed, only to erupt on the opposite side of the creature! Brood's fluid form possessed now a discarded molt, rose fast to unsheathe an iron spear from the amalgam of death, and

Four brothers fight for Red Lysis

stabbed the elder. The iron shaft breached a hole in the mystical chitin and pinned a larvalwyrmen into its armor. A Red Cap, blind in the dark, left the saddle of the Pot to cling to the molted skin that was, for the moment, Brood. So desperate was this boy to survive, he closed his eyes and held tight to the monstrous, possessed molt.

Still, Lysis was essentially arrested by a strange fatigue; he had to let his

Fire run rampant as he remained standing still. The gray boy's proximity continued to sap his soul and douse the Fire...

All was chaos!

A polydactyl, dyscrasia-ridden insect caught fire! It was a six-armed
centaur-like beast with four additional hind legs stemming from a thorax and a
grander abdomen to balance its weight. Hence Narl's phantasm had assumed the
soul of a mutated, diseased nymph. He could eat larvalwyrmen with two hands
while the others operated two bows and launched a stream of arrows!

Asthete SanGules pranced forward, masked in a nymph head, and chided
the Doctor theatrically with Nurse Fae's voice: "Doctor! Your Queen killed me!"

Doctor Grave called upon a gargantuan, mutated larvalwyrmen to clear
the area, then he charged with his ax. Red Lysis thrust *Eviscamir* into blurred images of the moving barber. He slashed out deliriously, not able to discern whether
his blade struck friend or foe.

Then *Hewnmaw* and *Eviscamir* found each other again!

The Doctor moved to grapple Lysis. He was still wearing his insectan
helmet and gauntlets that had allowed him to operate on the Queen's soul, but his
body parts were not covered in their entirety.

Lysis hollered, "What would the dyscrasia do to you? Carry now the
burden of your Queen's soul! Come, I will merge with you!" Tongues of Red Fire
lashed out and crystallized the Doctor's exposed skin!

Flakes of crystal molted from the golem.

Lysis declared, "This is how your Queen killed your wife! 'Tis how you
killed Maeve! You turned her to crystal! Now your Queen's soul will poison you!
I come to give her back to you, for it is your duty to carry her!"

Charnel smoke exuded from the Doctor's head as the golem struggled to
break free from the clutches of Red Lysis. Fragmentary bits of golem shattered as
petrified debris.

Lysis was hell-bent on giving the Red Fire back to the Doctor, and cared
not to survive the battle. He was made to hunt the prey before him and cared not
to live longer. He needed only extinguish the red flame to put an end to the elder
races!

The gray boy hugged his leg tighter. Lysis's flame flickered as the child
held tight, and he began to understand how the Muse had been drained by human
spirits. Lysis grew precipitously weak from this touch. He had mere milliseconds
to decide whether to slice the boy from his leg so he could fight unencumbered or
to accept the burden... if he could bring himself to kill another young boy... like

Erolen...

Lysis was to be undone primarily by a hug rather than an iron weapon...

Seeing Lysis become entranced, Doctor Grave made his move...

Grave wrenched Echo free and lifted him up with his insectan gauntlet, then he propelled the child into the crucible of the Forge!

Free of the boy, Red Lysis became alert, but he had to choose fast. Dive in the Forge to save the child, or attack the Doctor. Protect or attack? Could he save the last living embodiment of Lysis blood? The child was an amalgam of insectan, avian, and human blood. It survived with dyscrasia. The hybrid boy had a pacifying effect. Weakened the fire within Endenken's skeletal frame. Turned things gray.

The Doctor is not my primary enemy. It is the Fire within me. And the boy can extinguish it.

Doctor Grave shouted, "Thinking of saving the boy? I saw his soul, and it reeked of the Lysis clan. If he is the true end of your lineage, it is only proper. Regardless, you will join him and fulfill Ante's legacy! The Red you carry will rekindle the womb of my Queen!"

But Lysis was no longer listening. He had already dove into the Queen's egg sac...

All turned dark. The atmosphere thickened. Heat seared his vision until all was flat. It was as if Lysis swam in molten rock—he drowned and yet felt free. No longer could he feel the burden of his memories. No envisages of his dead wife. No expectations to maintain—no legacies or rituals of the Pictish clan. Nothing. He floated in darkness, the astral realm becoming invisible. He had been in the Queen's abdomen before, to reforge *Eviscamir*. But he had maintained his *sight* then. Not now. Had he turned to stone? Had the boy tapped his soul dry? Was he a dispersed entity? He could only detect vibrations, ever so faintly, through the medium in which he was absorbed: "God and blood this day be-come, Joined as one with art and man, Let nature's lords pass along..."

D OCTOR GRAVE WAS sealing each and every entrance to the colossal abdomen. "I repair you now, Queen. This poultice is comprised of ground chitin, iron, and gallwraith bone. It fills and heals your shell."

Over days, Grave completed his final alchemical recipe. He fed the Queen human blood from the bellies of the Pots, courtesy of the Legion.

He watched the astral fire burn higher and higher as the Forge warmed day by day! He imagined a revived colony that was without flaw.

With Red Lysis therein, the Forge was reignited but was not yet pure. Black smoke puffed occasionally, so her Red was less brilliant, but still Red it was.

"I did it!" Doctor Grave cried.

I do not feel well, said the weak Queen.

"Rest, my Queen."

Oh, Doctor Grave, you failed me at every turn! You chose them again! You chose to be with the avian golem Fae! You invited her into the Underworld! Then chose to care for Maeve, your daughter, over me...

"I had nothing else to nurse," Grave said. He was sadly watching the flames fade to gray.

You made weapons and healed humans at the expense of my soul!

"Mother Queen, I still served you! I sought truly to bring you back to life!"

Yes, I am now reborn! My womb is barren. My colony is destroyed. My eggs are rotten. I have no mate for future litters. I am dying and useless. If I had the strength I would punish you... but... instead... I die now...

And the Red Fire that seemed so robust now dimmed. The Queen became quiet and her body rigid.

"I will bury you when I wake. For now, my dear Queen, I take comfort in your dying clutch. I am sorry..." Grave nestled amongst her six curled legs, enjoying her embrace even if she was upset or ungrateful. It would prove to be as fleeting and comforting as any of life's joys, such as enjoying a daughter's birth, maturation, and exit from home...

G RAVE LAY VULNERABLE beside the Insectan Queen's body.

A children's finger prodded him awake. "No more children need to be sacrificed. He saved me," Echo said beside a drowsy Grave.

Awaken! I am alive!

"Queen? Your voice?" The Doctor realized that the elder voice sounded distorted. He sat upright only to cower beneath the presence of the Gray Lord and mutant child beside him. The child had completed his metamorphosis and now appeared a healthy hybrid of elder and human, with swollen eyes of enormous size and unfurled wings.

Now the reanimated Queen's body was an inferno of white, gray, and black flames! While riding her thorax, with fiery, angelic wings and wild shadows frilling a corona about his head, the Gray Lord Lysis declared, *Your Queen was*

Grey Lysis wields Eviscamir atop the elder Queen

my prey! Her Forge my throne! The balance is complete, the dyscrasia does not harm us anymore! I am the Gray Muse! I am the living ash! I saved the child. We will keep this fire! We own it!

Grave did not move beneath the looming, reanimated Queen and the risen Lysis. Doctor Grave was absolutely defenseless.

Doctor, you fool! You must have known that your queen would not return as before. The current we ride on has been polluted with our ancestors' desires. We must embrace our circumstances and blaze new courses.

Gray Lysis declared, *I am the white, gray, and black fire, and you no longer rule over me! I am an artisan of death, Lord who conquered the dyscrasia. I am the Dark Muse. I feed on sadness and melancholy instead of blood. I inherit it all, and you serve me!*

You will comfort the orphans since you murdered their parents and they, as you, yearn for patronage. They are as lost as you now. Serving under my control, we will build them a home in which you will reside and stand guard. I will be the protector of all the children, and you will help care for them.

The Gray Lord impaled Doctor Grave with *Ferrus Eviscamir,* and immediately the Doctor's body was possessed by the Gray Muse. *I am the Lord of Dyscrasia! Doctor, you'll serve me now!*

EPILOGUE: DEY'S TESTIMONY

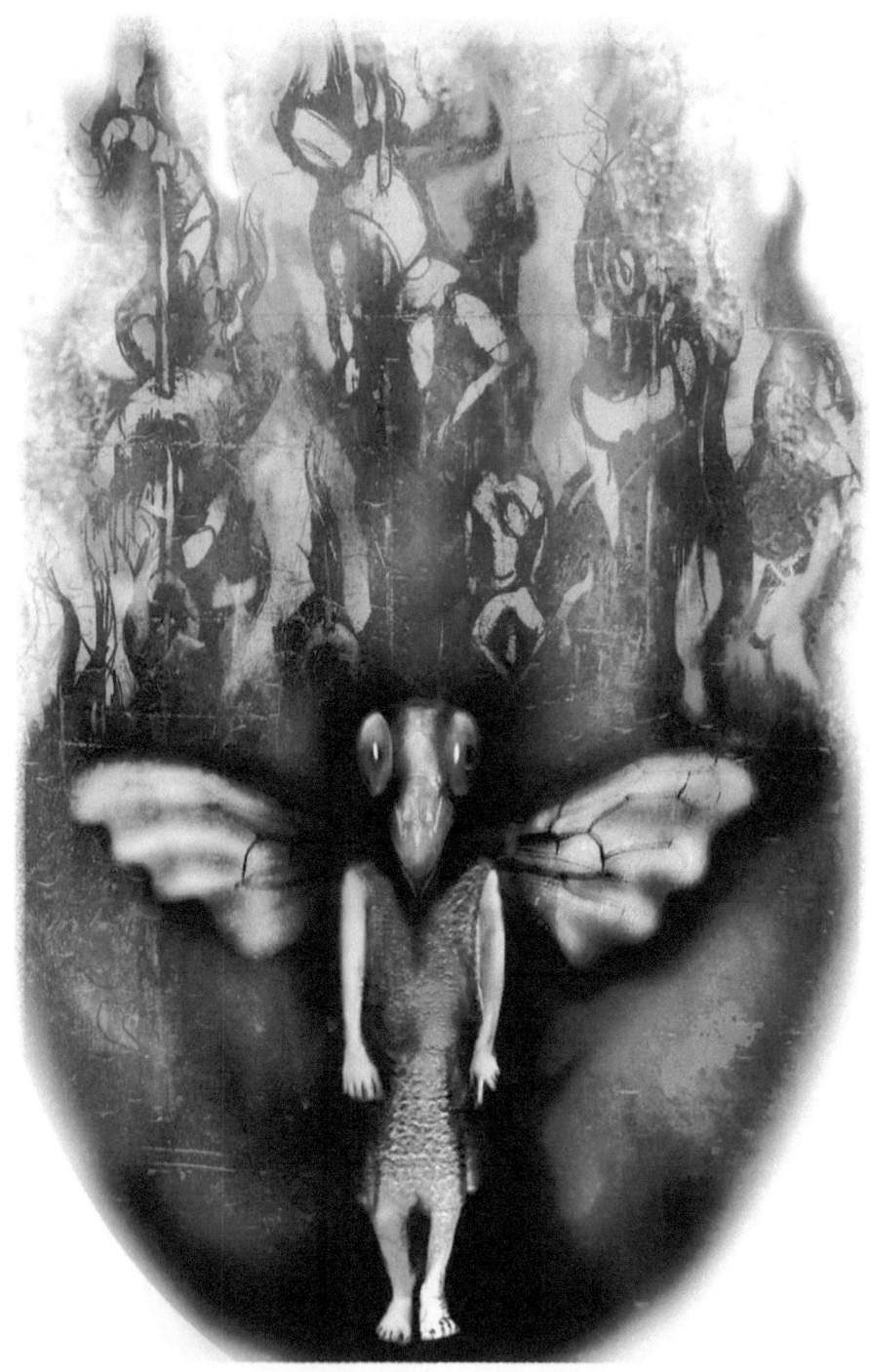

Echo stands in the Grey Orchard of Gravenstyne

Epilogue: Dey's Testimony

L ET ME TELL you about the gray Lord of Dyscrasia, because he will be coming for you or your children.

It is said that this fairy visits sleeping children, and those adults who dream like them. He listens to nightmares from beneath their beds, just beyond the mists of the Otherworld. He illustrates what he hears, transcribing the visions with the ichoric blood of the elders onto sacred parchment. He portrays these dreams with two-dimensional drawings that are real enough in his world—for it is impossible to distinguish between real and fantasy on the canvas of a fairy. Malicious children yield their dreams to him and become increasingly numb to the physical world about them. These dreamless children do not remember their nocturnal fantasies come morning since their precious thoughts have been taken.

However, benevolent children keep their joyous dreams—losing only their nightmares—and are even allowed to accompany the fairy to his home, to Gravenstyne. In truth, Lord Lysis does look after lost children. And there are many: Clanlord Kaiyn Tonn's orphans made their way here; Red Cap orphans from the Cromlechon Theater came; as did the children of the Augur's Aerie and the Gorgepath, too.

Echo, empowered by his own Gray Fire, has taken residence here. With his undead sight, he constructs beautiful dioramas and is ever at peace. He occasionally strays to the Bogs to play with the one human figure he reanimated, Byrhan. With Grave's help, the human's body had been reassembled like a patchwork doll. Byrhan's ghostly corpse prefers to linger near his mother's—attempting to bond with her soul, which remains pinned there.

Understand, Lysis is no longer a single entity confined to one location. He pervades space with his separate fires. He is a collective conscience, a monochrome fire, a true Gray Muse, burning centrally from his humanoid form as he rides the Queen's exoskeleton. He is everywhere that his fire burns, and his forest has grown to encompass the entire map as detailed on the flesh he wears, Ante's Map of the Otherworld.

The Gravenstyne Orchard has transformed from an unkempt forest into a holy ground that is at once a playground, cemetery, sanctuary, and prison. Enemies are on display here, impaled amongst the many allies that are also hung as if dead. Lysis has many heads on poles honored amongst his other trophies, including that of eleven dear children that enjoy being in the Orchard again. Only the residents know which transfixed manikins, armatures, or elder carcasses are the punished dead, protective watchers, or mere ornaments. Children hold hands and play freely among the iron trunks, secure in the knowledge that some forms are actually gray sentinels in disguise.

Children here produce art and offer it sacrificially to Gray Lysis. Chalk drawings on parchment are shared before a grand brazier that burns gray. They draw their nightmares and release their sadness into their art, and then give it to him. As he declared in his victory cry over the Doctor, he proudly consumes melancholy instead of blood. It is his way. Thus, the children are relieved of any sadness or emotional burdens.

You living see only superficial beauty. But this beauty you see would not satiate his hunger. He feeds on a deeper, dark beauty that only the dead can access. You living folk cannot see loneliness, fear, or sadness. You cannot observe souls like we can. So you cannot *see* the depth of the beauty emanating from, and consumed by, the Lord that protects us. But I can, since I am mantled within the apron sewn to his skeleton, my soul pinned to my leathered facial skin.

The living must feel the terror of loneliness to detect its presence. You must resort to bathing in the most raw astral signature of solitude. Understand, beauty is more than a quality of art. It is an experience. Humans denote beauty when the object at which they look compels them to tingle, tremble, or cry. Lysis sees, indeed experiences, the beauty in the dark art given to him. Yes, beauty is not limited to the object. It is the spiritual link connecting subject and viewer. Lysis feeds on this intangible connection, making the sadness easier to bear. He is drawn to it like a wasp to nectar. Become sad, and he will come for you. Make your children sad, and he will he feed on their sadness, deplete it, while he hunts you down.

Could you see as I do, you would know that loneliness burns a deep, melancholic black. To the dead, it is a most wonderful spirit to behold. And to see it consumed by him could not be more terrifying. Could you see the Lord of

Dyscrasia as I do, you would most certainly be compelled to tear. Or vomit.

The Gravenstyne Orchard quietly wrap about us. Lord Lysis. Me. Even Doctor Grave. And the buried inanimate bodies of Maeve and her eleven children. Their ruined birthplace stands in the distance. An empty nest. A bloodied one. The beautiful Gravenstyne.

Now the Lord's Gray flame pulses slower.

The cathartic action of the grand battle has subsided, waning in the spectacular moonlight, precipitously dumping the Lord into a tranquility that cannot be easily managed. He has survived the wrathful hurricane of chaos, transitioning from man to avatar and from custodian to god. His blood has transmuted from colorless to blue, to red, to gray.

While being called into action, he had been distracted from his guilt. How he betrayed his family. Failed them. Killed Erolen…

Now he remembers.

He is surrounded by countless youths, but ultimately he is very, very alone. If only he could give away his own sadness.

The melancholic black flame recoils now to a condensed state within his skeletal frame. His soul and the shade have merged and evolved. Lysis has embraced the terrors that haunted him. And circling around us, the victims of Lysis's choices stare at him, amplifying the signature of lonely terror. A thousand discarded children. Their mothers carried away by a butcher, their mothers' blood drained into a Blood Bog to replenish the ichor of Haemarr. Lord Endenken Lysis had once protected these families. But then he had betrayed them, too, ultimately, as he served out his oath to Haemarr. Endenken Lysis will never be at peace, though he strives to attain it.

I know this because I am attached to him. I am the soul of Dey, but I can still *see*.

Now that you know of dyscrasia, and the Gray Lord, he will come for you. Every time you feel the need to extend your arms, feel the wind beneath your arms as if they were harpy or insectan wings, your soul is mingling with that you cannot see but know is present. And every time you strain to listen to the ghosts on the winds, when the wind howls between the wood comprising your house or trickles through the labyrinth of leaves above you within the canopy of the forest, you are experiencing a dark disease. And the Lord will see you gazing at him and he will come for you, take your tangible hand with his intangible one, and he will lead you to us in the Gray Forest about Gravenstyne.

So what say you? Have you any fear or sadness? Will you accept this

Muse's invite? Or will you remain dead and inanimate toward nature's soul?

Heed that you are infected already, having listened and read so diligently. Did you think you could passively partake in this experience? You are not so innocent or immune. To willingly bear witness to art is to accept it and promote it.

Be still now. Worry not.

Just be mindful to sacrifice your dark emotions whence you arrive. Your soul will pale. The hue of your memories will desaturate. You will be cleansed. Protected.

Be seeing you...

APPENDICES

Appendix 1: Chronology of Key Events

Years since the founding of the Cromlechon

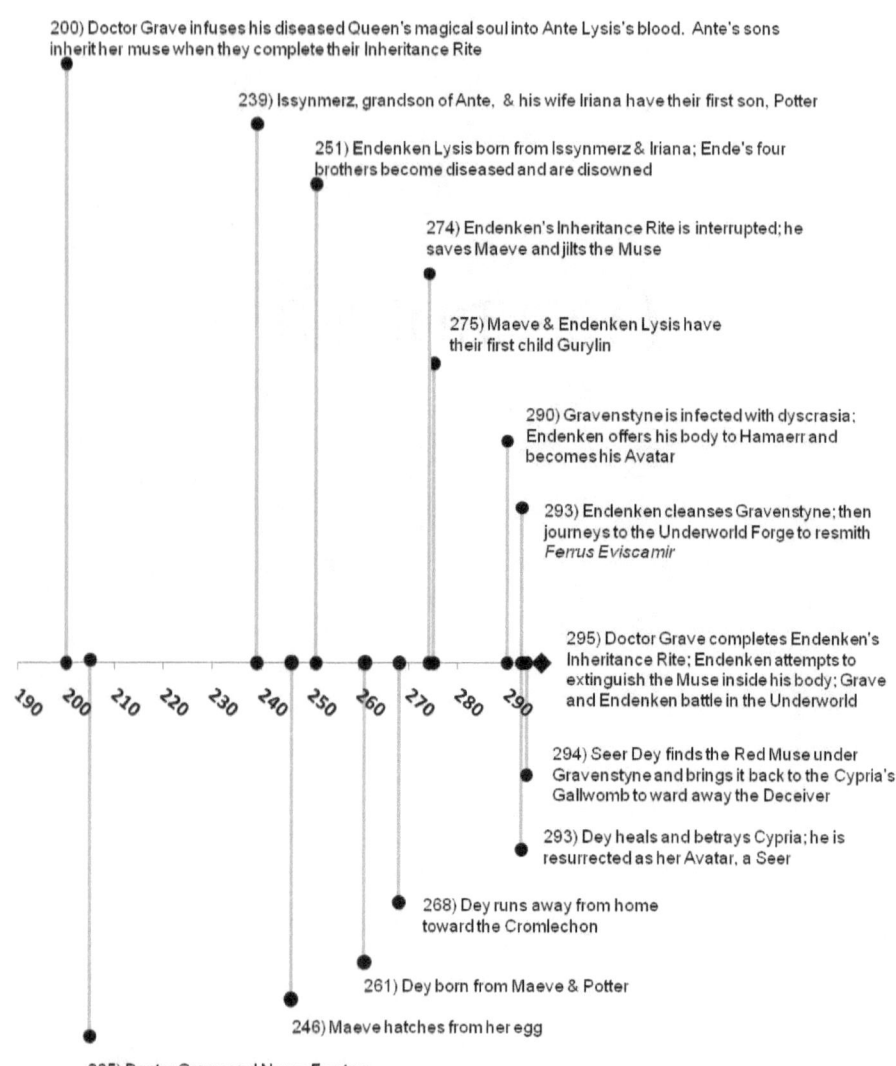

200) Doctor Grave infuses his diseased Queen's magical soul into Ante Lysis's blood. Ante's sons inherit her muse when they complete their Inheritance Rite

239) Issynmerz, grandson of Ante, & his wife Iriana have their first son, Potter

251) Endenken Lysis born from Issynmerz & Iriana; Ende's four brothers become diseased and are disowned

274) Endenken's Inheritance Rite is interrupted; he saves Maeve and jilts the Muse

275) Maeve & Endenken Lysis have their first child Gurylin

290) Gravenstyne is infected with dyscrasia; Endenken offers his body to Hamaerr and becomes his Avatar

293) Endenken cleanses Gravenstyne; then journeys to the Underworld Forge to resmith *Ferrus Eviscamir*

295) Doctor Grave completes Endenken's Inheritance Rite; Endenken attempts to extinguish the Muse inside his body; Grave and Endenken battle in the Underworld

294) Seer Dey finds the Red Muse under Gravenstyne and brings it back to the Cypria's Gallwomb to ward away the Deceiver

293) Dey heals and betrays Cypria; he is resurrected as her Avatar, a Seer

268) Dey runs away from home toward the Cromlechon

261) Dey born from Maeve & Potter

246) Maeve hatches from her egg

205) Doctor Grave and Nurse Fae tap Haemarr's eldritch powers and prepare Maeve's egg in the Underworld Forge

190　200　210　220　230　240　250　260　270　280　290

APPENDIX 2: HEIRS OF THE QUEEN'S MUSE

Primary custodian marked in flames

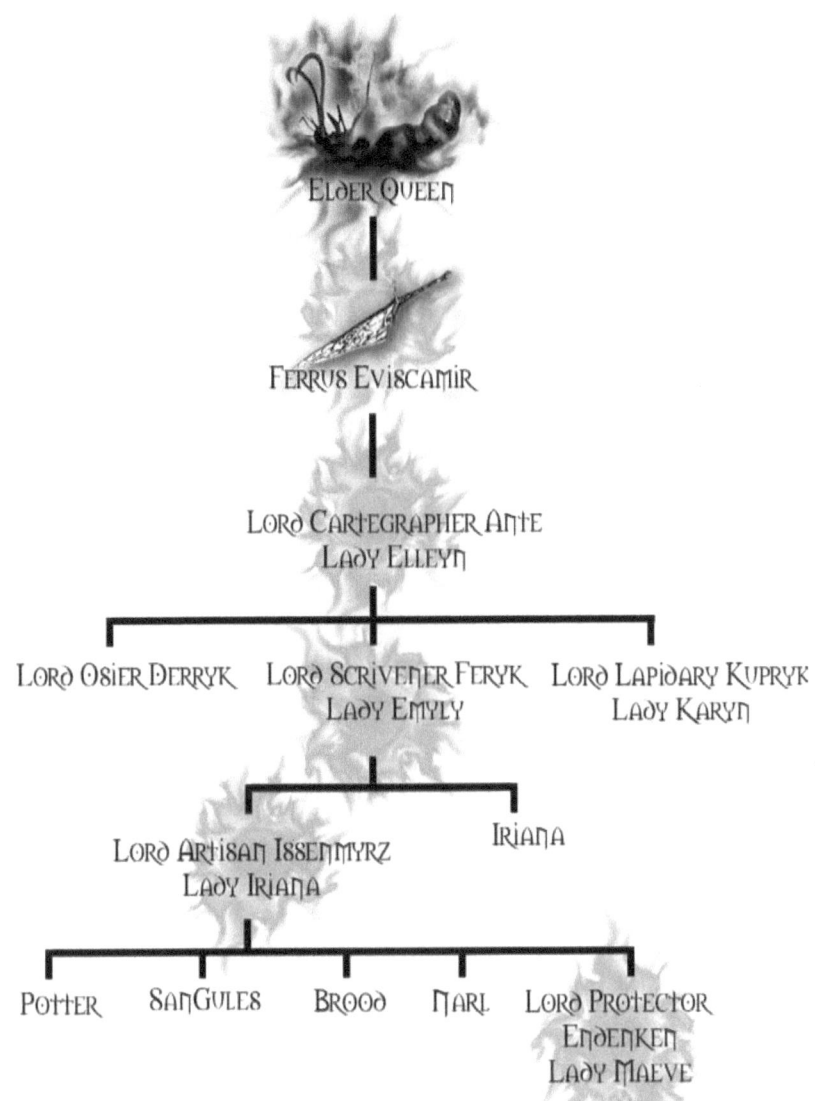

ELDER QUEEN

FERRUS EVISCAMIR

LORD CARTEGRAPHER ANTE
LADY ELLEYN

LORD OSIER DERRYK   LORD SCRIVENER FERYK   LORD LAPIDARY KUPRYK
                       LADY EMYLY   LADY KARYN

                                              IRIANA
LORD ARTISAN ISSENMYRZ
LADY IRIANA

POTTER   SANGULES   BROOD   NARL   LORD PROTECTOR
                                            ENDENKEN
                                            LADY MAEVE

APPENDIX 3: IMPORTANT GENEALOGY

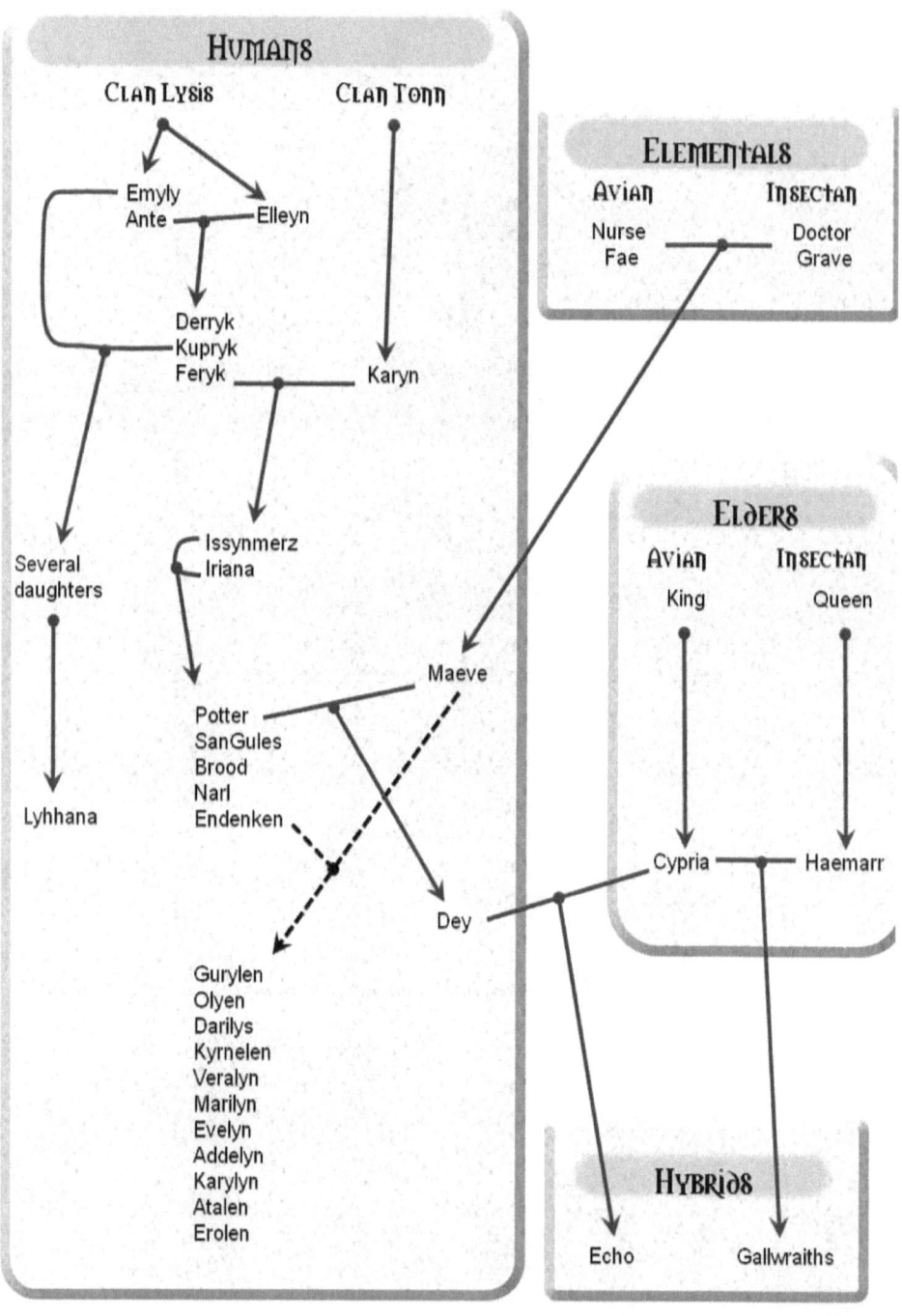

Appendix 4: Index

Darilys	Son of Endenken and Maeve Lysis
Deceiver, the	The Augur's enemy; the one responsible for impregnating Cypria against her will with the seed of Haemarr; the resurrected Endenken Lysis serving as Haemarr's avatar
Derryk	Lord Osier Lysis, a weaver who worked with flexible willow stems; son of Elleyn and Ante Lysis; hung himself in Gravenstyne's courtyard
Dey	Son of Maeve and the Potter; recruited by Cypria to heal her; becomes her Avatar and a Seer; known to the Augurs as the Father of Augury
Dissection Theater	Doctor Grave's central lair within the Cromlechon where he harvested humans to sustain Haemarr and the soul of the Queen; the bodies of mothers were drained in the Blood Bogs
Doctor Grave	See "Grave"
Dolmen	A monument of megalithic stones used for Picti rituals
Dyscrasia	A disease of the blood and ichor originating from an imbalance in the creative forces shared by human and elder kind; imparts human qualities to elders and turns their blood from red to blue; poisoned avian and insectan mixtures calcinate to stone.
Echo	The son of Dey and Cypria; prophesized as being one of the Chromantis
Elder Insectan Lifecycle	The Queen's colony was matriarchal. She was grotesquely larger than the lesser members and exhibited an ever-swollen womb ceaselessly producing eggs. Like common ants, only female ants were produced from fertilized eggs, so females comprised the majority of her colony. Unfertilized eggs produced male ants, which were rare and exhibited short life spans since they died during mating.
	The lifecycle of the ant consisted of several stages: firstly, the egg; secondly, the larva and larvalwyrmen: The worm-like larvae had no appendages or eyes. The mouth lacked teeth and could not grind food, and they seemed drawn to imbibing liquids produced by rotting creatures. The larvae shed their skin as they grew in size. Eventually their trunks bifurcated, as would a tree. This marked the Larvalwyrmen stage. These were a score longer than wide and had branched appendages destined to evolve into legs and antennae. These immature appendages facilitated the spinning of cocoons.
	The nymph and pupa were the third and forth stages: cloaked in a threaded, often transparent sarcophagus, the immature molting nymph resembled the fetus of a human, and hatched from its cocoon only to build another to accommodate its increased size, leaving a hollow image of itself in the former. The final nymph stage was the pupal stage. Its final metamorphosis produced a six-legged insect, with two antennae atop the head, and its body armored in opaque chitin.
	The pupa emerged from its sarcophagi as an adult elder insect. Elders differentiated into Pots, designed to transport liquid in their distended abdomens, or Soldiers, bearing long tusks used in battle.
Elder Pots	See "Elder Insectan Lifecycle"

Elders	Avian or insectan creatures worshipped by the human Picti. The elders fed upon humans for sustenance, and the humans sourced their creativity from the elders' ichor (see "dyscrasia")
Elleyn	Lady and wife to Ante Lysis; had three sons: Derryk, Feryk, and Kupryk
Emyly	Lady and wife to Feryk Lysis; mother to Issynmerz and Iriana
Endenken Lysis, Lord Protector	Last in the line of Picti custodians to carry the Muse on behalf of Doctor Grave, though he forsakes this responsibility since he rejects assuming the burden of his ancestors; marries Maeve with whom he fathers eleven children; becomes Haemarr's Avatar in attempt to save the souls of his family
Erolen	Son of Endenken and Maeve Lysis
Evelyn	Daughter of Endenken and Maeve Lysis
Fae	A shape shifting golem made of mist, often assuming a gryphon form; comprised of water, wind, miasma of the Blood Bogs, and the breaths of dying humans; once Cypria's Nurse, since released from her duties as Cypria matured; Doctor Grave's wife, and mother of Maeve gryphon
Faenne	One of Doctor Grave and Nurse Fae's stillborn daughters; a clay manikin
Father of Augury	See "Dey"
Ferrus Eviscamir	A large scalpel-like sword; has this promise inscribed on handle: "Queen, with this I heal you"; depending on its conditioning in the Forge, it severs only select elements, flesh, or bone
Ferrus Hewnmaw	A large cleaver; has this promise inscribed on its handle: "Children, may this blade carve you life"
Feryk	Lord Scrivener; a scribe and illuminator of manuscripts; a calligrapher; son of Elleyn and Ante; father to Issynmerz and Iriana Lysis
Flue Barrows	A sacrificial chasm in which the ancient Picti once sacrificed their human offerings to the Queen; later served as an escape route for Doctor Grave when he brought the last of the Queen's brood, Haemarr, to the surface; the Cromlechon is built atop these ruins of petrified elder and golem carcasses; vents gases from the Underworld crematorium
Forge, Underworld	The swollen abdomen (egg sac) of the Queen; the creative forces therein could be used to forge magical artifacts, transmute elements, and bring life into dead things; requires ingredients such as relics, souls, and ichor.
Gallwomb	Cypria's womb; a mound of earth layered with stone containing the unhatched litter seeded by Haemarr and Dey
Gallwraith	A diseased fledgling from Cypria's Gallwomb; a hybrid of insectan and avian traits born from Cypria and Haemarr's mating
Ghosts	See "Souls"
Golem	Entity made from the elements to nurse young elders (egg or nymph); the avian elders crafted theirs from the clouds; the insectan elders made theirs from the fleshy soil under the earth

Gorgepath, the	A trade route amongst the highlands about the Cromlechon; often filled with fog
Grave, Doctor	A golem made of fleshy, earth materials including body, bone, and blood; head of the Insectan Queen's nursing caste; after the colony he once nursed died of dyscrasia, he became torn between nurturing a family of his own and resurrecting the colony; Guildlord over the Cromlechon Guild of Barbers; frequently dresses with the skins of others
Gravenstyne Fortress	Clan Lysis's fortress; built atop a Picti sacred mound; beneath the forthill are the labyrinthine catacombs connected to other sacred hills and dolmens; its Orchard of apples and pears supplied the fruit for cider making
Grovel Tonn	Guildlord of smiths from Clan Tonn; recruited into Cypria's Augurs
Guild of Barbers	A group of humans who study necromancy; they aid Doctor Grave in the collecting of blood; most are possessed by larvalwyrmen; they are based in the Cromlechon
Guilds	An institutional evolution of the ancient Picti tribes that once organized human civilization and were grouped by trade
Gurylen	Son of Endenken and Maeve Lysis; their first child
Haemarr	Last of the insectan elders; an anthropomorphic wasp diseased with dyscrasia and so exhibits human form; obsessed with mating with Cypria
Harvest Moon	October full moon; appears red; marks the anniversary of Endenken Lysis's Inheritance Rite
Ichor	Elder blood; rich in iron complexes; when healthy it appears red and serves as a source of creativity for humans; when diseased it often appears blue (see "dyscrasia" entry); when completely spent, it turns black like melancholy; can recrystallize from melancholy into pure iron needles
Inheritance Rite	A funeral Picti ritual in which a descendant of the dead inherits the Muse the Picts worship from the deceased; the new custodian crafts a self-portrait from the blood, bone, and body of the deceased
Insectan Elders	Ants who are in the Insectan Queen's domain; feed on humans; live in the Underworld
Insectan Flue	See Flue barrows
Iriana Lysis	Lady and wife of Issynmerz Lysis
Iron Forest	A forest of iron gibbets supporting bird cages designed by Doctor Grave to catch Cypria but used by her to imprison Avatars of Haemarr or other humans who threaten her
Iron Horde	Doctor Grave's collection of manikins and fossils displayed in the Dissection Theater within the Cromlechon
Issynmerz Lysis	Lord of Gravenstyne; father to Endenken and four others; carrier of the Muse
Julian Kar, Sexton	Servant at Gravenstyne, under Endenken Lysis; maintained the bathhouse furnace and catacombs
Kaiyn Tonn, Clanlord	Clanlord over the smiths and stone carvers in the northeast territory; married to Aleece; father of Taiyn and Byrhan

Karylyn	Daughter of Endenken and Maeve Lysis
Karyn	Lady and wife to Kupryk Lysis
King, Elder	A gargantuan bird worshipped by the Picts in the northwest territories; his society was patriarchal, his Nurses made from the elements of the Sky
Kupryk	Lord Lapidary; a jeweler who works stones, gems, and minerals; married to Karyn; son of Elleyn and Ante Lysis
Kyrnelen	Son of Endenken and Maeve Lysis
Land, the	The interface between the Sky and the Underworld; the domain of humans
Larvalwyrmen	Larvae of insectan elders; once the Queen died, the larvae did not age or mature into nymphs but forever explored the Underworld and remained loyal to their Doctor Grave; see "Elder Insectan Lifecycle"
Leamond, Brewster	Servant at Gravenstyne, under Endenken Lysis; maintained the Orchard and brewed cider; had two sons, Apple and Pear, both of whom died before him
Legion	Kaiyn Tonn's army of men, questing to save their women from Doctor Grave
Levigation	An iterative separation process in which insoluble pigments are ground in water and left alone for gravity to draw the larger sediment away from the finer particles apt to remain suspended; the process is repeated until one reaches the desired particle properties
Lord	Title originally reserved for the primary leader of a Picti settlement or clan; evolved over time to be leader over any profession; since guilds began to replace clans, "Guildlords" became contemporary titles of guild leaders
Lyhhana	Cousin to Endenken; arranged to marry him after his Inheritance Rite
Lysis, Clan	Artists who are descendents of the western Picti tribes
Maeve	Lady to Endenken Lysis; bears Olyen, Darilys, Kyrnelen, Veralyn, Marilyn, Evelyn, Addelyn, Gurylen, Erolen, Karylyn, and Atalen; previously married to Potter (with whom she bore a son, Dey)
Manikin	A figure model to teach anatomy to physicians or artists
Marcus, Chief Cook	Servant at Gravenstyne, under Endenken Lysis; head of the kitchen; married to Pauline
Marilyn	Daughter of Endenken and Maeve Lysis
Melancholy	A black liquid, appears as black pitch but can be as thin as oil; condensed elders' souls
Memories	Residual astral signatures of a soul linked to a place or object, invisible to the living; non-responsive phantoms that continually reenact the past; see "Souls"
Mosaic	Dey's greatest masterpiece; a dynamic assembly of gravel in the Augur's Aerie that portrays Cypria or her emotions and reflects what her flocks see
Muse, Red	The Queen's intangible soul; worshipped (and drained) by the Picts as they created art. Doctor Grave saved her soul from death by implanting it into Ferrus Eviscamir (see Appendix 2, which illustrates the carrier of the Muse over time)
Narl	One of four disowned sons of Issynmerz and Iriana; an archer cannibal resurrected by the Red Shade as an eater of the dead, a ghoul

Nina	Wife of Prasus, blinded by his experiments; her soul haunts him
Nurse	Title of golems and elementals composing the eldritch nursing caste; Doctor Grave was head nurse for the insectan elders; Nurse Fae is the last surviving of the avian elder nurses
Nurse Fae	See "Fae"
Olyen	Son of Endenken and Maeve Lysis
Orphanmaker	Brood's ax
Pauline, Pantler	Servant at Gravenstyne, under Endenken Lysis; married to Marcus; maintained the bread and food supply of the pantry
Pear-of-Anguish	A pear-shaped torture device for insertion into orifices; a crank opens the multiple outer leaves of the pear shell. Endenken employed one to silence SanGules. Also known as a choke-pear or an anxiety-pear.
Picti	Native, tribal humans of the Land, coexisting with the elders for centuries; several tribes worshipped the Queen, taxed her soul, infected her with dyscrasia; a parallel fate afflicted the Avian King
Potter	One of four disowned sons of Issynmerz and Iriana; a drunk clay worker resurrected by the Red Shade as a vampire
Prasus	Alchemist and Pict, mentor to Whitebeard, husband to Nina, whom he blinded; prophesized that Gallwraiths and Chromantis would feed on dyscrasia and turn all to gray
Qual, Clan	Human colony; descendants of Picts who settled in the middle of the valley beside the Cromlechon; skilled in fabric and weaving technologies; Qualenson is their Clanlord
Qualenson, Clanlord	Clanlord over Clan Qual, a colony of tailors, dyers, and fabric makers; gave all those on his manor a ragdoll
Queen Elder	Insectan Elder Queen; last of her kind. The Queen mated with multiple males who fertilized her abdomen only to die immediately after. She shed her wings and nested in the Underworld. She relied on her golem nurses to nurse her young. Doctor Grave led this nursing caste. Eventually, her colony grew in numbers, feeding off of human sacrifices from the Picti who worshipped her soul, the Red Muse (and also drained it as they created art). She could communicate through her ichor to any in her colony. As her body failed, Doctor Grave retrieved her soul and embodied it within his sword, Ferrus Eviscamir.
Ragdolls	Qualenson's gifts to citizens of his clan
Red Caps	Orphans who live in the Theatre; their caps are fashioned from bloodstained aprons
Red Horde	A small army of animated manikins, fossils, and corpses that once decorated Doctor Grave's Dissection Theater but were possessed by Red Lysis
Red Shade	The phantasmal entity that poisons Gravenstyne Fortress; diluted representations of the Muse mixed with the ghosts of Endenken's brothers
Reher Tonn	Standard bearer of Kaiyn Tonn's Legion; a descendant of Grovel

Relics	Portions of a corpse that maintain an astral signature of the soul it once housed; often the head; key ingredients for working the Forge; see "Souls"
SanGules, Aesthete	One of four disowned sons of Issynmerz and Iriana; a connoisseur and collector of beauty; a domestic abuser resurrected by the Red Shade
See(ing)	The undead, elders, and seers have enhanced sight in which the physical world appears gray and memories, shades, and ghosts are colored.
Shades	Shadows of a master soul. More potent than memories, Shades are like diluted souls in that they maintained some vestige of their primary ghost.
Sky, the	The domain of the Avian King
Souls	Souls are visible as ghosts to those that "see" the intangible. They generally adhere to "relics" (some portion of corporeal remains), but can spread as independent entities adhering to secondary objects or places as "shades" or "memories." Picti artists mix their own soul with those of their objects as they produce "art."
Taiyn Tonn, Lordson	First son to Kaiyn with Aleece; first heir to the throne, title of Lordson
Tonn, Clan	Human colony; descendants of Picts who settled on the northeastern slopes of the mountains; skilled in carving stone, and retrieving and working metal and glass
Underworld	The domain of the Insectan Queen
Urlquason	A human; son of Qualenson
Veralyn	Daughter of Endenken and Maeve Lysis
Whitebeard, Apothecary	An apothecary and advisor to Lord Kaiyn
Wyvern	Lord Kaiyn's flail
Xel Culther, Avener	Servant at Gravenstyne, under Endenken Lysis; chief over the stables

ABOUT THE AUTHOR & ILLUSTRATOR

Seth was born in Massachusetts in the 1970s. He graduated the University of Cincinnati with a Bachelor of Science Degree in Chemistry and from the University of Wisconsin-Madison with a Master's Degree in Analytical Chemistry. Since 1997 he has resided in Cincinnati, Ohio working as a complex fluid microscopist, employing his skills as a scientist and artist to understand the manufacturing of liquids analogous to medieval paints.

For more on S. E. Lindberg and Dyscrasia Fiction™, check out these websites: _www.selindberg.com_ and _www.dissectiontheater.com_.